EUROPA

OMNIBUS EDITION

BOOKS 1-3: EUROPA, HELENA, VIKTORIA

BY

ELIAS J. HURST

Hi Kristine,
Sorry you couldn't be here,
but thank you so much
for always being so supportive
of my writing.

Elias J. Hurst

In Memory of Nick Jackson

Chapter One

"When I wake up in the morning, do you know what my first thought is?"

The woman in the chair across from Luka recoiled and cocked her head to one side. This was off script, way off script. Luka watched a little rage flash through her face as her eyes narrowed and her brow became severe. A stony resolve replaced it.

She pursed her lips and raised an eyebrow, signaling that he was clear to explain himself.

"I open my eyes and I think I've made a huge mistake," said Luka. He delivered the line deadpan, but with a hint of a smile tugging at the corner of his mouth.

There was a long silence after this too—long given that they were live on the air. The audience exchanged confused glances with one another. Then, like the first droplets of a building storm, they broke into gentle laughter. It gained force as more and more of the audience reached a consensus that this man had, in fact, made a joke. The host joined in with them, on cue, baring teeth as she laughed under her breath. She was a thin brunette about his age, but unlike him, she seemed at ease in the thick layers of makeup that a person had to wear for television appearances. It crinkled wherever his skin beneath moved, like a layer of dried lake-mud, and itched desperately as he sweated under the stage lights.

"Funny, Dr. Janovic, but there's some truth in humor, isn't there? So, we must wonder what makes you say that. Of all the best scientists and pilots and engineers in the world, only a handful were chosen. You are the brightest, the most physically fit, and you are even genetically screened I understand?"

Luka nodded as he spoke, "That bit is exaggerated, but yes. Every crew member underwent a genetic assessment and all of us have at least one thing in common. We carry a rare genetic marker for increased tolerance to long-term radiation exposure. It's an important predisposition for survival in space."

"So, what, you're cancer proof then?" said the host.

Luka laughed. "Not exactly, no, but you won't find it in our families all the same."

He leaned back in his chair and folded one leg over the other, assuming a relaxed posture, "and you are right to say that. It's the greatest accomplishment I could hope to be a part of. All of us should feel," Luka looked down at the floor, pretending to search for a word, "blessed that we were selected. This is the greatest endeavor in human history."

"Why do you hold so much regret then?" she asked, sounding concerned. Her voice suddenly carried more weight.

The interview was veering further and further from the script. His handlers would not like that.

Luka uncrossed his legs and shifted to the edge of his seat to lean toward the host. She reciprocated, leaning in, and closing the gap between them. It created an atmosphere of drama, like a secret was about to be told, "I may not be coming back. That's the part we tend to ignore. We're traveling six hundred million kilometers each way. We will be careening toward a distant moon in a plastic bottle strapped to an antimatter reactor. Every moment out there is an opportunity to fail. There is nothing to help us once we are on our way. Absolutely nothing. More than death, I am afraid of making a critical mistake."

The audience was quiet now, somber almost, with their funereal expressions.

"Well, when you put it like that, I guess we shouldn't be so jealous," the host said as she looked over to the audience. She pulled her lips tight into thin pink lines, curving them upward, and just like that the mood in the room lightened. Seeing the host smile, the audience smiled in return. Their faces brightened and they looked happy for the reprieve from gloom.

"If all of this is so dangerous, why bother sending people there at all? Couldn't a robot do this job, haven't we already sent them?" she asked.

Luka locked eyes with her.

"Yes, we could, and yes we have," he said.

He gave his response time to sink in, counting to three in his head. One-one thousand, two-one thousand, three. "There is no reason we could not manage the job with drones. There would be difficulties, but we could find work-a-rounds for all of it. On some level, this is a manned mission because we feel it doesn't count unless we've been there ourselves. That's the human spirit."

Luka tugged at the left-hand cuff of his shirt while he talked. The coldness of the metal cufflinks brushing against his skin agitated him. "But that alone is a terrible justification for the costs and the huge risk to human life. The deeper reason is that we must know that we can survive it. Resources are limited on Earth and if we are to continue progressing the way we are, we need to know that we can survive these missions. Someday they will become an important, even routine, means of collecting resources that we have depleted."

Luka almost said consumed, but at the last moment, he remembered that the Committee did not like that word. Consumed implied culpability. They did not want him to associate guilt with consumption. Depleted was technical, detached, and appropriate.

"So, this isn't just about discovery. It's about the future, for all of us. I can see now why you feel there's such a weight on your shoulders."

She paused and looked away from him, appearing to gather herself.

"You address the dangers of the mission, and your fears for what is to come, but you've had a harrowing journey already, haven't you?" she asked.

Where was she going with this? The muscles in Luka's back tightened. He shifted his weight and braced his spine against the curve of the chair-back.

"It has been, yes," said Luka as he forced a smile over gritted teeth.

"You not only survived the Megaquake, which put you into a coma, but you woke up from that coma six months after doctors said you would never regain consciousness. Then they said you would never walk again, but here you are now, fully recovered and a member of the Constellation crew.

4

It's an amazing story. A miracle even."

Megaquake. That stupid word.

He hated the word itself, it was a cheesy B-movie word, but he especially hated that everyone else loved it. One geologist used the phrase offhand. Then someone at a news channel, someone like the person interviewing him now, picked it up and used it in a broadcast. Now, he heard it everywhere and it did no justice to what happened.

On that day the Earth opened, and a wave swallowed a city of millions. Husbands, wives, children—whole families were erased. Not that he cared about them. He only cared that it swallowed her. It took Emma from him.

Well, it did much more than that. That would have been too kind. It tore her in two, literally, as the waters came rushing in. It forced him to watch with his back broken and pinned under a street pole.

He tried to scream at her. He wanted her to run, but with a collapsed lung, he could only mutter like an infant. The wave would come soon and she was trying to save him instead of finding shelter. While he babbled, with blood dripping into his eyes, she kneeled by him. She held his head in her lap and her palms were smooth and cold like the inside of an Abalone shell. Her hair, a vibrant red, looked ablaze with the sun low behind her. She smiled down at him and it culminated every good feeling he knew. He would never let go of that image, that moment just before it hit.

The wave did not drown him too. That would have been a kindness. It washed him out of the rubble and laid him on a grassy hill, nearly on the spot that Red-Cross set up camp after the water receded. The Earth itself did not want him to die. Nor did it want him to forget the terror on Emma's face

5

as it took her away.

"*Doctor Janovic?*" the host's voice cut through his thoughts, polite but commanding.

Luka shook off the memory. "Sorry, what? I didn't hear the question."

Someone in the audience chuckled, but the host leaned closer. She was careful with her expressions, practiced as an actress, but she held her head a little higher and that was her tell. She caught a scent that she liked.

"I asked what it was like when you woke up from the coma. What was your first thought then, was it of the mission?" she asked.

Luka froze.

"No, it wasn't. I can see that. You thought of Emma first, didn't you?" she said.

The cameras closed in on him. He watched them zoom on a stage-side monitor. Suddenly, he noticed the sweat beading in the crook of his back, and the tingling in his fingertips as muscles wrenched his spine.

"Waking up from a coma isn't like waking up from a nap. I had no thoughts. I was dead," he said.

"Hum. Interesting that you chose that word—dead."

She held the clicker of her pen to her temple and looked down at a notepad in her lap like she needed to brush-up on her line of questioning.

"Do you feel like you are a different person now than one

the Committee selected years ago? I mean to say, did her death change you?" she asked.

"I'm not sure I understand," said Luka. It was a plea. He knew they both understood her intent well.

"Well, there have been a lot of questions as to whether or not you are still fit for this mission, doctor Janovic. I don't mean that as an insult to your intelligence. You are undoubtedly the most intellectually qualified. It's your physical health—more so your emotional state—that concerns some of the public. I guess we are all wondering, are you up to the task?"

His nostrils flared and the veins in neck throbbed as he spoke, "I am aware of the rumors regarding my health and it is not the media's role to make these determinations. The Committee selected us, all of us, and they alone are qualified to make such a judgment."

Her pink lips curled into a smirk. It was a fleshed-out version of the excitement she held back earlier. "Let me say it this way, are you unhappy doctor Janovic? Are you hoping for a way out?"

His mind choked on a glut of words. He wanted to say too much, so nothing came out. He stared at her for several seconds and watched satisfaction wear through her veneer of professionalism.

"Fuck you," said Luka as he stood.

He stormed off stage and rushed down an office corridor, hoping to find the exit without knowing where to go. He ignored the sheepish glances of station employees as he went, and to the brave few who made eye contact, he returned venomous looks. When he turned a corner, his publicist,

Michael, intercepted him and rammed him into a wall with the flat edge of his arm. Michael's face puffed with anger and his jaw swelled as he gritted his teeth at Luka. Luka pushed back, throwing Michael's weight over his heels. Michael recovered and doubled the force over his arm. Luka's pulse hammered in his ears while they glowered at each other.

His adrenaline was fading, though, and in its absence, he began to understand his mistake. Luka let his shoulders go slack and Michael dropped his arm in response. They both let out a heavy breath as Michael stepped back and smoothed his clothing. This was a temporary armistice, he knew. Michael relented only because he would not have this argument in public. He had more control.

Michael jerked his head to in the direction he came from and they set off together. He led them through the broadcast station with Luka a step in tow. The whole building was a maze of uniformity and Luka did not understand how Michael made the correct sequence of turns through the series of white hallways and beige office areas. After what seemed like a century, they broke into a large open hall. It had a ceiling several stories tall and an empty floor, save for a few benches and indoor plants. A solid panel of windows comprised the outer wall, and it offered a brilliant view of the New Seattle skyline. In the forefront stood the modern towers. They were bright, monolithic structures that cast their light high into the night. Their collective glow stained the clouds above them a hazy orange. Looming behind them, not far in the distance, were the shabby remnants of Old Seattle. They were broken silhouettes extending from the brackish water of Elliott Bay. They gleamed in the light from New Seattle, but above them the sky was dark. Their fragmented shapes were wraiths emerging from the night.

Luka and Michael came to a bank of elevators, which brought them down to the main lobby of the broadcast station. It had a circular desk in the center of the room, where the receptionist sat, and an elegant LED logo hung above it. It was indistinguishable from the dozen others he saw in the past few weeks.

They stepped through the exterior doors and as he planted his feet at the door's landing, a motorcycle, a combustion motorcycle, rumbled by. The air hung with black smoke from its tailpipe—sulfurous and sweet, threatening and pleasant, all at once. Luka's eyes followed the relic until it disappeared over the hill. Then he noticed the swarm of reporters between him and the safety of their black sedan and his stomach churned.

Michael clenched his jaw and pushed forward with confidence. He knocked people to the side, dropping the guise of politeness, as he forged a path through the sea of bodies. Luka tried to follow in Michael's wake, but the crowd kept finding small inroads between them. They blocked his path little by little, and soon they isolated him. They stretched out their arms like antennas and forced their microphones into his face. They shouted their questions in volleys.

"Can you comment on tonight's allegations?"

"Will the Committee remove you from the mission?"

Luka knew this mission would be a spectacle. Even years ago, when the Constellation spacecraft was ones and zeroes in a schematic file and the crew were profiles in a list of candidates. Even then, he knew, but he never foresaw being at the mercy of public opinion.

They pressed in tighter against him. It was hard to breathe in such a dense group and the muscles in his back began to clench. They torqued his spine and pain radiated from the plates the doctors had used to repair it. Beads of cold sweat began to form along his brow and his vision fuzzed.

Michael looked back. They met eyes and Michael did an immediate about-face. He shoved his way back through the crowd toward Luka, knocking a few people to the ground in the process. He gripped Luka's arm and pulled him toward their car. The violence of his action tempered the reporters. Although they fired off obscenities, they parted for Michael as he pushed through. He yanked the rear door open and Luka slumped into the backseat. Michael slid in after him and slammed the door shut.

The cacophony died. The heavy tinting on the windows tempered the camera flashes too, which continued to snap long after the door shut. The cabin pulsed with the dulled white glow of the cameras firing beyond it. He felt the gentle pull of momentum as the car came to life and accelerated away.

Luka drew in a slow, deep breath. His face was hot as blood rushed back to it. Michael was massaging his forehead with a thumb and forefinger. He was only thirty-five, but already deep wrinkles crossed his face. Not that he looked bad. He had sandy-blonde hair with a masculine jawline and dimpled chin. His eyes were light and engaging. He had vitality, but also the look of someone who wore concern too often. His was the visage of a person who spent their life cleaning up someone else's.

"What the *hell* was that?" shouted Michael.

"I know, I know," said Luka.

"No, you don't," said Michael, continuing to yell.

Michael was still rubbing his forehead. A red spot had

formed where his thumb moved in a tight circle. The veins in his neck bulged like old roots breaking through a sidewalk and blood flushed his cheeks. Luka knew this look. Michael was not putting on a show. This was actual anger.

"Jesus, Luka. You're not as irreplaceable as you think. There are plenty of people behind you who are just as prepared to go and the Committee's been watching. You all have replacements, all of you. You can't be doing this. Not on an international broadcast. This will be all over the media."

Michael shook his head. "Christ, it already is. Who am I kidding?"

Luka turned to face him. "She crossed the line. You know that she did."

"Yeah, sure. It was wrong—and way off the script we approved—but that doesn't mean you can lose it *every single time* someone brings it up. It might still be painful for you, more painful than I can know. Regardless, she is dead, and you are not. To the rest of the world, this is a god-damn interesting story and so people will continue to ask about it. Bottom line is you're going to have to buck up because *this is* what you signed up for."

Luka nodded and the cabin of the car went quiet. He looked down at his right hand and studied the scar spanning from his forearm to the second knuckle of his ring finger. He ran a thumb along it. Years of healing and PT had not helped. All the skin on the upper part of his forearm was dead to the touch.

"Just made her career, didn't I?" said Luka.

Michael huffed. "Yeah, you did."

11

He gave his forehead a rest, slipping his hands into his pockets as he reclined back into his seat. His suit was the same shade of charcoal as the leather of the seats and his body blended into them, giving the impression that he was a disembodied head. He looked like a Cheshire Cat that worried constantly in place of smiling.

"And I'll do what I can to make sure you didn't just unmake yours," he added as he closed his eyes like he was about to take a nap.

He would come around. He always did.

Luka turned his attention back to his window. "So, what do we do now?"

Michael's eyes snapped open, and he exhaled. "You tell me."

"Honestly, I'm hungry."

"Not what I meant, but I'll have something sent over when we get back," said Michael.

He turned his attention to his interface. His eyes went dead as he manipulated the augmented reality in his mind.

"What I want is a steak."

Michael dropped the interface and shot Luka an annoyed look. "You know you're not allowed to eat that—even if I could, by some miracle, get my hands on an actual slab of cow."

"Why don't we cheat, try our luck? There's a place I know of," Luka said.

He knew he was being irritating. He counted on Michael to tolerate as much.

"Yeah, we're not going there. Answer's no," Michael replied as he returned to the digitized world of his interface.

Soon they would fit the whole crew with interfaces like Michael's. Most already had it. He was among the holdouts, those that preferred a device they carried. One that could be left behind. Soon he would have a memory chip implanted too. This would give him access to—memory of—the schematics for the power systems on the Constellation craft. He insisted to the Committee that he could memorize all this information without the chip, and he had, but they would not accept that risk. There would be no unplugging in his future.

"Do you ever get sick of that thing?" Luka asked.

"Only when I'm using it to clean up your messes," said Michael.

Luka could not suppress the small grin that crept across his face.

"There, I made sure the kitchen will have something sent over to your place by the time we get there. Something *approved* that is, just for you. Me, I might go have that steak. And you can bet your ass I'm expensing it to your account. Now, remind me again, what's the name of that place?" Michael continued.

Luka shrugged. "Be my guest. I could have a hundred steaks a night between now and launch and not run through my account."

Michael frowned. "It's not a one-way trip, remember? You might want a thing or two when you get back. Food and shelter come to mind. They're not going to let you live in DA housing forever."

"Odds aren't in favor of the crew returning. I say you have the steak, then at least one of us can."

"You know, someday, you might find a reason to want that money. You could meet someone, have kids. Big house, certified food, private colleges. All of that. Believe me. I can personally attest that you'll wish you had the money then."

Luka kept his eyes on the window and watched the passing buildings.

"Why don't you come over to my place and eat with us tonight? We'd be happy to have you. The kids will be asleep by now, but Rebecca said she'd stay up to eat with me," Michael asked.

"Pretty sure that's not *approved*," said Luka.

"Why do you think I'm inviting you?" said Michael.

Luka laughed. "Then I'm on board."

If they shared only a single point of agreement—and sometimes that was the case—it was that they found the Committee's rules aggravating. They were bureaucratically and inefficiently restrictive. Their scope covered even the extraordinarily mundane aspects of crew member's lives like what types of deodorant they could use and how many pairs of socks they could keep in their DA quarters. The constant nagging of these restrictions tried even the most patient of the crew and staff.

Their sedan slowed to a stop.

14

Luka and Michael both leaned toward the middle of the vehicle to peer through the windshield.

"Why are we stopped?"

Michael's eyes went blank as he pulled up the car's diagnostics on his interface.

"Martial blockade, it looks like. Everything's fine with the car."

"Any idea what they're up to?"

"No, but it looks serious. They're geared up. It isn't just some checkpoint."

Michael pulled out of his interface and looked over at Luka. "I don't like this."

"MP's?"

"Yeah, a lot of them."

Luka glimpsed Michael's interface. Military Police were forming up in front of the barricades ahead. They wore black body armor and full-face tactical helmets. The letters NSMPF were emblazoned on the backs and sides of their armor in bold cyan. Those forming the front line took a kneeling stance with their rifles braced on the barricades. Another squad was setting into formation behind them, standing so that their bodies staggered with the line ahead of them like checker pieces on a board. There were fifteen of them at least. Luka could not get an accurate count because the video feed on the windshield began to stutter. The frame rate dropped to a near frozen state as a high-velocity drone screamed overhead. The shrill whine of its engines pierced into the cabin of the car. Michael and Luka both clamped their hands down over their ears in reaction. Their eyes went wide.

Then there was a bright flash. Even through the tinting on the windows, it was blinding like an arc welder held at arm's length.

The vehicle went inverted twice over. His seat belt kept his body locked in place, but his arms flailed as the car tumbled.

It came to a rest upside down. The roof was buckled in. The windows were broken. Dust hanging in the air stung his eyes and he had to fight to keep them open. His brain felt foggy. Thoughts came slowly.

He looked over to his right. Blood was running from Michael's mouth. It dribbled down his forehead and fell to the roof in a steady, pattering trickle. It matted his hair and stained the blonde a muddy red where it ran. His head hung slack from his shoulders, and his arms dangled down to the roof of the car with his knuckles resting on the asphalt where the glass sunroof had been moments before. Luka could not see the source of the blood flow. He wanted to know whether it was internal damage or just a cut on his scalp; from this angle it could have been either. Best case Michael's face had smacked against the window, opening a gash on his head. Worst-case would be blood running from his ears—concussive damage. Michael's eyes were open but distant and confused like he was locked in his interface.

A peculiar odor began to fill the car and with it came a thin, caustic black smoke. Trails of it floated in through the broken windows, like will-o-the-wisps passing by. Luka remembered the smell, but he could not place it at first.

Then he knew. The battery array was overheating.

Oh no.

There were too many subsystems in place preventing a
cascaded failure. Regardless, it was happening. The smell was
unmistakable to him. Luka began fumbling with the buckle
on his seat belt, trying to release the clasp. When the battery
array went critical, the alloy frame would collapse from the
heat and in a few minutes, it would weld the chassis of the car
to the roof. Long before that, molten battery would leak
through the floor and consume them. It was difficult to guess
how quickly the failure would progress, but it was minutes at
best. Already he began to feel the violently exothermic
reaction happening above them. Heat radiated through the
floor panels of the car and into the soles of his shoes. His feet
were sweating. On the other side of some thin carbon fiber,
their end approached.

His mission training should have helped him to stay calm
in conditions of extreme stress like these, but it did not. His
adrenaline surged and it frenzied his heart. His hands shook
and the square-inch-sized release on the belt buckle became a
difficult target for his thumb. He kept looking over at
Michael. The puddle of blood beneath him had doubled in
size since the car landed upside down.

Luka pressed furiously at the button on the clasp, missing
often, but even when he made solid contact it would not give.
He took a deep breath, remembering to slow himself, and
braced his hand against the buckle. Carefully, he squeezed his
thumb down onto the release. The button did not budge. He
folded his left thumb over his right and squeezed with the
combined strength of both hands. Sweat from his chest was
now running down his chin and dropping into his eyes,
blurring his vision, and further complicating the process. He
tried the same process again. Still, it would not give.

The heat was building in the cabin. The air choked him. It

was like breathing fumes off fresh asphalt. The paneling along the floor felt spongy. He jammed his feet against it, trying to wriggle free from the safety belt's grasp, but it flexed in proportion to his push. He tried a few times more, but the result was the same. With the floor giving way he could not get any leverage and he worried his foot might punch a hole through if he kept trying.

Luka shoved his hands into his pants pockets, searching for anything he could use as a tool. There was nothing. He checked his coat too, but he came up short there as well. He searched around him. There was shattered glass and a lot of it. It was all around and within grasp, but it was safety glass. It broke into hundreds of neat little honeycomb shapes with no sharp edges. He would not be cutting or dissembling his way out.

The combined effects of the heat and the smoke made his head swim. It felt like a star was threatening to collapse in on him.

He focused his thoughts inward.

If he could not break the belt, his only remaining option was to work with it. He might free the tension on the belt if he positioned himself just right. The correct angle should ease the mechanism from its bind and allow him to unclasp it.

Luka found a grip for both hands on the bottom edge of his seat and pulled upward with all his strength. The belt sucked in tighter around him in response, constricting around his ribs. It was not the result he hoped for, but he continued. He pressed his right hand against the roof, and he pushed upward with all the power in his right arm while he reached for the buckle with his left hand. It was a sloppy effort, but his fingers found the clasp and to his immense surprise the button gave way. The buckle came loose with an innocuous *click* and the belt fell aside. It released him straight onto his head.

He should not have been shocked by this result, but he was. His body crumpled on top of him and the blood rushed away from his brain, stunning him. His vision fizzled out and for a moment he forgot where he was.

He shook it off. The array was near critical and he needed to keep moving. He needed to get them both free before the reaction ate through the floor panels.

It was then that he noticed it already happened.

Michael should have been shrieking in pain. The battery cells had melted through the floor above him and engulfed his foot in a dazzling yellow-white glow.

Luka swung his legs over to one side and rolled his body so he could face him. Michael's eyes were open, but glazed and dead looking. His pupils should have contracted in the intense light of the battery array meltdown, but they were dilated instead. Luka could only hope swelling had not already rendered Michael brain dead.

He fought with the buckle that kept Michael in place. The same principle that had bound his own had jammed up Michael's belt too. He grabbed Michael by the lapels of his jacket and rocked him with his left hand while he tried pressing the buckle with his right. It gave way after a few tugs and Michael crashed down to the ceiling of the car in a haphazard lump. Luka rolled through the pool of blood that had formed beneath Michael as he positioned himself to drag Michael out of the car. The blood slicked the right half of his body, and in the intense heat, it dried on his skin instantly. It crinkled and flaked away.

Luka slipped his hands beneath Michael's armpits and then used his legs to squat backward and drag Michael's body with him. He moved bursts, but it only took a few reps before his back was against the other side of the car. Luka spun around and slid his feet through the mangled frame, lowering himself into a prone position. He began snaking through the window. A ragged edge on the door frame dug into his back as he went. He shivered as he felt the metal slice through his skin. He clenched his teeth and pushed through the opening until his shoulders were clear.

He was reaching into the car to pull Michael's slack body through the window when a pair of hands clenched Luka by his shoulders. His first instinct was to fight off their grip, but the vice hands clamped down on him and jerked him up.

Luka screamed "NO!" in protest over and over as he was shoulder carried away. He writhed in the grasp of his captor and pried at their hands but the person carrying him was too strong for him to break away. They had a heavy weapon slung across their backs. It was a soldier, not a paramedic.

He laid Luka down on his side near an armored vehicle and ran back over to the wrecked sedan to help two others in dark gray uniforms yank Michael free. They moved efficiently. They freed Michael within seconds and not a moment too soon. As they carried him toward, Luka the frame of the sedan collapsed. The entire rear half of the car succumbed to the white glow of the super-critical battery cells and imploded.

Luka pulled himself onto his knees and surveyed the area. A cluster of MilPol vehicles surrounded them. Some of them were wrecked while others had polished black exteriors, having arrived after the blast. There was no fire. The only light came from the melting battery arrays on their sedan and the two destroyed MilPol trucks near it.

20

It was not an explosion that blew their car off the road which meant the source had to be a repulser—a momentary but massive magnetic wave that injected a viral code into the car's battery array. It was the only device capable of hacking the fail-safes while simultaneously hitting with enough force to send a car into a violent roll. It was high-tech weaponry and expensive enough that he thought only government-backed forces had access to it.

The three soldiers who had extracted Michael came running toward the armored truck behind Luka. The largest of them had Michael slung over his shoulder. Michael's head lolled like a rag doll as the man jogged toward Luka.

One of the other two motioned for Luka to climb into the truck as they approached. Luka complied, scrambling into the vehicle. He moved deep into the interior as he could and took a seat on a hard metal bench. The exterior of the truck was reminiscent of a 20th-century armored bank car, but the interior was modern. It was part assault vehicle and part ambulance. It was not MilPol. There was no insignia at all.

"He's been exposed. It hit bone, I know it. If it gets to marrow—"

Luka picked up a fragment of their conversation as they loaded Michael into the truck and secured him to a stretcher.

The men jumped into the truck, sitting on either side of Luka, and they continued to speak as if he were not there.

"Do we have the equipment to deal with that?" one asked.

"He could go toxic if we don't," another responded.

"Shit man. Where's the blade, do we have one?"

21

"Driver's side rear compartment."

"I'll get it."

"Don't," said the largest of them.

He was a hulking mass of body armor. He was so tall that he had to hunch over where everyone else could stand comfortably in the space.

"Just got word from on high. We need to get out of here now. There may be a second wave inbound. Our orders are to secure the DA assets and drop them at the facility. Their own people can deal with medical."

"And what about this one? You know this is serious," said one of the other soldiers as he nodded to Michael.

The big man twisted his mouth to one side. It was the exact motion of someone about to spit a wad of chew, but his mouth was empty as far as Luka could tell. His face was weather-worn like old leather. Deep crevices formed where his skin wrinkled at the corners of his eyes.

The first soldier pressed on with his point, "As long we deliver him still breathing, he's their problem. Not ours. If he dies before then, they will make it our problem. Right?"

The big man clenched his teeth and ran his hand across the stubble on his jaw. There was a tense moment of eye contact between the two soldiers. It might have gone sour, but gunfire picked again somewhere in the distance and shocked them all into action.

"We have to do this on the road," the large one announced.

Then he started fishing through a compartment to his right.

"Jack! You're up," he shouted.

"Lord, here we go," said the soldier nearest Luka as he removed his helmet.

His hair clung to his forehead, slick with sweat, "You guys know this is hard enough to do on a stationary operating table, forget a stretcher in the back of one these vans and with that asshole computer up front driving."

"Don't know. Don't care. Just get it done," said the large one.

"'Course you don't. Ain't your foot he's gonna be cuttin' on is it?" said the third soldier as the truck rolled into motion.

"Both of you shut up. I'm making the call here. His chances are better this way," said the large one.

The venom in his voice made it clear he was their ranking superior, though Luka guessed their insubordination suggested he had not been so for very long. The one they called Jack stood and shuffled his way along the side of the stretcher, headed for Michael's feet.

Luka gathered the courage to speak up, "Someone mind telling me what's going on here?"

It was a stupid question, but it got things started.

"We have to take your buddy's foot," said the commander.

"Yeah. I understood that much. I'm more concerned with whether you guys know what you're doing or not," said Luka.

23

Their commander took to this statement with maximal displeasure. He deadlocked eyes with Luka. His irises were sunken deep beneath a heavy brow, but they were a piercing gray-blue and they threatened to choke the life from him.

"Yeah, we do know what we are doing, and we just saved you back there, so I would check that tone you prick. You may be precious DA cargo, but I will not hesitate to end you if you challenge me again."

Luka maintained eye contact, but he knew this was not a contest he could win. "OK. I understand," he said.

"You understand what? See, I don't think you do. You're an engineer, right? Good at making things?" said the commander.

Luka nodded.

"Yeah well, Jack here's real good at cutting people's limbs off to keep them from dying." He clamped a hand on Jack's shoulder. "Jack here's an ace, ain't ya Jack?"

Jack did not acknowledge this flattery—which oddly gave Luka more confidence in him. The commander continued on, "So let us do our job and you do yours. You sit there quietly and stay out of the way until we get you back to your home."

"Just be glad it ain't you getting arced. We wouldn't want you to miss out on your *trip*," said the third soldier.

The commander shot a dangerous look at the third soldier, "That's enough. You shut up too Roger. Jack needs to concentrate."

The van slammed through a shabby wooden barricade just

24

then. The sudden deceleration threw Luka against the metal partition that separated the back of the truck from the motor compartment. He felt blood running from the gash on his shoulder blade. A wet throb of pain raced with his pulse. He did his best to ignore it.

The stretcher, though fixed to the floor, lurched forward hard and jostled Michael's limp body. Jack and Roger were both thrown from their feet. The commander, however, held his ground. He braced against the side of the van with a grip on a handle at the rear and seemed remarkably unaffected by the impact.

"Dammit, do you think that computer could warn me when it's going to do that!"

Jack lifted himself back up to his feet, took a wide stance, and began repositioning Michael's foot—the one he intended to amputate.

"I think it's fixed on just getting us out of here Jack," said Roger.

"MilPol isn't going to be happy we're just slamming through their checkpoints like that," Jack muttered as he prepped.

"I don't have time to care. Roger, go see if you can't poke your head out a window and let us know if we're going to hit anything again."

The commander jerked his head toward the front of the van, indicating for Roger to move. Roger jumped into action, making for a small opening in the partition between the two compartments of the truck. He launched himself through the hole and disappeared.

The commander made eye contact with Jack. "Get it done."

Then he handed Jack a rectangular black object.

Jack held down a flashing green button on the side for several seconds until an arch opened from one end. The surgical blade went online with a series of loud beeps and the back of the van filled with a harsh blue glow. Even over the rattling of metal and hum of tires, Luka heard a sharp crackling sound like high voltage wires overhead.

"What happened back there?" Luka asked as he shielded eyes against the light.

"Don't know. No time. Your friend's already showing signs of septicemia. His red cells are going toxic," responded Jack.

"What, why?" asked Luka. Strangely this was the first time he considered why they were amputating. He knew the biopolymer cells were hazardous, but he had assumed it was because of chemical burns, not toxicity.

"You're a scientist, aren't you? Biopolymer from the battery cells got into his blood. It'll spread. It'll mutate and kill the marrow unless I eliminate the source," Jack spoke while he disinfected a section of Michael's leg just above the ankle.

"No other way to stem it?" asked Luka.

"No. And you might want to take a deep breath now. This isn't going to smell nice."

Jack steadied a vivid blue light above the area he disinfected. His body went loose, absorbing the shock of the road so that even when he swayed with the movement of the van, his hands remained still. A blue horizontal bar appeared on Michael's skin, marking where he would cut. Three loud beeps sounded. There was a flash and a miniature crack of lightning.

Then it was done.

Luka looked down at his own feet, not wanting to see the result first-hand. He quickly realized that he should have taken Jack's advice because the smell hit him in an awful wave. Jack was busy putting an IV into Michael, seemingly unaffected, but Luka's throat tightened. His stomach rose, and he tried to fight it, but he knew it was coming. The odor was not objectively intolerable. It was almost sweet, like barbecue, but sickly charred too. It was the psychological effect of knowing the source that triggered the revulsion. He forced himself to swallow, over and over, hoping that he could avoid it. It was too late though. His stomach contracted and a watery-yellow liquid ejected from his mouth onto his feet, spraying the floor and splashing the walls.

Jack huffed. It was something near a laugh, "Told you." He began feeding a line of clear liquid into the IV he had set up.

The commander, who had been silent through the operation, also seemed to struggle. Luka saw that he was swallowing hard repeatedly, using the same technique that had failed him. The commander turned his head toward a corner and cupped his left hand over his mouth. His whole body shuddered while convulsed. He swallowed hard again after, pushing the bile down.

Then the commander rolled back his sleeve. He had an interface attached to his arm. Where Michael's interface fed directly into his brain, the commander's was a holoscreen that covered from his wrist to his elbow and wrapped around his entire arm. It looked like his whole arm below the elbow had been converted into a computer. The commander read from a screen on the inner side and was making strange gestures with the fingers on his left hand. There were repeated patterns and positions. It triggered actions on his screen. He had gloves on, so Luka could not tell if the commander's hand was also prosthetic but based on this, he assumed it was.

"ETA two. They've got med staff ready to transfer custody," the commander announced.

The van swung a right and hit the accelerator hard as the van was coming out of the turn, throwing them all—except the commander—from their feet. The van accelerated at full bore for at least a full minute and then came to a screeching halt. Its tires locked in a full skid as it passed through a series of open gates.

They came to a stop and the back doors of the van burst open. Emergency staff in blue Daedalus Astrodynamics uniforms crowded around the opening. They lifted the stretcher out and hurried Michael off in the direction of a research building. Luka jumped out of the van intending to follow the group carrying Michael, but one of the medical crew positioned herself in front of Luka and snatched him by the arm before he could take a step in Michael's direction.

Chapter Two

The woman guided Luka toward the medical facility. He watched Michael's stretcher disappear into one of the squat concrete bunkers that formed the research annex. He pulled in that direction but the woman kept a firm grip and steady pace. Two other medical staff approached Luka at a jog.

"No exposure. A laceration on the upper back. Non-life threatening. Take Dr. Janovic to section two. They want to debrief after we address the wound," she announced as the pair came within earshot.

"Dr. Janovic, follow me," said one of the new arrivals as he motioned for Luka to walk toward a set of doors leading into the primary wing of the medical facility.

Luka walked in front and waited at the threshold until his escorts came into sensor range and the doors opened with a quiet hiss. Of the buildings within the secured Daedalus Astrodynamics complex, the medical facility was the only one Luka did not have privileged access to. He hardly knew it. Every two weeks they underwent routine physical evaluations, and for this, they were granted access to only one specific subsection of the building. The sum of his knowledge amounted to the training facilities where the tests were performed and the hallways that led to them. As he passed through the doorway and as his eyes adjusted to the harsh white LED's, Luka was disappointed and reassured to discover it was much like the interior of any other part of the complex. This hallway was sterile and orderly. It was bright and isometric, not unlike his lab. Not unlike his living quarters either. Once inside, the med staff took the lead and directed Luka through a confusing sequence of white corridors and layers of biometric security. It was all identical to his eyes, and though he tried to keep an internal bearing, he was sure he could not retrace his steps should he find the need to.

Then, his surroundings changed. They passed through one more set of narrow walkways, one last innocuous laboratory space, and emerged in a large central chamber.

The room had an open floor plan. Entrances to more interesting looking labs lined the outside at regular intervals, but Luka could not focus his eyes on them. At the center of the room stood a massive white monolith of a machine. It was ten meters in height and double that in diameter. A spire-like metal structure extended from it and rose to the ceiling. He craned his neck upward as he traced it to its point. It was cast in a dull metal, which he reasoned was some alloy of aluminum or tungsten, and deep grooves traced its outer surface like canyons carved by ancient rivers. The ceiling was domed like the inside of a massive planetarium and it had a peculiar geodesic pattern. Ice filled his veins as a realization swept over him.

The spire was a heat exchange system and the domed ceiling was radiation shielding. It was the same pattern he designed for the electromagnetic shielding on the Constellation craft. Only a machine that consumed and released prodigious amounts of energy would need such an extensive cooling element and only a machine that used antimatter would need such radiation protection. He was told the government permitted Daedalus Astrodynamics to use antimatter strictly for the propulsion systems on the Constellation. The existence of this machine suggested that other agreements had been made. It meant Daedalus Astrodynamics had far more political leverage than he knew. It meant the stakes were higher than just being kicked off the mission. Michael had been trying to warn him of this before the attack.

They circled clockwise around the machine until they came to a break in its matte-white outer shell—a control hub and a small tunnel-like entrance into the core. Some technicians busied themselves making adjustments on screens and turquoise blue projections here. The curve of a reactor cell behind them removed any shred of doubt he still held. Antimatter powered this system.

"Welcome Dr. Janovic," said another member of the medical team as he approached Luka. "I doubt you've seen this particular instrument before. This a DNA matched bioreconstructor, we're going to use it repair that laceration in your back."

The doctor motioned to the massive instrument behind him, "the DMR, it uses your—"

Luka cut him off mid-sentence, still staring up at the spire, "I get it, it takes my DNA and prints tissue."

The doctor recoiled and anger flashed in his face for an instant, but he recovered and put on a polite face. "Ok then. Seems you have the gist of it. Well, uh, in that case, we need you to remove all of your clothing and then lay down there on your stomach here."

He motioned to a sled like that of an old MRI scanner. It extended from the cylindrical opening at the heart of the machine.

"First, we will need to render a 3-D model of the wound, then we will begin the reconstruction process."

Luka twisted his mouth and hesitantly pulled his shirt over his head. He threw his shirt to the floor and paused for a moment, wrestling with whether he wanted to climb into a device that channeled so much energy.

He undid his belt and let his pants fall to his ankles.

"Please remove your underwear as well Dr. Janovic," said the machine's operator.

Luka slid his underwear down and kicked his pants and shoes free from his feet. Between the doctors, instruments technicians, and other medical personnel, there were at least twelve people in his immediate vicinity. He looked around at them but not a single one of them seemed to register the sudden presence of a naked body. They focused on their tasks.

With Luka disrobed, the doctor used a box of alcohol wipes to clean the skin around the wound. The dried blood around the wound required scrubbing in some areas and the rough motion sent stinging shots of pain through Luka's body. He gritted his teeth and did his best not to flinch.

When the doctor finished his preparations, he motioned to the sled with an open hand. "Position yourself here please."

Luka climbed on the sled. He laid his chest down first and swung his feet up after him. Contact with the cold plastic sled raised goosebumps along his arms and legs and he shivered for a moment while his body adjusted. Laying prone with arms tucked at his sides and his head propped up on his chin, he felt like he was preparing to skeleton luge into the great machine.

"We are going to sedate you. The procedure itself is more or less a painless one, but we can't risk you moving."

At the same time the doctor explained this, a technician fixed an IV into Luka's hand.

"More or less? That's not very reassuring," Luka challenged. "Care to explain how—"

He tried to continue but all at once his brain slipped into sleep and he fell away from the present.

The next sensation Luka remembered was that of his mind being vacuumed out of a dreamless, black unconsciousness. His eyes opened, and he was sitting upright in a white leather chair. It was not a plushy recliner, not the type a person relaxed in. This chair was tightly upholstered, square-ish, and thinly padded. The hard edge of an armrest dug into his ribs where he slumped over it.

He looked down. New clothes—even his shoes were changed. Now he wore a navy blue flight suit, the kind they would wear for the duration of the mission. The material was a sturdy mix of synthetics, somewhere between neoprene and cotton. It was form-fitted but much more structured and breathable than spandex. On the right side, near the collar, it was embroidered with his name in light-blue lettering. On the left side, it had his title.

Dr. Luka Janovic. Chief Propulsion Systems Engineer.

His new shoes looked something like a boot but felt much lighter. He reached back and felt along his shoulder blade where he expected to find the wound from the accident. The area was hot with blood, but there was no open wound. As far as he could tell there was not even a scar. All that remained was some minor swelling.

33

Luka was busy running his fingers over the new skin when the door to the room slid open. A lean, bald man with a feminine gait entered. He wore all white and had sharp amber eyes set behind a pair of thinly framed glasses. As a kid, Luka had known adults who had a genuine need for prescription glasses but in this era, they were an affect. Anyone living in this world had vision impairment corrected well before adulthood.

The man spoke with the same grace and calm that he walked, "Hello Dr. Janovic, I'm Janus Claassen, I am chief liaison for Daedalus Astrodynamics and the Committee for Human Development."

He extended his hand in Luka's direction.

"I know who you are," Luka replied, ignoring the man's gesture.

Janus withdrew his arm.

"Ah, well then, no need for further introductions," he said as he took a seat across from Luka. "We are sorry for the difficult ride here. It is just that we needed to secure you quickly. Those were militant separatists that attacked you. We do not know why they went after you specifically. We monitor their activities and typically they focus their efforts only on government targets. This was an *out of family* event. It did not fit our models. You will feel reassured to know that we launched an investigation into this attack to determine all motives."

"I'm so relieved," said Luka as he rolled his eyes.

"We became aware of an impending attack during the interview broadcast. MilPol was on scene to intervene and we thought they could stifle the effort—we did not, however, anticipate the assailants would have access to repulser technology. An investigation has also been launched to determine how they might have acquired the schematics to build such a device. We are greatly concerned by this."

I'm sure you are, thought Luka. Repulser tech was discovered by Daedalus Astrodynamic when a prototype propulsion system failed during a power test. It wrecked a huge portion of their R&D facility. The cost to rebuild and replace all the electronics almost put them under. Dauntless as they were, they recouped the cost—and then some—when a member of the board of directors realized the military might be very interested in that technology. A division of R&D was then dedicated to weaponizing the technology that caused the accident. This filled their coffers and the propulsion systems team began work on a new design for the Constellation craft. This was when they appointed him as the lead designer for the propulsion system.

"We understand you sustained an injury. Did the DMR work satisfactorily?" asked Janus. The flat quality of voice indicated no concern for Luka's wellbeing, only an interest in the outcome of the procedure.

"Yes. There is some swelling, but as far I can tell it's healed."

"Any other side effects you've noticed? Headache, nausea—disorientation?"

"No."

Janus smiled, exposing teeth that were startlingly white even against the perfect bleaching of his clothing. "Excellent. We've spent quite some time developing that technology. In a way it is fortunate we had this opportunity. This was the first real-world test. That device is still in more of a proof-of-concept phase than a practical one. I am pleased to hear it functions outside of an experimental application."

"Me too," replied Luka, hoping that an obvious lack of interest in the goings-on of their medical research would end the conversation sooner. He was too groggy to be pissed yet at having been used as a lab rat.

His stomach lurched and his heart surged. In the fog of the drugs, he had forgotten.

"What happened to Michael? Is he alright?" Luka asked, his eyes wide.

Janus held his palm out. "He will be fine. Our team indicates he is stable, but it is too soon for visitors. We can discuss this in more detail later and determine a visitation schedule."

"Ok then. What now?"

"Good you ask. We are pulling all the crew members from their off-site housing and relocating them here. We're not taking chances; everyone will remain on campus for the duration of pre-mission. It was not our plan to initiate this phase until three months pre-launch, but given recent events, we believe it is best. You can return to your quarters now."

"And do what when I get there?" asked Luka.

"Captain Lorenz would like to meet with the team in two hours. Not everyone is on site yet, many crew members are still in transit. Aside from Captain Lorenz, I believe Dr. De Villiers, specialists Eilertsen and Widmeyer, and doctors Villa and Blair will be present at the briefing."

Janus said *believe*—as though there was some casual doubt

who would be present and who would not be. DA knew their exact whereabouts, always.

"Okay. I don't have clearance though. I'm certain that blast wiped my credentials," said Luka.

"You have clearance. The doors will recognize the signal from your biochip."

"What?" questioned Luka.

He heard it fine, but he needed confirmation to believe it.

Janus looked up and stared at him with that unnerving gaze that was his default form of expression. Luka went pale as the information sunk in. His heart sucked the blood from his extremities back into his core and his skin matched the fabric of Janus's suit. The room felt smaller.

Janus elaborated, "While you were under we took the liberty and implanted your biochip. It was more efficient that way, more convenient for you. This way there was no need to anesthetize you twice."

The panic crept in stronger. I felt like an anchor hanging from his neck and pulling him toward the floor. Luka fought to keep himself upright. He knew already that he would not like the answer to the question he was about to ask.

"I was told I was only being sedated, not anesthetized, and only so that the re-constructor could image me and repair me the wound in my back. Exactly how long was I under Janus?"

Janus folded his hands onto his lap and crossed one leg over the other. It was another odd mannerism of his. The position itself was not feminine, but the way he approached it was distinctly effeminate. He folded his hands delicately,

37

placing one on his right leg first and then gently laying the other on top of it. He did not cross his legs by laying one on top of the other but instead locked them together at the ankle as a woman in a skirt would at a formal occasion.

"Well, as you know, we must carefully monitor a patient's brain activity after the chip is implanted. There are extensive diagnostics that must be run, all with the brain in a controlled, stable state."

"How long?"

"Fifty-six hours, approximately."

"Jesus."

Luka stood. His legs shook, and the room dipped and swayed like he was wading in a gravitational mire. "You can't just do that without my consent. Fifty-six hours, are you kidding me?"

Luka meant to emphasize his outrage by standing but Janus did not meet his escalation. He sat in his odd way and stared into space. Without a reaction from Janus, Luka's gesture became awkward. He sat back down.

Janus pressed on like none of it was in the least bit strange, "Technically we can, and we did, Luka. It is stated in your contract that such a device would be implanted prior to launch. Please realize that I, of course, do understand your alarm. You also must see how it was the most logical set of actions given this sequence of events."

"What time is it?"

"Oh-eight hundred hours on Tuesday the twenty-fifth of August," Janus said. He recited it like a computer. It was odd to hear him utter such an arithmetical sentence when he moved and spoke with so many graceful embellishments. The use of military time juxtaposed his delicate manner.

Luka bit his lip. Janus waited.

"You should have told me ahead of time. That is a breach of protocol. I'm going to bring this up to the Committee," Luka said.

Janus nodded. "If you want, you may. We of course sought the Committee's approval before we took such an action. The circumstances of your arrival were unusual. We had to improvise. I doubt they will find your complaint to be consequential."

Whether Janus told the truth about getting approval or not, he was right. the Committee was not likely to take action on any complaint Luka brought to them. They already saw him as the prima-donna among the crew and he was sure that his recent performance at the interview would not help his cause.

"What about Michael? It's been fifty-six hours. I understood the need to wait when I thought it had only been a few hours. It's been days."

"Our medical staff says his condition is stable, but it is too soon to visit, as I said before."

"If his condition is stable, why is it too soon for visitors?"

"That is the determination of the medical staff, not my own."

Luka grit his teeth to keep from exploding. It was fruitless to argue with Janus. He was singularly rational.

"Fine. When can I see him?"

"As soon as his medical team clears him for visitors. Would you like to be notified when that happens?"

"Yes, obviously I would," Luka said as he stared at Janus. "Are we done here?"

"If you want to be," replied Janus, unfolding his hands and placing them on the armrests of his chair.

"Okay."

"Okay," said Janus as he stood, pushing off from the chair with his hands and letting his fingers drag behind as he did so. "Let me show you the way out."

He motioned toward the door, "Would you like to be picked up, your building is across campus?"

"No, I'll walk. Thanks."

"Hum. Yes, perhaps it is good that you stretch your legs after such a long sleep."

Luka bristled at his word choice. A drug-induced coma did not qualify as sleep. He bit his tongue.

Janus's eyes went foggy as he accessed his interface while they walked, "We'll need to arrange training sessions so that you may fully utilize your biochip—it can be a strange adjustment period. For now, I advise that you do not attempt to access it. We have already uploaded the power system schematics and it may overwhelm you the first time that you become aware of this information. It is no cause for major concern, but the sudden rush of data to the brain has been known to induce seizures—that is until the host learns to

40

manage the flow."

"And how exactly do I avoid accessing it then?" asked Luka.

"Well, in truth, we don't know. That's why the training is so crucial. Unfortunately, the triggers vary from person to person. It seems that, despite our advances, some of the brain's mechanics remain an enigma."

Janus smiled apologetically but the sharp look in his eyes made clear it was not.

They came to a set of double doors, and as they neared, a heavy set of locks actuated with an audible *thunk*. The doors slid apart at diagonal angles and bright yellow morning light flooded in through the opening. Luka shielded his eyes with a hand while his pupils struggled to adjust. It was typical of Seattle to be sunny on a day that he did not mind a few clouds and rainy on those that he pined for a bit of light. The warmth of the sun was a welcome change though, despite the glare. Being indoors so long Luka had no longer noticed how cold and synthetic the air in the medical facility was. It was like water distilled to such purity that it had lost its taste—all of the minerals and imperfections that gave it character, torn away.

"I know where to go from here," said Luka as he took his first step through the doorway.

"Very well. We'll be in touch."

Janus posted in the doorway, wearing a blank expression while he waited. Luka felt Janus's eyes on him as he walked away and made for his living quarters. He took at least a hundred steps before he dared to look back over his shoulder. When he did, he found that Janus was still standing at the doorway, still staring him down from across the ocean of asphalt that separated them. The bright sun reflected off of his white clothing and blurred his figure, but Luka felt the pierce of his gaze.

Ahead, it was empty. It was early enough in the morning that only a few of the sizable operations staff were active. Security drones busied overhead though. They moved like hummingbirds, zipping from point to point in quick bursts and pausing for short rests. Their undersides were painted a grayish-white and their rotors produced only a quiet hum, making them difficult to spot, but his eyes keyed to their motion. They were like shadows at the edge of his field of view. Although they appeared to be governed by chaotic patrol algorithms, it also seemed that one was never far from him. Maybe it was their sheer numbers that created this feeling, or then again, maybe this was a 'perk' of his new biochip. Even before it was implanted, Luka suspected this 'simple memory enhancement' would host a set of unadvertised peripheral functions. Janus confirmed as much when he explained that the biochip replaced his old security credentials.

He pushed it from his mind for the time being. He ignored the drone, and he kept eyes forward on the horizon until the entrance to the residential complex came into view. The building was six floors in height, shaped like an 'L' with a large square area set in the middle. It was boxy but modern. Delicate lines of white metal and glass defined a complex spiraling polygon, accented by brushes of deep navy and royal purple. What appeared to be glass was semi-transparent photovoltaic paneling, and in many places, the tubular sections of white metal were small-scale wind turbines. Every part of the building had hidden functions. His quarters were on the top floor of the left wing, nearest to the Captain's and Elise's. The remaining nine members of the crew were housed on the same floor, but in the larger right wing which formed the vertical stroke of the 'L'. Like those at the medical facility, the doors to the living quarters unlocked with a heavy sound and hissed as he approached. They hermetically sealed the environment inside.

This entrance opened to a lobby and a speckling of administrative offices. Above them were several floors of single bedroom apartments, intended to house the crew and some support staff once the mission entered the pre-launch phase. A ten-foot Aztec pyramid crafted from a light gray stone dominated the lobby. Water rose from its center and cascaded down its steps, collecting in a pool at its base. A bright blue paint lined in the pool's inside so that water took on a winsome turquoise glow. Pulsing and sparkling LED lighting enhanced the hypnagogic effect. He moved past the empty offices and toward the elevator to his floor. The office doors were open, but they were dark inside. They were asleep, remaining dormant until their hosts arrived. Within the hour the lights would click on, the computers would power up, and the offices would come to life as they sensed their users nearing. All of the DA campus was half-alive, half-intelligent, sleeping and waking in rhythm with its human counterparts.

The accident left him sore, and the long sleep made him lethargic, but at the last minute Luka opted for the stairwell instead of the elevators. A painful six flights up, the stairway opened to a large room filled by morning sun from an impressive dome of skylights overhead. Beams of light glared on the white couches and tables, giving the impression that the room was out of focus. Light reflecting from a midnight-blue accent wall at the far end of the room cast a bluish-purple glow over everything—like a neon light seen through drunken eyes. Luka squinted, but the room looked the same. Maybe there were drugs lingering in his system.

Eager to plan who he would harass so he could get in to

see Michael, he made for the hallway at his right that led to his quarters.

A voice stopped him.

"And he arrives, our own Jesus back from the dead—and *wow,* he's already in his flight suit. You do realize it is still weeks before launch don't you?"

His eyes snapped to the source of the interruption: a dark spot in the glare that he had not bothered to recognize as a human form before. Elise was sitting on a couch in the common area, with her feet tucked beneath her and an elbow propped against an armrest. She lowered the book she had been reading into her lap but kept it open in her left hand, pinching the pages beneath her thumb to keep her place.

He knew she was only joking in her boorish way of doing so, but she was not smiling. She never did, not really. The nearest he had seen in the three years was a sardonic grin. One that lacked any warmth.

She was scowling now with her face as rigid and tense as her body. She had the ultra-lean physique a person achieved only through compulsive exercise. It spoke to self-discipline that verged on self-punishment. She permitted no luxury, and she wore her skin with inexorable confidence. She was an unyielding and often unlikeable person—good as a crew member, but not a friend. She could not armor her eyes though. In them, Luka saw an acute intelligence and that somehow forgave so much of her harshness. He sometimes lost himself in this, wondering if her thoughts were as hard as the persona she created. Luka held onto that hope.

She was wearing a white tank top and navy leggings, both DA-issue, but no shoes. It was another announcement of her refusal to be tamed. She never followed the rules of the

44

common area.

"Not my choice, I was—" Luka started explaining.

"Luka, I know. They told us you were in the medical facility for like two days," Elise said as she rolled her eyes. "Why do you think I was giving you a hard time—you're kind of a drag, anyone ever tell you that?"

"You're not the first."

"That's shocking."

"Oh fuck you," Luka returned.

There it was. That near-smile she sometimes dared to show.

Elise untucked her legs and placed her bare feet on the floor. She drew out the action. It felt like slow motion. Then she stared at him with that violent, unblinking intensity that was her trademark.

"Fuck me? So that's what you want then. When? Should we do it here, she would do it right now?" she asked.

She knew. She knew how he looked at her in those moments that he forgot Emma. This was her way of calling him out on it. That is what he told himself.

Elise set the book down beside her letting it close, losing her page. She put her hands down on the couch, leaning in toward him.

"You know, you and I could go to your room, doctor, and we could see what it is you're after."

She said it with such intent, and stared at him with such an alarming severity, that he assumed she meant it only to intimidate. A voice in his mind screamed to walk away.

His body, however, responded to her challenge differently. His pulse quickened. His skin prickled. His higher mind fought the tide of feeling, but something more primitive in him, something much stronger, urged him to consider that she was serious on some level. It forced him to confront a truth. It was a condemning reality, and one that he hid poorly. *He wanted to say yes.* But even if it became more than a joke and they walked down the hall together. Even if she then ripped off his pants, and he removed her shirt. Even if they pressed together and her body tensed as he gripped the hair at the nape of her neck. Even if, at that moment, just before their lips met, he saw that opening in her eyes grow a little wider, he knew that he could not go further. It would always end there.

He shot her annoyed look and started walking in the direction of his room again.

"Luka."

He did not turn back to face her, "What?"

"How's Michael?"

Luka stopped full, but he did not turn back to face her. "I don't know yet—why do you want to know?"

"Come now, I'm not so heartless," said Elise.

"Excuse me if I'm not convinced." He was facing away, paused mid-step, "—and I think most of the crew would agree with me on that."

"Well, how are we ever going to find out if you never give me the chance?" she asked.

He looked back to see Elise putting on a vainglory. Her hair was pulled back tight into a ponytail, which she liked to tuck over the front of her shoulder instead of letting it rest at her back. She was a classic vision of Scandinavian ancestry. In a lot of ways, she was a modern Viking. She was tall, fit, capable, and determined. Her coldness, that profound satisfaction she wore when she twisted someone to her will, was nauseating. Yet, she charmed people with it—himself included.

Maybe it was only her looks that enabled her. Men were always more accommodating of beautiful women than they were of good women. Maybe it was her confidence that attracted people. Whatever was the case, she took great pleasure in it. It came easily to her and Luka fell into it.

He turned on his heel to face her. If it surprised her to see him turning back and walking toward her, she did not show it. He choked down the panic welling in his torso and moved with as much intent as he could muster. She watched unflinching, like a predator anticipating a meal. Her was her prey, his eyes dull-eyed and hypnotized by her danger.

"What's going on here?"

Luka recoiled at the sound of another voice, that of Captain Lorenz.

It was not his instinct to fall in line at a command, even after his time spent at White Sands, but he did. Captain Lorenz elicited this response in him—in all of them. The effect was immediate. The spell broke, his eyes moved from Elise to the Captain.

Olivia's expression was a mix of irritation and exhaustion, her face slack and heavy.

"I have no idea," said Elise.

Elise had deftly changed her face since Olivia's interruption. Now, she too was apparently confused by the situation. She raised her eyebrows dramatically.

"Never mind, I don't want to know. You two know protocols. Keep it in your pants. Or for god's sake at least keep it out of the open," said Olivia while she waved it off with a hand.

Every crew member was nearly the same age, the oldest at thirty-five and the youngest at twenty-seven. Olivia was only a year older than him and yet she was scolding them like a mother walking in on teenagers making out in her home.

"Actually, no. Listen," said Olivia.

She looked stressed, something Luka did not notice before.

"We are under even more scrutiny now. The Committee is nervous that NASA will back out of the mission. I'm doing my best to hold everything together, but I just don't know. Luka, you've been under so you probably haven't heard. Ever since the assault, there's been talk of putting Seattle back under full martial law. These attacks may derail the mission. The Committee can risk the capture of antimatter."

She paused.

"Whoever attacked you took out that entire MP unit in seconds. That's not supposed to happen. The MP are untouchable. All the tech and bioenhancements those guys have—and the access to surveillance—they should have the advantage always. The repulser was something unexpected. It had modified wave frequencies. They're saying it overloaded any biochip in a quarter mile. Preliminary reports show it was about ninety percent lethal to anyone with tech hard-wired to their nervous system. Considering that most of our military and political higher-ups fall into that category, it's a serious problem."

Olivia rubbed her forehead, speaking to the floor. "We fall into the category. Luka, so do you. Now."

This was a strange gesture for Olivia. She was never one to avoid eye contact when speaking. Luka took it to mean she knew much more than she was telling them now.

"You're lucky you got out. That's all I can say," she added.

Olivia exhaled when she finished speaking. Her cheeks puffed out as she pushed the air through her lips.

Elise meanwhile listened on without an attempt to disguise her boredom. She slouched in her seat and picked at her cuticles. She had a low tolerance for gloom and she wanted to make certain that Olivia knew it.

Luka watched Olivia, who normally would confront Elise on this, slump down into the white leather of a nearby armchair.

"Let's wait until the others get here."

An hour passed with none of three speaking. Elise returned to her book. Olivia followed form, picking one up from a shelf along the back wall. Luka did nothing, more or less. He found a seat, and he starred at the sun refracting in through the windows, awash in his thoughts.

49

He worried for Michael, who was no doubt strapped to some machine in a hyper-sterile corridor of the medical facility. He could only hope they were doing more good than harm because it was his fault that Michael was there at all. He threw a fit, he stormed out. He threw off their schedule. The interview was supposed to last another fifteen minutes. If he had not lost control, they would have been at the news studio during the attack.

Luka had never met Michael's wife Rebecca, but he knew Michael loved her deeply. He knew that she was good to Michael too. After the coma, during all those awful months, Michael had been there to help him. Michael slogged through the pain of recovery with Luka while his surgeons repaired his spine in a series of agonizing surgeries. He came out alive because of Michael's efforts. Michael had been there to talk him down late at night and to keep him moving forward when the pain was severe. Michael missed so many days and nights with his family during that time, and Rebecca had been remarkably patient with all of it.

Michael had daughters too. Luka wondered if they were scared. He wondered if he should call Rebecca, or he wondered if DA had already done so.

Luka, Elise, and Olivia all flinched as the double doors leading into the common snapped opened. Olivia set her book down and looked back over her shoulder toward the entryway. The latest arrivals were Dr. Hadrien De Villiers and Dr. Rafaela Villa—both employees of Daedalus Astrodynamics, both exceptional systems engineers.

Olivia shot upright and trotted in their direction, greeting them with a warm smile and genial handshake. Villa smiled and she shook her hand. Haddy, however, wore a more guarded expression. His lips were pulled into a thin line. Luka knew him well enough to recognize it as a happy expression. It showed in the wrinkles near his eyes.

"Haddy, Villa, so good to see you both," Olivia said.

Her eyes looked glassy and concerned. It was unusual for Olivia to show so much emotion. He wondered if she had been worried whether they would arrive at all.

Haddy slung a bag down onto a nearby couch and surveyed the room. He and Luka exchanged a nod. Elise was too busy with her book for greetings or at least pretending to be.

Haddy starred directly at her and cleared his throat. "What, are you too good to say hello now?"

Elise lowered the book. Her face dripped with malcontent. They glared at one another, both immovable. The room went silent while their ritual played out. Haddy looked like he might try to strangle her. Elise's looked not the least bit concerned by it.

Then she winked, exaggerated and cheeky. Haddy smiled and chuckled.

"Good enough. I know not to expect too much of you," he said.

His expression hardened. "Where's the rest of us?—I thought Villa and I would be the last."

He looked in Elise's direction but the question was to the room at large.

Olivia nodded for Dr. Villa and Hadrien to take a seat. They took the cue. Haddy positioned himself beside his bag while Villa took an open space next to Elise.

51

Olivia then began explaining that Tara and Dr. Blair were also supposed to be here at this point but were "indisposed" for reasons Janus would not disclose. Luka imagined they were presently in the medical facility, having chips attached to their nerve cores without their knowledge, the same as had been done to him.

Hadrien was busy cross-examining Olivia in his thick Afrikaans-slanted English. He had a habit of dropping the h's from "this" and "that" and when he swore—which he did often—it sounded open and throaty like 'fock'—with the 'u' rolled into an 'o'. The 'ck' came out as a guttural click sounding from somewhere low in his throat. It was a sound Luka did not think he could imitate even with years of practice. The more agitated he became, the more clipped and strung together Hadrien's words became. There came the point where it was difficult to understand him at all as he slipped in and out of his native tongue.

"*Blicksemse* fock. *Indisposed?* How does he get off saying that? I can't be the only one here who thinks it's bizarre they're not telling us."

"No, no you're not. I'm fed up with him too, Haddy," Olivia answered, "but he is *their* gatekeeper, whether we like that or not. You've worked for DA for years, you know how they are. Everything must be compartmentalized—information is a disease."

"It's not right," Haddy added.

Olivia gave him an icy look to make it clear her patience for the topic was fading.

"We all feel the same. We end it there," she said.

There was a silence then. No one seemed to know what to say. They looked around to one another like students all hoping that someone else would speak up and answer the teacher's question.

Villa, who had been sitting in silence since she arrived, took this opportunity to enter the conversation. She spoke with a cool and even, "So what are we expected to do now? We are here well ahead of Pre-Launch, if I am to begin final diagnostics I will need the whole crew to be present. Without their direction, a subsystem may be overlooked. It creates complications. It leaves room for oversights we cannot permit."

Luka knew Villa well enough to recognize her cool tone a symptom of extreme stress—much the opposite of what it appeared. He admired her ability to remain composed when others went ragged. Conventions had changed since his childhood. It was more socially acceptable than ever for a man to be emotional, and all the mental health professionals who tried to guide him out of the bog of Emma's death wanted him to express his feelings. They saw the weight of his feelings and thought that opening up would alleviate the pressure. He obliged them. He cried, he broke down, and he lashed out. He let loose on those who would hear it. In the end, however, he felt no release from it. He found only exhaustion in it. He discovered that for everything he let out into the world, he somehow took more back in. These were the gallows of anxiety—to search for catharsis and to find regret instead.

Villa fiddled with the collar of her shirt and stared at Olivia, waiting for direction. Olivia sat perched on the edge of the chair with her neck straight and spine arched. The coldness that took her face earlier faded as the topic shifted away from Janus.

"The Committee has decided that we will begin Phase One in three days. Everyone is supposed to have arrived by then. In the meantime, we will be left to look after ourselves. Stay out of trouble and hold tight. I'm sorry I can't offer more than this. The assault on Luka and Michael disrupted our timeline."

Villa nodded in casual acknowledgment of Olivia's statement. She then sat back in her seat, satisfied with the directive—limited as it was.

At Villa's resignation, their collective urgency waned, and the day passed, more or less, without event. Olivia and Elise sought refuge in their books. Luka chatted with Haddy for a while. Villa joined in for a bit too, but as the day wore into afternoon, she disappeared into her sleeping quarters. As the shadows grew long, Luka was left on a couch by himself. Olivia and Elise remained in opposite corners of the room, seated near the large panes of glass. Their bodies traced dark lines against the vibrant orange and red sky beyond.

Chapter Three

Luka wanted the calm that took the room to find him too, but he was restless and fidgety. His chair groaned as he shifted his weight from hip to hip and as he tucked and untucked and re-tucked his legs beneath him. He tried to put his mind somewhere peaceful, but the slakeless thoughts of Michael and his conversation with Janus fought their way forward over and over.

Elise, meanwhile, lost herself completely in her book. She offered no respite to him. She had the habit of swinging between extremes of imperiousness and complete detachment, and she was living in the latter now. She was the gargoyle of their little world, and it bothered him how unburdened she was by the concerns of the rest of the team. Once, he tried to break her exterior, and he succeeded. He did not, however, find what he expected. When he pried, there was no Disney princess hiding beneath all of her anger. It was not a girl looking for hope or love that peered back at him through the tiny opening he created when he pressed her about her childhood. Instead, it was the same hardened look he saw in the soldiers at White Sands when they tested weapons on insurgents. He knew then that her armor did not protect her from the world. It protected the world from her. She knew how to kill. She had killed. He did not know the when, where, or how of it, but he was certain of what he saw in her face. Every time he thought of interrupting her, he remembered this.

Luka gave up on waiting for Elise's attention to sway from her book. It was nearly dark when he finally stood and took his first steps, shuffling down the hallway to retreat to his quarters. Elise was not more than a shadow now, and she seemed quite content and surprisingly able to read in near darkness.

He closed his door behind him with a cold click and sat and sank on the edge of his bed. He stared at the wall while he organized his thoughts. His mind was not a library anymore. Once it had been clean and orderly, but now when he looked inward he saw a shanty town—more wreckage than structure. It was cold and the tin roofs were always making a racket in the wind. The threatened to blow away into a low orange sun.

Luka folded his arms against his chest. He already knew he would not succeed, but that was an insignificant detail. He was going to try to get to Michael. He owed him the effort at least.

He knew it was impossible for him to travel anywhere in the facility without being tracked, especially so with his new biochip. He also knew that Janus, for whatever reason, did not want anyone from the crew near Michael right now. His reluctance to share details on Michael's condition or to commit to a visitation date advertised this plainly. Daedalus Astrodynamics would be monitoring access to the medical building with extra scrutiny. Given the right resources, and the time, he could have planned a successful approach. Their security was advanced, but every system had faults, shortcomings—workarounds. Resources were rarely an issue on the DA campus, but time he did not have. They would move Michael soon, and that if they did so, he might not see Michael ever again.

It left one option, and a terrible one at that. He could run it like a gauntlet. He could strike sooner than they expected and hope he made it far enough before he was caught. It was more than nothing.

If he was caught, he could pretend that he had wandered over to the medical building looking for help with his biochip. It would not be a convincing excuse to Janus, but it was good enough for anyone else he might encounter. So long as he was a member of the Constellations' crew, they would play nice with him.

Not if he was caught, but when, Luka reminded himself.

Luka lifted himself from the bed and wrapped his fingers around the handle on the door. He turned it, slowly, so that the internal workings silently retracted. The hinges were oiled and smooth. They made no noise as he exited.

Luka slid down the hallway, moving along the wall, hugging shadows. He stopped at the edge of the hall and peered around the corner into the common area. Elise was gone. That was a bit of luck. No matter his reason, she would not have let him pass unfettered. Fortunately, it appeared everyone had resigned to their own quarters for the night. Still, he paused, he listened. His pulse thumped loudly in his ears and made it difficult to hear. He took a deep breath. He waited while his heart stilled.

It was quiet.

He hurried across the room, placing his feet carefully, but quickly as he went. He opened and closed the stairwell door behind him with the same caution as the door to his quarters. Then trotted gently down the stairs.

He avoided the lobby with the pyramid and instead exited through a one-way side-door that connected to the stairwell for emergency exits. It sealed with a hiss after he passed through. He waited again and listened as the door settled.

No voices, no movement.

It was and cold in the way New Seattle so often was. A layer dew instantly collected on his face and clothes. His breath fogged even though the temperature was far freezing.

A heavy overcast blanketed the sky. It was opaque enough to drown out the moon. With no moon and no stars, it was an astonishingly dark night. In the far distance, the lights of New Seattle glowed with a rusty orange against the cloud cover. The tallest buildings looked cramped by the low ceiling.

Luka could not see the drones but if he listened carefully between the heavy thumps in his eardrums, he could hear them buzzing in their air around him. Nighttime gave the impression of privacy, but it was only that—an impression. He suspected they operated on wide spectrum cameras, seeing in UV, Visual, and Thermal spectra. Day or night did not matter to them. For what he knew, they were equipped with biologic sensors as well—mass-spectrometers constantly sucking in air and monitoring for pockets of skin oils or pheromones. Whatever their means, he was sure the drones knew he was here with them. There was also no sense in trying to stick to dark spaces or to be especially quiet. It was too dark out for anyone to spot him from their windows, and with the buildings being sealed, no sound could reach anyone inside.

Luka took his cue, putting on an air of someone assigned an important task, and set off at a brisk pace toward the medical facility.

In the damp night, the mist quickly soaked him. His DA-issue clothing repelled the moisture and kept him comfortably warm, but the water dripped down his chin and matted his hair to his forehead. Although he was not cold, Luka instinctively hugged his arms to his chest as he walked.

He pushed forward through the fog.

Light from the two lamps marking the east entrance to the medical facility began to bleed through the mist. On a clear night he could have seen that they were huge LED's forming the characters 'M2', but tonight the water vapor in the air muffled their shape into fuzzy white orbs. It was a view pulled straight from an impressionist painter's nightscape.

Luka approached the East Wing doors. The glow of the letters flooded his eyes and blacked out his peripherals as he neared. The drone activity around him gained intensity as he got closer. They hung around him, no longer wisps of movement, but a thick swarm of bees that projected an audible hum into the still night. He ignored them, acting as casual as he could as came into arm's reach of the secluded set of doors that led to the crew's training and exam rooms. They unlocked and slid apart. Luka held a blank expression as he slipped through the doorway and waited while they sealed behind him.

Inside, the overhead lights inside were at half power. They blanketed the hallway ahead in a dim red glow. Heavy shadows occupied the corners. They swam in his peripherals and evolved into dangerous silhouettes. His senses prickled. He knew it was only his nerves, but his eyes darted from side to side, watching for threats. There would be others here working, parts of the medical facility operated twenty-four-hours, but this wing was entirely dead. The red-washed corridor ahead was empty.

Luka set off down the hallway, deciding to make for the training lab and then find his way deeper from there. He would run into issues with security permissions, but he hoped a feigned need for help with his biochip would get him further than his standard permission set.

As he walked, the lights directly over him intensified their glow to a fuzzy white, then they faded to a dull red again as he passed. It was a means of conserving power, but the localized power system was difficult to adjust to. Lights and doors came to life just as he approached and it induced a kind of panic when the world sprung to life and died just behind him. Horror movies used this same trick to announce the approach of something malignant and Luka could not shake that image. The hair on the back of his neck tingled and urged him to look over his shoulder. He struggled to keep his eyes forward and his mind on his target.

He passed through entry into the training lab and crossed the walls of treadmills, weights, instrumentation. There were two doors at the far end of the room. He tried the right-hand one and it opened. Another long corridor stretched ahead, as blank and featureless as any other, and the dimmed lights made it difficult to see to the end of it.

He paused.

Inside the medical building, there were no signs at all. This facility was not intended to accommodate visitors and the medical team all had floor plans uploaded into their biochips. As a consequence, signage was obsolete.

If the Committee intended to—or already had—installed a biochip in Michael or any of the other crew then the bioreconstructor was the best place to start looking. It was at the heart of the facility, in the most secure zone, and while there were no obvious indications of where he should go, he knew it was generally deeper in.

He closed his eyes. He had seen the whole DA facility from the air, once, several years ago. The M2 Medical Facility was near the southern edge of the campus. He held the image in his mind and focused on the view from the side bay of the helicopter as they had circled over the south-west section of campus. There were three buildings in his mind. The smallest he knew was the bunker entrance to the research labs and antimatter housing. The other two were considerably larger. One was a chubby "L" shape, most likely their residential building, and the other something like a Z with a large square in the middle. If he had to guess, the M2 medical facility was this Z-shaped structure and that the bioreconstructor would be somewhere in the central square. They need a large open space to accommodate the huge cooling spire and shielding dome. He pictured his entry point, traced his steps thus far, and then approximated a heading that would lead to the center of the building.

He moved down the corridor and chose a door at his right near the end. It opened too.

Several more corridors and random selections followed. He kept his internal north aimed at the core, and as he progressed deeper into the building, he became aware of an increasing number of biometric scanners. His stomach turned over each time they let him pass. This was more good luck than he deserved.

In theory, these sensor systems were undetectable, but sometimes he would catch a whisper of a click as some mechanism actuated, or sometimes he spotted a tiny red LED at the instant it blinked on. If this building employed the same security as the research labs, then they used microphones and magnetic resonance to listen to the heartbeat of every person in the vicinity and to track their movements. From these basic datasets, behavioral algorithms could detect shades of anger, anxiety, sadness—a whole spectrum of emotions. They were compared to baseline signals from each employee's profile, and from this, the security systems estimated who might be a security risk. They had real-time monitoring of a person's biometric credentials and a simultaneous measure of their intentions. It was far more advanced than anything he saw at White Sands.

Fortunately for Luka, it seemed he did not need to worry about any of it. He breezed through all the security, even has his anxiety grew and the behavioral algorithms should have tripped the alarms. Somehow, they did not. Best case was that his biochip was in a diagnostic state and the medical team knew he might need to return to the medical building in a rush if it malfunctioned—giving him temporary credentials for any choice that led him nearer to the lab where the biochip was installed. He knew better, that was not his life, but he kept moving anyway.

He found that by taking the doors that readily opened to him, he could maintain a course to the center of the building and that the walls beyond each successive threshold were thicker, more reinforced. He was getting closer, and with the progress, a seed of hope grew.

Then, suddenly, the lights went up.

They flipped to full intensity, full-spectrum LED, and in an instant, he was standing in the sun on a clear day. It blinded him while his pupils struggled to contract and stop the onslaught of photons. He shielded against the glare with a hand stretched across his brow.

His stomach dropped.

Someone was approaching, someone who had override authority.

There was a door just ahead on his right. Luka sprinted to it, ripped it open, and darted through. He pulled it shut behind him, using all of his strength to force the pneumatic hinges to move faster.

It was not immediately clear to him what an unlucky choice he made. The door hissed as it sealed shut and only then did Luka's ears go haywire. The door he passed through led directly into the DA facility's anechoic chamber. Gravity swam and he stumbled backward. He thrashed in the dark as he struggled to find something to anchor him.

Next, there was a moment, a brief moment, where he was in suspension. His feet left the ceramic edge of the pool and he hung in the air. Then his body broke the surface of the water. The world snapped back into focus as water erupted around him and his senses returned. His clothes began to take on weight. They could repel the weather, but the seams around his hands, feet, and neck were not sealed. His body shuddered as cold liquid washed over him and flooded his shoes.

The force of his fall had pushed him a few feet under and his now water-logged clothing began to drag him deeper. Water filled his ears and pressed painfully against his eardrums. His sinuses stung and the pressure inside his head multiplied as he sank.

He opened his eyes.

This pool was nearly twenty meters deep, not for recreation, but for simulation of low gravity environments. The room that housed it was cut off from the outside world— perfectly lightless and anechoic. Its purpose was to disorient. Subtle reverberations were a vital aspect of human balance. A person could get used to functioning without them, but it took practice. This room trained a person to fight the creeping disorientation of lightless and soundless environments. Sudden immersion overwhelmed anyone.

Lost to his inky cocoon, Luka let himself drift deeper. His lungs begged for him to swim to the surface and his veins burned as carbon dioxide levels rose, but he ignored their protests. He pushed these thoughts out until they went quiet. He focused and drew his thoughts inward.

His heart slowed.

He rationed the precious oxygen that his body had left.

Thump.   *Thump.*   *Thump.*

He sharpened his focus, looking deeper inward until he found a point of semi-consciousness and his pulse dragged even slower.

Thump.   *Thump.*   *Thump.*

In this state he knew could last for several minutes more, maybe ten, before his brain succumbed to deprivation. He hoped he could hide long enough, but part of his mind became aware of a light filtering down from above. It flowed from a single point with great intensity and formed a neat column of light down to him.

It was a spotlight.

He slipped out of his meditation. As his pulse rose, his legs began to twitch. Drowning was imminent.

The fight was over.

Whoever was up there knew he was down here. It was a waiting game he could not win—but despite the lethal buildup of carbon dioxide in his blood and despite the tremors racking his body, Luka hesitated. A voice somewhere in his mind suggested another path. It said he could sink instead. If he only held on a little longer, all of it would be gone and then he could rest.

Luka shook it off.

He unfolded his legs and began to kick his way to the surface. The first few strokes into the tunnel of light came easy, but the powerful muscles in his legs quickly consumed the little oxygen he had left. He had overestimated his conditioning and a grave reality set in—he might not make it to the surface.

Panic welled, and he lost his practiced swimming form and as he gave in to terror. With his higher mind gone, his body reverted to a frenzied thrashing upward. His heart slammed irregularly behind his ribcage and felt like it would explode with each beat. His vision darkened and his ears rang as his brain moved dangerously close to unconsciousness.

He breached the water in one final frog-stroke up and took in a desperate gasp as his face met the air. He pulled some water into his lungs in the process and broke down into a fit of coughing between frantic, shallow breaths.

Janus waited at the edge pool. He was standing in front of a huge light source—its beam was a meter in diameter with an intensity of hundreds of thousands of lumens. His figure cast a long shadow across the pool.

Luka could not look directly at him. He raised a hand to his brow to shield his eyes from the glare while his other hand worked to stabilize him in the water. He was bobbing up and down at its surface, his body still racked by bouts of violent coughing as his lungs rasped.

Janus waited, looking down at him with that socially inept stare of his. When he finally spoke, he sounded as casual as ever.

"You know you're not supposed to be here Dr. Janovic."

At the sound of his voice, adrenaline rose in Luka. Although his body was exhausted, the sound of it filled him with a new resolve like dying coals fanned back to a flame.

"Oh you think, do you?" said Luka. He tried to shout, but he was too out of breath to manage it.

He swam to the edge of the pool, near Janus's feet, and rested his elbows on the pool's lip so that his legs could stop kicking.

"You know why I'm here anyway. Tell me where he is."

Luka cupped a hand over his nose and cleared his sinuses loudly. It yielded a palm full of murky slime, which he then flung it in the general direction of Janus' shoes. It hit his mark with a satisfying splat.

Janus did not react. "No, I will not indulge you right now."

Luka trod water, equal parts dumbfounded and angry.

Janus continued, "You are here, in the M2 complex, wandering corridors that you have no business in when you well know that you should be in your quarters given the heightened security on campus and the unstable nature of your biochip. This demonstrates a certain disregard for protocols and consequences. Your apparent interest in disrupting this mission concerns me. It is not a healthy behavioral pattern for a crew member."

"And I'm sure you're quite an expert on normal behavior," Luka replied.

"Well yes, I am. As I'm sure you know I hold degrees in many fields—among them are doctorates in psychology and medicine. I think I am well qualified to make such judgments."

"You missed my point."

"Hardly. I chose to move beyond it. I'm hoping to find a resolution, Luka."

"And what resolution is that, Janus?"

"I'm hoping that you will exit the pool."

Luka grit his teeth. "If I do, will you kindly leave me be?"

"I'm afraid not. I have a matter I must discuss with you," said Janus.

Luka slicked his hair back with both hands and exhaled loudly, "Okay."

Luka dragged himself out of the water, putting his forearms up onto the edge of the pool and lifting upward. He flopped onto the surrounding tile with a heavy slap. The doors to the chamber had been opened and several sound-absorbing panels had transitioned into smooth surfaces. The sound of sloshing water reverberated around the room. With light and sound both restored, the disorienting effect vanished.

Luka pushed himself up from the ground and swung his legs under him. They shook as they were forced to bear weight again. He stumbled but steadied himself—working hard not to show his weakness.

With his balance regained, he took a long step forward to close the gap between him and Janus. He adopted a military posture to try to match Janus's height. It was a mark he could never reach, but he did his best to stand nose to nose with him. In the wash of the spotlight, he and Janus looked like two scrawny boxers taking promo photos for their faceoff.

"I did my part, now get on with it," said Luka.

Janus waited—hesitated, maybe. Luka struggled to read him.

"Very well. I know why you're here Dr. Janovic and the answer to what you are going to ask is no. You cannot see him."

A dirty glut of words choked Luka's brain. What managed to come through was the least effective of all.

"Fuck you, Janus."

Luka conjured up whatever chlorinated, slimy discharge he could pull from his sinuses and spat in Janus's face. It landed squarely on Janus's nose and Luka expected that this at least would elicit some emotional response.

It did not. Janus dispassionately produced a bit of cloth from somewhere inside his overly tight clothing and gently wiped his face clean. He took his time, meticulously removing all traces, and when it was done, he neatly folded the cloth and stowed it away in an inner pocket. He acted as though none of it had happened.

Luka clenched his fists. "You're going to let me see Michael or I will raise hell with the Committee. I will go to the god-damned press and I will blow this up. I will tell the public everything that I know and everything that I suspect."

The words echoed and died. Janus almost smiled. The edge of mouth crinkled and turned ever so slightly upward.

"It is not simply a matter of whether I will or I will not. Michael has been transferred to another facility. It is not an option for you to visit him there."

"Where!" barked Luka. "Where did you send him?" It was a question, but he delivered it as a demand.

"The morgue," said Janus.

Luka's body went slack. His legs wobbled and his arms went limp at his sides.

Janus kept speaking, "I assure you that we intended to let you know—when it was appropriate of course." Janus shrugged. "I would say that I'm sorry for your loss, but in truth, I am not. We were becoming concerned that Michael was not a good influence on you. Please return to the housing facility. This mission is over for you. There will be a briefing in the morning."

Luka knew he was not a skilled fighter but a hate so intense overtook him that he was willing to try anything. He would tear Janus limb from limb. He would open his gut and strangle him in his own entrails if he got the chance.

He took a monster swing at Janus's chin, putting his full body weight behind the punch like a drunken brawler. All in all, it was a quick and powerful punch for a person who had not thrown many in their life. Luka was impressed with his own ability.

Janus leaned back and watched the strike fall short of its target like Luka was moving in slow motion. It was in an impossibly swift and fluid reaction. A practiced fighter might have dodged the strike, but not like that—not so effortlessly. All Luka caught with punch was air and he fell forward under the momentum of the strike. His legs were too lethargic to compensate for his shifted center of gravity. He could not recover his balance. He took the fall on his shoulder and skidded on his side across the wet floor.

He scrambled back to his feet and prepared to strike again. Janus turned to face Luka, his postured relaxed— upright, feet together, hands folded behind his back. Luka charged forward and closed the gap, leading with his shoulders as he prepared to tackle. Janus sidestepped it at the last moment. He reacted so quickly that it seemed like precognition. Luka was so close that he felt his shoulder brushing against the fabric of Janus's suit. It was simply too late for his strike not to land, he thought, but suddenly he was throwing his shoulder into air instead of Janus's body.

It compelled him to consider a terrifying reality. Janus was bioenhanced.

The tell was not the movements themselves, but his reaction times. His reflexes were so quick that from an outside perspective it seemed predictive. It outpaced human physiology. His brain could not have transferred the signal to legs quickly enough to sidestep at that moment. It meant that Janus had an optic relay in his spine. It was a mini, synthetic brain that boosted reaction times by circumventing the need to move signals up to his head. It was the most advanced, and no doubt most expensive, neural tech available and until now Luka had doubted that the technology existed at all. On base at White Sands spec ops trainees had insisted to him that it was in field-use. They boasted that when they got their bioupgrades, they would be able to dodge bullets. They were fond, in particular, of a tall-tale about a Wild-West style initiation ritual. They said that trainees would pair off and would go out into the desert at high-noon and draw pistols at ten paces like the old movies. A soldier only made it on a spec op crew if they survived. The trick was, no one ever got hit. Luka had dismissed these as stories fed to young soldiers to get them excited about killing people. Now, seeing the way Janus moved, he had to accept their reality.

Luka hit the ground again, this time sliding on his stomach as his momentum died. He climbed back to his feet and shuffled closer to Janus. He was preparing to launch another punch when he noticed Janus's fist headed for his temple. It landed.

His body went limp. His nose smashed against the ground on the way down and then he felt the cold tile against his face. A knee pushed down hard into his back and a stinging pain rang through the entirety of him. His mind flooded with images. The deluge of thought felt like fluid filling his head, and the sensation of expansion was so great, he thought it would fracture his skull. At first, he could not make sense of it because of the intense pain, but fragments began to form wholes. He saw flashes of circuit diagrams and calculations. They seared into his brain like hot iron. He tried to hold on to the rush, but it overtook him in a flood. He slid into some empty, faraway place.

Chapter Four

Luka woke to a hand cupping his mouth. His first reflex was to inhale at the shock of it, but the palm clamped down over his lips and choked any sound that might escape him. His eyes went wide with panic. He pried at the hand holding him down and lashed out, grasping around him to get leverage.

His hands found sheets, ordinary white sheets. He was in his room, in his own bed. His last memory was Janus's fist making contact with his temple and he had no explanation for his current location.

In the darkness, he recognized the shimmer of her eyes first. Her pupils were drawn to their maximum and effulgent with hunger. Elise was straddling him. Her weight pressed down on his chest and the inside of her legs clamped in against his torso. He rocked his shoulder hard to one side and tried to twist his hips to throw her off. Her center shifted and leaned to one side, but she recovered and moved the hand that had been cupped over his down to his throat. Her grip pinned him down like a manacle.

She lowered her face down to his so that their lips were nearly touching. Silvery strands of hair brushed his cheeks. Her skin was smooth and cold and her breath was sweet as it invaded his lungs. For a moment their pupils synchronized, and they looked into each other. His body eased. She might be luring him in to kill him, and he knew he should not give in, but he did. Her lips pressed against his, the aggression of it matching the predatory look in her eyes, and Luka's hesitations dissolved. He pulled his lips free from hers and brushed his mouth along her neck. She shivered.

Her mouth rested near his ear. The moisture of her breath prickled his skin.

"Just listen," she whispered.

The hum of climate control almost drowned it out.

Luka pulled his face away from her neck. He cocked his head and narrowed his eyes, but her lips moved to his collarbone then, pressing lightly, and he no longer cared. She traced a line along his clavicle and rested her lips on his shoulder. Then she bit him, swiftly and hard. His eyes went wide, and he became aware of his whole body as his muscles twitched and he snapped out of his half-daze. His heart, already quickened, threatened to break through his sternum as his body prepared to fight. It did not draw blood, but her teeth left angry a red impression in the meat of his arm and it throbbed with his pulse. He lurched upward, using the strength of his hips and back to throw her off. She rocked forward in response and slammed her forearm down onto his throat before he could raise his head. His Adam's apple pinched into his windpipe and it locked him in place. She smiled as she stared down into his eyes and waited. When she was satisfied that he would not struggle again, she lowered face and pressed her cheek against his. Her breath flooded his ear with a pleasing warmth again.

"They're going to kill you."

She said it so softly that he was, again, not sure he heard it.

It made little sense. He was lost in a corridor of mirrors, thoughts reflecting on to each other. Part of him said he should be fighting her off right now, part of him wanted it, and another part screamed that something more important was happening.

Then it sunk in what she said. It pierced through his confusion like a cold spear in his gut. He opened his mouth to question, but Elise slapped him hard across the face before he could speak. It rang through his bones and rattled his teeth. His mind swam. She slapped him so hard that the only reason he thought of it as a slap, was that it happened to be open-handed.

"I said keep your mouth shut," Elise said as she sprang back to her feet.

She left in a fury, jerking the door open as forcefully as the pneumatic hinges would allow. She ripped a book from his shelf and threw it at him for emphasis just before she disappeared through the doorway and stormed down the hall.

Luka lay still, dazed not only from the strike but from the sudden egress too. A wave of guilt and a catastrophic wanting came over him in Elise's wake. His guts twisted with regret. No, he had not broken the promise he made to Emma's memory, but the intent was there. The painful erection he had now left him no deniability.

He wanted to let the tears welling in his eyes come forward, but another voice inside him would not allow it. These were problems, but there was something worse yet. It called him from a dark hollow, ringing like a cold church bell. It was distant at first, but as his attention turned, it rose to a scream.

Something was desperately wrong—something he had forgotten to remember.

Michael was dead.

His throat tightened and his mouth filled with saliva. A lump rose from deep in his stomach and burned his esophagus. Bile ejected from his mouth and splattered all over his pillow. He heaved again, and again, until there was nothing left to pull from his stomach. He collapsed to his side and curled his body into a ball. The tears he pushed back earlier found their way through. He sobbed, loud and ugly. His body shook as it passed through him. He cried in a way he had not since Emma's passing. Time lost him. It went on and on until it seemed he depleted every fluid he could expel. Rigors shook him, but there were no more tears to be had. His mouth was cottony and a dry tongue offered no relief to his cracked lips. He rolled over, exhausted, and laid flat on his back. His eyes closed and he drifted toward sleep.

Something dug into his side by his kidney and would not let him relax. He crooked his arm and fished the object from beneath him. Luka held it up and studied it. It was the book Elise threw at him, a copy of Bram Stoker's *Dracula*—decades old. Its deep maroon hardcover was tattered edges, and the pages were yellowed and more brittle than they ought to be. But none of this was remarkable.

Luka sat up and swung his feet over the edge of the bed.

This was not one of his books. It was a stranger. He knew every object in this room. Their living areas were Spartan by design and they trained themselves to memorize, in great detail, every article around them. It was to prepare them for the monotony of the Constellation's interior, and the aching and unchanging months they would spend in transit to and from Europa. In the context of high-risk space flight, it was useful to be accustomed to boredom and to be attuned to small deviations in their environment.

Luka flipped through the book and the must of aged paper filled his nose as the pages rolled over. He smiled weakly, placing its origin. This was the book Elise had been reading a day ago in the common room. It suited her. His shoulder ached where she dug her teeth in.

He stood and paced the room as he examined the book. He dragged his fingers across the binding and the edges of the pages. All the pages had significant fatigue, but some were especially broken and had been dog-eared many times over and then smoothed back out. They were flagged for attention.

The last of these was page 477—evidently where Elise stopped reading the previous night.

When Luka opened to the page, he found that the 477 in the upper right was scratched out and the number 15 was written in its place in blue ink. He turned to another of the flagged pages. Here, the number 54 was inked out and a bold 4 was penned in. As he moved through the book, Luka found four other dog-eared pages were similarly defaced. There was a code to it:

10 was 20

54 was 4

121 was 6

138 was 3

152 was 9

477 was 15

It was a simple book cipher. The numbers scratched on each page pointed to a specific word on that page. Those wishing to hide a secret in plain sight had used this method throughout history. The one used here seemed to be the most simple variant, and following that convention, he should note the 20th word on page 10, when reading from the top left: *Meet.*

The 4th word on page 54 was *Water.*

Following this code, he got a set of six words:

Water, Meet, Old, Rain, Front, Next, Heavy.

They were scrambled, but not random. Reordering the words, a few coherent messages could be formed, but they distilled into only one concept that spoke to him:

Meet Old Water Front Next Heavy Rain.

Elise told him *they* were going to kill him. This was book was connected to that message. She was giving him instructions on what to do with that message. She literally threw them in his face. He did not need to guess much at who she meant by 'they' but it left him with questions. *Was she telling the truth,* and if so, *why had she told him?*

Luka chewed on his lip.

Given his recent confrontation with Janus, and Michael's death, his answer to the first question had to be yes. Her warning was genuine. He was a pain-point for Janus, and the Committee, and the boldness of his recent attempt to breach the medical facility warranted an equally bold response. He sought to expose something they hid and now they sought to disappear him. Action, reaction. The second question, the *why* of it, troubled him more though. Elise was not caring. She liked him enough, he thought. Enough that she harassed and taunted him, like a schoolyard crush. That, however, was not a motive. In every situation, she acted only when she gained from it. The second question transformed. It was not

77

why did she tell him, it was *what did she gain from telling him?*

His lip was bleeding. His mouth was dry and his anxious chewing broke through several layers of skin. He sucked the blood into his mouth and cringed at the metallic taste.

He believed her message was sincere, so first, he needed to live. The rest he would solve later.

He turned his mind to the message of the cipher.

Old Water Front referred to the wreckage of the Hotel Waterfront at the edge of Old Seattle. *Next Heavy Rain* was not so specific, but Luka thought he had the general idea of it. Biochip data transmissions ran on millimeter wave pulses. It was a wavelength capable of handling large data packages and it was also considered safe enough to be transmitting directly through brain tissue. While the avoidance of brain tumors was a massive advantage of using this transmission band, it had a major disadvantage too. Millimeter wave communications were susceptible to rain-fade. The molecules of water in the air could absorb the energy of the transmission through vibration. A heavy rainstorm harried and slowed transmissions. This offered an advantage, however slight, to a person trying to disrupt the tracking functions of their biochip. The rain made it hard for them to ping location with accuracy. It also would diminish the capability of the drones patrolling the DA the facility. The data-intensive communication packages they transmitted—like visual, thermal, and AI—leaned heavily on millimeter wave technology. The rain could create distortions and gaps in their data cycles. If it disrupted the sensor that fed their behavior algorithms, Luka stood a chance to evade them. The time to move would be during the next heavy rainfall.

A storm alone, however, would not be enough to mask his location. It would dull it, and the drones would suffer functionality losses, but he needed something more if he was going to leave the DA campus undetected. Shy of wearing a lead-lined helmet, he knew of nothing that would block the biochip signal entirely—and the weight and conspicuousness of such a helmet made it unusable. He could, however, broadcast his own signal. If he analyzed the biochip signal and then emitted his own anti-aligned signal, their descriptive recombination would significantly reduce the range and clarity of the biochip signal. If this and the rain-fade worked in tandem well enough, he might achieve full anonymity—as long as the storm lasted.

Luka stayed up well into dawn, laying out the schematics for his signal disruptor in the back pages of Dracula while he drank coffee. His ears hummed from the high dose of caffeine in his blood. It took some improvising and less efficient workarounds, but by morning, he had a design that used only components he could scavenge from his lab.

When he stood from his desk, satisfied with his design, it was 6:00 AM. He slid the book into a space on his shelf to disguise it among the others he owned, and after a quick check of his armpits, decided a shower and a change of clothes were in order before anything else. He didn't know if he would have another opportunity before he left. The weather forecasts predicted rain in the evening, but only a sixty percent chance due to prevailing winds pushing the cell north. Nonetheless, he had to be ready. Based on the radar images, if the rain hit, it would be a torrent. It would be exactly the kind of storm he needed.

After showering, Luka pulled on one of the identical Daedalus Aerodynamics uniforms from his closet and left their dormitory, making a direct line for his lab.

The sky was a flat gray, the color of brushed sheet metal, and the morning sun glinted behind it. He frowned and picked up his pace. Today he did not need to pretend. This was his routine. The drones knew his rhythms, and they paid him no mind when he moved in the direction of his work.

His R&D facility looked like a 20th-century missile silo from the outside. The portion on the surface was a squat concrete bunker with narrow rectangular slits for windows—the type of structure a person observed a nuclear detonation from—but it was a facade. The R&D building was an iceberg, extending many floors beneath the surface, and it was not subterranean for security reasons. The deepest points held the greatest danger. This anachronistic bunker on the surface conveyed the appropriate message about what lay beneath. *Stand back.* The antimatter reactor he built, housed on the lowest level, was cataclysmically powerful. If the reactor ever went critical, it would wipe out all of New Seattle—Low City and High City both. It did not matter how deep they buried it. The force might even extend to the remnants of Portland and Vancouver. It would crater the Pacific Northwest like a hundred Mount-Saint Helens. Antimatter was a different kind of power. It had the force to reshape the earth like nothing else. It was God's own dynamite. Luka's blood rushed every time he entered the building, not with fear, but with excitement, and his pulse quickened as the topside bunker doors opened.

On either side of him were two DA security guards. They sported similar navy uniforms but carried heavy combat rifles and had thick panels of body armor over their torsos. There was a limited rotation of guards at this post as it required a higher clearance than most. Luka never spoke to them beyond a gruff 'good morning' or a 'good night,' but he knew their faces. Today on the right was the one with the comically thick mustache. He looked like a cross between a 20th-century porn star and a cowboy. His eyes were more tired than usual.

80

He did not react to Luka's presence, but his companion nodded hello. Luka nodded the gesture and passed between them.

They were a last line of defense only, a bastion of an older time. The real security protocols here were the unseen ones. Even he didn't know the full extent of them—but he knew a barrage of scanners and sensors were sizing him up now. He waited until a thick set of double doors extended out from the once flat wall and slid apart. They opened to a bright elevator cabin. Luka stepped in. Despite their heft, they glided back into place, and the cabin began to fall. His stomach lurched at the sudden acceleration. It took a full two minutes to reach his lab. The doors opened, and it was like stepping a century into the future. However drab the R&D building was on the outside, it was by far the most impressive building of the Daedalus Astrodynamics and NASA network on the inside. His level was officially labeled Subsection 166 East. Chunky black letters on an old whiteboard to his left announced its unofficial name. WELCOME TO NEW MANHATTAN, they said. The research team had taken to calling this level New Manhattan for the obvious parallels to the original Manhattan Project. They played with dangerous energies here.

Luka stepped into the bright laboratory entrance. Overhead white LEDs lit the entire space, but it was sectioned into separate work areas by walls of clean, bluish glass. The walls turned opaque or transparent as needed and were mobile. Huge as it was, this entire level could be rearranged with this network of glass panels. They constantly adjusted the floor plan to accommodate their needs as projects gained momentum or were phased out.

Luka navigated the corridors with ease, taking a direct route to his office and personal lab space. Despite the early hour, many people were already in their labs working.

Fourteen-hour shifts were not uncommon for the dedicated staff—especially during pre-launch. A group of three engineers looked up from the huge metal device on their table as he passed. Rather than showing up early, more likely they were still here from the night before. Their eyes were bloodshot and glazed over from the combined effects of too little sleep and too much caffeine. Luka wondered if they had not turned to more potent stimulants. In his early days, during the core research phase, he had developed an unhealthy reliance on quasi-legal stimulants himself. It helped him push through sleepless nights and it helped him focus to find breakthroughs. For a long time, he allowed amphetamines to carry the weight of his ambitions. There was a time after too, when he decided he could not crutch his intellect with stimulants, that he turned to alcohol to soothe his anxieties. It left him more empty than full.

Luka turned his eyes away from the group and focused ahead. Thankfully, no one was waiting for him at his lab. The glass door glided open and a refreshing serenity greeted him. Pristine white counters opened ahead. All of his tools and equipment were organized exactingly. Every metal surface gleamed. Not a speck of dust rested anywhere. It was his small bit of control in so much chaos. His mind quieted at the sight.

He set to work straight away, pulling components from drawers and collecting tools to begin assembly. He worked in a trance, oblivious to the world. Hours passed.

Luka flinched when the doors to his lab hissed. He whipped his head around to see them opening and instantly recognized the intruder by his easy, loping gait. Haddy wore a wide grin as he strode in and he raised an exaggerated eyebrow as he surveyed the room.

"Keeping yourself busy I see."

"You know, Janus won't like that at all," he added as he nodded to the spectrum analyzer Luka tore apart for components.

Once it had been an impressive instrument with a price tag circling in the millions. Now, it was a carcass. The plastic and aluminum chassis remained intact, but Luka had ripped the innards out and laid them into neat categorical rows and columns. He sorted by function. It was an organized process, but the hollowed chassis and dangling wires suggested the image of a gutted animal.

"What I mean to say is, by all means, *please* tear everything you can get your hands on apart. Since I can't strangle Janus myself, I might as well irritate him to the maximum—and as far as I can see you're doing a better job than ever I could," Haddy continued.

He laughed at his own joke. His body shook with it. In other circumstances, Luka would have joined in and laughed too in his reserved way, but his mind was too dark, too focused at the moment.

"Haddy, they killed Michael," Luka said.

Haddy's jaw went slack. The humor died. He stared at Luka for a long time with his eyebrows pushed close together.

"Wait. You mean killed, literally?" he asked.

Luka's mouth tightened, his lips becoming thin lines. "I... I don't know, actually. That's what Janus said. I tried looking for him but Janus."

Luka stopped mid-sentence, realizing his mistake. Ignorance would offer Haddy some measure of safety.

"What? Why are you here if Michael is dead? What did Janus do?" Haddy's face darkened as his muscles tensed. Anger picked up in his voice and his shoulders squared to Luka.

Luka shook his head. "It doesn't matter Haddy. I'm sorry, don't worry about it. Michael died in the accident. I'm just upset."

"You said killed, not died. What are you holding back?"

Luka was looking off to his right, half present, half in thought while he planned his exit from the conversation.

"You know I have your back," Haddy asserted.

Luka nodded but said nothing. He could not involve Haddy any further. It was not a risk worth taking.

Haddy narrowed his eyes. "I won't step into this. I couldn't say why, but I know you have a reason for not telling me what I can. All I can say is that I hope you will turn to me when that time comes."

Haddy turned his body in the door's direction. "I have my own work to do, so I best get to it."

Luka nodded again in silent agreement.

"Let me know," Haddy said as he approached the exit.

It was a simple phrase, a casual idiom. *Let me know if you want to hang out. Let me know what you want to eat. Let me know when is good for you.* When Hadrien said it, however, it was not casual. He was pleading for Luka to let him help.

Luka said nothing and Hadrien turned away and left. He returned to his work and began assembling the remains of his equipment into his new devices.

The storm arrived that evening.

The winds died and a dense rain cell moved in over New Seattle. When Luka exited the elevator and saw the darkened skies, he smiled. He put on an old jacket he carried up from the lab and raised the hood over his face as he stepped outside. Rain pattered against it as the first drops of the storm fell.

Wherever they kept Michael—or his corpse—he would not find it. He could try a run at every building on campus, but he would lose that game. They would kill him first and make it look like an accident. Within campus, they defined the processes, the laws. They controlled everything. Beyond their campus, however, Daedalus Astrodynamics struggled to hold their place in the world. This facility was unbelievably expensive to maintain and their above-the-law attitude earned them a share of enemies. External pressures were his best chance at getting any answers about Michael. He had powerful contacts, and if they did not work, he would raise hell in the media. The Europa mission was over. Daedalus Astrodynamics was over.

First he needed to get out. The building storm and his newly built signal jammer shielded him from the omnipresent drones, but they would not help with the traditional security systems. DA had an on-site militia of at least a hundred armed soldiers and a two-meter thick concrete wall surrounded the entire complex. This was further fortified by layer of razor-wire topped chain-link fencing. There were snipers too. He recognized them by the rifles they carried as they headed out to, or back from, their posts. He didn't know their positions.

DA designed the place with only one way in and one way out. So that's what he would use. If he could not blast through the walls or climb over them quickly enough to escape, then he would disappear out the front door and hope he made it far enough before they noticed. Some of the staff, like himself, lived on site. There were various kinds of residences available on campus for them. The majority, however, lived somewhat normal lives and commuted in from the towers in High City.. Every day they arrived on one of nine shuttles that dropped off at 8:00 AM and every day they left on 1 set of 3 shuttles that departed at 5:30, 6:30, or 7:30 each.

His presence on one of these departing shuttles would be an anomaly. The shuttles had DNA and facial recognition and would know it was him. There was no avoiding that. Their programming would flag his presence as an out-of-norm event and feed it back into the server—but he guessed that system prioritized anomalies involving entry to the facility over those involving an exit. The guards faced outward. They rarely looked at who was leaving. It was a guess, a gamble, but so long as the flag was given anything other than urgent priority, no one would stop him immediately. It would go to the core for analysis first, and then into a human analysts queue for oversight. They would look at it, and upon review, they would escalate. It would reach Janus, and he would promptly soil his pants. Then they would lockdown the shuttle and turn it straight back to the facility, delivering him to security like a package courier.

The circle of communication left a window of time though—one where he might get beyond their reach before they realized it. The first shuttle stop in High City was twelve minutes out from campus and he might have that long. With the GPS signal from his biochip muddled, they would not know exactly where he was, only vaguely. If he made it off the shuttle, he could disappear into High City and make his way for the Old Waterfront from there.

It was 6:18 now and he needed to make the 6:30 shuttle.

Luka set off across the expanse of asphalt, and as he walked away, he looked over his shoulder at the bunker one last time. His work here had carried him through many painful days. Once, he had even thought of his time here, his role in the mission, as some great humanitarian achievement. He learned that none of it was about advancement or discovery. The mission was for resources. Rare earth minerals were too rare it turned out. Oil dried up, and the world collapsed until a new technology came to save the day. Now, this world built on tantalum and gallium electronics would die when the Earth stopped coughing them up too. Mines ten kilometers deep marred the landscapes of China and central Africa. From space, they looked like the impact craters of Earth-destroying meteorites. Their yields declined every year.

It was NASA's mission at the start. They wanted to go to Europa to find microbial life beneath the ice. It was only a dream, though, without the money to fund it. With its deep pockets, Daedalus Astrodynamics stepped in to save the day. It seemed like a great deal for NASA, but they did not advertise the details of the contract. Along the way to Europa, Daedalus Astrodynamics would drop off a payload of mining probes in the asteroid belt. They would locate and claim the asteroids with the largest deposits of Platinum, Tantalum, Gallium. A few rich specimens could have the worth of nearly the entire global economy.

And there was something else they needed from NASA to make that happen. Despite its poor funding, NASA still had one major bargaining chip. Getting that far out into space required special fuel. Daedalus Astrodynamics had the satellite and probe technology for the mining operation, but they did not have access to the antimatter or the propulsion systems it fueled. For that, they had to cut a deal with the government; they would fund the exploration of Europa if they could launch their mining probes along the way.

Luka pulled his eyes away from the bunker and picked up his pace. In the short time he spent reminiscing, the rain had shifted from a gentle shower to a freezing torrent. He clutched his arms against his chest and kept his head down while he trotted for the shuttles.

Just ahead a mob of employees huddled beneath the glass roofs of the pickups bays. The wind blew the rain at a harsh angle and those around the edges held their umbrellas held out horizontally to guard against the sheets of sideways precipitation. Their dense formation brought to mind a Roman Testudo, but disorganized and strangely colorful with their assortment of umbrellas. They looked like a field of wildflowers being battered by a thunderstorm.

Luka pulled the hood of his jacket in tight against his face and made the nearest bay. The wind whipped at his sleeves and sprayed rain into his face.

The employee shuttles served the same essential function as a school bus, but they were macabre visions of the friendly yellow objects of his childhood. These were heavy armored vehicles, outfitted in carbon hulls, that gave them an ominous matte black finish. The windows were blacked out too, with one-way glass. They carried two security guards and up to fifteen passengers, and yet they were agile. They did not stop for anything beyond their routes. They were programmed with traffic priority, same as an emergency responder. The navigation systems of other vehicles were forced to yield to or avoid them entirely with alternate routes. The public at large hated them. They sped around the High City with impunity. They varied their daily routes. It was an excellent security protocol, but the unpredictability of their location made them especially dangerous to pedestrians. They had taken a few lives. As of yet, no one of real importance. So, as of yet, there was no collective outrage.

The 6:30 set pulled into the bay.

Luka kept his head down and fell in at the back of the crowd as they shuffled one by one into the vehicle. He took a seat near the middle of the shuttle and soon after the vehicle went into motion. It drifted through the facility, but as soon as it passed by the guards at the gate, it took off. It maneuvered at an alarming speed, taking corners with an uncomfortable g-force that seemed it should tip the vehicle over. Although they were thrown about just as much as him, no one else seemed to mind the jarring ride. They were, evidently, accustomed to this balls-out commute. Luka stared out of the window and focused on keeping his heart rate low. He didn't know if sensors on this vehicle would detect his uneasiness. He tried not to panic, but the seconds drug out and the rough ride made it worse. His stomach lurched with every bump and he watched the security guards in his window's reflection, weary of every twitch.

Outside, High City streaked by in a stream of immaculate glass and marble buildings. There were few people out in the streets during such an intense storm and it made the world outside of the DA facility feel empty. The sky crepitated. Thunder rumbled and lightning flashed across the mirrored exteriors of High City's building. His throat tightened.

It couldn't be long.

They had to be getting close to the first stop. He was at 11 minutes 42 seconds now.

He scratched at his palms.

12 minutes, 15 seconds.

Bile churned in his empty stomach, threatening an uprising. He should have eaten before leaving. A gnawing stomach made his anxiety all the worse.

13 minutes, 12 seconds.

In the window's reflection, he saw one guard whispering across the aisle to the other. His body tensed. In his pocket, he gripped his homemade stun gun—a last-ditch means of defense, built from scraps in his lab.

Something was wrong.

Luka planted his feet on the ground and prepared to make his stand, but then the shuttle slowed. It rolled into the first stop and a few people began to file out. Luka rose, his legs shaking, and fell into the queue. He kept his head down as he brushed past the guards.

The humidity and cold shocked his body as he stepped down outside of the vehicle. It was an unpleasant greeting after the dry-warmth of the shuttle, but an overwhelming relief accompanied it. The shuttle ride was the riskiest part of his plan—and he had made it. At this point, he was mostly free. *Yes, the rest was dangerous too, but how bad could it be?*

Luka let out a huge exhale and set off at a brisk pace away from the shuttle. He was out of the facility, yes, but High City was still in the reaches of DA and the Committee. He needed to hurry. True safety was in Low City. They would find trouble if they followed him there.

Five blocks from his drop point there was an elevator that spanned the considerable drop from the High City Deck into the Low City shopping and nightclub areas—collectively known as the Light District. A private company owned this elevator, and it mostly served the needs of High City revelers wanting drunk-stumble into the wild parties of Low City. It was the quickest route into Low City, but Luka, could not use it. It was a convenient bridge between two economically contrasted worlds and this meant there were considerable security protocols protecting entry. A special chip had to be purchased and implanted in an undisclosed location of the body to use it. Since he could not use the main roads either, he had to go the long way around. This was an old stairwell at the far end of High City that dropped into the empty and water-logged industrial districts of Old Seattle. This field of warehouses was a neither-place now. It was unclaimed and forgotten. Luka hustled down side streets and footpaths of High City as he made for this stairwell, his exit from his old life.

Chapter Five

~Get Higher~

Bright pink letters floating in a smoke trail formed the slogan while vibrant blues and greens shaped the body of an overgrown caterpillar beneath it. The colors shone against the bare concrete of the decaying building, even in the gloom of the storm.

At the caterpillar's feet stood Alice—but not canon Alice. This was High City Alice. She was ghostly pale, with vulpine features, and she wore a garish gold dress. Glimmering lines traced arrows, and moons, and astrological symbols along her collarbones and wrists. Her hair was pulled back tight. While the upper class of High City opted for a muted sense of fashion, for the partygoers that ventured down into Low City, these were the fashions of the day. Her dress alone made it clear which caste this Alice represented.

She was terrified. The Caterpillar, which looked more like Jaba the Hut than the Carroll's Hookah smoking Lepidoptera, had his tongue wrapped around her waist. Thick lines of saliva dripped from his lips and smoked seeped from the open corners of his mouth. His bloodshot eyes bulged like they would burst from his skull. The image on this mural was a message, the other mantra of Low City: *Eat The Rich*

Ever since The Rise, when the dikes finally broke and Old Seattle flooded, it had been two cities. There was New Seattle, and the Northern Districts, which prospered and became known as High City. Then there were the flooded remnants of everything else. People took to calling these areas

Low City. Elevation defined the borders, and that the start, the names referred only to the topographical differences. Over time, however, they grew to have a double meaning. The economic connotation of *High* versus *Low* underpinned the current circumstances of the residents in each.

The Committee forbade travel through Low City. It was for a good reason. Luka would have gone anyway—just to annoy them—except that he himself was not keen to wander down here. Criminals in Low City had bigger plans than standard muggings. Organ harvesting was a common ordeal for a healthy person like himself caught in the wrong place. His chest cavity was ripe with dollar signs and extracting his organs was far less trouble than trying to extract a ransom. Low City was rife with gangs too. None of them had the firepower to threaten the Military Police, but all among them were eager to move up the hill and carve out a sliver of High City. LCG, in particular, was a source of increasing anxiety for High City. They amassed wealth with alarming efficiency, and the richer they got, the higher they moved. This was the perverse gravity of New Seattle; it pulled upward at the heaviest pockets.

Luka knew of two routes to the Old Waterfront from his present location. Both of them were bad, but in different ways. He could pick his way through the slums and risk the hunt, or he could travel through the markets of Low City and risk being sighted by a drone or MilPol informant. Right now the threat of having his organs removed was far scarier than Janus or the Committee, so he decided the road more traveled was the better.

He left Alice behind and began working his way deeper into the random puzzle of streets that formed the outskirts of Low City. There was a lot of graffiti. It was a forest of marquees for LCG, as far as he could tell. The majority were sloppy cursive tags and monochrome symbols, but periodically he saw another mural like the scene from *Alice in Wonderland* that he left behind. As much as he tried to keep his eyes forward and his feet moving, Luka could not help but to stop and study some of them. They were huge works, spanning whole walls of buildings tens of meters wide, and the artistry, by-and-large, was impressive.

There were more scenes from Alice. Luka grinned at a mural of two cigar-smoking, anthropomorphic, playing-cards—an Eight of Clubs and Ace of Spades. They were using the heads of tuxedo-clad High City businessmen as croquette mallets and, what he assumed were these men's testicles, as the croquette balls. The playing-cards wore heavy gold chains and white suits reminiscent of Tony Montana in Scarface. The artist achieved a grotesque level of realism for such a cartoony scene.

Two buildings down from this was a massive image of an emaciated blonde woman snorting cocaine off the ass-crack of a curvy stripper vixen. The stripper wore a bright purple thong and cocked her ass high into the air from her hands and knees so that she gave easy access. The blonde buried her nose deep, not wanting to waste a fleck of the powder.

For what felt like hours, he wandered through these wrecked industrial complexes. The murals offered some interest, but mostly the streets were filled with garbage and occupied by drug addicts. He hugged close to the walls, walking with his hood pulled low over his face. In his pocket, his right hand gripped the crude stun gun he had fashioned back at the DA facility. Adrenaline urged his feet to move faster, but he slowed down. If he moved too quickly, he might draw more attention from the dealers and the addicts—or the other desperate-looking people that shuffled around the shadows of these collapsing buildings. If he looked like he was running, he might incite a chase.

94

He was picking his way through a rubble-clogged street
when he stopped dead and cocked his head toward the sky.

Was it?

He pulled back his hood to listen.

Yes, it was.

He ducked into a nearby alcove and pressed his back to
the wall. A sheet of water ran off the crooked edge of a ruined
roof overhead, drawing a curtain in front of him. It was hard
to hear through the white noise of rainfall, and the crackling
thunder, but he already knew he was right. He heard the
high-frequency hum of a heavy-class military drone. It was a
sound he could not purge from his memories of White
Sands.

It would struggle to find him in the storm, especially so
when he tucked himself into a water-logged corner like this.
Still, it was getting closer. The hum was getting louder and
that meant it had at least a general idea of his location. There
was a critical distance where the effects of his jammer and
rain-fade would no longer hide him.

Luka pressed his palms flat against the wall behind him.
He urged his body to move but his feet were anchors and his
legs were rubber hoses that barely held him upright.

Once, at a test facility near White Sands, he saw a military
drone fire a round at a fleeing insurgent POW. The bullet,
more of an artillery shell given its caliber, ripped the
insurgent's leg clean off just above the knee. Well, no not
clean off. The remaining bit of leg was ragged and torn like
the stump of a weed ripped from its roots. It looked fake, like
CGI, to see a limb separated from a body and sent tumbling
down the street. Only there was the smell, and the screaming,

and the gray pallor of the man's face as he bled out. That was not movie magic. The man cried for help for much longer than Luka thought possible. He cried for home as the other POW's watched him die.

There was no malicious intent in the drone's s behavior. It was a machine. It had calculated that blowing off the fleeing prisoner's leg was the most effective action. The man's agonized screams chased the fight from all his comrades—one shot made ten men surrender instantly. From a tactical perspective, it calculated correctly. The drones were programmed not just for maximum efficiency, but for maximum impact. The general concept was not new. Militaries from every country used extreme shows of force to demoralize their enemies. To implement it in a drone's programming, however, was novel. Some at White Sands, like him, found it hard to reconcile the brutality, but the results silenced any protest. When it switched from clean kills to lethal maiming, the drone ended the fight faster. It drove the resolve from its other targets and this led to more surrenders. They could interrogate live enemies. They got more intel for less effort. There was no arguing against that.

The hum was a roar now. It rang through his sinuses and deep into bones. His body shook and his legs barely kept him aloft. It would not be long now.

Luka's breathing rose to a pant. He pressed his back in tight against the wall and he wished the brick would let him sink deeper.

If the drone came even a few meters closer, it would get a signal lock.

Luka held his breath. He closed his eyes.

A crack rang out through the air. It was louder than the thunder. Much louder. His eyes snapped open. The heavy *whomp* of a high caliber revolver followed. It had to an old weapon, something someone in LCG would carry. Modern pistols were sharp and whispered. Only old weaponry was slow and deafening in that way. This reverberated through the concrete like a heavy bass tone.

To his surprise, he did not feel any pain. Luka patted down his body, starting at his chest and moving down his legs, but there was no wound, no blood. He assumed the shots were aimed for him. Then he realized, he was not the only one aggrieved by the drone's presence.

The drone would shirk a revolver round, no issue—even a .44 magnum. It was like using a slingshot on a bear, but it was a welcome distraction for him. The drone would drop its hunting directive and locate the source of the gunfire instead.

A second crack, not of the revolver but of the drone's 120mm shells, filled the air. The ground shook and a cloud of fire and smoke erupted two blocks over.

A rocket-propelled grenade launched from the roof of a nearby building shortly after. It hissed as it spiraled down toward the drone and erupted in a ball of flame. Even though the missile was headed in the opposite direction of Luka, he ducked and covered his head with his arms when he saw it go off. The drone would shirk that too. It might be thrown off balance by the impact, but no more than that. Its carbon hull paid no mind to light explosives. Whoever made the unfortunate decision to take on the drone apparently did not know that they needed heavy artillery to pierce its armor. They were amateurs, LCG thugs or the like. Only a person with zero military experience was stupid enough to fire an RPG at a heavy-class drone.

Luka stood back up and watched the exchanged. His legs tensed as he prepared to run, hoping to make the best of the distraction, because it would not last long.

But something odd happened before he could take the first step out beyond his shelter. He felt the distinctive push of a repulsor wave. It slapped him back against the concrete behind him just as an odd blue flash filled his vision. It was the color emitted by a blown transformer, but a hundred times greater.

Pain like fire rushed through as his brain as his biochip reacted to the repulsor wave. It burned throughout his body like a wave of molten iron crashing over him. As the EM field grew, and the virus code entered, the pain went exponential— it expanded until nothing else filled his mind and he passed from reality.

Then the warmth was gone. The fire left his body, and he returned to his reality in Low City. It felt like only a few seconds, but when Luka returned to consciousness, he was cold, very cold. The concrete and water had sapped every bit of warmth in him. He opened his eyes and tried to roll onto his stomach. His vision wobbled as it adjusted to the new angle. As he reoriented, panic crept back in. He remembered the drone and prepared to run when he looked over to his right where it had touched down. There was a lot of smoke and a lot of rubble. He did not hear the characteristic hum of its propulsion, though. There was no thunder from its guns either. There were no sounds of fighting at all. The drone was dead. Someone did him a massive favor. His arms went slack and let his face rest in a puddle. The grimy water ran in through his lips and he spat it back out in a great exhale. The feeling of relief was greater than the discomfort of the cold, polluted water. It superseded everything, for a moment. He might have stayed that way, but an erratic shiver took hold and reminded him he was wet to his core and dangerously cold.

He needed to fight his way back to his feet. He needed to move, to generate heat, and get away from the sapping concrete. He clenched his jaw as he prepared to move. Some street grit had found its way into his molars and it crunched unpleasantly as his teeth tightened down. He pulled his legs up to his chest. Then he rolled his weight over onto his knees so that he was on all fours. His movements were jittery and odd, like an actor on a damaged roll of film. He pushed up with his arms as hard as he could. They quivered but held. Now he had to stand. He pushed upward with his hands on one knee and landed one foot under him.

Nope. It gave.

He stumbled to his right and fell hard into a deep puddle. There was not enough time to get his hands under him to break the fall, so his right shoulder took the punishment instead. A sour taste filled his mouth. He would have gritted his teeth from the pain, but they were chattering from the cold and the shock to his nervous system caused by the repulsor. He dragged himself over toward the wall with his limp legs in tow. A pitiful gutter creature, he blended in better than ever.

He repeated the same sequence of moves, this time with a hand bracing against the brick as he stood from one knee. It worked. His other foot followed and planted beneath him as he forced his body upright. His balanced swayed and his body shook, but he held on.

Luka took a step, and then another. He walked, slowly, dragging a hand along the walls for stability—even so, sometimes gravity would sway and he would tumble sideways and slam into the wall. Step by agonizing step, he laid down kilometers behind him. In time his nervous system calmed, and his body warmed a little and his speed increased.

With every few blocks, the buildings became taller and cleaner. He saw less wrecked concrete and more glass and marble as he progressed. The graffiti disappeared and elaborate LED lighting replaced it. The lights were blue, red, purple, or white and their hazy glow made Luka feel like he was walking through a nebula. There were normal people in these neighborhoods, just going about their night. Well, normal-ish. They were ordinary in the sense that they were not undeniably drug addicts or gang members—though they might still be. They moved with a different kind of confidence than the people he knew in High City. There was less self-importance in it, more fortitude. Many openly carried heavy side arms and vicious looking blades. They wore black hoods and occult symbols dominated the designs on their clothing. It intrigued and frightened him at the same time.

Ahead, a woman more 'Low City' than any other he had yet seen, exited a building. The landing of her doorway thrust her out onto the sidewalk in such a way that she and Luka were obliged to meet eyes. They locked onto one another. She watched him with her head cocked at an angle. Curiosity glimmered behind the hardness in her eyes. His wrecked and soaked clothing disquieted her.

No, it was not that. Luka studied her harder. She sensed his unbelonging. She knew he was a native of a higher place and her eyes narrowed as she tried to figure out why he was there. She wore tight black leggings with reinforced sections along her hips and thighs. Traces of blue and gray highlighted these armored sections and accentuated what might have been a holster. On top she wore something like a drab black motorcycle jacket, but with a heavy, oversized hood. Her hair, so blonde that it was near white, stood in stark contrast to the black silhouette of her figure. There was a faint yellow-white glow near her neck. It pulsed gently, reminding him of a firefly on a muggy summer night.

Her eyes widened and her mouth, pulled tight just a second before, opened to say something. Luka puzzled at this.

Then his vision fizzled out to static.

The base of his skull throbbed.

There was little coherent thought populating his brain at that very moment, but he sensed he was being dragged across the concrete. The fibers of his clothing pulled at the porous rock like Velcro and the wet streets seeped into any remaining dry area on his back.

Some day.

Luka felt his body come to rest. He was in an alleyway, occluded by two overflowing black dumpsters. The stench of putrefying garbage wafted into his nostrils and it turned out that this smell was an effective alternative to smelling salts. His olfactory cortex sent out alarms to the rest of his brain and slowly his other senses roused to the call. He lolled his head back and forth as his brain came back into focus.

Luka pressed his palms against the ground, thinking to sit up, but just then a boot clamped down hard over his esophagus and pinned his shoulders and head to the ground.

The foot did not exert enough pressure to collapse his windpipe and completely block airflow, but it was enough that he struggled to fill his lungs. His body writhed and his hands wrenched at the ankle attached to the boot. His circumstances did not improve.

As his vision cleared, Luka became aware of a glossy black set of teeth smiling down at him.

It was an odd sight for someone who grew up in a world of perfect white veneers—the incongruence of expectation and reality frustrated his brain. These teeth were not blackened from rot. These were too perfect, too clean, too straight—but somehow dyed or veneered to look like black stone. The man looking at him had an unsettling onyx smile. Luka's skin crawled and his as he took in more of him. The whites of the man's eyes were tattooed a deep purple. In the dreary light of a stormy day, it was hard to distinguish between the pupil, the dark iris, and the rest. It gave the effect that they were completely blacked out. They looked like two pools of spent oil swimming in a pallid and gaunt face. They were the eyes of a person possessed by a vicious will to live. The man looked old and ragged, but there was something young in him too. He was old beyond his years, aged by a hard life.

The man twirled Luka's homemade stun gun in his right hand, the way one would fidget with a pen out of boredom.

"Well, where in the hell did you get this yeah?" the man said.

"Something like this isn't easy to come by I'm supposing," he added.

He used too many H's when he spoke. They were harsh and hissing. There were too many Y's too, casually tacked onto words where they had no business. He clipped most syllables and drew out a few uncomfortably long. Though it bared little phonetic resemblance, Luka assumed the phrase "c'b-m by" to mean "come by." It was like listening to a person speak in cursive.

The man was threatening him, but he found himself puzzling at the accent instead of fighting. It was nothing he recognized, nothing from overseas. It had to be the product of being born and raised in Low City.

"Anyone carrying a toy like this is from up there, on High."

The man jerked his head in some direction that was not necessarily toward any part of High City, but Luka got the point.

"I ain't seen tech like this. I got a sharp eye and I know a find. I'm going to take this and you, well you are going to walk with me—to meet some of my friends. They're going to like what else you have to offer."

The man's eyes went wide as he said he the word *offer.* It was monumentally stupid of him to respond this way, but Luka felt the words forming on his tongue before he could pull them back.

"Friends? I don't think the pusher whose cock you suck to get your next fix counts as a friend. I'll take my chances," Luka said.

The man smiled. Thin, pale lips pulled tight against his perfect black teeth. Deep fissures appeared in his lips as his grin grew wider. "Ah, done it. Okay. Joke's on me then?"

The cracks wept little trickles of blood and Luka thought he could smell the rot in the man's breath even over the reek of the dumpsters.

"We can see who is laughing in a moment."

The man jammed his foot harder into Luka's neck, bent down deliberately slow, and pressed the contacts of the stun gun tight against Luka's chest. Luka knew the killing power of the thing he made, the thing now pressed right over his heart, and he thought of asking the man to stop. For a second, he even thought to beg, but there was no time to follow through on his thought.

An iron pipe swung into Luka's view and connected with the man's face. The strike threw the man sideways and when he hit the ground, the stun gun went skittering across the concrete. Luka scrambled to his feet and raised his fists.

It was her holding the pipe, the woman who locked eyes with him just before he was attacked. It occurred to him that she may have the same intentions as the man with black teeth, but he was too drained or too stupid or too desperate to listen to his paranoia at the moment. He dropped his guard and so did she. The pipe clattered to the ground by her feet.

They both struggled with what to say. Silence hung heavy between them.

"I hope you can understand that, here, down here," she pointed to her feet, "we don't usually get in the middle of things like that. I let it play out how it will—but he was going to kill you."

She had a narrow jaw and large eyes, framed by high cheekbones that lent her an alien quality. The gruffness of her voice contradicted her delicate frame. She spoke like someone who shouted too often or smoked heavily.

She pointed off to her right. "Head east two blocks and one north. There's a shop there, Black Lane—B L V C K," she said as spelled out the letters. "Go there, change your look. You'll die walking around in clothes like that. You are begging people to drag you into an alley and do what he did."

He should have nodded in agreement, or walked away, or did anything other than stare at her stupidly, but that's what he did. He was soaked in garbage water, bruised, and shaking from the cold—and she was going to help him. He felt achingly meek.

A disapproving frown overtook her face.

"Take this. It will get you some credit, enough to get some clothes I hope," she said.

She held up a small plastic case that contained about half a dozen neon green pills. Luka stared at her outstretched hand, still looking brainless.

"Do you know what these are?" she asked.

Luka shook his head absently. She flicked at a pebble with the toe of her shoe and sighed, exasperated.

"Of course you don't."

She grabbed his wrist and pushed the plastic case into his palm, forcing his fingers to wrap around it, to protect it.

"Drugs. They are drugs. Popular ones. Make you feel good, make you have a good time. Use them to barter."

She released his wrist. "Do you get that concept?"

Luka nodded slowly, somehow wading deeper into the transaction without a single word. His sluggish mind, meanwhile, worked on a thought.

"Why are you helping me?" he asked. His voice quivered as he spoke and his face flushed as a result. "You said yourself, you don't get in the middle of things."

The woman smiled, not openly, but the corners of her mouth tugged upward and the crow's feet at her eyes became a little more pronounced.

"Guess you're not so dumb," she said.

"I have my moments," said Luka.

"I know you," she blurted out. She must have spoken louder than she meant to, because recoiled and pulled her lips in under her teeth. "I mean to say I've seen you on TV. You're supposed to be a genius."

There was another silence between them and a shuffle of awkward expressions.

"They call it P-H-D smart. It's like brilliant and stupid at the same time—but more often stupid," he said.

The woman almost laughed. There was a smile and an audible *harrumph.* She reigned it back. Seeing that she understood his joke, the tension in his spine eased.

"But my question stands, why help me?" he asked.

She shoved her hands into pockets and shrugged her shoulders. It was an adolescent looking gesture and Luka questioned his initial assumptions about her age. He revised downward. *22, 23?*

"That news lady is a bitch. I saw the interview ... and then I read about you ... and uh, well it's just that I get why you did what you did. Down here, we would have slit her throat."

106

She paused.

"*That,* and I guess I have a thing for pathetic creatures that need rescuing—just ask my ugly ass cat." She nodded over her right shoulder, toward a window. Luka made out the silhouette of a lanky cat peering down at them. A set of yellow eyes watched. *What did you call it when an owner and their pet looked alike?*

"The guy who runs BLVCKLANE, he'll want what I gave you, but he won't take kindly to you showing up with it. Tell him these came from Lady Luck, get what you need, then get out. Don't linger in there."

Her face wore a gravity that wilted any questions growing in Luka's mind. He pocketed the plastic case of pills. His eyes darted from side to side while he thought what to say next. She looked up at her cat in the window. It was time to go, but there was no social protocol for this kind of goodbye. They had become too personal, too fast. Now they had to leave, and they both seemed to realize that they did not know each other. The goodbye was necessary and unnecessary all at once. It was discordant. Luka thought about shaking her hand, but that felt too forced, so he just said, "Thanks."

The man with black teeth was dead. The rigid state of his body and foamy spittle at the corners of his mouth were evidence enough, but to add to it, he could smell that the man had shit his pants. He knew it was a petty gesture, but he spat in the man's face before he turned and left.

The shop was exactly where she explained and he was immensely grateful that it was only a few blocks away. Relief washed over him as it came into sight and the small measure of safety it promised urged his feet forward. The front looked a little like a rundown sex shop, or maybe an old dive bar. Its brick facade had been painted over in matte black and any windows had long since been covered. Some tired red lights framed the doorway and above it, in a glossy black, were the letters B-L-V-C-K-L-A-N-E. Luka trotted to the building, clutching his ribs as his breath picked up. He pulled the door open and the power stench of stale cigarettes hit him so hard he had to take a step back.

The man behind the counter at BLVCKLANE was not at all what Luka pictured in his mind on the walk over. Given the Lady Luck's appearance, he expected some skinny goth kid who wore too much jewelry. The dilapidated front should have cued him to expect otherwise, but the reality scowling at him now shocked him. The man had a long stringy beard with touches of gray and his face was pock-marked. He sported what was best called a beefy build. It rode that line between being buff and just plain old fat. Altogether he looked like a member of an old school motorcycle gang and everything about his appearance cautioned Luka not to mess with him. His bloodshot eyes gave Luka a hard look as he passed through the entryway and into the main floor of the store. They said that Luka had about ten seconds to give his reason for entering or he would not ever leave.

In a panic, Luka jammed his hands into his pockets and shuffled around to retrieve the little plastic case. The man drew a blue-black semi-automatic pistol in a blink, and before Luka could flinch, he had the barrel pointed at Luka's temple. The man's face was stone, his eyes laser focused. His aim was solid and his hand did not even shake in the little way it should from holding a heavy object at full extension. This was a familiar stance for him. He was big too. He must have been sitting on a stool when Luka walked in because now he stood a full head taller than Luka, and he had an impressive gut to match.

Luka froze, leaving his hands in his pockets. "It's pills, that's all."

"From Lady Luck," he added quickly.

The man grunted in acknowledgment, but the pistol did not change its aim.

"What kind?" the man asked.

"You tell me, they're not my thing," Luka replied.

The man's face did not soften, but nor did the situation escalate. Luka gripped the case in his pocket and withdrew his hand in slow motion. He placed the case on a nearby countertop.

"Any weapons?" the man asked.

"No?" Luka responded, his eyes narrowed in confusion.

The man dropped his aim and held the pistol at his side. "People like you are too stupid to lie when you should. You still think good nature exists," he said.

With his free hand, he undid the clasp on the little case and lifted the lid, displaying the bright green pills. Then he did something odd. The man sniffed the pills. He sniffed them hard. As far as Luka knew, no pill should give off any odor. If it did, it implied some level of volatility and impurity—the opposite of the qualities a pharmaceutical should have.

The man exhaled and breathed in so hard through his nostrils, and with the pills so close to his nose, that Luka thought the man would inadvertently snort one in a nostril. The man performed this procedure twice more, closed the case, and then tucked it into an inner pocket of his jacket.

"Ammonia. The good ones use ammonia in the extraction. Sometimes you can smell it, just barely," he explained.

He held his hand over the part of his jacket that now concealed the case like he was about to pledge allegiance, "And you're in luck, these are good. Which is how I know you did get them from her. Which is also why I am not going to kill you."

Luka nodded in agreement with this statement, though he was not sure why. He had no reason to believe she gave him pills of better quality than any others.

"What is it that you came for?" the man asked.

Luka opened his mouth to answer, but the man butted in first, shaking his head as he spoke, "Never mind, I know."

He bent down and pulled an ancient looking revolver out from a drawer somewhere out of Luka's view and set it on the counter. The steel on a revolver was supposed to have glossy bluing, but the specimen in front of him now was pitted and dull all over. The hammer looked like it was rusted into place.

"This, "the man pressed his sausage-like finger down on the cylinder of the revolver, "This relic does not fire anymore. But it does look the part. Take this and whatever clothes you need and get out. You have two minutes."

Luka jumped into action like he was on a timed sweepstakes giveaway. From the old department store racks to his left, he grabbed black pants, a black shirt, and a heavy Davy's-gray coat that had a hood and seemed to be waterproof. With the clothes bundled in his arms, he walked

110

back over the counter and shoved the little revolver into his pocket.

The man's eyes followed him as he exited BLVCKLANE.

Outside, the rain had slowed to a mist. It increased the danger that he could be tracked, so he kept to the edges of the street where water was sheeting down from the gutters. He circled around the block until he a secluded area where he could get into his new clothes and ditch the old ones. His ribs ached as he bent at the waist to slide his legs into the new pants and they hurt even more as he raised his arms to pull the new shirt over his body. As painful as it was to dress himself, the warm clothes were a godsend. With his body finally rid of the biting wet-cold, he felt renewed. His thoughts came faster and his coordination improved. He felt ready to face the last leg of the trek—well, almost. He took a piss in the corner, adding a fresh layer to the stale urine that stained the concrete there before he set off again.

Looking the part of a native, he moved with more confidence. He kept to the wet corners wherever possible, but with each passing kilometer, they became more scarce. The buildings improved, and the streets became more populated as he got closer to the Light District.

The people here were still armored, dressed almost exclusively in black, but there was a burgeoning high fashion aspect to it. He saw several women wearing contoured black dresses with intricate patterns of diamond and triangle shapes made to look like interlocking pieces of body armor. From a passing glance, he could not decide whether the armor was functional or just imitation. To shield from the elements, people wore heavy black cloaks with ragged and rakish angles. They were half tattered, half chic. Gentle lights in gold and white hues pulsated within the hoods themselves and backlit the faces they shielded from the rain. It had a hypnotic effect.

Luka made prolonged eye contact with people even when he knew very well that he should not.

There were facial piercings too, a body modification he had never seen in High City. Lips, nose, brow, cheek—people used any part of the face that had enough skin to pinch and pass a needle through. Only a few had multiple piercings, but almost everyone seemed to take part in the practice. Some—women and men both—had pastel-colored hair. Blues or lavenders or silvery whites were the most common. If not one of these colors, then their hair was impossibly black. Natural tones were almost non-existent.

The deeper he moved, the more the nightlife presented itself. Clubs and late-night shops lined the streets. There was open drinking and a lot of drugs. Needles, pills, pipes, tabs—all were used as openly as a cheap bottle of vodka.

People laughed and had a good time, clinging to one another as they stumbled from place to place. People fought too, sometimes lightheartedly, and sometimes in full-contact bloodsport. Luka saw split lips and swollen faces, and again, the gender did not seem to matter here when it came to drinking, drugging, fighting, and doing anything else that was unambiguously illegal in High City.

Jesus. Wasn't it a Tuesday?

There was a chaos and a strange beauty to it. Despite the violence, it captivated him. It was liberating. As he walked, he found himself wishing he had not spent so many years in the sterile wealth of High City and the rigor of remote military bases. He rewound his life in his mind and pictured an alternate path filled with raucous nights in Low City instead of the cold, lifeless nights at White Sands.

He turned a corner and suddenly he was there, the center of it all. It had been described to him, he had seen photos before, but the real thing took his breath away. He could not have imagined that a sight so stunning existed in this violent underworld. Ahead, the city glowed in the brilliant colors of a supernova. Blues and pinks and deep ultra-violet purples washed over the buildings in every direction. It consumed his whole field of view like a fog washed in color. The sidewalks glowed yellow under the steps of people as they moved through the square. Pulses of color erupted around their feet like raindrops as they walked. This was Lucida of Low city, the Light District, the last reason Low City had not devolved into total feral decay. Here, Low City reached the pinnacle of its opulence. It was not the same kind of extravagance found in High City. It was lavish in a wild and irreverent way, and he loved it.

Chapter Six

No matter how poor the odds, someone will be the victim of chance. There is only implausibility, never impossibility. This principle guides the hidden physics all around us. It encodes everything. Probability silently shapes our lives.

These were his professor's opening words in statistical mechanics during the spring semester of his sophomore year. His professor intended to explain a principle of quantum mechanics, that probability, not certainty governed all subatomic behavior—that even the most unlikely interactions could not be disregarded. It was an attempt to create some drama in an otherwise dull and math-intensive topic. His efforts were not so successful. The warm summer air had come early that year and the sounds of other students chatting and flirting in the quad floated in through the windows of the classroom. It was tough competition for a professor. Most of the class had their eyes locked down on the syllabus, calculating when exactly they would need to start studying for the midterms. Luka, however, had looked up just then, right at the very moment that his professor spoke those words. They made eye contact, and while the line was meant for the class as a whole, it felt like it became his alone. For Luka, that one innocuous moment seeded every unfortunate event since.

Someone will be the victim of chance.

He thought of that now. He blamed it for the absurd sequence of chance that brought him to this point. He was standing alone in a freezing downpour, hoping that the person meeting him would not try to kill him. Luka looked down at his feet and clenched his jaw as a quiet dread pulled through him. To slow his mind, he tried to focus on the wind-driven rain pelting his jacket. The storm had picked up again since he left the Light District. Now, large drops fell and made a clamorous sound as they struck the wooden planks of the pier. If he closed his eyes, they felt like fingers tapping politely at his back.

This is where they were supposed to meet. *Waterfront* could only have meant this mess of boards and bridges that used to be a pier by the Waterfront Hotel. He was certain of the location, but he did not know for whom he should be waiting. It was Elise that warned him, but his gut told him it would not be her that he would meet here. She warned him by means of a cipher in a book. It was a clue he might have overlooked. It meant she wanted to tell him but that she needed to keep her actions covert. She was playing an inside game that was not yet over.

He also did not know how long he should wait for them. Elise's instructions did not give him a specific time, and now he wondered how the person, or people, he was supposed to meet could know when he would arrive. Strictly speaking, this was not even the *Next Rain* from the time he got her message. The stormed had died down for a while as he crossed through the Light District and only recently picked up again. *What if they had come and gone during the first downpour?*

In the pattering drone of the storm, Luka did not hear the boards creak as someone approached. Heavy rain had darkened the night to the point of near blackness and he could not see the figure moving toward him through the webs of wrecked structure. It came to a stop just in front of him. He flinched at the sudden presence, but forced down the alarm and eased his body back into a calm stance. Water pooled where their combined weight depressed the age-softened wood.

"Can you swim?" they asked in a muffled voice.

The faint glow of his eyes revealed their synthetic nature—two blue points burned bright amid an otherwise hollow face. Of all the reasons Luka knew a person would elect to have prosthetic eyes, most were for combat. His pulse quickened under the scrutiny of these burning blue cameras. He wanted to shuffle away, to put more space between him and the man, but his feet were anchors. He was ready to move forward, not back.

"Well enough," Luka said, wondering if he should have spoken softer.

The man spoke softly, it was barely audible over the bluster of the rain and wind, but he did not appear alarmed at Luka's comparable loudness. "The water is cold and the currents can be strong. So I'll ask again, can you swim?"

"How far?" Luka asked.

The man nodded his head out toward one of the half-submerged skyscrapers that used to be downtown Seattle. It did not look far. Not that far, anyhow. Even through the rain, he could make out the shape, which suggested a manageable distance. The thing with swimming was that distances were deceiving and that the conditions of the water mattered greatly. Close as the building may be, it would be at least twenty minutes in the water—frigid, oil-slick water.

Luka chewed on his lips. He began to doubt whether it was even possible to go that long in that cold without slipping into hypothermia.

"Yes or no. We need to move now," the man pressed.

"Does it even matter? You know I am going to try whether I'm a good swimmer or not," Luka said.

"Last chance—yes or no?" The man repeated, his tone unchanged.

"Yes," said Luka.

"Follow me," said the man.

He turned on his heels and hurried through the tangle of wooden beams. Luka followed, working hard to keep close behind. They hopped, and crouched, and shuffled through the mess of wrecked wood. It was chaotic, like a dead thicket in an old forest, and rife with sharp edges. They moved fast, and even with all of Luka's physical conditioning, he struggled to keep pace. The man moved with a fluidity that Luka could not imitate. He seemed to route ten steps ahead so that no obstacle slowed him, and he placed his hands and feet in just the right positions each time. His legs pushed and his arms pulled with the exact force required. His progress was seamless forward momentum. Luka kept up only through reckless imitation of the man's movements and a complete disregard for his aching body. He gritted his teeth and pushed the pain of his aching ribs from his mind.

The man stopped. Luka almost carried on forward and slammed into his back, but he stopped himself just short so that he stood uncomfortably close behind him. The boards came to an abrupt end. They were at the water's edge. Without wasting a moment, and with the same efficiency that he moved through the pier, the man removed his outer layers of clothing. Pants, jacket, and shirt were all shed until an inner layer was exposed that, at least by appearances, was a wetsuit. No sooner had stripped his excess clothing than the man entered the water. He dove off of the edge of the broken dock they were standing on and swam back underneath it. Luka shivered as he watched.

Within a minute, the man resurfaced with a black dry-bag in tow. It floated, bobbing behind him like a sad and deflated balloon. He lifted himself back up onto the dock with the ease of a practiced motion and he tossed the bag into Luka's arms. Luka caught it on instinct alone and it was heavier than he expected. He rocked backward as he recovered his balance.

"Remove all of your clothing and put this on. It will help you survive the cold and it will dampen the signal from your biochip until we are inside. They will track the device you brought," the man said.

Luka studied him while hugged the bag to his chest like a child clutching a stuffed animal. He found it difficult to read the man's expressions—if there were any to be read. Luka added to his mental tally of non-organic traits the man possessed.

Inside the bag was a skin-tight suit identical to the one the man was wearing. The material felt like neoprene, but it had more complexity beneath the surface. There were rigid metal fibers woven throughout in intricate patterns. It prickled with electricity like it was statically charged and when he held it closer to his face, heat pulsed through his spine and dizzying sensation grew from deep within ears. From his recent experience with a repulser, he knew this is how it felt when an external signal played havoc on his biochip.

Luka ignored its discomforting effects and held it close to his face to study it. His jammer did not cause the warm sensation, nor the vertigo, which meant it did not use destructive interference. Instead of targeting one organized signal, it masked all signals using a massive and chaotic electromagnetic output. His jammer was a precision silencer, this suit was more like a pillow hastily stuffed between a pistol and its target.

"Hurry," the man said, some waver of concern now present in his voice. He nodded to the suit in Luka's hands.

Luka complied, hastily unzipping his jacket and unbuckling his belt. He pulled off his pants and yanked his shirt up over his head. In seconds, he was naked except for his underwear. With his back and chest exposed to the freezing rain, his body slipped into an intense, myoclonic shiver. His hands shook, and he struggled to undo the zippers and clasps on the suit. Fighting to keep his body steady, Luka slipped his legs and arms in to the suit and pulled the zipper up the back. It was baggy on him at first, but almost as soon as he noticed this problem, it shrank and form-fitted to him. It provided an immediate reprieve from the cold. The metallic fibers in the fabric radiated warmth. His tremors slowed. Seeing that he was properly suited, the man nodded to Luka that it was time to go, and threw the Luka's pile of soggy clothes off of the dock and into the water. They sank. Their gentle wake was a punctuation mark on his point of no return. Luka took a deep breath. Then, he and the man entered the water. They slipped off the dock like seals sliding in from a sunning rock.

The bay water was briny and smelled of hydrocarbons. It was a sweet but unsettling odor. The water was icy. The warmth of the suit protected his core, but his feet and hands were exposed. They ached as they adjusted to the frigid cold.

The man broke into an easy breast-stroke toward the ruined skyscrapers. Luka followed form, trailing about a few strokes behind him. His ribs still hurt where the man with black teeth kicked him, but something about the suit's construction reinforced his body. The pain was a fraction of

119

what it had been. He picked up his pace, suddenly feeling sure he would make it. Then the first wave crashed over him and quashed his optimism. The force of the falling water drove salt through his sinuses into the back of his throat. He coughed in rejection, but it felt like more water went into his mouth than out.

By the third wave, he was short of breath and struggling to stay afloat. He kicked and pulled his way through the water, doing his best to maintain good swimming form, but desperation was taking hold.

One arm forward, pull it back. Now the other, pull it back. Then turn your head and breath. Repeat. Keep kicking. Again. Again. Again.

His shoulders ached after only a few minutes of swimming. He tried to find a rhythm, but the water kept finding its way into his lungs to interrupt him. He coughed constantly and breathed in hard fits between. It drained him, quickly, but he kept fighting and they progressed.

The outcrop of ruined buildings that formed Old Seattle was on the horizon now. The waves became smaller as the buildings ahead broke their strength. Luka spent less time choking and more time breathing. His strength returned.

New challenges took the place of the heavy waves. The nearer to the structures they went, the thicker the layer of oil on the surface water became. The government had the means to clean this contamination up with oil-hungry microbes—but did not care about this place. It was the past. It was forgotten and left to suffer. They left it as a reminder. *Be with us, or be forgotten.* The sweet scent of gasoline now permeated his entire respiratory system. He thought of benzene as he took in the pollutants and his mind filled with the resonant structures of all the carcinogens that might be running through his nose and swishing in his ears.

Swimming through the oil slick felt like the equivalent of running through mud. His legs were numb, his eyes stung, and no matter how hard he focused, he could longer able to perform fluid strokes. It sapped his energy even faster than the strong currents and waves he faced minutes ago. His arms hit the surface of the water in heavy slaps. His shoulders were spent. He struggled and thrashed like a fish on shore. The man, however, looked comfortable swimming through the oil slick. He cut its surface like a canoe. He was so far ahead now that Luka could only spot him by his wake. Luka's stomach tightened. The man was getting further ahead with every stroke.

In time, the water became placid. Its surface shined like a black mirror. The approach had been terrifyingly gradual, but suddenly Luka was amidst the ruined buildings. He was in the sunken city and the hope of stopping soon reinvigorated him

They swam toward the tallest of the structures. It was a building made of black marble and black glass that now had a thick layer of slime growing several meters up from the waterline. The man glided up within arm's reach of the largest unbroken section of the exterior and pressed his palm against the glass. He swiped his hand across its surface, tracing a large triangle. A vertical crack appeared in the wall, starting about three meters up from the water's edge and creating a seam down beneath the surface. Luka was a few meters back, but he glided in closer he could feel the vibration of motors from somewhere inside the building. A huge panel of glass lifted out of the exterior and slid to the left. Water poured in over the edge of a newly opened portal. The man swung a leg over it and lifted himself inside, nodding for Luka the follow.

Ahead, a rusty stairwell led downward into a dark corridor. The stairs and walkway were made of old metal grating and the water pouring into the building from the over the entrance's edge flowed down the walls and collected into a series of gutters along the bottom edges of the room. It disappeared into drains at each corner.

At the end of the corridor was an antique steel airlock that, from the looks of it, had been salvaged from a 21st-century nuclear submarine. It sealed and unsealed by means of a rusty wheel in the center of the door. The man cranked the wheel. It took considerable effort, even for him. It groaned and screeched in protest as the steel latches locking it in places retracted. When the locks surrendered, he gave it a hard tug, and it swung open.

The man waited by the outside of the airlock but nodded for Luka to go through ahead of him. Luka took it to mean that everything from this point would be a solo mission and it made him uneasy. This man was not an ally, but his prowess reassured him. Under his watch, there was some notion of protection. Beyond this door, he was alone, and the man sensed it. He locked eyes with Luka. His glowing irises offered no human connection, they were like staring into CCTV cameras, but his throat was tight and a hint of concern angles his eyebrows. He nodded one more time, urging Luka to pass through the hatch. Luka swallowed hard. Salt and oil coated his throat as he forced the thick saliva down.

Luka nodded in return and pulled himself through the doorway like he had seen people do on warships in movies. He put his hands through first, gripping the sides, then he ducked his head and swung his legs through like he was jumping in. He did not know if it was necessary to do it this way, but it felt natural. He had only just cleared the threshold when the door swung shut and resealed behind him. The creaking and scraping ring of metal reverberated through the room as the steel latches worked themselves back into place. In the time it took him to stand upright and recover from the disorienting shriek of the door, someone had positioned themselves in front of him. They stood with their arms crossed, blocking the way ahead—no more than a silhouette in the dim incandescent haze.

BOOK TWO

HELENA

Chapter Seven

"I didn't think you'd make it," said the skinny teenager standing in front of him.

His eyes scanned Luka from his feet and up to his shoulders.

"They told me you would, but *I* didn't think so."

At first glance, Luka guessed the person in front of him was no older than sixteen. He had the slouchy posture of a sullen high schooler and he wore, with pride, a wispy patch of facial hair that could be loosely described by the word *goatee.* He looked remarkably like Shaggy from Scooby-Doo and this did not oblige Luka to take him seriously. His eyes, though, had the hardness of a person who made lots of errors in judgment and learned to survive through a mountain of mistakes.

"Welcome to the Rabbit Hole," he said with arms extended out in a mocking welcome gesture. His voice dripped with sarcasm and his inflection was some miscellany of Low City slang and British English. The confusing mix of speech and gestures reminded Luka of a dorm room neighbor from college, who took mushrooms too often and seemed to always be in the throes of a psychedelic flashback. Through all of the drama, Luka could not decide whether the kid was being facetious or if that was the actual name of this place.

The kid jerked his head to the side to shake a mass of unkempt hair away from his eyes and now both yellow eyes were visible. "I personally wanted to call it Atlantis—but people thought it was too hokey. And well, I guess this place is a little too shitty for that, in the end."

Luka's eyes narrowed. "Right."

"So you agree, huh? Not even here for ten seconds and already you're jammin' on the place." The kid rolled his eyes. "Some thanks I get for rescuing you."

"That's not what I was saying," Luka interjected. He took a slow breath, inhaling and exhaling audibly. "Why the Rabbit Hole, then?"

The young man considered this while he rubbed the peachy hairs on his chin.

"Because we are in the nowhere between the real world and uh—well, whatever else. You'll see. I'll warn you now though, don't get your hopes up. It's all full of scary-fuckers and psychopaths down there. I'm telling you now. Just don't say I didn't tell you."

"Okay?" questioned Luka as he raked a fingernail down the stubble on his jaw.

"Hey. Don't say I didn't tell you things get weird down there. You'll come to find that being here in no-man's-land isn't so bad though. Didn't take me long, that's all I'm saying."

"I'm sure I won't," said Luka.

He cocked his head. "Wait, when you say down, do you literally mean we are going down below us? As in under The Sound?"

Luka pointed to the floor.

"Yeah. Duh. Since when do people like us live in skyscrapers and shit?"

The kid snorted at this.

"Get it, huh? 'Cause we do live in a skyscraper!"

He motioned in a wide circle to the wrecked building around them and a disquieting smile crept across his face. He acted like everything he did was a part of some unfortunate hazing routine he had for newcomers.

The kid clapped his hands and began rubbing them together vigorously. He picked one, sober-sounding High City accent and stuck to it the whole way through, "So let's get down to business. We got you here, now you owe us. It's time to settle your bill."

"Okay, and what did you have in mind?" asked Luka.

"Funny you use that phrase when it's more about what you have in yours. See, what you've got in that head of yours is precious to us. It'll more than pay your way if we can have a look-see."

This he said cutely, but there was something ominous in his promise to cut into Luka's brain.

"Don't worry, we're not after the chip. No extraction. We just want what's on it is all," the kid added.

His insistence to not worry did little to that end. A chill spread through Luka. Blood was fleeing from his limbs.

"BOOM!" The kid shouted as he slammed his fist on the wall next to him. Luka jumped as a hollow thud rang through the room. "We've got big plans for that data."

The cold feeling grew stronger. Beads of sweat formed on Luka's forehead. He shifted his weight as the muscles in his back began to lockdown and wrench his spine. He took a deep breath again.

"You already know who I am," Luka said. His voice quivered.

The kid's eyes went wide. "Yeah, and?"

"And before you start cutting on my skull, I think it's fair that I know your name," Luka continued.

The kid rubbed his chin again. "Humm."

"Alright, alright," he nodded. "Lark. Pleasure is yours, I'm sure."

Luka raised an eyebrow, "Lark?"

"Yeah," the kid replied.

"Seriously?" Luka frowned. It was all getting tiresome—the stupid names, the bizarre act.

"Yeah. Lark. Don't be a dick okay." The kid jerked his head again to swoosh the hair away from his eyes. "God, keep it up and you will fit in just fine with all those assholes down there."

"I am guessing that your parents didn't name you Lark is what I meant—and I don't think it's unreasonable of me to ask for a real name given what I'm going to agree to do," Luka pressed.

It made him uneasy to admit it to himself, but he was at this kid's mercy. However much Lark acted like a perma-stoned idiot he, in a big way, controlled access to some underworld. People respected him for a reason he did not yet know and that meant Lark was dangerous in some way he had not yet seen. It was best to tread lightly.

"Okay, okay. Well, you caught me tough guy," Lark said while he put his hands in the air like he was about to be arrested. "They didn't name me Lark. Big whoop. But the thing is, they never really liked me anyway and I never really liked them back. So, what's it matter what they called me? And I'll tell you what I did like, huh? I had a pet bird that I loved more than anything. I named it Lark. I know, I know, I have no idea where that came from but I was a kid and it was the name picked."

Lark waved his hand in the universal gesture of *don't even go there.*

"If you didn't gather as much from the moment you met me, let me tell you now that I wasn't too popular in school. Kids didn't seem to like me much. I didn't get invited to many birthday parties. That shitty little bird was the about the only friend I ever had. It was a fragile little thing. I caught it outside in my front yard, it was nearly dead and I nursed back to life. Well, guess what then, *Doctor.* See, my mom was a fucked up drunk and one day she decided that Lark *smelled like shit,*" said Lark, mimicking his mom's slurred speech.

"So she took him out outside and drowned him in a bucket of water. What a great solution! I found him floating in the water when I came home from school that day. I cried. I really did and I don't care if you know that I did, *tough guy*. I hope that Lark pecked the shit out of her. He was a little guy, but he was feisty. I'll never know. She was always piss-drunk and accidentally burning, or cutting, or scratching herself anyway, so there was no telling where any injury came from. Well, anyhow, with Lark dead and my only friend gone, I had no reason to stay. I left home the next day and decided that from then on, I was whoever I wanted to be. So my name's Lark and—and don't fucking mess with me!"

Lark lunged at Luka and put a fist up to Luka's face like he was going to punch him. To Luka's surprise, he flinched and jumped backward. Lark seemed surprised too. His eyes doubled in size. It took an uncomfortable few seconds for them both to collect themselves and stand down. Lark brushed at some wrinkles in his shirt.

"Uh. Okay. Follow me." Lark finally announced.

He swept the hair away from his eyes as he walked. "through here is the primary control room. I want your suit back. Those things cost me a pretty penny and more than a few hours to make. Looks low tech but it has a pretty cool EM emitter. It will block your signal until we have more permanent means of disabling your biochip. But then I'm guessing you already kinda knew what it did, didn't you doctor?"

Luka nodded.

"There will be side effects you know," said Lark.

"You mean from this suit?" Luka plucked at the skin-tight wetsuit he was still wearing.

130

"No, wow you're a slow study. From us extracting the data on your biochip, duh. Shit's WAY encrypted. Like, you don't even know the kinda shit they got protecting that thing. They got these security protocols that will hit your brain stem. It'll give you the ax if we're not careful."

"Okay then. What *are* the side effects?" Luka asked.

Lark craned his neck over his shoulder to make eye contact with Luka. "Death," he said.

It was the first time Lark said anything to Luka without a measure of sarcasm or flippancy. The floor tilted and the edges of Luka's vision went fuzzy. He fought to keep himself upright, straining his back, but he was losing hold on gravity.

"Ha, ha, ha! I'm just fucking with you man! I'm way too good for their shit. Man, you should have seen your face. You ... you went all ghosty on me!"

"Hilarious," Luka said through his teeth.

"You're a real buzzkill," Lark shot back. Then he broke into a rapid-fire, matter-of-fact, speech, "Temporal dislocation is the most severe and most common of side effects. Headache, Nausea, and Vertigo are also reported. You may experience brief periods of vision loss or a burning sensation in your spine, along with confusion. If this does happen, please contact your medical professional immediately as it may be a sign of a more serious complication. But in short, your brain will go all wonky. You might not know where the fuck or when the fuck you are for a while."

"I know what temporal dislocation is," said Luka.

Lark's speaking became furious. He slung words at Luka instead of exhaling them like lazy trails of smoke. "Look, be an ass all you want to be, but remember we're the only people capable of shielding you from big bad Daedalus Astrodynamics. You have realized that they are into a hell of a lot more than just space and stuff right? Please tell me you have. You can't possibly be that dumb."

Luka froze and Lark shook his head.

"Well. Oh. My. Shit. You really are that thickheaded. Well, let me explain. What you know as Daedalus Astrodynamics and the Committee is only a branch of something much bigger. The Committee has wider ambitions than silly little space missions."

Lark looked down at his feet and his eyes darted back and forth rapidly as if he lost his place and was searching for the words he needed. Then, he clapped his hands together and snapped back into the moment like he had not missed a beat.

"But let's not get into that right now. First the data. Then we disable. Then we talk. Then you can go on your not-so-merry little way. Good? Agreed? Do we have an accord?" .

Lark drew out the syllables on *accord* and imbued with as much mockery as a word could hold.

Luka's legs shook with the urge to run. His heart surged and everything in him shrieked *run*. Lark was childish and strange, but he was also the sort of person who enjoyed burning an ant's antennae and ripping the legs off of grasshoppers. Luka was just his latest plaything.

"So? What's your answer doctor?" asked Lark.

It felt like someone else was saying it, like he was floating over his own shoulder watching the words slip out. "Yes. We have an agreement," said Luka.

Lark sucked in his lower lip and stared at Luka with creepy wide eyes. "Let's get crackin' then."

Lark pointed to a ragged chair in the next room. Luka obeyed, shuffling to the chair, and taking his position.

"I must sedate you, of course," Lark announced as he rummaged through a cabinet somewhere behind Luka.

"Of course," Luka parroted.

Seconds later, Luka felt the prick of a needle in the back of his neck and the world faded.

When he came to, Lark's face was only inches from his. The unpleasant heat of Lark's breath filled his nostrils. His breath smelled like cat food—fishy and revolting. Whatever sedative Lark used on him, it was quality chemistry. His brain snapped back into focus and he did not feel hungover in the least. There was a dull ache, though, at the back of his skull where Lark must have been prodding.

"We seem to have a tinsy problem," Lark announced.

Luka locked eyes with Lark, expecting him to continue. Lark's gaze, however, drifted off—he was looking straight through Luka. His mind was somewhere else.

Lark shook his head, clearing the thought, "Oh. Right." Then he pulled his face away from Luka's and began to pace the room.

"The data on your chip is corrupted. Some kind of safety feature, maybe. I don't know," Lark scratched at the back of his head, "Either way, it puts us in quite a predicament. See 'cause we brought you here and all, but now you haven't held up your end and all. Get what I'm getting at? Hum?"

"Yeah. I do," said Luka. He put on a stony face and held his shoulders square—like he was staring down an animal about to charge.

"I'm not so sure," said Lark. He scrunched his mouth to one side. "See, you're here," he pointed down to his feet, "and I can't let you back out there." He pointed to in the general direction of the airlock.

Then Lark bent down and yanked on the rusty handle of a drawer in an old wooden roll-top desk. It was a relic of an older world, sun-bleached wood and poorly cast iron. It surprised Luka that he had not noticed it earlier, because now it dominated the room. Its age and heft made it an oddity in the room full of sleek, modern instrumentation. Lark yanked on the handle again, harder this time, but the drawer did not budge. Instead, the whole desk lurched forward with a loud screech.

Lark crouched down and peered under the desk, trying to find what was catching the mechanism. "But all the same I can't let you through there either," Lark said as he pointed over his shoulder with his thumb, vaguely in the direction of the next room.

"That doesn't leave me many options," Luka said. He maintained his steeled expression—his mouth straight with his lips pulled thin.

Lark lowered himself onto the ground in front of the desk, sitting flat on his butt with his feet braced against the legs of

134

the desk. "It leaves you just one. There's a phrase I like to use in these situations. Learnt it in a book. Blood in, blood out."

"Do you know what it means doctor?" Lark asked.

Luka froze.

Lark, meanwhile, shifted each foot until he seemed content their positioning. Then, with both hands wrapped through the drawer handle, he began to pull back using the combined strength of his legs and arms. He locked his jaw and put his full weight into it, lifting himself from the ground.

The handle broke first. Lark skidded backward across the floor. "Fucking humidity," he hissed as he came to a stop, splayed out flat on his back. "My gun's in there," he added.

Lark picked himself up from the ground and brushed the floor grime from hands onto the sides of his pants. Stun-locked, Luka watched while Lark collected himself and retrieved a hammer from a nearby cabinet. It was more like a mini-sledge with a hefty square striking surface and longer than typical wooden handle. Lark began furiously smashing the old desk. Each blow landed with a sickening crunch as the old wood gave way. Shards and splinters flew. They clattered against the walls and skittered across the floor. The sudden and reckless onset of violence was disturbing on its own, but that alone did not freeze Luka. It was the open smile on Lark's face, his fetishistic arousal at the destruction. Luka knew he should try to run—or to fight. He knew he should do something, but the absurdity of it captured him. The whole scene was so strange that he could not bring himself to feel afraid of it.

Lark broke the desk way beyond the point of necessity. It was only when there were no more whole pieces left to be broken, only pieces to be broken into smaller pieces, and when the satisfaction of any one blow waned, that Lark stopped. By the end, he was just half-assedly swinging into a pile of irregular fragments. The diminishing returns determined his endpoint. In less than two minutes, he had reduced the desk to a hefty pile of scrap wood and tinder. Objectively, this was an impressive feat. The desk looked well built, a relic of an age when people desired furniture built from slabs of expensive hardwoods.

Lark turned his attenuation back to Luka. His eyes were razor focused and he white-knuckled the hammer in his left hand. Sweat and dust cemented his hair to his forehead, some of it covering his eyes. Lark's intent was clear now: *blood out.*

With the business end of the hammer, Lark pointed back to the pile of shattered wood. "My gun is in there somewhere still ... but ya know it occurred to me about halfway through that I didn't really need it."

He was breathless from the effort and took heavy pauses between words.

Lark looked down at the hammer and judged its heft. "That fucking shitty chip ain't gonna work when I'm done. Don't you worry doctor."

Now, Luka's body unlocked. He felt his muscles tensing, coming to life. His adrenaline rose. His hands swelled as he balled them into impregnable fists. His nostrils flared, and when Lark's eyes turned away to look at the desk again, Luka considered taking the first strike.

In his mind, however, he played the same three seconds of reel over and over. He saw the arc of the hammer swinging. It moved like jagged frames of 8mm. He saw the impossible power of Lark's skinny arms. He saw the wood crunch as the hammer ruptured the desk. The sound was haunted him, like the splintering of his bones. He remembered his own back shattering across a telephone pole years before and the fight drained from him.

He could fight, true, but he would lose. He could run too, but if he ran, he would not even know where to run to. They were losing options. He still possessed something of value, though, and that gave him a third way out.

"You're after the schematics," said Luka. His voice betrayed his conviction, quivering on the first words.

Lark's eyes snapped to Luka. His pupils sharpened. His appearance, which earlier conveyed the idea of a child, transitioned into one of a predator. He was wound tight and eager for violence. Luka understood him now for the schism that he was.

"You have nothing." Lark burst out. His tone bordered on hatred, but all the same, his arm went slack and his grip on the hammer eased.

"No. We both know what you are after. You couldn't get the data you wanted from my chip, but that doesn't matter."

"I didn't need it to begin with. I know everything on it in perfect detail. I have every bit of that data memorized," said Luka as he pressed a finger to his skull.

He continued, "Listen up, Lark. You can do your best to smash my head with that hammer—and you may succeed—but I have what you are after and you'll lose it if you do that. So, I'll cut you a deal. You help me take down DA and I help you build whatever it is you are trying to build."

Luka took in a deep breath. He saw the knuckles on Lark's fist turn white as he firmed his grip on the hammer's handle again. He bent his knees preparing to dodge the first strike and he shifted his weight to the balls of his feet.

But Lark's let the hammer slip from his hand. It clattered to the ground. His eyes softened and that eerie grin reappeared. "We have a deal, doctor Janovic."

They shook hands and like that, Lark was a teenager again. The hate and violence bled away.

"I took care of your biochip," he said.

"What?" asked Luka.

"I mean I couldn't get the data, like a said, but no signal will be comin' from that thing now! Oh, I fucked it up good."

Luka turned his head and stared at Lark with a skeptical sideways glance.

"Thanks. I guess," he said.

"Which means you don't need my suit anymore! So come on, cough it up!"

Lark held out his palm and flapped his hand.

The idea of stripping down in front of this bizarre person made Luka queasy. It was yet another layer of vulnerability to be naked, and he already knew he could not trust this person. Nonetheless, he pulled the zipper down his back, peeled the suit away from his chest, and slipped it free from his legs. The mass of electronics warmed the control room, so at least he was not shivering. He held the suit in a sloppy bundle in his outstretched arms. Lark snatched it from him and then set off down a corridor in the opposite direction. The legs of the suit dangled free and dragged across the grated steel floor as he went. Luka broke into a jog to catch up with him.

"So, do you have something else I can borrow for the moment? Your friend had me leave my other clothes back at the pier," asked Luka.

"Yeah, yeah, yeah. We have that stuff. Come on," said Lark.

Ahead of them were the doors of what looked to be an elevator. The doors opened as Lark approached and inside was a drab 20th-century elevator carriage, probably original to the building. It had separate buttons for each floor—one to forty and sub-levels P1 to P6. Lark pressed the button for P2.

"We retrofitted the old parking structures. Pumped all of the water out, sealed it up, and modernized it. We dug some of our own too. The water above helps to conceal our communications and heat signatures," he explained as the elevator began to glide downward.

The original display that told the rider what floor they were passing was broken, so Luka had no idea of where they started and how far down they needed to go, but it seemed to take a long time. He counted a full forty seconds before the elevator slowed to a stop. The doors opened with a *ding*.

It was not nice, but it was better than Luka expected. The room ahead was a like a shabby dormitory, but with dull orange lighting so that it had the mood of a doomsday bunker. There were chairs, couches, a kitchen, and bunk rooms. It had the basic things people needed to survive and work on whatever 'projects' they had. Regret welled in Luka's stomach and settled like a heavy stone as he took it in. His limbs ached. All of him throbbed with exhaustion and his back was twitching, threatening to spasm. He traded his prison at Daedalus Astrodynamics for this new, worse one. This was every bit their dormitory, just a bad version of it, and there was no turning back. They killed Michael. Now he would ruin them.

"How many people live down here?" Luka asked as he counted the visible beds.

"Twenty to thirty on any given day. Most are gone right now though, getting supplies. Probably for the better. Their assholes. You wouldn't like them," Lark nodded to his left, "You can sleep in that room over there. You will find clothes in there too. I suggest you do that first."

Luka bobbed his head in agreement and hurried off to the room at his left. To his relief, the promise of clothes and a bed was not another of Lark's jokes. This room was an actual bedroom with closets and drawers, and in them were things he could conceivably wear. It was all drab tactical clothing in blacks, grays, and deep olive greens, but it would do the job. He tried on various combinations of underwear, pants, and shirts until he found one of each that fit reasonably well. He found a set of boots and socks in a storage container and took them too.

When he left the bedroom and came back to the main room, Lark was standing in the exact place he had been before. His eyes were foggy and distant. If he was aware of Luka's presence, there was no outward sign of it. Remembering the incident with the hammer, Luka decided to wait it out rather than disturb—and possibly startle—him.

It was not long. Within minutes, Lark's eyes slipped back into focus. His pupils narrowed and he blinked rapidly as he returned to the present. He waved Luka back toward the elevator and they rode down a few floors more.

140

Lark was silent now, especially so for such a garrulous person. Wherever he had been a moment ago, it was not a happy place. Luka knew that look in himself.

This time the doors opened to a lab. It was a lab remarkably similar to his own in New Manhattan at the DA facility. It was perhaps not as clean or modern, but unnervingly good given that they were several floors underwater, occupying the ruins of a skyscraper's substructure. Lark had a lot of the same equipment Luka did. Not just the same sorts of things, but the exact same equipment—make, model, year. Lark was replicating DA experiments in his own lab. Specifically, those involving antimatter.

"How do you power your containment field?" asked Luka, taking a stab at his hypothesis.

Lark turned on his heels and his pupils contracted to pinpoints. A little of that violence returned to him and surged in the veins of his neck.

"Containment for what?" Lark asked.

"You know what."

Lark cocked his head, rubbed his tongue along his lips. His eyes darted and back and forth. Luka nearly smiled.

"How did you power yours?" Lark volleyed back.

"You first."

Lark chewed on the inner part of his cheek. Luka saw him suck it in and gnash it between his teeth. It left traces of blood on his teeth.

"Nuclear primary. Tidal secondary—and a fuck load of diesel generators in case things really get hairy!"

"Jesus," said Luka, his eyes wide. "We're lucky you haven't leveled New Seattle already. Diesel, that's your back up? No combustion generator is going to have the stability you need."

"I buffer with my battery array."

"It's stupid, and you know it is. Stop defending it."

"Not all of us can afford redundant nuclear reactors, alright. Don't you think they might draw just a little too much attention to our operation down here? Huh, smart guy?"

For a second time, Luka almost smiled. "Not a reasonable excuse. If I'm going to be involved in this, we will first start with improving your containment redundancies. *Then*, we can start building whatever your heart so desires. Though, I already know you are trying to recreate my antimatter reactor and power system."

Lark did not enjoy being bested. Luka saw the veins in his forehead throbbing harder than ever. The animal who destroyed the desk was just beneath the surface now. His arms were shaking and he was pulling more skin from the insides of his mouth. He was ripping the hairs out of his arms too—but he made no move at Luka. He kept the bit. It meant he truly needed Luka's help.

* * *

They spent two weeks retrofitting the batteries to stabilize the containment field.

Then they started on the plans for Lark's device. It was a repulsor, but antimatter fuel drove the power up on an exponential scale. Lark needed the repulsor wave to penetrate the shielded central communication server at the DA facility. It would inject a virus into the system and relay it to any biochips that matched the virus's signature. It would be a massive strike against the shadowy management of DA. Lark already had the most difficult-to-obtain material for the build, the antimatter, the fuel. Luka wanted to know how he managed to get it, but when he pressed, Lark became agitated and evasive—and again the animal in him would rise to the surface. It would take time to get that answer. Lark offered it in fragments. Antimatter aside, they had a challenging list of components they needed to build the reactor. He focused on those for the time being.

Their device had to contain and transfer obscene amounts of power. That meant this list of items would be difficult to procure. A lot of them were military grade. There weren't many sources. Fortunately, Luka knew one place where they could find just about every component they needed. Unfortunately, it was White Sands Missile Base. They stored the prototype of his antimatter reactor system there. From it, they could build Lark's new device. It was terribly convenient—and terribly stupid.

"Great, so we just need to break into a military base," said Luka.

"It's not as bad as you think," replied Lark.

"Have you been there?"

"No, but well, that's my point. You have right? Inside job. Should be easy for you."

143

"I agreed to help, not do the whole thing myself," said Luka.

"Relax. Ray-la-ha-tay señor. I have a plan." Lark held his arms out, palms up like he was reciting The Lord's Prayer at a Sunday Mass. Luka rubbed his eyes with the thumb and forefinger of his right hand.

"Should I be worried that you are speaking Spanish?"

"No. Just practicing," said Lark with a smile.

Luka knew Lark was baiting him to ask why. This was Lark's favorite game, luring people in the direction he wanted them to go. In the past two weeks, Luka grew to know it well.

"I know some people that may be able to help, that's all," said Lark.

"Oh, great," replied Luka

In these two weeks, Luka had also learned that Lark was corresponding measures of brilliant and terrifying. He was a skilled lateral thinker. He sought unconventional solutions almost exclusively. He slept only two hours a night, but never seemed tired. Altogether, Luka imagined it was like being roommates with a serial killer. Maybe not just *like it*, but maybe it *was that*.

At Luka's dismissal, he and Lark drifted in different directions. They both needed space to do their best thinking and so they wandered off without goodbyes. Luka shuffled in the direction of the bunk he had begun to think of as his bed. He laid back on his pillow, tucked his hands beneath his head, and busied his mind with remembering the security layout at White Sands.

144

His first memory was of the dryness—air so devoid of moisture that it made his ears ring. He remembered the constant nosebleeds in his first month. The bleach-white sands around the base were not formed of silicon dioxide like most deserts and dunes in the world. They were gypsum, a natural desiccant. It sapped every bit of humidity from that valley. He remembered cold winter afternoons, with high winds, and a low orange sun on the horizon.

They killed a lot of people there. Guantanamo Bay was a soft place by comparison, a place where a person imprisoned on the pretense of terrorism may be released with changing political winds. No one was ever let go from White Sands. Prisoners there were already dead on the books. They were fodder for war games. They let people go sometimes, or rather, made them think they had escaped. It was only so they could tune the tracking algorithms on the military drones or so they could test new ultra-long-range rifles. They used next-gen 0.338 rounds to cut down 'escapees' at a distance. Luka knew the layout. He knew it—but his brain would not let him see it. Instead, it replayed these memories of people being ripped apart by drones and rifles. His heart raced.

"So, did he tell you the story about his pet bird?"

A voice broke his concentration. A voice he knew, though not well. It was another of Lark's cronies. Whether he was here by choice or another person forced into this company, Luka did not know. His name was Aldin or Edwin— something that started with a vowel and sounded like a character from a medieval fantasy novel.

Luka rolled his body over and sat up so that his legs dangled off the top bunk.

"Yeah?"

"Humph. It's a lie you know."

A deep crease formed above the bridge of Luka's nose. "What?"

"All of it."

His eyebrows pushed closer together. "You mean about his mom?"

"No, I mean all of it. He never even had a mom," said Aldin.

"Not sure I'm following," Luka replied.

"He was created in a lab. Grown. A genetic experiment—he's a soulless lab rat. That's what I'm saying."

Luka bit his lip while he digested this. It was not all that surprising given Lark's physical and mental abnormalities.

Aldin looked at him expectantly with his mouth already open and ready to say more.

"How old is he?" Luka asked.

Aldin smiled. "Now you're on to it."

His teeth were painfully crooked and few were black with rot near the base. He was a Low City druggie—or was at some point. There was no other reason for him to be that skinny and for his face to be so pockmarked. He had to be intelligent, or valuable in some other way, though. Lark did not keep any other kind of person around.

"He's older than you, I'd guess. He doesn't seem to age like us—you and me I mean. Real people," Aldin continued.

146

Despite his own misgivings and fears concern Lark, the judgment felt wrong. However irritating and frightening Lark could be, he did not deserve quite that much cruelty. The value of a soul was something people gave themselves, not something bestowed by a higher order. Lark was no more— and no less—soulless for having been created rather than conceived.

"Oh, and don't let on that you know. I don't think he likes us knowing. Just between you and me huh?" added Aldin.

Luka nodded absently. "Yeah. It's safe with me. Thanks for the intel."

Aldin scrunched his face to one side, lips tucked in over his ruined teeth. "You have tech in your neural system, tech he can mess with. Just remember that."

The words snapped Luka's mind into focus and the hair along his arms prickled. He narrowed his eyes and looked at Aldin, but Aldin would not meet his gaze. He was looking off to his right and running his tongue along the side of his mouth. Luka took it to mean that something along those lines was done to him. It was a genuine warning.

"I get it," said Luka.

Aldin nodded. He wrapped his knuckles twice on the post of the bunk bed and then he left.

Luka had no idea what function Aldin served, or more importantly, know why Aldin had shared so much information. For a long while, he ruminated on this. He sat at the edge of the bunk and let his legs dangle until his feet tingled and threatened to go numb. In one way the conversation read like a warning, in another, a test. It was possible that Lark sent him, that Aldin was part of Lark's fear game. Lark might have shared the information so he could leverage it against him later.

Luka laid back on his bed and tucked his hands beneath his head as he let his mind drift back to his time at the military base.

He left White Sands fifteen years and five months ago. He flew out on a military transport, landed at Vandenberg, and then they released him to civilian life. From there he bought a cheap car just off base. It had only the most basic autonomous features. He was not certain it was highway legal but tried his luck anyhow. He worked his way southward first, toward Los Angeles. He tried to settle in an affluent neighborhood there, a place that was at that time, called Silver Lake. He felt like a prison-lifer released into the wild. He could not adjust. The city was so condensed and frantic. There were no rules, or routines, or boundaries. There was no purpose. Rich people were strangest of all. They spent all day deciding where and when to eat and drink. He was used to having his meals prepared, being told when they were available, and how long he would have to eat them.

There were also no drugs at White Sands and there was very little alcohol. Both were abundant in Los Angeles. He got drunk his first three nights in a row there and on the last night of his bender he got mugged. At the White Sands base he carried an MK23 sidearm. He shot close groupings. It was one of the few tolerated recreational activities out there, so he practiced often. Now, as a civilian, he could no longer open carry. After ingesting some party drug he didn't know the name of, and a garbage can variety of liquors, he stumbled home through an alley.

A lanky, wolfish sort of person stepped in his path. The man had wild hair. It was greasy and matted in some places and stood on end in others. He did not bother hiding his face with a mask or bandana. It was gaunt and lost in the mess of beard and hair.

He pulled a knife and Luka reached for his pistol—with the intent to kill. He did not even feel a sense of danger. It was a reaction, a muscle memory, but his pistol was not there for the follow-through. He reached for his left hip with his right hand—cross draw they called it. It was slower, not recommended by the truer gunman on base, but he was not a soldier and he liked the feel of it. In his mind's eye, that moment was in slow motion. He swung his hand across his body to draw his pistol, but he grabbed air instead of the grip of his MK. A horrified look swept over the man's emaciated face. His jaw dropped open, and in the orange glow of street lamps, he looked a lot like the man in *The Scream.* He recognized Luka's intent. Their meeting in the alley started as an attack of one on the other, but now they both felt they were defending their lives. The fight turned feral and he lost.

The man only stabbed him once—and half-heartedly at that. It sliced through some muscles and cartilage on his chest, but it did not penetrate his rib cage. He punched Luka once too, hard in the solar plexus. As soon as Luka went down, he ran off. The blood poured from the wound. His blood-alcohol concentration was way beyond reasonable and his vessels did not want to clot. When the shock of the blow to his stomach wore off, he lifted himself back up to his feet. He stumbled out toward the main street, leaving a heavy drip trail as he went. The front of his shirt soaked through and a syrupy stream ran from a torn edge along the hem. He sat down on the sidewalk and leaned back against a street pole, clutching his chest.

It was the early hours of the morning, but eventually, someone happened upon him and called an ambulance. A night at the hospital and two weeks of rest righted the damage. After that, Luka decided that he was not ready to be in a city. He bailed out of his pay-by-the-day rental, packed what he had into two duffle bags, and headed north. The span through Ventura and Santa Barbara was unbelievably beautiful. The turquoise water and cliffs reminded him of childhood trips to Croatia. He spent more time staring out at the horizon over the water than on the road. He hugged the coastal routes wherever possible and stuck to the small towns. They were easier to navigate. They were safer and slower. The drinking continued beyond LA, though. He was driving drunk for long stretches of that journey, and it got worse with each day.

Northern California passed in a blur. After a few days, the sides of the road transitioned from coastal scrub to evergreen trees and the sky became gray. The once turquoise water faded to a muted blue.

One afternoon, with at least two bottles of wine sloshing in his stomach, he fell asleep at the wheel. He drifted off the road and into a tree. The autonomous functions of his car should have prevented it, but the sensors were either disabled or broken. He had been ignoring the warnings on the dash ever since he bought it. Lucky for him for there was not much of a ditch at the shoulder and there was plenty of thick underbrush to slow him down before he struck a huge spruce.

He was not hurt, but the old car was done. Smoke poured out over the hood and the front right tire was buried in the wheel well. It took some doing, but he managed the pull the car away from the tree and pushed it a few meters further into the forest so that it was no longer visible from the road. Then, he passed out in the undergrowth. He was drunk, so he did not bother with a blanket, or jacket, or anything between him and the damp ground.

When he woke it was night and his buzz was gone and his body was numb with cold. Either the impact with the tree or the effort of moving his car had split the seal of the gash of his chest. He could not remember which. The wound was mostly healed, but the tissue welding failed in the deepest part of the cut. It wept blood and the front of his shirt was sticky with it. The cold It may have been a blessing. It dulled the pain in his chest and staved off the worst of his hangover. He picked himself up off the ground, brushed as much mud from his pants shirt as he could, and fished a metal canteen out of the car. He took a couple of swigs and used the rest to splash his face. He decided to ditch the car. The DMV might eventually ping his GPS and figure out that he abandoned the vehicle, but he bet that the signal was not very good out on these roads and that crossing state lines would complicate that process. A fine would show up in his account someday—and a ding on his license too. Not likely they would suspend him. Not likely they would put a warrant out for that. He grabbed his two duffels out of the back seat and set off in the direction nearest town. It was four clicks to the north along the same stretch of highway he had been driving.

The walk went fast, though the warmer he got, the more he regretted that he tore open the cut on his chest and especially regretted his four-day bender.

He came upon a hotel at the edge town and paid for one night on credit. The room was dumpy, with faded red curtains and musty carpet, but it had a bed and a toilet and those were his only two considerations right then. He took a long piss, stripped to down to his boxers, and settled into the sagging mattress.

He woke to a knock on the door. It was gentle at first but after a few rounds, it turned to pounding. He sat upright. It was morning. Light snuck in under the crack of the door. He threw the covers to the side and rubbed his eyes. The pounding continued.

"Yeah, yeah. I'm coming," Luka shouted.

He slipped his pants on and stumbled over to the entrance. A screen beside the sliding lock came to life and from the doorcam he saw it was a cop on the other side. The man had a sour expression, lips pulled to one side, eyes locked on the door. He did not recognize the uniform. It could have been federal or local. The police in LA wore tactical armor, all business. They were imposing. This man's uniform was anachronistic, friendly almost. He had gray slacks, polished black shoes, and a button-down shirt. He still wore armor, but under his shirt instead of over it. It was the thinner, less protective kind. He even wore a tie. Most departments ditched those a decade ago. It was a cold morning, so he wore a knee-length black overcoat too. Luka could not see what kind of weapon he carried.

He tapped the screen and the bolt on the door released. The door opened.

"Luka Janovic?"

Luka nodded.

"Detective McCallum."

The officer flashed a badge, but it was too quick for Luka to read the credentials.

"Did you forget something last night?" McCallum asked.

"What?" Luka asked.

"I asked you if you lost something on your way into town."

152

Luka's mind was foggy from a lack of sleep and alcohol withdrawal. For a moment, he did not see where this was headed. Then it clicked.

"That was fast," replied Luka.

McCallum snorted. "Not really. Refresh on the signal is ten minutes in city limits. Took six hours out there."

Luka huffed. "You always come after people when they park somewhere odd?"

"Well you didn't just park out it out there, did you? If that's all it was I wouldn't be here. Just would've docked your profile and moved on with my life."

Luka rubbed his forehead. His head was throbbing and the yellowy morning sun was doing him no favors in that regard.

"What time is it? You don't have better things to do than wake-up calls on abandoned vehicles?"

McCallum smiled tightly. "It's 7 A.M. and no, I don't. Sunday morning. Coos Bay. Not a lot happening around here."

Luka scratched the back of his head. "So, how much trouble am I in?"

"Ah, to the point. I can appreciate that," said McCallum as he fidgeted with the collar of his jacket.

"Not much. Why don't we just agree that you had car trouble and settle on a fine for littering? That and towing costs. Someone has to pick up that junker," he continued.

"How much is that?"

"Oh, I don't know. Twelve, thirteen hundred."

"Ouch," said Luka.

"From what I see it looks like the lesser of your worries."

"Point taken."

McCallum studied Luka for a moment. "Are you in some trouble I need to know about?"

"No."

He locked eyes with him. "We saw all of the empty bottles in the car you know."

"Who's we?"

The man cocked his head and studied Luka. "Me and my partner, but that's none of your business."

Luka looked away, down at his feet. "Fair enough. I'm guessing that you would not believe if I said that I didn't drink any of it while driving."

"You'd be guessing correctly."

McCallum made a pistol with his left hand and fired at Luka. "Though, that's not what interests me the most."

Luka blinked slowly, trying to shake the headache and clear his mind. "Okay. What is it then?"

"What interests me is that I pulled up your records and there's a whole lot missing from the past few years. No car

154

registration. No license renewal. No infractions. No place of employment. No rental. You get the point. Can you explain that to me?"

Luka shook his head. "No, I can't."

McCallum's mouth pulled thin. His jaw clenched.

"See, that's not going to work for me," he said.

Luka exhaled loudly. "Now I know why you showed up."

"Now you do," said McCallum as his hand drifted inside his coat, resting on his belt near his hip.

Luka's throat tightened.

"Did you see that I'm a researcher, a scientist?" asked Luka, his voice cracking a little.

"Yes."

"Look closer at the record. I can't say where I was, and it won't exactly either, but I have a feeling you'll catch it."

McCallum's heavy brow sunk low on his face. He was staring Luka down when someone two rooms over ripped open their front door. Luka and McCallum both looked over. It was a man in his mid-forties with skinny arms and a sizable potbelly. He was fully prepared to *let 'em have it*—with his fist in the air and his red face swollen with anger. His mouth snapped shut and his arms wilted when he saw that at least one of the men was a police officer. He retreated and locked the door behind him. It was like someone had just played a tape of the scene in reverse.

McCallum set his gaze back on Luka and reached into an inner pocket of his overcoat. He pulled out his cell phone and started searching, still keeping one eye on Luka.

"You drop off the record in Las Cruces New Mexico and appear again in Lompoc California."

Luka nodded.

"Okay. I get it. I don't know what you are doing all the way up here," said McCallum.

Luka cut him off, "Just got out."

"Alright. All the same. I don't know what brought you here, or what you went through, but I need to know you won't do this again."

Luka looked down at his feet. "I'm done with it."

"You sure? Because I'm cutting you a break here. I can't have that coming back to me," said McCallum

"I mean it. I'm done," replied Luka.

The same man that had opened his door earlier to yell at them was now peering at them through a crack in his curtains. He must have thought he was discreetly observing, but the curtain flapped back and forth every time he repositioned himself and Luka's peripherals kept hanging up on the motion. He glanced over to his right. McCallum did the same.

Luka pointed with his thumb in the general direction of his neighbor. "Seems like you might want to knock on his door next."

"Seems like it," answered McCallum.

"I've got a question for you," said Luka.

McCallum's eyebrows narrowed. "Shoot."

"If I went back to sleep for," Luka counted to three on his fingers, "three more hours, is there a place around here that would still be serving breakfast?"

McCallum snorted a second time. It was nearly a laugh, but shy of approving. The sound existed somewhere in a gray area between irritation and amusement.

"Twenty minutes on foot, down the main road. It's called The Hungryman's Cove."

"How clever."

"Not actually. It's the name of that cove over there." McCallum pointed to a hazy bit of land across the water.

"One last one for you, Mr. Janovic."

"Okay."

"How long are you planning on staying?"

Luka looked down at McCallum's polished shoes. He pretended to be from around here but they were out of place in a town like this. The air here smelled like salt, and rot, and evergreen. It was the kind of place that people wore boots most of the year and sandals for those few warm days in summer.

He shook his head. "I'm not planning on anything."

157

McCallum weighed this, chewing on nothing. Luka held still, trapped in a bear's gaze. Then McCallum shrugged, casually, in a way that said *no big deal.* He slid his cell phone back into the pocket of his coat and turned his feet to walk away.

"None of us are," he said as he set off toward the motel's front office.

Luka watched McCallum take two steps away before he closed his door and fell back onto the lumpy bed. Sleep came quickly again.

He woke around noon with his hangover much improved, but with his body dehydrated. He cupped his hands beneath the faucet in the bathroom sink and drank water by the handful until his stomach distended. He showered and took another long piss while he was at it.

He did not have much in the way of clothes, but at least two items in his bags did not reek of booze or smell bad from a general lack of washing. He picked a faded blue T-shirt, a dark gray sweater, and some black jeans. Dressed, he made for the café McCallum had suggested. He walked along the curb of the main road with his head down, focusing on his feet.

To his great fortune, The Hungryman's Cove served exactly the type of food one wanted to eat after a bad hangover and a long sleep. It was greasy and carb loaded and he ate all of it—with lots of coffee. For the first time since leaving the base, he felt almost good. The cafe was a cheery, busy place. The walls were aqua blue with accents of orange and minty green. The service staff hustled from person to person, tapping orders into their tablets and running plates back and forth between the kitchen. The air inside was stuffy and rich with the smell of burned grease, but every time someone entered or exited, a flood of autumn ocean air rushed through the room. The pungent air of a cold ocean was pleasantly sharp against the stifling warmth.

Two women, travelers he judged from the size of their backpacks, were sitting in a booth next to his barstool. They sat shoulder to shoulder with their backups piled into the opposite bench of the table. They had a paper map unfolded in front of them and they were scribbling notes in pencil at various locations.

Luka did not mean to stare, but the heavy food had put him into a daze, and he was drifting off with eyes resting on their map. He did not even notice them laughing and whispering into each other's ears. They stared back, straight-faced until the intensity of it cut through his daydream. He jolted back in his seat. A fork went clattering to the floor. They smiled and laughed again.

"Sorry," he said.

The one nearest him waved it off and shook her head, "No, no. Don't worry about it. Sorry for messing with you. Couldn't resist."

Her friend, the one nearest the window, didn't chime in but wore a wide grin too. She had brilliant red hair that she kept in a neat braid. She had vivid amber-green eyes that flashed against the gray sky in the window behind her.

"Are you from around here?" the woman nearest him asked. Her friend stayed silent.

"No, just passing through I guess."

"Vacation or what?"

His pulse rose. "Vacation, in a way."

"What about you two?" asked Luka, turning the questioning back to them.

"We're doing a road trip up the coast and into Canada."

"What do you mean *in a way?* That's a bit mysterious. If you are going for the good-looking and mysterious thing, it is working. Dark clothing, long hair, vague ambitions. We're intrigued," she said as she made eyes at her friend.

Luka's face flushed. He was not sure if it showed, but he felt it turn hot. "I uh—I quit my job a few weeks ago. Is it still considered a vacation if you're unemployed?"

"Oh yeah. That counts. I'm Chelsea, and this is my sister Emma. She speaks too, I promise."

Chelsea laid an elbow into Emma's ribs. Emma winced and her nose crinkled up.

"Hi," Emma said.

She locked eyes with Luka. Because she had not spoken to this point, Luka had expected that she would have a soft or mousy sort of voice. Even from a single word he could hear that that was not the case. It was confident, with a touch baritone and rasp—like a jazz singer.

"I'm Luka. Nice to meet you both."

He waved at them in lieu of a handshake and they waved back.

"Luka, what did you used to do for work before you became a bum like us?" asked Chelsea.

"I'm a scientist."

"Ok, what sort?"

"High energy physics."

"Whoa, sorry I asked," Chelsea said as she grinned, "is Luka a code name, or is that your actual name?"

"You know the saying. If I told you, I'd have to kill you."

Maybe not the best thing to say to two women you only just met.

Chelsea laughed but pulled the smile into a stony expression and leaned in toward Luka. "Now that you've given away your secret identity *Luka.* I must tell you that I am not Chelsea and that she is not Emma. Our real names are Vladlena and Oksana and we are Russian operatives sent to assassinate you."

Luka did his best to mask his smile and mimic Chelsea's tone, "Assassinate me? I must be pretty important."

"You must be. They don't send us for just anyone," said Emma, jumping into the conversation. She and Luka met eyes again and he knew then that he could not pull his eyes away from her again.

In his bunk, Luka drifted into sleep thinking of Coos Bay and the first time he met Emma. Sleep came easy when his mind filled with good memories.

When he woke up, he did not know how long he had been asleep or whether it was night or day. It was difficult to keep track of time in Lark's bunker. It destroyed his circadian rhythm. He had been losing his grip—working when he felt awake, sleeping when he felt tired, and eating when he felt hungry. No schedule. A few weeks of living in an environment without daylight and he was untethered.

He swung his legs over the edge of the bed and hopped down. The shock of the cold concrete ran through his body, starting at his feet and prickling up through his back. He shivered. A clock on a wall panel just outside of his bunk read 22:18 in red digital characters. He had slept for five hours or so. Enough, he reasoned.

Luka slipped on a pair of socks and his boots and shuffled out of the room toward the elevator to the lab. He moved down the hallway that led to their primary lab space and on the other side of the glass he saw Lark busy tinkering with what appeared to the be the main block of a diesel engine from one of the backup generators. It was odd to observe Lark when he thought no one was watching. He was at his most alien when he was alone. Around others, he had some veneer of social function, but that fell away at times like this. A normal person might pace the room to collect their thoughts. They might scowl in deep reflection, or rub their temples, or scratch their head—or take breaks. They might listen to music. He did none of this. Lark hated music. It agitated him. Luka tried once to put on some music through a computer in their lab and Lark threatened to shiv him with a dull screwdriver. Given that it was Lark making the threat, Luka had to assume he was at least partly serious. *No music.* Lark worked with a blank face and a slack jaw. He snatched tools, parts—whatever he needed without looking at it. He worked at such a frantic pace that one would assume he had a pistol pressed to his head, ready to fire if he did not meet some arbitrary deadline. His arms and hands moved so furiously that it was almost cartoonish. His eyes were locked forward and focused.

"Mouth breather," Lark shouted from his lab as Luka approached.

Luka jumped. He was not sure whether Lark had seen his reflection in the glass or if he heard him breathing from so far off. To his knowledge, it was not possible to hear anything through the thick transitional glass surrounding the workspaces.

Luka pressed his palm to the glass on the door. It read his biometrics and registered access with a quick blue flash. The door slid open to the left and Luka passed through.

"I told you those were not reliable," said Luka as he pointed at the engine block.

Lark spoke without looking up from the engine, "You would be right, except that this isn't one of my generators, which are reliable. This is part of a different diesel system, one that we will be using soon. I thought it would be better to give it a once over beforehand. Dick."

He reached back to a counter space over his shoulder and retrieved a wrench to start reassembling the cylinder heads. "This is part of an engine from an old research sub. I modified the sub to be electric, but it has biodiesel engines too. That's what you are looking at here. I make the biodiesel in-house from algae, but it does gum up the valves—hence I'm replacing them."

Luka raised an eyebrow. "You have a submarine?"

Lark pulled his attention from the engine and anchored his thousand-yard stare on Luka. Those yellow-amber eyes made Luka's blood run cold. They were frighteningly perspicacious.

"Now, would I lie about that? Me? Certainly not."

Luka shirked his gaze, choosing to look out through glass walls at nothing in particular. "You probably would, if you thought it would impress me."

Luka pretended to be interested in the steel joinery that reinforced the bunker. Lark scoffed and returned to his work.

"During The Transition the government was pretty AWOL. I was able to buy a lot of things then that would have raised red flags now. On the cheap too. I made sure plenty of records went missing, and a few people along with them. So yes, I have a submarine. It's a modified NR-1 type, to be more exact. Not that you would know what that is. Dick," said Lark.

"What, did you just learn a new word and couldn't wait to use it?"

Lark shook his head but did not look up from the engine. "I've known that one for a while just never had cause to use until today."

Luka yawned and stretched his arms out in a wide 'V,' doubling down on his bid to irritate Lark.

"Alright. You win. When and why will we be using this?" he asked.

Lark slammed a socket wrench down on the table. "I am SO glad you asked. I thought you never would Doctor."

Luka flinched when the wrench made contact and he was sure that Lark noticed. He did his best to stand with his shoulder square and his spine straight.

164

Lark continued, "We take the sub to an airstrip on an island north of here. On this island I have a jet—also procured during the transition and placed under the holdings of about ten layers of shell corporations. We will fly said jet from here to Mexico. From there, our team will make an assault on White Sands."

Luka shifted his weight. "Listen, I was thinking about how we might get in but—"

Lark cut him off. "I know you can't figure it out, shithead. That's why I've already got it worked out. I've been planning this for years. You've only just come along. I only told you to work on it so you would go away and give me a damn moment's peace. Come-pren-day?"

It took Luka a moment to register the assault. His head jerked back and his face twisted in confusion as the words sunk in. "Okay. You already have a plan. Can you elaborate?"

"Smash and grab. That's it. All you have to do is direct us to it and we will handle it. Do you think you can you handle that much? Do you come-pren-day?" said Lark through his teeth.

Luka's adrenaline rushed. His eyes scanned the wrenches scattered around the counter. He thought of picking one up and knocking Lark across the back of the head with it. Then he remembered that old desk in Lark's server room, reduced to splinters by a hammer in Lark's hand. He thought of the hate and glee in Lark's eyes when he swung.

His heart slowed. He thought better of it. It would be more effective to snub Lark verbally anyhow, to keep his cool, if he could.

"Well, now I know why you've been speaking Spanish at least," said Luka.

"What?" asked Lark.

He had gone distant, lost to his engine. Too late.

"You told me to relax earlier and you just asked me if I understand, both in Spanish," pressed Luka.

"Oh. Yeah."

Lark spoke dispassionately, uninvolved. He was on autopilot now. The rest of the world was static to him. Luka knew the look and knew that it was an impregnable state. It was time to go. He lost this round. Luka turned on his heels and exited the lab.

Chapter Eight

Lark did not lie about the submarine. He did own one, and they were going to use it. They were in the elevator now, moving down toward the lowest level of the bunker. The doors opened to an antechamber with an old naval airlock door at the far end—a door just like the one Luka had passed through when he first arrived at Lark's complex. Lark motioned for Luka to go first. He stepped out of the elevator and cranked on the heavy wheel that released the latches on the door. It squealed with each turn, but the lock gave way, and it swung open. Beyond the door was a docking room where the water rose to half the height of the ceiling. The submarine sat beside a grated metal dock. It was half submerged, with its topside deck and entrance bobbing above the waterline.

It was not big, maybe ten meters long, and they had a lot of equipment to pack into it. From the elevator, they carried bag and after bag of firearms down to the sub. They had at least eight combat rifles, an equal number of pistols, and two long-range rifles. They also had tactical armor, a few bricks of high explosives, and crates of ammunition. It stacked from floor to ceiling, two rows deep in the back of the submarine.

For food, they packed disaster relief rations: complete, high-calorie meals neatly packed into durable plastic pouches. They looked like military rations, but lower quality, and less appetizing—which in Luka's opinion was a backward accomplishment. He had seen, and eaten, many varieties of military rations. He knew which were tolerable and which were abhorrent by the look of them. None were good. The dull gray packaging containing these meals was stamped with DRR in large black letters and below that were single line

167

descriptions of the contents. Among those they packed were: Chicken and Peas, Ham and Peas—there were a lot of peas—Lentil Stew, and Salisbury Steak with mashed carrots. The real coup de gras, however, was a meal described as "Imitation Meat Taco." Luka set it aside, near Lark's belongings. He did not seem to mind these meals in the least. In these weeks, Luka had learned that most of what Lark ate came from those plastic pouches.

It took them a few hours to get everything loaded into, and secured, in the submarine. Once they had all the equipment on board, Lark flopped down into a seat at the controls. He flipped a few overhead switches and pressed his hand to a tablet console at his right and the submarine came to life. The main hatch closed and sealed. The ballast tanks pulled in water and the submarine's sail dipped beneath the surface. Luka took a seat at the communications hub. The main lights clicked off and an eerie red light overhead bathed the cabin in a dull glow.

The submarine was autonomous, but Lark remained at the controls, adjusting the Heads-Up Display on the forward windscreen. It showed an image from a rear camera. They were gliding backward through the first air door. It closed behind them and this new chamber filled with water. Then, the outer lock opened and the submarine flipped a one-eighty, and they faced out into Elliott Bay.

The water was murky and black, with visibility less than two meters, but the sonar and EM sensor systems rendered a high-definition image of their surroundings onto the forward glass. There were some crevices and sea ridges out in the distance, but in their immediate vicinity, it was all flooded structures. It was a complete lost city, a scummy Atlantis, and they picked a treacherous route through it. Buildings of varying heights entrenched them. Some had collapsed and formed narrow tunnels that they had to pass through. Others appeared structurally sound from a distance, but as they approached, scaffolding and I- jutted out into their path and threatened to shred the hull. The sub navigated through all of it effortlessly, moving with a slow but steady assuredness.

Within an hour they were in open water and their speed increased. The diesel engines kicked into action and filled the cabin with a gentle hum. Luka got sick of staring the communications controls and meandered his way toward the bow of the sub. The copilot's chair was near the front of the vessel, to the left of, and slightly behind, the main control chair where Lark was seated. He plopped down into it.

From his position, Luka could not see Lark's face, so it was hard not to know if he registered his presence at all. His body did not move. Luka shifted in his seat, intentionally making noise as he settled in, but Lark did not react. He appeared to be looking forward at the HUD, but his stillness suggested that he was in one of his trances.

Luka cut into the silence, "What was your mom like?"

The words echoed. The cabin was mostly metal and Luka's voice bounced around until the hum of the engines swallowed them. He saw Lark's head turn to his left, just barely, like he was about to look over his shoulder at Luka.

"Really? You want to talk about this shit? You are a sappy mother fucker," said Lark.

He was shaking his head in disapproval. Luka was sure he meant it to be every bit as condescending as it sounded. That meant he was on the right path.

Luka pushed forward. "We both already knew that. So, what was she like?"

169

"She was a miserable goddamn drunk, I told you already," Lark shot back. He spoke with so much force that he was almost yelling.

"No, she wasn't," Luka challenged.

He expected it to enrage him. Instead, Lark rotated his shoulders, turned his head, and smiled at Luka. His smile was somehow so much worse than his anger.

Luka swallowed heavy but held his course. "You already know what Aldin said to me back at your base, so why don't you tell me your version."

Lark kept on smiling. It was not a happy smile, but an amused one. He was enjoying this for a reason Luka could not yet figure out.

"Aldin told you the truth. Minus some detail, and not so eloquently, but the truth," said Lark.

"I'm not interested in eloquence. I just want your version of events," said Luka.

Lark broke eye contact with Luka and, little by little, drifted his gaze up to the ceiling. His eyes began stutter from side to side. His jaw fell open and his head dipped back. Whatever was going on with him it was either extremely painful—or the exact opposite of it, pleasurable. Whichever the case, it made Luka's teeth itch and it made his stomach churn. He wanted to look away, but he didn't. He couldn't. Lark sucked in air and arched his back. The angle became so extreme that Luka worried Lark might crack a vertebra, but then, suddenly, his body relaxed. His spine straightened out and he set his hands on the armrests of his chair as he turned his eyes back to Luka.

"No, no thanks," he said.

"If you want the reactor to work, you'll give me your best effort. Information for information."

"That's not our arrangement."

"Like hell it isn't."

"I rescued you. You already owed me."

"Do I irritate you Lark? Do I ever piss you off?"

Lark huffed.

Luka continued, "Yeah, that's what I thought—and yet I'm still alive, which tells me the information I have is worth more than our original arrangement acknowledged. I'm changing the terms. A little back story is a fair trade for my expertise."

Lark ran his tongue along his teeth and studied Luka with narrowed eyes.

"I'm allowing you to help, so I suppose it's fair that you know why," he said.

Luka nodded, trying to accept the victory as obsequiously as he could. He needed Lark to feel he had the upper hand.

"There was a lab. Let's start with that," said Lark. "There were others there with me. I was the only one who turned out as intended, but there were plenty of other *me's* there. Some of them lived long enough for me to know them. Well, sort of."

The lights in the submarine flickered. Through the vibrations in the floor, Luka felt the diesel engines sputter and rev up hard. Lark paused too, listening. His hands clenched the sides of his chair. His spine went rigid. They both froze until the vibrations stabilized. The engines settled in again—just a hiccup.

"There were a lot of retards and deformed ones. They were pathetic, awful creatures—non-verbal and in constant pain. I'd hear them shrieking at night and struggling in their restraints. I'd hear their heart monitors flat line. Sometimes I'd wake up to that. No one ever came rushing in to save them, so the alarm would keep going for hours. For a long time, I'd cry when I heard them go. Those are some of my earliest memories."

"I know, I know," said Lark as he held both hands up in the air and rolled his eyes. "I was a sap like you then. Only difference is I grew out of it."

Luka kept quiet. He felt adrift now, caught by a stronger force.

Lark settled down and started into his story again, "Our creators would wait until morning to collect the bodies. I'd wake again to the sound of a cell door next to me creaking open. Two would carry the body to the incinerators and a third would hose out the cell. It was all very rinse and repeat—to be so literal. They wore these yellow biohazard suits that were complete overkill. A little excrement would not hurt them. They were made of that stuff."

Horrible as it was, Luka could not help but grin a little at this dig.

"I was special, so sometimes during the day they'd let me roam the halls. I'd wander by the other cells and stare in through the bars at the different iterations of me. If the non-verbal ones weren't shrieking or crying, then they were gaping off into space. I liked them better when they were wailing and struggling, it gave me hope they hadn't given up, but I always wondered what they thought about during those quiet moments of theirs. I wondered if they were as intelligent as me, just trapped in a body that wouldn't let them express it. I sometimes tried to communicate with them in other ways—tapping on the bars and such. It never worked. They were stupid after all."

Luka could not be sure, it was dark in the cabin and the red lighting made it difficult to track movement, but he thought he saw Lark shaking. Whether it was with anger or sadness did not seem to matter. Lark was exposed.

"They made a girl version of me too. We were biologically the same age." Lark shook his head. "I have no idea how that relates to when we were born."

Luka cut in, "I don't follow what you mean by that."

"I don't age at the same rate as you. My telomeres are better."

"Got it," said Luka, although he had only a vague idea what Lark was implying.

"I'm so glad. Are you going to let me talk now?" said Lark.

Luka opened his mouth to apologize but held it back and nodded instead.

"We were basically identical in appearance, gender mirrored, and we talked sometimes. I thought of her as my twin sister. She was the only thing like family that I ever had, or that I will ever have. In the end, she was the most unlucky creature of all."

Lark was chewing was on the inside of cheeks in between words. Luka saw flecks of blood on Lark's front teeth.

"They were always trying to impregnate her—in the ways you are thinking, and also so many creative other ways on top of it. Oh yeah, they started with the modern techniques, the science, In Vitro Fertilization. When that didn't work, one of the docs took the great burden upon himself to go ahead and try it the old-fashioned way. He was going to give his own DNA a shot at the championship. When that didn't work two of the guards decided they should give it the college try too— you know, just to be scientifically thorough. It was very analytical of them, those bastards. One day I slit their throats with a bit of broken glass. I cut my hand in the process, but boy did it feel good," said Lark.

He held up his hand to show a trace of a ragged scar extending from his forefinger down to the heel of his palm.

"Well, eventually, they caught on that she was sterile. Then some weeks after that, they got tired of fucking her. Or maybe they were afraid I would kill more of the guards. I don't know. I do know that they couldn't be satisfied and accept that she was sterile. This was science, they could not stop until they had exhausted *all* options. They anesthetized her and tried to transplant in a new, working set of reproductive organs. They must have had a difficult time matching the donor organs to her genome because the transplant didn't take. They tried again, and then once more. Turns out it didn't matter how genetically compatible the donor was, her immune system just wouldn't let the foreign organs be. She died of septicemia. Even her genetically superior body had limits on the trauma it could sustain. After she was gone, they suddenly, truly, noticed me. I was their prodigal child, the sole survivor of their science. Experimental perfection. They wised up and they wouldn't let me just wander around the facility anymore. They started running

174

more tests, draining more blood. They had this machine to jerk me off—can you believe that man? At the time I didn't even understand what it was they were doing to me. They harvested a lot of semen, A LOT. Turns out I was sterile too. They wanted some prized Arabian horses, but she and I were just a couple of dirty old mules."

Lark was an adept liar, he was adept at most things, but this did not feel like a lie. It was too pure. He didn't add any of his strange accents to it. It kicked like straight cocaine.

"Your lovely Committee—Daedalus Astrodynamics and all that. The same assholes that were going to kill you. They did this to me, all of this. That was their lab. They tortured and killed her and who knows how many more like us. To a God that doesn't exist, I am Lucifer, and they will suffer by me."

Luka swallowed hard, but his Adam's apple stuck in his throat like he was trying to swallow a boulder.

"I'm going to teach you one lesson Luka, and I am your elder, so listen the fuck up. Never cage something that is smarter than you."

Lark held up the index finger of his left hand to emphasize his point, "I got out of my cage and I killed as many of them as I could on my way to the surface."

The shaking was obvious now and adrenaline wore through Lark's voice, "When I say *as many as I could,* I do mean that. I was indiscriminate. Any person associated with that place was, and is, guilty. I'm going to kill a hell of a lot more of them. Yes, that makes me a murderer. I'm sick in the head, but at least I know it. You just need to know, however sick I am, they are sicker. What makes them worse is that they don't see it."

175

Luka studied feet. He could feel Lark's eyes on him still, but he could not meet them. His stomach was turning over on itself and gurgling. There was a tightness in his chest too—a deep stress-tension that might arrest his heart. True, he was willing to kill Janus—and a few other higher-ups at Daedalus Astrodynamics—if that meant he could find Michael, or at least expose what happened. He was willing to kill the upper echelon of DA if it pushed their behind-the-scenes activities into the light and meant they could never rebuild. But in his head, he had pictured himself like a comic book vigilante, with the end justifying the means. Something about Lark did not fit into that image.

"You know they were going to kill all of you on the mission, right? Olivia, Tara, Zheng—anyone not in their circle," said Lark.

Luka pulled his eyes from his feet. "What?"

Lark smiled. "Oh god, you didn't? Oh, you sweet child Luka."

Luka shook his head. "I'm not following."

"You were never going to Europa," answered Lark.

Luka rocked back in his seat. His eyes darted back and forth while he tried to piece it together. He did not want to ask, but he knew he was missing the wider implication.

"Okay, humor me," he said.

Lark's smile widened until his teeth showed. The corners of his eyes crinkled with glee.

"You know that part of the bargain with NASA, where Daedalus Astrodynamics get to launch their mining drones into the asteroid belt along the way?"

"Yeah, that was the general agreement."

"For them, that's the whole mission. They were going to drop off their drones, kill all of you in some *accident*, and then come back home with core samples worth trillions. Once they have claims on the best specimens, it's all over."

Luka sucked his lips in under his teeth and chewed. The hum of the engines filled the cabin again as they both went silent.

"That's a wonderful story," said Luka. He put his on the sides of the chair like he was about to stand up. "For some reason, despite your constant lying, I believe that this lab existed. I believe that what you say happened there, did. But don't feed me this crap about the Europa mission."

Even in the dark cabin of the submarine, he saw Lark's pupils contract to pinpoints. He pressed on anyway, "You expect me to believe that they were going to kill half of the crew and abort just after they've finished their objective? No one would fall for that. There would be absolute hell to pay when they got back. You can't just screw the government and walk away untouched."

Lark's voice became ragged and distorted as he bristled with rage. "Really? Because rich people do it all the time. You suffer from limited scope, doctor. The metals in those asteroids are worth some measurable fraction of the entire global economy. They could buy the government's debt and jack the interest rates to bankrupt them. They can do whatever they want once they own those rocks. With enough money, they become the government in all things but name."

Lark stood from his chair and ambled over to Luka, running his finger along the ceiling as he went. He stumbled back and forth a little as he walked like he was drunk. Luka could not decide whether Lark needed to stabilize himself that way, or whether it was an affect of his current persona. Lark leaned in so close that his horrid, fishy breath filled Luka's nostrils.

"That's why you and I are doing what we're doing."

Luka stood to meet him. His heart hammered behind his ribcage. "Didn't you just finish explaining that we were doing this because of what happened to you and the others in that lab? Why is it now about some ludicrous scheme to become a world power? Stop lying to me."

Lark tilted his head and studied Luka. His pupils were still laser-focused and threatening. Luka clenched his jaw and met his glare.

Spittle erupted from Lark's mouth as he spoke, "So it's both. Do you have a problem with that?"

"I do when it's not the truth," Luka fired back.

Lark's whole body jerked as a convulsion racked it. He clenched his fists and he began to pant. His chest moved in quick, shallow heaves. Luka knew this was the edge of Lark's control. If Lark went over the cliff, he would tear him apart, so he froze. He waited while it passed. It took minutes, not seconds, but his fists released and his breathing slowed. He pulled his head back upright and spat a thick wad of bloody mucus onto the floor.

"Maybe I don't care about their big scheme, maybe I just want to kill them ... but that does not make what I said any less true. They intend to kill the NASA crew. I saved your life when I brought you to my base, and if you stop this mission, you save the rest of your crew too."

Lark leaned in again. Their noses were nearly touching.

"Do you have a problem with that?"

The world was gray, but it still had sides. Luka wondered which he was on now.

"No, I don't."

Wrinkles formed and pupils relaxed as satisfaction crept once more into Lark's eyes.

"Good," Lark said.

The next twelve hours passed without another word between them. Lark went back to the pilot's chair and gaped into space. Luka dozed off in his chair. The diesel engines would sputter and rev periodically, pulling him from his nap, but otherwise the smooth hum inside the submarine lulled him into a shallow sleep. He came out of his torpid state when the diesel engine shut down for good with a heavy clunk and the sub switched over to full electric.

The Heads-Up Display showed them gliding into a small cavern on some island to the north of New Seattle. This was not a built-out dock like the one at Lark's facility in Elliott Bay, but a rocky alcove that centuries of rising and falling tides carved into the cliff. Jagged edges along the walls threatened to rip into hull and Luka watched on the forward screen as they slid through the narrow passages. The autopilot program was more skilled than a human, it had perfect reaction times and could monitor all the sensors at once, but it was a tight fit and there were unpredictable shifts in current as waves plunged and pulled water through the cavern.

Vibrations made by rocks dragging against the belly of the sub made Luka's skin prickle like the silverware screeching on a dry plate. He kept looking over to Lark, wondering if he should be concerned. Lark, however, was serene as ever. He was either immune to anxiety or outright reckless.

The cavern gradually opened up and on the far wall ahead there was a crude metal stairwell with a hatch built at the top. The sub slid up beside it and a set of electromagnets anchored it to the metal railing with a thud.

Lark got up out of his chair and started toward the rear of the sub near the main hatch. "He will have prepared the plane already, so we need to hurry," he said as he walked.

Luka jumped up out of his seat and followed at Lark's heels. "Okay. Who's *he*?"

Lark stopped and looked back over his shoulder. Luka almost bowled into him

"My friend. The one who met you in Low City."

It was strange to hear Lark refer to someone as a friend.

"How did he get here already?" Luka asked.

"He had other means of transportation," Lark said as he worked his way up the ladder to unseal the main hatch of the sub.

"I guessed as much. The point of me asking was that you and I had to take this circuitous route to keep us off of DA's radar, but this other guy was somehow able to get to the airfield well in advance of us."

Lark huffed and looked down at Luka from the top of the ladder. "Circuitous, where the fuck did you learn that tenpenny word? Does it matter how he got here, doctor? When he met you at the pier and swam you across the bay, did he strike you as the sort of person who makes mistakes— the sort of person who would accidentally blow our cover?"

"No, I guess not."

"Then stop fucking asking and just follow me."

Lark rotated a heavy bolt on the door and the hatch opened. A rush of cold, salty air poured into the submarine. A shiver ran through Luka. He had gotten used to the stuffy warmth of the recycled air and the ocean air chilled him.

By the time Luka climbed up the ladder and stepped through the hatch, Lark had already laid down a gangway between the submarine and the stairwell leading to the surface.

"Why are you empty-handed?" Lark shouted as soon as Luka came into view.

He was busy securing the gangway and the mechanism that fixed it to the railing seemed to give him trouble. As far as Luka could tell, Lark had not looked up from it, but somehow he knew that Luka had not brought up any of gear with him. As it so often was the case, Luka could not figure out whether it was only a good guess, or if Lark had some other way of 'seeing' him. Without a word, Luka descended the ladder again. He grabbed two bags, slung them over his shoulders, and worked his way back topside. Lark secured the gangway by the time he returned. When Luka popped through the submarine hatch, Lark stepped to the side and motioned for Luka to go up to the stairs.

The stairwell opened onto a rocky coastline near the edge of a spruce forest. From this spot, the area looked uninhabited. Luka threw the bags aside, flinching when they hit the ground as he remembered they might contain explosives. He looked out over the water. The ocean was an unending expanse of chaos. A hard wind whipped across it, drawing up white caps. They crashed into one another from all directions, losing any coherent pattern. The sharp smell of evergreen and cold ocean pulled Luka back to Coos Bay. His mind became with a maelstrom of memories, pulling him inward.

Emma's hand touched his face. He breathed in the warm, piney smell of her hair. He felt the warmth of her body as she shifted her hips in close against his while they slept.

His spine tingled and the muscles in his lower back began to twist. They clenched and torqued his body. Luka collapsed to one knee. His breath rose and his heart thundered. A panic was creeping in. Luka gritted his teeth and pushed himself back to his feet. He dug his nails into the meat of his arm and the pain brought him back to the present. He threw himself into the task of unloading the gear.

He and Lark went in alternating shifts. It took a dozen trips to retrieve the emergency rations, water, and various firearms and explosives. When they finished, they had a huge grid of equipment laid out on the rocks. Lark had it all organized by type. Huffing, and red-faced with exertion, Luka flopped down on a bit of grass next to the stairwell when they finished the last load. Flat on his back, with his chest heaving, he sucked in deep breaths while he tried to regain control. He was in decent shape from mission training, but moving up and down three flights of stairs a dozen times with a hundred pounds of equipment on each go, was not a trivial task. Lark was unaffected by the exertion. He didn't even sweat, yet alone breath hard. He took a seat on a large black rock not far from Luka and looked out at the ocean while Luka regained his breath. In the distance, a branched cracked. Luka bolted upright and turned in the direction of the sound. He scanned the horizon. The sound of crunching rocks and snapping twigs grew louder. A large two-seater ATV appeared in the clearing, moving toward them from an inland location. Luka looked over at Lark, wondering if he should make for one the guns, but Lark watched passively as the vehicle approached. Luka eased back on his elbows and did the same.

The driver's eyes glowed even at a distance. It was the man who met him in Low City. Just as Lark had promised, he was here. Luka felt a pluck of attachment—*or comradery?* He had not seen him since the swim from Low City. This man had guided him through an ocean, he had reassured Luka to step through the door into Lark's domain, and so far Luka was alive. He owed him that.

The man offered a subtle nod in Luka's direction as approached, but did not speak. The ATV came to a stop Lark jumped into action, and Luka followed suit, loading their equipment into the trailer at the back of the ATV. Between the three of them, it went quickly. They piled their gear high into the trailer—higher than seemed stable to Luka. Some of it had to be loaded into the passenger's side of the vehicle too. They stacked bags of rifles and munitions from floorboards to backrest. Lark gave the big pile in the trailer a quick shove to see what might shift and when nothing fell, his mouth curled into the upside-down U-shape of *good enough*.

The man jumped back in the ATV and it crawled to a start. They plodded through the forest. Luka and Lark walked behind the vehicle, ambling along at a slower pace than either liked. They moved deep into the trees and forest transitioned into old-growth evergreen. Some of the trunks were meters in diameter. They stretched up far into the sky

183

and faded into the thick marine layer before Luka could see their tops. It was eerily quiet too. A few squirrels chittered. Once, a crow cawed a warning as they get passed beneath its perch. The spaces between were dead air, though, and it heightened his nerves. His peripherals went wild.

The trees eventually broke away into a small airfield. There was one landing strip, one classic half-cylinder-shaped hanger, and one tower of an unimpressive height at the far end of the clearing. In days past, someone would have lived out here to act as an air traffic controller when arrivals were expected. Now an algorithm handled it. The tower housed servers and a processing system. People did not come here often, the forest was fighting its way back into the clearing. Vines covered the lower portions of the hanger and overgrown shrubs camouflaged the base of the tower. It looked deserted aside from a single gleaming jet that sat in the middle of the runway. Its shape reminded Luka of an early 2000s era luxury cruiser—the sort an important businessperson would have used to travel from London to the Amalfi coast for a weekend away.

The ATV set course for the jet and picked up speed thanks to the smooth ground of the airfield. Luka and Lark jogged to keep pace.

The plane had a pearl-white finish with some gold accents that glinted even in the filtered light of the foggy island afternoon. The wingtips turned up at ninety-degrees near the end of the wing, suggesting agility, and it had more engines than a vessel of its size needed. There two turbines near the rear of the fuselage and another two fixed to the wings. It was not a stock configuration. The rear-fixed turbines looked period accurate for the 2000s, but the two wing-fixed engines were a more recent design. Luka noticed it only as they approached the front of the jet and he could see into the engines from a front-on view. They did not have standard circular compression fans at the front, but an axisymmetric intake. It was clever. At a glance, the plane looked like a vintage cruiser, but in reality, it was probably as fast and as agile as the most high-end modern jets.

The forward door slid open when the ATV got near and a staircase extended down onto the tarmac. The man wasted no time. He began pulling gear from the trailer and hustling up the stairs as soon as the ATV stopped. Luka and Lark ran to catch up and jumped into the effort.

Based on the exterior, Luka had expected to a gaudy interior—white leather, dark wood, a plush couch along one wall—all of that.

Instead, he stepped through the doorway and was immediately reminded that this was Lark's plane. Lark was banausic. Creature comforts did not concern him. The inside was stripped. The entire passenger space had been converted into cargo space like a narco jet. For seating, there were five small folding chairs fixed to one wall. They looked uncomfortable, flimsy, and completely insufficient for a flight of more than an hour. As far as he could tell, there were no bathrooms either. A bucket at the back of the plane that reeked of urine answered his question about how they relieved themselves.

Together, they loaded and strapped equipment to the floor and walls with tie-downs. When they loaded the last bag, Lark drove the ATV over to the hanger and jogged back across the runway. The forward door closed behind him. Lark swung down a heavy red bar to lock it in and made for the cockpit.

The engines started warming up. An oscillating hum rang through the cabin. Luka recognized the pulsing frequencies

185

and confirmed his suspicions. They were hydrogen cell engines—modern and powerful.

The man pulled down the chair next to Luka and took a seat. He was already wearing ballistic armor, which was an odd choice. It was not the heaviest variety, but constricting enough that it must have been torturous in such cramped seating. He had a pistol in a chest holster. It looked like a normal .45 caliber but with a wooden grip, which was uncommon for tactical weapons, and it had a clip that extended out far beyond the butt of the handle. The clip was so large relative to the pistol that it was almost comical. Some soldiers at White Sands only used burst fire, never single-shot. It depleted the clip fast, but they insisted it was more effective when fighting against light armor. It had a higher chance of penetration and more knock-down power. To them, those benefits were worth the risk of frequent reloading. Luka took the presence of this clip to mean they were expecting armored resistance wherever they were landing.

Although he had nothing in particular to say—or to ask—he felt a strange urge to talk to the man. It reminded him of his college days, bellied up to a bar, working up the courage to approach a girl. It was a clawing desire to speak but absent the will. He opened his mouth at one point and then closed it.

"Relax. It's a long flight," said the man, sensing Luka's tension.

He spoke in that same hushed voice he used back on the pier in Low City. At the time Luka assumed it was to avoid being overheard by a drone, but it seemed now that it was his natural way of speaking.

"Between him and me," he pointed his thumb toward the cockpit where Lark sat, "You'll be fine."

186

He gripped the neckline of his armor and let the weight of his arm pull it down. "Just stay behind cover. The most you'll need to do is lay down some suppressive fire. If things do go sideways, aim true and conserve your ammo."

Luka nodded, pretending he understood. He knew how to fire a weapon, a few different weapons in fact, but he knew very little about what to do in a real firefight.

He almost spoke again but could find nothing to say in return, so he closed his lips and leaned back in his chair. The engines roared up to the full thrust and they surged down the runway. The force of it almost threw him sideways out of his seat. The jet went airborne in less than a hundred meters of runway.

The rest of the flight was painfully uneventful. It dragged on, fretfully, minute by minute while Luka prepared his mind for whatever would be next. He ran through the drills and techniques he learned at the firing range. He tried to picture himself moving from cover to cover, laying down suppressive fire. Twice, turbulence rocked the cabin so hard that he had to cling to some nearby netting to keep his seat. It offered a brief, but welcome reprieve from his thoughts.

The changing pressure of descent alerted Luka that they were approaching their destination. He yawned to open his ears and let them adjust to the changing strain. The right complied with a satisfying pop, but his left ear felt like it was full of water. The pressure built in his sinuses and his left eye ached. The jet banked hard to circle and Luka spotted an airstrip in the distance. The scenery outside the windows had transformed drastically. When they banked southeast after leaving the airstrip outside of New Seattle, his view had been lakes and forests, all murky blue-grays and deep greens. Now it was an expanse of bone-dry sand. It was beige in all directions. The earth looked wind-whipped and desiccated.

Craggy ridges rose from the desert floor in the distance, carving dark spires against the horizon. A deep fissure had opened in the ground below. Its depth was abyssal and it stretched for as long as Luka could see. He stared down into it.

A cold sweat came over his body.

Half coherent, he heard a voice.

"I used to get nervous, too," said the man. "You can call me Roland," he added.

The jet continued circling downward until Lark straightened it out and made a final approach toward the airstrip. The jet touched down lightly, but the weather-worn airstrip was not smooth asphalt or concrete. It was riddled with potholes and covered with a layer of slick dust. The cabin shook violently as the flaps came up and they roared into deceleration. Their equipment rattled and jostled, but the tie-downs and straps held. The bucket in the back, however, ricocheted around from floor to ceiling and bounced its way uncomfortably close to Luka. The stench of urine wafted over him. He grimaced.

The surface of the runway evened out further on and the shaking abated enough for the brakes to come on. They kicked in hard, throwing everyone and everything inside the cabin forward. The layer of dust on the runway prevented the tires from keeping track and the plane started skidding at an angle. It drifted sideways down the runway like a performance car in a sharp turn. Lark adjusted the flaps to right their orientation, but they had lost too much speed for the wings to help. The plane tipped dangerously to one the side, but their momentum arrested just it before it could roll. It skidded to a stop.

Not a second later, Lark appeared from the cockpit, wearing a wide grin. "Fuck man. That was crazy!" he announced as he made for his gear at the rear of the plane.

Luka had been expecting them to hit the ground with bullets already flying but it was quiet now, save for the whine of the engines cooling down and the gusting wind outside.

Roland jumped into action too, retrieving his assault rifle from its wall-mount. It was a modern build, but a simple one. He didn't have any gadgets fixed to it: no laser sights, no scopes, only fixed iron sights. The rifles Luka and Lark took had night vision, IR, and UV capable scopes. They had laser sights, aim assist, and contextual HUD's too. The absence of these enhancements on Roland's rifle hinted at the capabilities of his synth eyes.

Roland opened the forward door of the plane and went down into a kneeling position at its entrance, sweeping his rifle across the horizon. Nothing. The stairs unfolded from the belly of the plane and touched down to the ground. He moved down them, keeping low as he went. He swept his aim across the horizon again, wider this time. Then, he moved to the back of the plane and checked their rear. He repeated the process on the other side of the plane and at the front. When he completed a full three-sixty sweep of the plane, he held a thumbs up to Lark.

He moved back up the stairs and they started loading up packs. They each took a rifle, a sidearm, a knife, ammo, food, and as much weight in water as they could stand to carry. Luka tightened up his boots, adjusted the straps on his pack one last time, and went down the stairs. Lark and Roland followed. The stairs retracted and the door on the plane sealed shut.

Despite the heat, Lark and Roland both had bandanas pulled up over their noses and mouths to protect against the stinging gusts of sand carried by the wind. Luka chided himself for not bringing one of his own. He turned up the collar of the light jacket he wore. It did not keep the stinging pellets away from his face, but at least it kept some of the sand away from his neck.

With their gear settled, they nodded to one another and set off toward the dark mountains in the distance. They walked single file with Lark at the front, Luka in the middle, and Roland at the rear.

Chapter Nine

There were three of them.

They wore ratty black dresses that whipped and thrashed in the desiccating wind. They looked like tattered flags on high poles. Their faces were painted matte white, the shade of sun-bleached bones and their eyes were lost in a trance. Golden slivers of iris gleamed in the depths behind the empty sockets of their skull-masks.

They moved in sync. They followed a rhythm that no one else could hear—Ultra-low frequencies. the resonance of the Earth moving through space, guided them.

They began to twist their hands and arms in strange ways. They contorted into inhuman positions. The angles should have broken joints, but they flowed through the poses with wicked celerity. Their fingers, slender and spider-like, made the movements all the more frightening as they flicked through odd patterns.

Lark had his rifle shouldered with a finger held tight against the trigger guard ready to fire—but he didn't. Roland stood beside Luka, with his arms slack at his side. He was lost, cervine now.

Their movements intensified and began to resonate with one another. Luka's vision distorted and sparkled. The three women began to phase in and out of each other like apparitions.

The hair on his neck went rigid as the prickle of static filled the air. Electricity was building around them. They were creating it—drawing it in and concentrating it inside their bodies. It pulsed from them in time with their movements, like electric eels. The world around all of them went still. The fervor of their movements increased. Luka's eyes began to drift focus, moving from a far depth of field to a close up without his consent. As the charge in the air grew, so did a huge magnetic field. Rock and dust containing paramagnetic ore, iron or otherwise, began to align into patterns in the sand. A geometric spiral emitted from them and overtook the ground for ten meters in every direction. Deep in his brain, a voice called to Luka. It told him to run but he could not. The same trance that captured Roland tightened its grip on him.

The cloud of electricity sparked memories in his brain as it harried his biochip. Their movements flashed through his consciousness in uncontrollable waves of senses—color, texture, and emotion blended all at once. These rushes muddled into complex meta-feelings that merged incongruent aspects together—color-sound, sight-feel, anger-pressure. Images of the of the Constellation's power systems—which should have been corrupted as a result of Lark's tampering— were sliding in and out along with a chirping sound. These memories had a peculiar metallic taste. It was ferrous like blood.

He fought the waves at first. He struggled to stay in the moment and keep his mind above the tide, but the sensory wash began to feel like a warm cocoon. In his mind's eye, dusk was fading to dark. A deep night and a thick cold settled. A heavy mist came in with it, blanketing the horizon in a soft white. There were stars too, where for years there had been nothing but a wash of orange sky. Now, yellow orbs of fire hung low in the blackness. They flickered and crackled and threatened to collapse on him. A heavy moon rose where before endlessly setting sun had rested. It mirrored a cool blue light and it was so big that he felt like it might swallow him.

Then he saw Emma. She emerged from the glow of the moon and glided down to him. She was looking down into his eyes again. Her hair was a vibrant red halo.

Then came flashes of the years of physical therapy.

He was strapped in the sled of an MRI machine. There was a sterile white glow to everything and the soft voice of a technician telling him to be still. There was a biting pain in his hip that ran up his spine. Narcotics in his blood dulled his nerves and added a fuzzy texture to the memory.

Then he was walking again, for the first time. A nurse in stupid cartoon-mouse scrubs held him at the elbow and another pushed his chair behind, ready to catch him. The arches of his feet protested the most. They had forgotten the burden of bodyweight. His legs quivered as he forced them rigid beneath his body. He lifted one foot and pushed it forward. It was a shuffle, not a walk, but the nurse at his side smiled encouragingly and a sweet taste filled his mouth.

His knee buckled. He fell. It turned bitter.

Time moved forward several months. He was walking outside of the outpatient clinic, staring up at the trees in their deep autumn colors. It hurt to walk but he could cover some distance now. He was alone. No one felt it necessary to be at his side. It was cold.

The sky flashed and thunder followed, but this was not part of a memory. Something new interjected, something from the present.

Luka slid back into reality just as a potential formed

between two points in their air. A blinding blue-purple bolt cracked across it like it was ripping space-time open. In the same instant, the space filled with a web of arcing electricity like someone flipped the main switch on a Tesla Coil. Lightning rained around them. He and Lark kept their feet, but Roland collapsed under the pressure of the electric storm. His eyes rolled back in his head. Being synthetic, there was no need for his eyes to roll back in his head the way their biological counterparts would to protect the cornea—but like blinking, the reflex persisted beyond its necessity. Their undersides were a shimmery gold-copper inlaid with a maze of circuitry.

The pressure of the storm began to weigh on Luka too. A burning wave spread through his body, stemming from the biochip at the base of his skull. It was same the feeling as when the repulsor wave hit him in Low City, but an order of magnitude stronger. It locked his muscles as it traveled through him.

Luka thought Lark was paralyzed too. Until, from the corner of his eye, he saw Lark take a step forward. The strain in his movement made it clear that he felt the same weight on his body, but he pressed forward somehow. Maybe it was sheer force of will. That, he had.

Lark took a few steps more. The blue flash of the storm engulfed him, leaving only a nebulous silhouette. He ripped off his mask and his helmet and threw them to side. The helmet tumbled a few times over and then the magnetic field captured it, and it rose into the air.

Lark stepped forward again. He was almost within arm's reach of the storm's eye.

The field dropped.

The dust and rocks fell. His helmet clattered as hit the ground. The weight lifted from Luka and he gasped as his muscles released.

With the wind and storm gone, he could see the faces of the women clearer. They were Lark's sisters. The relation was unmistakable in lines of their faces. Or they were his daughters, or his mothers, or his clones. It was hard to know, but they were about the same age in appearance, so he instinctually thought of them as Lark's sisters.

Like a herd of elephants, they knew their own kind. Their demeanor changed when they saw Lark's face. Their stances softened. The stood upright. Their shoulders relaxed. They and Lark stared at one another, silent. They were calculating. Luka knew the expression from watching Lark in the lab.

Lark lifted the sleeve of his jacket and showed them something imprinted near the crook of his elbow. They mirrored the gesture, each rotating their right arm so that the soft skin of their inner arm faced out toward Lark. Another long paused followed. They studied each other for a while longer. Lark lowered his rifle, letting it slip out of his hand and fall at his side.

Roland had recovered consciousness. Luka watched as he willed his body to stand. It did not want to cooperate fully yet, his legs quivered and stumbled while he found his balance, but he did find it. When he saw Lark's rifle slip out his hand and fall to the ground, a wild expression overtook his face. He drew the automatic pistol strapped to his chest and aimed at the three women. His synthetic eyes always had a dead look to them, but every other part of his body screamed irrationality. His shoulders tensed and his mouth tightened into a line. He leaned forward into his aim while he trained his pistol on the middle of the three women. His arms shook, but Luka guessed his aim would be true enough to hit its target even with the tremors.

The women did not appear alarmed—or they simply did not notice Roland. They were eye-locked with Lark like an intense conversation was happening, but they never spoke.

Luka walked over to Roland and laid his hand on top of Roland's left arm. Roland did not react to this. He kept his eyes down the sights and the muscles in his shoulders tensed. He held his finger at the trigger. The twitching in his hand threatened to set loose the rapid-fire pistol.

Luka gripped Roland's forearm and pressed downward. To his surprise, Roland complied. He lowered his pistol, then let his arm go slack at his side so that the barrel pointed at the ground. He kept a tight grip on the handle though—and he kept his eyes on Lark.

Nothing had progressed between Lark and three women. They were staring at one another, the same as before, and were eerily motionless. The wind had picked up again. A gust tugged at their clothing and whipped up the powdery dust that had settled around them. It cast a haze around the group. Luka and Roland squared their shoulders to them and watched and waited.

Roland was impatient. Luka saw him shifting his weight from foot to foot and rolling his shoulders. He took a step forward, about to set off in a march toward to Lark, but Luka snapped his arm out across Roland's chest to bar his path. Some mix of shock and irritation flashed through Roland's face, but then he nodded gently and the muscles around his mouth relaxed. He took a step back and waited beside Luka.

Whatever this ritual was, and however long it took, Luka knew it needed to play out slow and steady, but even he did not expect it would drag out straight into the evening. Hours slid by until the sun was getting low on the horizon. It bathed the desert in an orange-yellow glow. The mountains in the distance ahead became inky carvings against the vibrant backdrop of a desert sunset. Lark and the three women were a dark circle of statuary.

Luka had to take a piss. It was inopportune, but the urge had been building for hours until, now, when he thought he might rupture. He shifted his weight from side to side, fighting it, but he had to relent. He turned his back to the group, walked about ten paces into the distance, and went about his business. His bladder ached as he let loose, but the stream withered soon. It was a disconcertingly small volume. The color was much too amber. He was dehydrated, and not just a little bit. The three of them had depleted their water a full three kilometers before they encountered the women. With night approaching and the temperatures dropping, he would be okay for a while longer, but his time was limited. Dehydration was a creeping form of death, that kind he could ignore right up to the point it killed him.

Luka zipped up his pants and turned to face the group again, hoping that his interruption had somehow impacted Lark and the sisters. It had not. For a moment he considered intervening—but he shook it off. Patience paid twice what impulse did. He walked back to his post and resumed guard beside Roland. They exchanged sideways glances and then they both settled back into the stillness.

The sun was gone now. It dropped below the horizon and the only remaining trace of day was a faint bluish wash against the growing black. It stretched up from the western skyline and faded into the abyss overhead. The far side of the sky was kettle black and riddled with bright white spots from stars and satellites. In the middle was the foggy purple and yellow-

197

brown glow of The Milky Way. A dark chasm at its center threatened to swallow the Earth.

Luka was nearly asleep on his feet. He nodded off and swayed. He was about to topple over, when for no reason he could discern, the standoff ended. He stumbled forward, caught his balance, and saw that the statues were moving. At first, he could not make sense of what was happening. The women formed a single file line and hurried off into the night. Their black clothing faded in the distance. Lark followed behind them, not in perfect single file formation like the three, but several meters behind and a little off center. He walked right passed Luka and Roland without a word. It was the ultimate anticlimax to half a day's waiting.

He was ten meters out when he finally looked back over his shoulder and said, "We are going to follow them."

He jerked his head in the direction the women had disappeared. Luka and Roland jumped into motion and jogged to catch up with Lark.

Though the ground was flat, it was difficult to walk in the near-total darkness of a moonless night. Luka found himself high stepping to avoid tripping over the small rocks that littered the chalky desert floor. He could only just keep the pace set by everyone else. He pushed his feet forward, edging the line between jogging and walking. The women were far enough ahead to be out of sight for Luka, and no matter how quickly he tried to move, he could never catch more than a glimpse of one of their cloaks trailing behind them. Roland had synthetic vision, and was probably running on UV and thermal-vis, so his effortless steps made sense, but Lark too seemed to move better in the dark than the average person. Luka alone had to walk through an unfamiliar wasteland, in the pitch black, without aid.

They hiked through the empty desert for over an hour. Slowly, they worked their way in toward the deep fissure that cut across the desert floor, until they were moving parallel along it. They walked dangerously near the edge. The three women flirted with disaster. They stepped along the cliff, sometimes with their toes hanging over it. The dirt gave way as their feet fell, but never collapsed fully. Luka clenched his jaw watching them, waiting for part of the wall to fall away under them, but they covered kilometers toeing the line like this—without incident. They knew the desert.

Gradually, they came to a section of the fissure that widened out. It was hard to gauge in the dark, but Luka guessed it to be a hundred meters across. It was still deep, twenty meters at least, but the walls were not as vertical here. Luka had thought it was still too steep to traverse down safely, but soon enough they were all moving down it at a tenuous angle. It was a constant battle with traction. His feet continually slid toward the deep, threatening to cast him down into the bottom. To keep from falling, he had to lean in hard against the sandy slope. He dragged a hand along it to steady his balance. They moved at a plodding pace downward until they reached a craggy and bouldered wash at the bottom.

The women, like Lark, appeared overly-thin and fragile but possessed deceptive strength and agility. They maneuvered through the treacherous basin with ease. They casually hopped over trenches and effortlessly scaled up the rock faces that blocked their way.

Luka, however, could barely summit the smaller boulders that lay in their path. His arms and legs ached. His lips were cracked and bled from dehydration and his throat felt like it was worse than his lips. He sucked the blood from his lips and swallowed whenever there was enough built up to do so.

199

The taste made him nauseous, but it provided momentary relief from the burning in his esophagus.

It was slow going through the wash. They never explicitly waited on Luka, but he noticed that the group slowed whenever he lagged especially far behind.

His head swam. Dizziness set in. His blood pressure was dropping. With only starlight to see by, it took all of his focus to make sense of his surroundings and navigate his way forward.

Luka had no idea how far ahead the others were now.

He stumbled along the wash with little thought, operating on autopilot like a blacked-out drunk, when he ran flat into a three-meter rock. His face made contact first. His nose cracked and a stinging pain ran through his sinuses. Blood trickled from his nostrils. He reached up to touch it and smeared it across his lips and chin. It dried almost instantly in the moisture-less air. Luka placed a hand against the boulder in front of him. He felt an easy hold beneath his fingertips, but he could not climb it. He was about to collapse backward and let himself fall deep into the sand. Once he went down, he did not intend to get back up again.

A dark figure appeared in front of him before he could. It steadied him with a firm grip on his shoulders. It took several seconds, but his vision came into focus.

It was one of the three women. She watched him, her eyes appraising him. They were a lot like Lark's, but where Lark's irises were a raw yellow, hers were a rich gold. They shined like an eclipsed sun in a shadowed sky. She slid her hand down from his shoulder and clasped his hand in hers. Her skin was cold and smooth. She pulled him up the rock. She led him forward. Depleted as he was, Luka no longer held a firm sense of time. He staggered onward in semi-consciousness for an indiscriminate eternity. It was dust, and rock, and more dust. It was stars overhead and a cold hand guiding him.

Then they stopped. All of them were there. They huddled around an odd bit of wall in the basin. It was hard as concrete and formed of straight angles. It was inorganic and there was a door in it. At first, it looked the same as the rest of the wall, but a seam formed. The door slipped a few centimeters backward and then slid away to the right. The two women in front filed in, Lark followed with Roland behind him. The woman who had stayed behind to help Luka waited. She said nothing. She made no gesture. She just waited. Luka watched her, but she appeared to be unaware of his gaze, unselfconscious to an inhuman degree. She had her black hood up, but it left a sliver of her face exposed and the glow from the room beyond the door provided enough light for him to truly see her. She had high, rounded cheekbones and a square-ish jaw. She had full, pale lips and a prominent philtrum. Where Lark was boyish, she looked more mature in age. She was young in appearance, but also weathered, experienced.

It took a couple of minutes for Luka to figure out that she was waiting for him to pass through the door. When he realized why she was standing absently at the entrance, he felt his face flush. He hurried through the door and she fell in behind him. She slid the door over and pushed it into place after they passed through.

The entrance led into a long hallway lit with a dull orange glow. Luka could not find a direct source of the light. It seemed to emit from the walls themselves. He pressed his hand to section and glowed a little brighter from the warmth. He dragged his fingers along the wall as he moved further down the hallway and it left scares of orange lines behind him, like claw marks.

The hallway opened into a large common chamber. At first glance, it was like Lark's bunker—drab but functional. If these women were responsible for its construction, they were industrious like Lark. However drab it was, it was an impressive structure to build so far into the desert and so deep into the earth. It suggested they and Lark had the same instincts: escape, fortify, go on the offensive.

In the center of the main room, there was a large garden. It fostered an eclectic mix of plants—there were vegetables, succulents, and some poisonous looking jungle types with broad, purple leaves. It was a micro-ecosystem. He did not know much about botany or agriculture, but Luka understood the intent. The variety offered balance. Some were there for pH, some for nitrogen fixation, and the rest were there for food production. A steady trickle of water flowed down a glass wall and under the soil. An empty column of concrete extended up to the surface. At the top, there were panels of glass. During the day this was a sunroom. It was, however, dark and lurid now.

Luka stood at the precipice of the main chamber, observing, watching. The woman who helped him through the basin brushed by him and joined her sisters. His stomach sank. The group did not talk to each other. Silently, they formed a half-circle and they looked back at him.

Five sets of eyes watched. Five sets calculated his worth. He was different from them. He was primitively human, and in this strange home that was far out in a forgotten desert, that made him an outsider. He did not understand how they felt— nor could he ever. He did not understand what they accomplished in the twelve-hour standoff. He could not ally with them, not truly, and now he knew that.

Lark spoke first, "They will be helping us accomplish our goal." He took a step toward Luka, breaking the arc. "I know you will have questions because you always do, but for now you need to shut up and hold it in."

He took another step forward, further distancing himself from the group and closing the gap between Luka and himself.

"They don't like to talk." Lark nodded his head back toward the three women. "To be clear, *they can*, they have the necessary biomechanics and language. There is nothing deficient in them, but leave them alone."

Lark continued, "I know you see some physical resemblance between us. We are not clones. We are not siblings. Do not act like we are. We are not the same."

He paused, looking down at the floor. Usually, Lark said what he wanted in a steady onslaught—never short of words. It was unusual to see him collect his thoughts.

He took a few more steps forward, and Luka moved forward too, passing through the threshold of the door and into the main chamber. He and Lark were now nose to nose.

"It is clear we need to improve your physical conditioning. You will be on our program for here forward. When it came to science in the lab, you had a voice. Here you do not. You do as we say."

The room went quiet. Luka wanted to fire back but his mind was blank—or rather it was filled with everything else. Lark was only taunting him, he knew. It was a tactic to show his authority in front of the others and it made him choke his impulses.

"Why am I here?" Luka asked. Despite his exhaustion, he straightened up his posture. "You've made it clear that I have no function and that I am a hindrance to the others, so why?"

Lark smirked. "You traveled all of this way, you nearly died in that canyon, and you only now ask why?"

That was hard to counter. They both knew why Luka was here. He lacked any better options, but he could not say that. He was dead in High City, he would not last long in Low City on his own, and he did not have the means to escape DA's attention elsewhere. Here, at least he was alive—if only clinging to it at times.

Tension built between them. Luka thought of the hammer, knowing that he was the desk in this standoff. He was holding what Lark needed to accomplish his goal and Lark would smash him to pieces if he could do it without losing the information Luka held. It reminded him to play cautiously. He needed to play for the long game.

One of the three women stepped forward and placed a hand on Lark's shoulder. She pulled him back, creating space between Luka and Lark. Luka saw now that, while the three women were near identical, they were each unique in small ways. There were variances in the shapes of their eyebrows and lips. One carried herself differently than the other two. She had a slouch, her back rounded near her shoulders. The others maintained a firm, idyllic posture. Another had a habit of flaring her nostrils when she breathed.

Lark fell back into the group and the woman stepped forward into his place, as close to Luka now as he and Lark had been a moment before. It was her again, the one who helped him. He knew her eyes. She smelled like the desert just before the first rain of the season, when the wind blew in cold air from an approaching storm. Her scent was petrichor—but with a sharp undertone in it too, like ozone, like a crack of electricity.

She took his hand into hers. Her touch was delicate, like the brush of a leaf, but it prickled with energy when she clasped his. A shiver ran down his spine, but a pleasant one, like a breath in his ear. It was not rational for it to affect him in this way, but it did. Without words, he understood her. A calm overcame him.

They slept on the floor that night, all of them in a common room. There were no blankets, but the room was held at a comfortable temperature by a means unknown to him. There no pillows or cots either, and Luka missed those more. He removed his jacket, balled it up, and slipped it under his head. It wasn't much, but it helped. There were no typical human comforts. From the limited background Lark give him, Luka knew that Lark endured awful conditions in the lab where he grew up. These women likely did too. Their choice to sleep on a bare concrete floor reflected what they grew up knowing. Luka's throated tightened when he thought of it.

Despite his exhaustion, Luka could not sleep except in short stints. He turned and fidgeted, partly because of the unrelenting pressure of the stone floor on his joints, and partly because of awful, cyclical dreams of the DA-owned labs Lark described. He saw Lark and his sisters, but they were locked in separate cells. The room was bare concrete, like this room, but cold, too cold to sleep. There were rusty metal drains in the center of each cell and yellowy-fluorescent lights flickered overhead. In the dream, he was a guard and dream-him relished the opportunity to beat them and torment them. He hosed them down and watched them shiver in fetal position. He whacked them with whatever blunt instrument was handy and he watched them cower in a corner as he strolled passed their cells. They avoided eye contact with him—except for one. She stared back at him, more defiant each time he tried to break her. The gold in her eyes glowed molten-hot. The more he tormented them, the stronger she alone became.

As morning washed over the desert, the central chamber filled with sunlight, and Luka gave up on sleeping. He opened his eyes and rolled over from his hip onto his back. His body ached horribly from the previous day's exertions. He was nauseous and his hands were numb and cold. The stone floor sapped his body despite the pleasant air temperature in the room. Above all else, he was desperately thirsty. He pushed himself up from the floor and shuffled over toward the garden in the center of the room. It glowed with vibrant shades of green. Light scattered all across the room in fractals of minty and deep forest hues. Behind it, there was an antechamber. Through the foliage, Luka saw Lark, Roland, and the three women sitting at a large rectangular table. It was hewn from dry-rotted wood and certainly handmade. Lark and Roland were eating emergency ration meals. Luka could smell the salty odor of the mysteriously preserved meats in the entrée packets even at a distance. The women sat together at a far end of the table, eating greens of indistinguishable varieties that were piled high on hardened clay plates. The whole group was drinking a murky brown liquid out of crystalline glasses. The glassware looked expensive and antique—much too fragile to have survived the journey out into the desert. The breakfast ritual looked like a perverse model of the apostle's last supper.

He hobbled around the garden, toward the table. The combination of dust and sweat in his boots during their trek had formed blisters all of his feet. The cool stone floor soothed them when stood still, but walking was excruciating. He took each step gingerly, rolling his foot down from heel to toe. There were two chairs open at the table and he took the one nearest the sisters. The liquid they were all drinking came from a large rough-ceramic pitcher in the center of the table. It had the same color as the desert and looked to be made from local mud. He took one of the glasses and poured some liquid into it. It smelled earthy and vaguely of lemon. He gulped the glass down. It was not exactly palatable either. It seemed to satisfy his thirst though. He poured another glass and downed it too. The third glass he drank slower, and with each sip, he felt the exhaustion of the previous day and the fog of a restless night lifting from him. It spread through his body in a soothing wave.

There was an emergency ration on the table for him. Luka grabbed the package, ripped it open with his teeth, and began laying out the meal pouches in front of him. There was stewed beef for the main course, peas as a side, and a brittle cracker. It crumbled to powder at the slightest touch. He tried it first, but it was like putting chalk in his mouth. It instantly soaked up what little saliva he had and made it impossible to swallow. He took a swig of the tea, hoping to wash it down, but that only reconstituted the cracker into a muddy paste. With another swallow of the tea, he got the first bite down but decided to move on to the rest of the meal before revisiting the cracker. The beef and the peas tasted as awful as he imagined they would, but he was ravenous so they went down easy. Luka finished his ration, left feeling a little sick, but full at least. He waited at the table for the others to finish eating, for lack of knowing what do next. The group sat in silence, chewing and swallowing quietly. The meal passed without a single word between any of them.

The sisters got up first. They finished the food on their clay plates in its entirety, and then they stood and began to move toward the exit of the compound. Lark motioned for Luka to follow them. They exited the compound and started to walk out into the desert, barefoot. He did the same, hopping down from the table, and jogging to catch up to them. Outside, a powerful crosswind whipped from left to right. It tailed the women's loose black clothing out in long strands to their right as they walked.

The first two kilometers were agony. His blistered feet protested every step and he fought to keep his body upright. Eventually, though, his brain gave up. It decided that he would not stop, no matter how much pain it gave him, and so the pain faded. His feet became numb and he fell into pace with them.

They walked several kilometers more. They walked until even the mountains in the distance disappeared from the horizon and every direction was just endless, flat, ivory sand. The sisters sat down with their legs folded in front of them and closed their eyes. One, the tallest of the three, motioned for Luka to do the same with a wave of her hand. He squatted down and sat. After walking so long, it provided immense relief to his feet, but every other part of his body ached and he wished that he had thought to bring some water. His throat and lips were cracked. Whatever recovery the murky liquid at breakfast provided, he was back to square one now.

At first, he splayed his legs out in front of him and laid back on his elbows like he was sunning at a beach. He rested for a long time like that, letting the wind dry the seeping patches of new skin on his feet. He waited for some further instruction, but three women offered no further guidance. They sat perfectly still, with their perfect posture. They were oblivious to his fidgeting.

He stood up and touched his toes, stretching out his hamstrings. He kicked some dirt around, watching it float up into the wind. He laid flat on his back and stared up at the sky for a full hour.

They did not move all the while. Then it came to him. He bolted upright and folded his legs in, doing his best to mimic their posture.

He closed his eyes. He had never meditated before, and beyond the acts of sitting and breathing, he did not know what else to do. He tried to *empty his mind.* He had heard that phrase before, but he had no idea what it meant. If he pushed one thought out, another came rushing in its place. He found no emptiness. He shifted his weight. One of his legs was going numb. His ear itched. He scratched it. His shoulders started to slump. He straightened them.

He shook out his arms and laid them his lap. He breathed in deep and exhaled. He tried again. He listened to the wind. He concentrated on it—not just the howl of it moving across the desert, but the faint rattle of individual grains of sand rubbing against one another. His mind revolted at the boredom of it, but he maintained focus. He noticed a faint static charge in the air. It plucked at his skin in gentle pulses. He slipped into a rhythm with it.

When he opened his eyes again it was near sundown. He did not know when he had truly drifted off into meditation, but based on the movement of the sun, it was several hours ago. He looked around him and he was alone. The sisters were gone.

He leaped to his feet and turned a three-sixty, scanning the horizon in all directions. It was empty. He was alone. His heart rate shot up and his pulse throbbed in his ears. He brimmed with anger while he paced in circles.

He paced and paced until his heart settled. Slowly, he realized, he did not mind his circumstances. He thought he should be indignant or angry about being left behind, but in actuality, he was not. They were gone, yes, but he knew the way back. They left footprints in the sand and they were deep enough that wind had not erased them yet.

He brushed the dirt from his clothes and set off toward their tracks. The burning pain returned to his feet, but he ignored it, and as before, it eventually went away. He was walked well into the night, stumbling forward while he tracked their footsteps by the faint light of a waxing moon. When he finally made it back, he nearly collapsed at the entrance. He did not know how to activate the door, but it opened as he approached regardless, and he stumbled down the hallway. He stripped off his jacket, laid flat on the floor, and fell asleep instantly. It was a dreamless, dead night—the opposite of the night before.

The next day was the same routine, only this time they allowed him time to put on his boots before he left. The three went barefoot again.

Day three and day four were the same as this. On day five he fell into meditation quickly and came out of it just as they were preparing to leave.

On that day he broke Lark's rule. While they walked back to the compound in the dying orange and purple light of the sunset, he broke the code of silence.

"Do you have names?"

"Yes," answered the tallest of the three.

Luka stopped dead in his tracks. Although he asked them straight out, he did not expect an answer. They stopped walking too.

Another of the women spoke, "I am Maria, she is Stanya, and that is Helena."

Maria was morose and dead-faced like her sisters, but she had a lightness in her voice that made her seem the most accessible of the three. Stanya, the one who spoke first, was a few centimeters taller than the other two and had a habit of slouching, as though willing herself to be shorter to better conform with her sisters.

The third, Helena, was the one who had helped him through the basin on his trek in. She was brutally abstruse. She seemed to be adrift in an existential plane that only they understood. In her lucid moments, Luka would catch her watching him from beneath her hood. She had a fondness for rubbing chalk and ash on her face in the pattern of a skull and it unnerved him to be under the gaze of such a threatening and beautiful presence. He found that he sometimes watched her too.

"Luka," he said as he offered them a quick, polite smile.

Maria nodded in return and they resumed walking.

They were not like Lark. He was strange and readable, like them, but he was still of this world in many that they were not. He had humor, for one. However bad it was, it humanized him. He had his acid sarcasm and he had annoying habits like talking about himself too much or loudly clearing his throat of phlegm in the morning and leaving the byproduct in the sink basin. He was not likable, but he was relatable in some ways. These women were distant and strange on a different order of magnitude. They were lost to another mode of perception. It was like they had seen the afterlife and returned.

They arrived back at the compound just as dark overtook the sky. Lark and Roland were cleaning their weapons on the floor. They busied themselves scrubbing at the actions and slides, trying to work sand out of the grooves. The powdery grit in this part of the desert was murder on the finely machined auto-pistols and burst rifles. He knew—or had known—whole squadrons who preferred older, slower weapons that had wider tolerances on their machining for this one reason. The rate of fire mattered little if the weapon jammed.

The sisters went at sat at the table. Stanya retrieved a clay pot from a stove across the room, whose flame burned a bright blue like a gas flame. Given the confined quarters of the compound, and the difficulty of maintaining a natural gas source, that seemed unlikely. It was probably algal biofuel—something rich in ethanol, like what Lark used. He had not examined the garden in detail yet, but he supposed they had a hybrid algal culture somewhere in there.

Stanya set the pot out on the table and the sisters drank the murky tea from their crystal glasses. Luka considered cleaning his weapons too, but he was dehydrated and not eager to be in Lark's company. He passed Lark and Roland and sat down at the table with the sisters. He drank the tea too. In his peripherals, he saw Lark casting murderous looks in his direction. Luka smiled to himself while he looked down at his drink. Time passed slowly in silence.

An hour later, the sisters all rose in sync and moved to the empty room where they slept on the floor. They slept more than an average person—twelve hours at least—and they spent much of their waking life in a semi-conscious state. They meditated or otherwise drifted off in a daze. For the first few days, he was so exhausted from trekking in the desert, that he easily adjusted to their long sleep pattern. Tonight he could not. He stood and headed for the exit. He had not adjusted to their hypogeal lifestyle either and he craved the surface whenever he was inside the compound.

Lark was absorbed with cleaning his weapons, but he snatched Luka's wrist at precisely the right moment as Luka walked by.

He did not look up from his weapon as he spoke, "You've had enough time to acclimate to the desert now. Tomorrow we start training."

He tightened his grip. "And your gun better not fucking jam."

"OK," said Luka as he twisted his wrist free from Lark's grip and went on his way. He smiled to himself again as he made for the exit.

The doors opened, and he stepped out into the basin. The cold struck him first. He thought of it as a desert and therefore assumed it to always be warm. In his time away from White Sands he had forgotten the true nature of this place, that it had extreme temperatures in both directions. Tonight he was wearing only a t-shirt and thin pants. The cold wind bit through it. Goosebumps rose along his arms. He flexed his feet in the sand. The rest of his body ached from the cold, but his feet at least relished it. He looked up at the night sky. The abyssal maw of The Milky Way grinned down at him amid the thousands of stars.

The cold settled in deeper. He rubbed his arms to generate heat as he started making his way out of the basin, treading over boulders and climbing ridges until he reached the flat plain of the desert floor. Here, the expanse of the sky never ended. Millions of stars filled his eyes. Luka laid flat on his back and gazed upward while he faded into sleep.

The next day brought hours of strenuous exercises under Lark's direction. He ran sprints, he did pushups, he did sit-ups, and he did more sets of lunges and squats than he could

213

count. After that, they ran through tactical drills. It was a little silly with only an empty desert to practice in, but they practiced formations and fire protocols. Lark berated him for small errors in movement or weapon handling. They ended in the afternoon. Lark and Roland returned to the compound. Luka, however, made his way out into the desert, where he knew the sisters would be meditating.

He reached them near the end of their session. He sat down, mimicked their posture, and fell into a trance too—for what time remained. After a few hours, they all came back to the world. They rose to their feet and began the trudge back to the compound. Luka shuffled along at the back of the line.

"How long are you going to stay?" asked Maria. The flat tone of her voice made it sound like an accusation.

Luka wrestled with it. They walked almost a kilometer before he responded.

"Only until we complete our mission," he said. He tried to mimic her lack of emotion.

They kept on walking through the desert, Maria at the front. Their form was exacting, nearly to the point of stepping into each other's footprints. Luka drifted to the left and the right, stepping out of line, adding a chaotic variance to their trail.

"Are you loyal to him?" Maria asked.

It had been nearly an hour since anyone spoke and the question shocked Luka out of his daze. It was also a difficult question. He did not know her loyalties and yet he needed to align with them. The more he thought on it, though, the more he understood his answer did not matter. They could kill him should they want to, and he was dead already anywhere else. Honesty was his only path.

"Only as far as mutual interest," he said.

His words went out into the wind without acknowledgment. They just kept going. It should have worried him, in a way, that she did not immediately affirm, but the more time he spent shuffling through the barrens with them, the more he understood their nuances. She weighed what to say, just as he had.

They were beginning the descent into the basin, slipping downward on the unstable banks when Maria responded.

"It is the same for us," she said.

Luka stopped walking. Maria and Stanya kept moving, but Helena stopped too. She looked back at him while her sisters slipped away into the blackness of the night. Her expression was ashen behind her dead-face paint, but her eyes were wild and alive. Even in the darkness, they shined back at him. Luka nodded and she turned away and started walking again. He followed.

They continued toward the compound, Luka a few steps behind Helena, with the other two sisters out of sight ahead.

When they got back to the compound, Lark was busy modifying some electronic device. He did not even notice them passing—or if he had, he did not care enough to acknowledge it. Luka joined the sisters at the table. As with every night, when the meal concluded, they stood and exited to sleep. Luka sat alone, wishing he had some alcohol, or opioids, or anything to pass the time and numb his body. He did not want to sleep, but his body ached for it, so he did.

The next day was another full day of strength training and tactical exercises with Lark. Luka bumbled through it. His body was sore and lethargic. When they finished, he did not have the energy or the time to walk through the desert and join the sisters. So, he returned to the compound and sat with his back against the glass wall outlining the garden. He stared up and watched day slip to night in the skylight.

Dinner was business as usual. He ate some terrible emergency ration that was supposed to be beef and it left him feeling like he ingested six days' worth of salt in one sitting. After dinner, the group went to sleep. Luka tried. He laid down and closed his eyes and let his thoughts fall away, but he could not sleep. He tried over and over, but his mind would not go blank so that sleep could enter. He gave up.

He stood and exited the compound. The night was exceptionally clear. He climbed on top of a large boulder a few meters down the basin and sat at its edge with his legs dangling into the chasm beneath. His mind went blank. He laid back on the rock and let his eyes slip in and out of focus as he looked up at the stars again. This desert was quiet. Every other place he had known buzzed with insect life at night, but here it was only hallowed silence.

A scorpion made its way along the rock by his hand, attracted to the warmth of his body. It was tan—the same color as the dirt around him—and small. It was the dangerous kind. His body begged him to jerk his hand back in reaction, but he thought better of it. The scorpion was making its way along his sleeve, moving toward his shoulder.

Another hand appeared in his peripheral and scooped it up.

Luka's body jerked this time. His heart rate surged and he almost rolled off the boulder.

Helena sat beside him. She slipped down at his right while she let the scorpion crawl across the top of her hand and up her arm. When it started to move along her shoulder, she scooped it up with her other hand and gently set it aside on the rock. It hurried off and disappeared over the edge.

She fixed her gaze on Luka. So often Helena's eyes would be slack and distant, like someone high on MDMA, but right now they pierced him. Her pupils were drawn wide in the darkness, but the remaining sliver of her irises shined with the rich color of starlight.

Luka broke eye contact, looking down at his hands. He ran his tongue along his lips. They stung, chapped as they were from his days spent in the sun and wind.

He laid back at looked up at the sky.

Helena copied him. She laid flat with her legs over the edge of the rock and folded her arms over her stomach. They were shoulder to shoulder. She smelled like rain and the heat from her body radiated into his. The rock beneath them chilled him, but his skin burned hot from a quickened pulse.

"Which is yours?" she asked.

It was the first time he heard her speak. Her voice was soft, not breathy like a whisper, just delicate. It had the timbre of a celesta.

He wrinkled his brow. "I don't know what you mean."

Helena lifted an arm and pointed up into the night. "The constellations, which is yours?"

Luka's eyes fixated on the black rift at the center of the Milky Way.

"I don't believe in any of that," he said.

He looked over at Helena and from her profile, he thought he saw her smile. The skin beside her the corners of her mouth creased.

"Belief is irrelevant," she said.

Her lack of inflection made it difficult to gauge her mood. Luka could not decide whether she was correcting him or just stating her own opinion.

"Which is yours?" he asked.

She lifted a hand from her stomach and used her finger to trace a shape in the sky, connecting a line of stars low on the southern horizon. The figure had a long curved tail that stretched up from the horizon, and at the top, it forked into five branches.

"The scorpion. Like our friend," she said.

She nodded in the direction she had released the scorpion earlier.

"Which is mine?" he asked.

"Lyra," she said.

She pointed back over her shoulder to a set of six stars in the northern sky. "It's there, to the north."

From his supine position, Luka had to arch his back and stretch his neck to see where she was pointing. The constellation was an elongated diamond with a triangle connecting at one corner.

218

"It may be hard for you to see it, but it is clear to me," she added.

Luka could not work out whether she meant *see* in a literal sense or a metaphoric one. It left an opening to ask a question that he had held in for some time already.

"When we walk in the dark, you have an easier time with it—all three of you. Well, Lark too. It's not just that you know the way. You have better night vision, but is it more than that?"

Helena placed her hand on his forearm. The hair on his arms bristled with the electricity in her fingertips. She turned her head and met his eyes. He swallowed hard, fighting his breath down.

"It's not the same for all of us. I am more attuned to it than Stanya or Maria—but we understand more colors than you," replied Helena.

"I saw that your skin flushed when I laid beside you and I see that you are cold now," she continued.

She turned her eyes up to the sky, "There's no darkness, not anywhere. I see best at night. In the day it is ... washed out."

She hesitated on the last word. Luka interpreted the pause to mean she was unsure of her choice.

"I understand," he affirmed.

Given what he knew of their connection to electromagnetic energy, it made perfect sense that she could interpret a wider set of wavelength combinations. From her statement about color, he knew she at least had more cones

219

in her eyes. If she also had a tapetum lucidum structure in her eyes—like a nocturnal animal—it would explain both the improved night vision and the odd shine in her pupils.

Her mechanism for perceiving heat, he could not guess at.

"Why Lyra?" he asked.

"Because you are like Orpheus. You are in the underworld, trying to bring someone back," Helena answered.

He tried to suppress it, but the adrenaline hit his bloodstream and there was no turning back. His back clenched and his spine twisted, sending waves of agony through him. His breath quickened and his mind filled with a hundred hateful words. The abyss opened in his vision and his skin burned white-hot. He pushed himself upright and opened his mouth to speak.

Then he thought of Michael, red-faced while he lectured him in the car after the TV interview. Michael warned him not to lose control every time someone brought up Emma. Luka bit down on his lip. He reigned back the hate. He replayed Helena's words instead of listening to his own.

She knew what was happening. She was even stiller than usual. She could not have fully known what she had ventured into, but she must have seen the change in him understood on some level.

"I'm not trying to bring her back," said Luka.

Helena nodded, agreeing. Her face was dark, unreadable.

They both were quiet for a long time then.

die in the desert. Tonight the air between them had changed. The contact was intentional. He felt it, but he could not bring himself to accept the obvious truth. A frenzy grew in him.

He looked down into the blackness of the ravine below their boulder. The barrier to anything more than this was immense. He imagined himself leaning over and kissing her, or pulling her into him, or just speaking plainly about his thoughts, but it all felt too forced, too artless, for her.

He looked down into the blackness and lowered himself into it. He pressed with his triceps until his arms could lower him no further and then let himself drop the remaining few meters.

He hit the ground flat-footed. His feet had grown stiff from sitting. A painful shock rang through his heels and up his shins. He ignored it and made for the bunker.

Chapter Ten

They breached the outer fence with ease. It was aging chain-link, more a nuisance to their progress than an obstacle. Lark carried a canister of liquid nitrogen and made quick work of it. He outlined a rectangular shape with the nozzle of the canister, roughly like a door, and when he yanked on the links, the metal gave way like bits of uncooked pasta. Fragments fell to the hard desert floor and scattered. No alarms sounded. The engines of heavy diesel machinery roared in the distance and the high-pitched whir of drone turbines filled the air too, but so far, none approached. They ducked through Lark's doorway, one by one, and moved to the next barrier. This fence was also chain-link, but it hummed with a lethal electric charge. Lark drove a heavy metal rod into the ground and produced a bit of cabling from his pack. He connected an alligator clamp at one end of the cable to the metal rod and then snapped the clip to a link in the fence. Sparked erupted upon contact and then the hum died. They had rehearsed all of this, but still, Lark's efficiency disquieted Luka.

Lark tapped the back of his hand to the fence to test it. There was no reaction. Satisfied, Lark repeated his trick with the liquid nitrogen and motioned for them to follow through. Beyond the second fence, Lark took a knee and held his arm out a right angle, making a fist with his hand.

HOLD.

They waited. A patrol drone approached. Its engines were much quieter than the military drones in the distance but distinctive with their near-ultrasonic pitch.

This was the most dangerous part of the breach. Beyond the second fence, there were no physical walls, only sensory barriers. A security drone like the one that approached now had no offensive capability, but it could discover the intrusion and trigger a team of military drones. Like the one Luka had encountered in Low City, they could arrive in a matter of seconds.

Lark froze, eyes locked on the drone. Luka tried to follow it too, but it moved in blurred bursts that his eyes could not track. In the darkness, it was only a wisp of shadow. There might have been two. And then there might have been three converging on them.

Luka swallowed hard. One drone was a curiosity, but if a team of drones was coalescing around them, it was a prelude to a full alarm.

Shadows swirled around them. The drones' algorithms sensed a disturbance, but it was not enough yet to confirm and raise the alarm.

Luka watched. Only his eyes moved.

As the cold set into his body and his muscles tensed, he thought of hunting deer with his dad years ago. They drove a whole day without stopping. They slept in their car that night, cramped between the back hatch of their SUV and the second row of seats. They hiked into the woods before dawn the next day. It was early spring. Most of the snow had melted away, but the air and ground were cold. They pushed up a hill and he sweated from the exertion of lugging a daypack and rifle up a mountain. Then, when the terrain leveled out again, his heart slowed and he shivered as his wet base layer wicked heated away from his core. His dad was not a hunter. The trip was a whim, and while they sat at the edge of a bog before dawn, Luka resented him for it. He was only fourteen and his body tingled uncomfortably as numbness set in from the combined cold and stillness. He wanted to shiver or shift his legs to ease the needles in his feet, but whenever he moved, even slightly, his dad would shoot him an angry glance through the corners of his eye.

They had their backs up against the largest tree they could find at the edge of the clearing, but even at that age his shoulders were wider than the trunk of the tree, and it made an odd silhouette against the forest. The deer approached the bog just as a yellow-orange sun was rising in the eastern sky. The herd trotted to the edge of the clearing and among them was a large fallow buck—their intended target. His palmated antlers cast long shadows across the grass. He charged out into the pond and tramped and snorted, showing off. The does with him, however, waited in the tree line and eyed Luka and his dad. They did not run. Luka and his dad wore camouflage clothing and there was no wind to pick up their scent, but they knew something was amiss.

The patrol drones behaved like these deer. They converged near the group, aware of something out of place, but kept their distance while they calculated. Time was running out. While his body was stone, his mind frenzied with thought.

They were sensitive to a broad spectrum of electromagnetic waves, same as the drones on the DA campus. They must have keyed to the change in local EM from the downed electric fence.

Luka inched back to the opening in the second fence. He stretched his arm through the doorway Lark made with the canister of liquid nitrogen and found the grip on the clamp fixed the spike in the ground. He pulled it loose and the fence buzzed back to life. Roland looked back at him, his eyes wide with alarm at first, but he nodded approvingly when he heard the fence come back to life.

The drones, however, did not disperse. It now seemed there were five. He could not track them with his eyes, but he listened to the collective whine of their engines as they darted from place to place. They were swarming and they were seconds from a full alert, but Lark looked unconcerned by all of it. He was still on one knee with his fist in the air, signaling for them to hold.

The drones started to move away. He could not see them flying into the darkness but heard the change in their engines—the Doppler shift as the sound waves pitched down. They were moving toward the central part of the base.

A second later, at the other side of the base about a kilometer away, all hell broke loose.

The arcs of military drones flashed across the night sky as their turbines launched them toward the east perimeter. Rockets let loose in bright flares. Deep concussive rattles followed. The explosions and flares washed over their faces in pulses of orange and white. Luka's stomach lurched while he watched the storm of fire on the other side of White Sands. Despite the distance, he thought he felt the heat of the blasts.

Helena was somewhere in it. She was harder, more formidable than him, but he had first-hand experience with the drones. He knew the malice in their programming so he imagined the worst. He saw the drone team flanking the sisters, maiming one to distract and slow the others. Their *capture before kill* protocols gave no credence to injury or dismemberment. As long as the wound was not immediately lethal, they met the algorithm criteria for capture. The act of maiming fed positive feedback to their pseudo-AI's. It was the nearest thing to happiness that their machine-brains felt.

The explosions paused.

The fleeing patrol drones began to move erratically, nearly falling from the sky. Lark broke into a sprint and Roland followed at his heels. Luka hesitated. They were several strides ahead before he broke into a run behind them. Lark and Roland carried the heaviest packs, but they were faster, way faster than Luka. For every ten meters they ran, he fell a few more behind. He pushed harder, running as close to a sprint as he could manage with his equipment. He was sucking in air to feed oxygen to his legs, but the dust and dry climate irritated his airways. His lungs burned as they churned through dirty air. Their target was a low bunker a hundred meters ahead. They stored his prototype antimatter reactor five floors down in this complex.

When Luka made it to the bunker, Lark was already assembling a plasma torch from a power supply and gas canister in his pack. He hunched over beside him, with his chest heaving as he gulped in deep breaths, and watched him work. A multi-point biometric authentication secured the lock. That would be extremely difficult to fake, but the door had external hinges—a serious oversight in construction. The door itself was too thick to cut, but around the hinges, the metal thinned. They would exploit that.

Lark lined up the first cut and a shower of white sparks and slag erupted as he squeezed the trigger. It was loud and blindingly bright, but the firefight across the base had resumed and drowned out any amount of noise their team made. It took six cuts to break away the outfacing areas of the hinge loops. Lark packed a thin strip of explosive charge in the crevices beside each hinge. He waved them back and Luka and Roland huddled around the corner of the bunker. The explosive detonated with very little fire but a massive concussive force. It rattled Luka, even sheltered around the corner of the thick concrete wall.

The door broke free of the hinges and hung by the deadbolt at the biometric lock. Lark began cutting at this last bit of umbilical holding the door. He worked with a precarious mixture of fury and control, but this metal was taking much longer than the hinges. It was a stronger alloy, it did not even glow under the direct blast of the torch, and it was thicker. He passed the cutter over it a dozen times, but it did not yield, and the cutter was beginning to flicker and shoot sparks.

A large clot of reflected slag had damaged the cutting tip as a result of his hurried work, but Lark pressed on, unconcerned by the cutter's imminent failure. He made another pass over the metal, now holding the plasma tip so close it was nearly touching the deadbolt. Between the flashes, Luka could see that deadbolt was scored, but cut not even halfway through. He guessed the plasma torch would not last long enough to finish the job.

He was right.

After two more passes, the plasma died and the darkness flooded back in around them. Without hesitation, Lark threw the cutter to the ground and looked over his shoulder at Roland. Roland rolled his shoulders, stepped forward so that he stood beside Lark, and planted his feet in a wide stance. He and Lark launched powerful front kicks into the door and they landed in sync. Their combined strength shook the concrete walls of the bunker, but the metal did not give.

They reset for a second round. These kicks landed in a clumsy one-two sequence, but the metal at the bolt twisted and nearly tore through. Lark kicked again, this time by himself. The last threads of twisted metal snapped and crashed into the hallway of the bunker with a deafening metallic rattle.

The corridor behind it erupted with gunfire. Lark and Roland rolled away from the doorway and took defensive positions at each of its sides. Luka was too slow.

The orange flashes of muzzle break willed his body to move, but his legs could not translate the signal fast enough. He took a round to his flak vest. It hardened when the bullet struck and dispersed the force outward across his body. It prevented the bullet from penetrating and diffused the strike enough to avert internal injury, but the momentum of the impact knocked the wind out of him and drove him from his feet. He landed hard on his back. Bullets zipped over him and struck the ground behind his head while he gasped for air. He rolled until someone yanked him to his feet by the back of his vest. His body quivered, but his legs held beneath him. He shook his head clear and steadied the butt of his rifle against his shoulder.

Lark, meanwhile, rounded the corner of the bunker and rolled a black metallic ball down the hallway. A blue-purple light erupted from the doorway. Luka's vision wobbled and the world went quiet for several seconds. Lark and Roland moved down the hallway in its wake. There was no more gunfire.

Luka rounded the corner at their heels with his rifle drawn up and swept from left to right as they moved down the hallway. He stepped over two bodies at the end of the hallway, training his rifle on them as he passed. They were dead, not unconscious. Thick, black veins marred the skin on their faces and bulged in their necks. A pool of blood collected beneath the limp hand of one of the soldiers.

The hallway led to an elevator and a set of stairs. The elevator had been locked out, probably by an alarm triggered by the two men, so they had to take the stairs. They stored antimatter reactor and power converter prototypes were five floors down, or least they had when Luka first built them. The improved, 2nd generation devices, were in another, more secure, part of the facility. They kept the prototypes as emergency backups. He was banking on them still being here—forgotten since his departure from the base.

Lark took the stairs two at a time, moving downward in a controlled run. Roland followed at his heels, able to match Lark's pace, though he could not bound down two steps at once. Luka had to take the stairs one a time also, but even moving so fast that he risked missing a stair and tumbling the rest of the way down, he could not keep up. By the second floor, they were already a full floor ahead of him.

When he reached the landing for the fifth floor, Lark was busy bugging the lock on the door. This was an older device, fingerprint and six-digit code only—easier to fake. He produced a severed finger from a pocket. Blood dripped from the stub where it had once been attached to a hand. He rubbed the fingertip against his jacket to clean it and pressed it to the scanner. A green light blinked beside the device. Roland, meanwhile, fixed two electrodes to the keypad with the wires leading back to a set of electrodes in his forearm. He closed his eyes and a few seconds later the door unlocked and slid open.

Once again, gunfire met them. Muzzle flares erupted from the far end of the room and bullets ricocheted off the surrounding walls. At least one shot connected. It struck Roland in the calf—whether it was a ricochet or direct strike, Luka could not tell—but Roland did not break his stride. He dove forward and rolled into cover behind a structural pillar at the left of the room. Luka back-stepped out of the hallway and took cover at the right-hand side of the door. Lark did the same and took cover opposite him.

Lark swung his pack from his shoulders and dug through it until he found a matte black case about the size of his hand. He opened the latches and set the case on the ground with the lid opened toward the door. A dark metallic object, no larger than a hummingbird, burst free from the case and zipped down the hallway. Lark froze and his eyes went distant.

Luka peeked around the corner to watch, but another pulse of fire met him and retracted his head. Bullets shredded the concrete near his face. The doorframe was not a sharp line anymore, but a ragged edge. Chunks of it fell loose and littered the floor.

Lark held his palm out, facing it flat toward Luka so that he could see it from across the doorway. He projected a video on it. It showed the room ahead. Luka saw Roland carefully positioned behind a central pillar in the room and he saw a large combat drone trying to flank him.

Lark's video feed was analyzing the drone. It flipped through thermal, X-ray, and UV-Vis data feeds. It searched for a weaknesses.

Their attacker was a medium-class drone, but a model that Luka did not recognize. It was flightless, probably. He did not see any of the heatsinking needed for jet propulsion, but it otherwise looked like a miniature version of the military drones up on the surface.

On the video, Roland took the machine pistol holstered at his chest, swung his arm around the pillar, and blindly emptied a clip at the drone. Brass rained to the floor beneath the pistol and at least half of the shots connected with their target. Violent sparks erupted from the drone's hull, but its exterior shirked rounds without a lasting effect. Based on the

X-ray analysis from Lark's feed, the rounds did not even scuff its armor.

"DO YOU KNOW THIS KIND?" Lark shouted over the cacophony of gunfire as Roland emptied another clip.

"NO!" Luka shouted back.

The fire died down for a moment.

Lark killed the video feed, returning his grip to his rifle. He bit his lip, looking up. The situation was becoming dire. Roland was agile, but the drone was maneuvering him into a corner. It would pin him down soon, and it was clear Roland's weapons would be nothing more than a distraction to the drone.

Lark turned his head and glared at Luka, "Any ideas, Doctor?"

"No, but guns won't work."

"Yeah. Duh."

"Can the drone you deployed do an EM pulse?" asked Luka.

"The pulse is too weak to knock out anything more than another surveillance drone."

"Get your drone as close as you can and pulse it. As soon as your drone's systems are back up, have it do a scan on the harmonics of the signals coming from the mil drone."

Lark smiled. "Hang on."

His eyes went distant again.

"Done," said Lark.

"Okay. Analyze the signal and look for oscillations in its transmitting band," said Luka.

Lark paused.

"It's solid. No oscillation. Almost no leakage. Immune to EMP and hack," he said.

Luka grimaced. "Damn."

"Yeah, damn," Lark replied with eyes wide. "What else you got? You oughtta know this shit better than me."

Luka exhaled and closed his eyes. He let the world slip away around him and a gentle hum filled his ears. At the back of his mind now, he felt the Constellation's schematics. They were fragmented and disorganized, Lark's attempts to access the data had corrupted them, but some of the splinters held complete concepts. He knew everything about power systems without the aid of the biochip, but he was searching for information it held on a peripheral system he knew little about: thermal management. In the shards, he found it—a 3D render of a graphene heatsink. The geometric pattern of this heatsink's fins was identical to that on the drone in the next room. The heatsinks on the Constellation were made of an extravagantly expensive graphene polymer. It was the only material NASA had found that could accommodate the tremendous task of exchanging heat from antimatter reactor while in space. If this drone had the same type of heatsink, then it produced a huge amount of heat. Thermal management was its weakness.

Rifle fire broke out in the room. It was slower but heavier than the machine pistol fire.

"RUN THERMALS. FIND A HOTSPOT," shouted Luka over the clangor.

Lark's eyes went blank.

The rifle fire stopped.

"Got one," he said.

"How much charge is left on the battery from the plasma cutter?" asked Luka.

"Some. More than half. Cutter gave out before the battery."

"Bad technique."

"Fuck you."

Luka flinched as shots rang out again. "CAN YOU MAKE THE BATTERY GO CRITICAL?"

Lark looked down at the ground, rifle pinned in against his shoulder at the ready. "Yes."

Another exchange of fire broke out, this one more sustained. Lark poked his head around the corner and began emptying a clip in the general direction of the drone, adding to the chaos.

"I GET IT. WE'LL HAVE TO GET CLOSE," he yelled as he unleashed bursts of rounds.

The clip dropped free from his rifle, empty, and he withdrew from the hallway. He pressed his back flat against the wall at the left of the doorway and jammed a new clip into his weapon.

"We get the bunker door from upstairs, drag it down here. I don't think the drone's carrying a caliber that can penetrate that much metal," said Luka.

Lark nodded in agreement. "I'll get the door and the battery. You stay here and lay as many rounds as you can into it. Distract it, buy us time."

Lark took to the stairs at a sprint. Luka rounded the corner of the doorway with his rifle up and began pulsing rounds at the drone. He aimed for the joint at the drone's top left shoulder, where ammunition fed into its primary machine gun. His bullets would not penetrate the armor, but if he could jam enough rounds into the feed area, his bullets might clog up the ammunition flow and disable the machine gun. He squeezed the trigger five times in quick succession, each time landing a spray onto the drone's shoulder, but the shots deflected out and away without effect. The angles were wrong. That plan was a bust, but it drew the drone's attention away from Roland. Under his barrage of fire, the drone retreated into a covered position. Luka advanced, moving deeper into the hallway to get a new angle. He flicked his rifle to full auto and fired the remaining fifteen rounds in his clip into the same crook on the drone's shoulder. There was still no discernible damage to the machine, but it triggered a change in its directive. It abandoned its patient maneuvering to pin Roland down and went an offensive strike. It turned its front to Luka and emitted a blinding white flash like burning magnesium and a deep, concussive crack. It dawned on Luka then that the machine had drawn him into the open by appearing to retreat.

The plugs in his ears identified the threat of the noise and blocked it out, but the flash happened too quickly for his glasses to adjust. He stood blind, in the middle of the hallway, exposed to the drone. Five rounds struck his flak jacket in quick succession. His feet slipped out from under him and

236

the back of his head struck the ground. His helmet took to the blow, but his brain jostled back and forward in his skull.

He opened his eyes, but it was all fuzz and stars. Even through the adrenaline, his abdomen burned like someone had dug a hot poker into his stomach.

He rolled onto his stomach and got up all fours, his back turned to the drone. One round hit the armor over his left hamstring and Luka collapsed down flat again. The pain sharpened his senses. The stars cleared from his vision. Lark appeared in the hallway then, with the heavy exterior door in tow. He hoisted it in front of him like a shield and strolled down the hallway. He stepped over Luka and stood it on end in front of them to create a barricade. The drone went berserk, firing continuously at the door, but its rounds could not penetrate the metal.

"YOU'RE BLEEDING," said Lark.

"Oh, great," said Luka, barely speaking over the gunfire.

He sat up and kneeled beside Lark. Blood oozed from a ragged puncture in his flak jacket. There was evidence of several other strikes on the armor, but it appeared only that one got through. It entered on his left side, just below his ribcage and exited below his shoulder blade. Without warning, Lark jabbed a needle into Luka's neck. The plunger of the syringe hammered down with a hiss and the burning sensation in his chest slipped away almost immediately. Then his vision came into perfect focus.

The drone stopped firing, accepting that it could not penetrate Lark's new barricade. It retreated from the hallway.

"That'll carry you through for now," said Lark.

Luka rubbed his neck where the needle went in. A welt was rising already.

"We need to press forward behind the door until we're close enough," Lark added.

"How are you going to stick the battery to him? I didn't think that part through," asked Luka.

Lark was grinning crazily. "I'm going to weld it to the fucker." He held the plasma cutter in his right hand like a trophy. The slag that clogged the tip had been broken away—it looked like he used a rock to do it.

"I'll stick it to him with a couple of quick tacks. Then I'll pulse the battery with an override code from my drone and it should go critical," said Lark.

Luka stared. Lark had mangled the torch. He didn't think it would even light again, but he had no better ideas.

"How many clips you have left?" Lark asked.

"Enough," answered Luka.

"Keep pumping rounds at it as we get close, then break off to the side and make for the pillar."

Lark whistled at Roland to get his attention. He peeked around the corner of the pillar he had taken shelter behind. They exchanged a set of hand gestures and then Lark looked back to Luka expectantly.

Luka pulled a fresh clip from his hip, loaded his rifle, and nodded at Lark.

Lark moved with the door held out front, shielding them both as they progressed down the hallway. The drone had resumed its mission to pin Roland. When it came into view, it was rounding the pillar in a counterclockwise circle, pushing Roland into a corner without an exit. Luka and Roland both unleashed automatic fire onto it, concentrating on its head where most of its sensor systems were positioned. They had little chance of damaging them, but it might disorient it.

Their tactic seemed to work. Under the barrage, the drone fired wildly in all directions. Luka and Lark moved closer to it. Lark lit his plasma torch. It cracked and hissed sickly, but to Luka's surprise, produced a cutting tip anyway. He motioned for Luka to take charge of their shield. Luka swung his rifle over his back and gripped the door with both hands, almost falling forward under the weight of it as Lark released his grip. Luka took a wide stance and steadied himself. The drone concentrated its fire on Roland once again, but he continued to unload clips into its sensors, exposing himself to its fire. Bullets struck his shoulders and arms, but his aim did not waiver.

Luka took another few steps, struggling to shuffle the immense weight of the door forward. When they got close enough, Lark leaned around the door and used the slag he had broken from the cutting tip to tack the battery to the drone. It clung to an armor section just beneath the drone's left shoulder. It looked like a grapefruit-sized tumor growing from the drone's armpit.

Lark took control of the door, shoving Luka behind him, and they retreated backward out of the hallway. Lark's drone flashed its EMP just as they passed the doorframe.

There was no effect, not immediately. The drone continued to pummel Roland's position with machine gun fire while they huddled behind the cratered door, but after a

239

few seconds, a trail of black smoke rose from the drone's back.

Roland took full cover behind its pillar and the drone drilled rounds into the concrete with an increased fire rate in response. It had whittled away at the edges of the pillar until the pillar was scarcely wide enough to cover him shoulder to shoulder and then it began to circle counterclockwise. As it turned, Luka saw the battery streaming smoke. The entire case was orange-hot and its white-hot core was beginning to shine through. It looked the drone was carrying a miniature sun on its back. The heat of it glowed on Luka's face like the lick of a bonfire on a cold night even from their position several meters back. Luka flipped his rifle into burst fire mode and steadied the barrel against the left edge of the door, preparing to expend what ammo he had left.

Before he could fire, the drone lost sense of the room. It zoomed backward into a wall and hit with a heavy thud. It took several seconds to recover from the impact. Then it fired off a few rounds in the general direction of Roland, but most of the bullets went wide of their target.

It tried to resume its tactical directive to keep Roland separated from Luka and Lark while it destroyed his cover, but its movements were muddled. It zig-zagged into the center of the room and started to make an arc around the pillar and then smashed back into the wall again as its sensors failed it.

The entire battery glowed blue-white now. The heat emitting from it was no longer a faint wash, but direct sun on a summer day.

The drone's movements became increasingly erratic. It zipped from one side of the room to the other and launched into a paroxysm of random gunfire. They all watched wearily.

These movements were its throws of death, but the random bullets could still find a target.

Lark got impatient. He stood from behind their door and began firing single shots into the drone, aiming for a spot just beside the battery. The armor caved in under the combined stresses of heat and the impact of the bullet. He flipped to auto and emptied a whole a clip into the opening his first shots created. The drone stopped dead.

They regrouped near the lifeless shell of the drone. Roland's armor was scuffed and tattered, but he himself looked none the worse for wear. Lark was shifting his weight from hip to hip and staring at Luka impatiently. Luka pointed to the door at the right of the room that led to his old lab and Lark motioned for him to take the lead.

This one had a keypad like the previous door, but no biometrics. He keyed in 1-4-9-2 and a green light blinked on the keypad. They hadn't changed the code in ten years, idiots. As the door opened, the LED on his helmet flicked on and flooded the darkness ahead.

Glass panels on the front of the huge bank of servers shined back. Along the floor was a network of onyx-black metallic piping—the front end of his prototype power converter. The pipes were a permanent fixture in the building. Those, they could recreate back at Lark's base in Low City. What they needed was his conversion cell, the heart of the antimatter reactor, that lay at the central junction of the pipes. It took the massive bursts of energy from antimatter annihilation and generated a stable stream of electromagnetic energy. It had been painstakingly machined over months out of exotic tungsten alloys using a one-off obsidian-tipped CNC mill. He followed the pipes until his headlamp lit up the unassuming cube of metal. He retrieved a hydraulic wrench from his pack, kneeled, and set to undoing the bolts that fixed the onyx piping to the front of the converter. Lark, meanwhile, worked at the bolts mounting the conversion cell to the floor.

Roland trained his rifle on the entrance to the lab, keeping watch. Luka removed the pipes from the cell, one by one, and then bolted metal caps onto each of the open ports to keep dust from entering the cell. Next, he set to the power conduit, freeing wires in a careful sequence. By the time he severed the last wire, Lark had finished freeing the bolts that held the cell to the floor.

Lark waved Roland over and Luka stepped aside as they hoisted the conversion cell. With considerable effort, they began shuffling out of the lab, past the wrecked drone, and into the hallway. Though he was the least experienced in combat, he was also the least capable of carrying a three-hundred-kilo chunk of metal up several flights of stairs, so assumed the role of lookout for the group.

Lark and Roland managed the task, slowly, painfully slowly. While they moved, Luka scouted a floor ahead. He ran up the stairs each time, and then he sprinted back down and rejoined, moving a few steps ahead while they hoisted the cell stair by stair. When they reached the landing of the ground floor, Lark and Roland were both sucking air and dripping with sweat.

Lark spoke between breaths, "I'm calling in the helicopter now. We need to move quickly. There won't be much of a window."

Luka took point and waited while Lark and Roland prepared themselves to sprint the cell out into the clearing between the bunker and their hole in the inner perimeter fence. He poked his head out of the bunker and swept his rifle in a wide arc across the open space. His scope came back null—no heat signatures—so he waved the team forward.

He broke into a run toward the clearing with the butt of his rifle locked into his shoulder, ready to fire. Time slowed. His eyes tried to pierce the darkness, and the scanners on his helmet watched for heat or EM signatures—but the night was empty. There were no signs of chaos that had erupted before they entered the bunker. The lights were out base-wide.

A pang of worry twisted in his stomach. The quiet could mean that Helena and her sisters had retreated, or it could mean they had been killed. His throated tightened. He amped up microphone sensitivity on his plugs, reaching out in the distance to find voices or the sounds of drones. All he heard was the chuff of helicopter rotors approaching. He looked behind him, over his shoulder. Lark and Roland exited the bunker. They each hoisted the power converter with one arm and were jogging it forward, but they had to stop every few meters and shake out their arms. At the halfway point, they switched their technique and each gripped with two hands instead of one so they could move with one person in front and one in back. They could not jog as fast this way but covered a greater distance between stops.

The chop of the helicopter grew to roar as it swooped in overhead. His earplugs ratcheted down their sensitivity and dampened the sound as the helicopter's rotors began to whip up dust around him. He looked up just the helicopter swung into view overhead. It descended over him. A rope and harness dropped from its belly and it hovered patiently while Lark and Roland did their best to jog the power converter over.

Luka was prepping the harness when a barrage of rockets streaked across the sky like meteors. It over-saturated his vision, leaving him momentarily blind. He fell to the ground and covered his head even though he had a helmet.

The helicopter erupted in flames as the first missile struck. Eight more found their target in quick succession and the helicopter disintegrated in midair. Fiery bits of shrapnel the size of hailstones rained down around him.

A few peppered his flak jacket, and some found their way into the cracks between his amour, but whatever Lark had dosed him with made him immune to pain. From his prone position, Luka looked over to Lark and Roland. They watched the missiles destroy the helicopter and neither appeared concerned by it. Their expressions were blank, their body language relaxed, as their plan was erased from the sky. Anger welled in veins.

Fear replaced the anger as six military drones set down in the space between him and the rest of his team. Their heavy chassis connected with the ground with reverberating thuds. Through a small gap between them, Luka saw Lark pointing toward the perimeter fence.

"RUN!" he screamed.

Luka's body snapped into action. He scrambled to his feet and ran for the fence with a speed that only desperation could fuel. The dust-caked crust that formed over the bullet wounds in his torso cracked open and fresh blood seeped down his right side. It dripped from his torso and left a trail in the dirt behind him. The fence was too far out in the darkness for him to see but it did not matter. In his mind, he saw a drone blow the leg off of a fleeing insurgent, only now he was that insurgent. He ran as hard as he could, knowing all the while that he would be cut down at any moment. All he could do was run.

But a peculiar sensation filled the air again. The hairs along his neck rose first and then the feeling spread to his arms too. A magnetic field rose. It pulled at his biochip and made it burn like a hot coal. No pharmaceutical could dull that.

Luka fell to his knees and clutched his neck while he gulped in air. He looked back at Lark and the drones. The drones that should have been maiming him right then were fixated on something else. They did not like the magnetic field either. All six of them turned their attention in the opposite direction of the fence. They unleashed another barrage of missiles and followed it with a roar of gunfire.

"KEEP RUNNING SHITHEAD!" instructed Lark's voice through the confusion.

Lark and Roland passed him at a sprint and Luka jumped into a run behind them. Blood surged through his body and it poured out of the entry and exit wounds in his torso. He was light-headed, unable to focus, but possessed by some force beyond physical sensation. He scurried through the holes in fences they made in their way in and he kept running into the night while the desert behind him glowed with fire.

BOOK THREE
VIKTORIA

Chapter Eleven

The jet was in sight when he collapsed. Luka's body gave out all at once as the last traces of the drug Lark injected him with left his bloodstream. There was a drip trail of blood through the desert from the seeping wounds at his chest and back and the parched earth beneath him drank it in greedily. His limbs were going numb. He knew the feeling of life slipping from him. This was his second go at it. A deep cold welled where existence retreated. His ears rang and he saw the wave again—a dark enormity on the horizon. It washed over him. It took the sun and it pulled him into the abyss. Underwater, he lost his sense of gravity. His consciousness faded. In the black, he heard a voice echoing down to him.

Not yet.

It pulled him to the surface.

Luka woke to bright white light. They were inside Lark's jet, already airborne based on the roar of the engines. The midday sun bounced off the clouds below them beneath them and filled the cabin with a brilliant glow. He squinted as his pupils struggled to adjust.

Lark was looking down at him, smiling. He was ugly in the direct light. His skin was rough with large pores and pockmarks. He was too pale and a touch yellow—jaundiced from a life spent underground. His was not a happy smile, but a smirk like he was telling a joke that only he thought was funny.

"Nicely done, doctor," said Lark. His mordant tone matched his sneer.

"Screw you," Luka choked out.

He coughed, trying to clear his throat of dust. He regretted it immediately. A stabbing pain ran down his spine and spread through his torso to remind of his bullet wounds. His hand instinctively went to the wound at his chest. There was a clean bandage there, taped down in a neat white square. He did not need to reach over his shoulder to know he would find the same on his back.

"Well you're about as useful as tits on a bull," announced Lark.

Luka cocked his head. It was an old phrase. Certainly not something Lark heard in person. His whole personality was like that—changing day-to-day, hour-to-hour. He built from scraps he collected along the way. Luka guessed that Lark must have watched some western and decided that today, he felt like a cowboy.

"Not my fault," Luka rasped. He tugged at a corner of the tape and pulled the bandage on his chest away. "Drones," he added weakly.

Beneath the bandage was a seam of skin. The surrounding area was puffy and red, but the wound itself looked healed.

"Relax, we fixed you up good. Pumped you full of synth to replace the blood you lost and closed up the holes," announced Lark.

Luka prodded at his ribs around the wound. He winced and inhaled sharply, finding that it was extremely tender.

Lark smirked. "Not much we can do about the bruising, though. That shit just takes time."

Luka shook his head and coughed up some muddy spittle. The pain of coughing took his breath away.

"What now?" he asked when he recovered.

Lark grabbed a plastic canteen from beside him and tossed it to Luka. He snatched the canteen from the air with two hands, wincing again.

"Drink some water. You sound like my mom the morning after a bender," said Lark.

"You didn't have a mom," Luka rasped.

"You knew what I meant."

Luka popped the cap on the canteen open and sipped slowly. His throat itched as the water seeped into the cracks and expanded the withered cells. He cleared his throat again and took another long drink from the canteen. He groaned as he sat upright and scooched himself back so he could lean against the cabin of the plane.

"Okay, *now* what?" he asked.

"You mean now that we don't have an antimatter converter?" Lark shot back.

Luka rubbed his hand across his forehead, massaging the deepening wrinkles there. The small bit of water he drank awakened his body enough to bring on a throbbing headache.

"Yeah, that."

Lark pursed his lips. "Don't worry. I never expected you'd pull the mission through. We just needed to spook them into transferring the equipment to another site."

Lark paused. "I'll pick it up in transit."

He did not understand how Lark intended to accomplish that but was too exhausted to press it.

"You're going back to Low City," said Lark.

Luka's eyes narrowed. "For what?"

"She got the encryption keys we need."

A crease formed between his eyebrows, "You mean Elise?"

"Yes. Who else did you think was helping me? I thought you would have figured that out when she helped you escape the DA base. She warned you and she made sure you got to High City when you made your move."

He knew that Elise was working with someone on the outside. He had not, however, until this moment, considered that she was a directive operative of Lark's. He also had assumed his escape succeeded because of his planning—with maybe a bit of luck. It turned out luck did not exist. Elise had both spurred and facilitated the escape.

Luka forced his face to take on a placid expression. "Okay. Where in Low City and when?"

Lark wore a feral smile. "Oh, you're not going to like that."

Low City did not particularly scare him now. He had crawled through the gutters there once already. He had made it this far. Lark was trying to rattle him, to manipulate him, but he couldn't guess yet why.

Luka stared at Lark intently, unflinching. He adopted a surly tone as he spoke, "Probably not. Now when you're done getting off on your own cleverness, are you going to tell me what needs to be done?"

A collage of emotions washed over Lark: shock, anger, amusement, and then anger again. The muscles in his neck twitched.

"You're dead without me. Let me remind you of that. If I hadn't disabled your chip, it would never matter how far you traveled or what you did. They would track you. You think you know pain because you lost some girl along the way? You think you know pain because you had to leave a cush life in DA care? You don't know shit and you don't even realize it. I may look younger, but I am much older than you, and to me, you are just some petulant kid who fancies himself tough because he spent a couple of years on a military base. Don't forget that *you* owe *me*."

Luka's heart raced. Blood whooshed in his ears with each pulse. The bruises on chest ached and his back spasm, threatening to lose control. He closed his eyes. He let out a breath and looked inward until his heart slowed and the tension his back eased.

When he opened them again, he set his eyes on Lark with a dogged stare. "I haven't suffered like you, sure, but I don't lie about it either. I don't make up stories. I don't pretend that I've had some life that never existed. I don't pretend that I had some screwed up family as an excuse for my actions. If you are done with this contest of *who's had it worse*, I would like to be productive. I want to move forward."

Lark met his stare. He stood with his mouth wide open and ran his tongue along his teeth. For a long time, he did only this. Saliva dripped from a corner of his mouth. He made no move clean it. When he finally unfroze, he returned the cockpit took the copilot's seat without a word.

He eyed him until Lark sat and then Luka laid down on the bare floor and did his best to fall asleep. Exhaustion overcame him, but he never fell into REM. The vibrations of the jet's turbines rattled through his body and the hard floor offered no comfort. His ribs ached where his weight pressed against them and he had to switch between laying on his side and laying on his back constantly. He drifted in half-sleep for hours as the jet pushed toward the Northwest. When he became cognizant again, they were descending onto the island where Lark stored his jet. Luka's ears popped as the plane changed altitude. He yawned as he tried to equalize the changing pressure.

The jet touched down hard. It had to. The crude runway was slick with rain and if they did not want to hydroplane, they had to break the surface tension of the water. The wheels of the landing gears slammed down on the aging asphalt. The flaps turned vertical, the brakes engaged, and the jet roared to a stop. The force of it threw Luka into the air and he crashed back down on his side. He gasped and clutched at his ribs as they throbbed.

They left most of the gear in the jet, only taking the weapons, ammunition, and some water to the submarine. They did not speak the whole way. Lark stayed far ahead.

The inside of the submarine was damp and cold. With the batteries and biodiesel engines offline for so long, the ocean had sapped the warmth from it. Luka opened his mouth wide and exhaled, watching his breath form mist in the cabin. Lark shoved passed him and headed for the pilot's chair. Luka followed, taking a bench formed along the hull of the sub. Roland took the copilot's controls. He inclined his head at Luka, discreetly, as he passed. Luka nodded in return, but after, stared at his feet while he puzzled at the reason for the gesture.

They ran through systems checks and soon a rushing sound overtook the cabin as seawater flooded the ballast tanks. The sub sank beneath the waterline. Motors came to life and then they were gliding homeward through the black ocean.

They stopped two kilometers offshore from the outer edges of Low City. Lark brought the sub up from a depth of fifty meters and held it a few meters beneath the surface of the water. Waves broke overhead and crashed on the hull like muffled thunder.

Lark stood from his seat and walked back to Luka. As he brushed by Roland, he snatched the machine pistol Roland kept in his chest holster.

"This time, take a gun that works," said Lark.

He flipped the pistol around so that he was holding the barrel with the handle extended to Luka. This was the first time they spoke since the exchange in the jet and Lark's relaxed posture and sarcastic jab were too friendly. He acted like he had completely forgiven and forgotten—neither of which he ever did. Luka took the grip. He looked over to Roland as he closed his fingers around the handle one by one, but Roland offered neither an affirmation nor a refutation.

Luka closed his hand and pulled the pistol free from Lark's grasp.

"Keep that pistol visible at all times. It's the best protection I can give you. Hardware like that isn't common out there. They'll think you're MP or a high-level gang enforcer. Less likely they'll try you if they see it," said Lark.

Roland stood, undid the claps at the sides of his chest holster, and slipped it free from his shoulders. He fished six clips from his bag too. With the holster in one hand and the clips in the other, he extended both arms toward Luka. The gifting was uncomfortably intimate. It was too gentle of a display for Roland. Luka looked at his feet while he took the clips and slid them into the ammo slots at the back of his belt. Then, he took the holster. He slid it on one shoulder at a time and the straps instantly synched in to form to his chest and shoulders.

"Elise will meet you at Dead Man's Hand. It's in the Light District. DA might have patrols or informants in the better parts of LC so I can't risk dropping you anywhere near there. You'll have to cross through the slums again," said Lark.

"Okay," said Luka as he fixed Roland's pistol to his new holster. He tested the reach twice, raising his hand from his side to the pistol's grip at his sternum.

"I'm going to upload an aug map into your chip. I marked it myself. You'll know where to go and where to avoid—and it'll help find a way out if things go sideways. Not that they will, right?" continued Lark.

Luke lowered his hand. "Sure."

"That's the spirit," said Lark.

From behind his back, Lark produced a device that looked like a chunky black collar. It had a gap at the front so that it formed a deep crescent shape.

"I made this just for you," he said as he held it out to Luka. "When I killed the tracking function on your chip, I damaged the wireless transfer functions too."

Luka took it and flipped it over in his hands as he examined. A smooth silicone material formed the exterior. It had two delicate hinges at the midpoints of each arc that flexed and allowed it to adjust its shape.

"Slide it around your neck so that the back portion sits near the base of your skull."

Luka flexed the points of the arc out and slid it around his neck. The hinges constricted and it sat tight around his throat, just beneath his jaw.

"Here we go."

Luka felt an odd rush of thought in his brain. He was trying to make a thousand decisions at once but he could not focus on any single one. It was both logic and emotion. It swept over him like a daydream of past life. Suddenly, he perceived, and he judged, and he *knew* things about Low City. All at once, he was disappointed, overjoyed, and left with a deep fear that rattled his amygdala.

"Give it a moment. Your brain needs to adjust to the metadata," said Lark.

It took only milliseconds in real-time—but the flood of information in Luka's mind dilated time for him. He had years of new memories, and as they populated into his hippocampus, he understood why he would, now, never need

255

interfaces or heads-up displays to direct him through Low City. All of the information he needed to know about Low City was there—in the form of first-hand experience. He knew the city as well as he knew the layout of his childhood home. He knew dozens of people who lived in Low City. He knew their personalities as well as he did his own friends. Suddenly, he understood the character of the whole city. He knew the streets and their topology and their secrets. He knew where to find the people he might need. He knew which places carried what types of goods and where he could hide. If someone shot him, he knew of three buildings where a pay-to-play doctor might help him. If LCG got ahold of him and tried to harvest him, he knew a name to drop that would freeze them up and buy him time. He knew Low City the way only a local could. He knew where Lark had arranged the meeting and now he understood why Lark told him he would not like it.

"Wow," muttered Luka under his breath, "jesus."

A proud grin spread across his Lark's face. "I improved on their embedding algorithms."

The glut of new information dazed him, but his higher cognitive functions were recovering from the shock. That fear that settled in his amygdala surged forward. What Lark gave him was far too useful to not come at a cost.

"I know it wasn't to help me. Why did you do this?" Luka asked.

"Yes, it was."

"No, it was not," said Luka as he ripped the device free from his neck. "Why did you give me this information?" he pressed.

Lark snorted and snatched the collar from Luka's hands. "The same principle that makes it twice as functional for you, will make it twice as lethal to them. You're the alpha test, and I am *so thrilled* to see it worked so well. From the look on your face, it worked even better than expected. You should be thanking me."

Luka chewed on his lip while he thought and the fear rushing through his brain a moment ago withered to a gentle, anxious hum. As explanations from Lark went, this was not so bad. Only self-satisfaction thrilled Lark, only things that fed his ego. In this context, his motive made sense. Luka could have been upset at being a Guinea pig, but it was far in his life the first time that someone used him as an experiment. The doctors did everything to his back. They took enormous risks. This would not be the last time it happened either. He just hoped he could keep cashing in on other's successes.

Luka grabbed the device from Lark's hands. "How much space is left?"

"You mean on the collar? It doesn't store anything. It just facilitates the transfer."

"No, I don't mean the collar."

Lark cocked his head. "Your chip. Why?"

"Just answer."

"I don't know, not exactly."

"Take your best guess."

"A lot, I think. The data I put in is compressed. It works like real memory. It's all there, just not always accessible. You have to find a thread and trace it backward to remember it.

Right now it's all fresh—and it will be for the next few days—but after that, you'll feel some of it slipping away from you. It'll work its way into your long-term memory gradually. It will be part of you. Then it will take longer to find it, just like your real memories, but it will always be there."

Luka shook his head. "I know you didn't try an upload without knowing the capacity of my biochip. Why don't you know how much is left?"

Lark's mouth tightened and his jawline hardened. He spat the words out, "Because I don't know how much space the Constellations schematics are occupying in there because their implanting codes are stupid. It's like they're storing in a binary format that works for silicon transistors but not for human cells and it doesn't bother to follow the sequencing the brain uses at all—which is why they told you it takes so much training to use it. It shouldn't. Lazy work on their part, as usual. Then they've got these layers of encryption on top of their shit encoding. Accessing those plans is like learning another language for you. The data I put it, it's already been translated. It's native."

Luka scratched at the stubble on his neck while he considered this.

"What other data do you have?" he asked.

There was a long pause. Then, that unsettling smile crept across Lark's face. "You're a junkie already."

"I was thinking of other information that might be helpful for my next task."

Lark's grin faded, but not in irritation. His eyes fell to the floor while his mind slipped into concentrated thought.

He looked up after a few seconds. "Tactical, you mean? Like combat and shit? I don't think you want those memories."

"What's a few more bad memories. You said yourself that I'm not very good. Help me be better."

Lark snickered. "For once not a bad idea, but don't say I didn't warn you. I need thirty minutes."

"I can wait."

Lark drew his eyes wide. "Yeah, I know, idiot. You're in my sub. I don't think you're fucking leaving without us knowing."

Lark moved back to the pilot's section of the sub and busied himself at a console. Luka took a seat and swung his feet up on a nearby bench. He leaned against a rafter curving along the inside of the hull. The cold metal drained the warmth from his back and soothed the inflammation in his ribcage. He closed his eyes and pictured Low City. The new information in his chip was an alternate life that had been grafted into his memory. It was like a daydream that became real. His brain elated at the opportunity to explore it.

His clothes were soaked through again. The drone roared overhead and his heart raced. This time though, he knew precisely where to go—two blocks away there was a flooded underground parking garage where an LCG rival operated a safe house. They could hide him presuming he had money, and a lot of it. The best route to the Light District from there took him on nearly the same path he chose at random on his original journey. Here, his mind snagged on an awn of discord.

The woman who helped in Low City existed in both his real and his biochip memory. His brain struggled to make sense of the confused data on her. His real memory had impressions and feelings about her already. He knew her for the pills she gave him to barter, and for a gun and clothes, he got in return. When he thought of her, he saw those neon disks laid out carefully in a plastic case. He saw the concern in her eyes right before someone bludgeoned him and dragged him into an alley. The new memories intruded on these old ones. They sought to overwrite his impressions. He knew her by the pseudonym she gave him, *Lady Luck*, but her real name was Viktoria. From his biochip, he knew she was only twenty-six—much younger than he assumed when he met her. From his biochip, he knew that she had ties to LCG's chief rivals, The Drowned. They operated in the slums and outskirts, shying away from the glitz of the Light District. A man named Dominik supplied her pills in bulk. His new memory told him that she had considerable clout with The Drowned, although she was not officially initiated. She moved product into LCG dominated clubs and they respected her for that.

Luka sat upright and rubbed his eyes with his hands balled into fists. Then he stared into the red lights overhead and tried to focus on the rafters of the submarine, but his field of view swam with black pools and bright fragments of Low City. He shook his head to clear them. He tried to coerce his mind back into the present by squeezing his eyes shut and then releasing them, but the visions persisted.

In this schism between his real memories of Viktoria and his newly implanted ones, a thought persisted. It tugged him back. It glared like a cynosure in the map data. With the added information from the new memories, he understood how much she risked helping him. He knew it would endanger him to find her, and he knew there would be consequences, but he could not ignore her. He had no idea what he could offer that would be valuable or useful to her. He thought of guns or money, but she had enough of those based on the gang ties in the biochip narrative.

Luka opened his eyes again. Lark stood in front of him with his folded arms folded across his chest.

"Ready?"

Luka struggled to stay in the moment. All of the new data in his biochip churned beneath the surface of his consciousness like a dream fighting its way forward. It muddled his vision with swatches of color and abyssal nothings.

"Yeah," said Luka, nodding absently.

Lark handed him the collar and he slipped it around his neck as before. It hit him instantly. These memories were sharp. They moved like ice bristling through his brain and they formed crystals in the paths behind his eyes. The sensation was intense and sharp, but there was a pleasing form within it too. It felt bright and cool as it settled. At first, he could not see through it, but as the wash of memory thinned, his conscious mind came forward.

A dull red glow bathed the submarine, but even this soft light felt like staring into a white-hot star. He raised his hand across his brow in reflex, like he was shading his eyes from a calescent sun. It did not help. He squeezed his eyes shut and opened them again but the intense glare would not abate.

"What the hell's happening?" Luka asked as he continued to blink.

Lark took on the intonation of a pre-wave Californian teenager, "Relax, dude."

Luka hunched over and rested his elbows on his thighs. "What the hell is going on?"

"It's fine. Chill out, man," said Lark.

"Will just tell me what is going on?"

"Like I said, relax, it's fine."

"I'm going to kill you—blind or not."

Lark smirked. "It's not a big deal. We overloaded your chip a bit. It didn't have quite the capacity I assumed it did. DA's fault, really. They stuck you with second-rate gear."

Luka cut in, "Ok that doesn't explain what's happening to me. Tell me now or I take the gun you just gave me and start shooting in random directions."

Lark put his palms up in surrender. "Okay, okay. Easy. Your chip is uh—like bleeding off some extra, dude. We put too much data in and it's going to vomit some stuff back out. Some extra electrons are floating around in your brain and it's apparently doing some strange things with your optic nerve. It'll pass."

Lark twisted his face into a confused look. "I'm pretty sure, anyhow."

Luka clamped his hand down on his chest and drew the pistol that hung there. He tucked his eyes into the crook of his elbow while he straight-armed the pistol in the direction he assumed Lark was standing.

Lark put his hands in the air. "Whoa, whoa, whoa. Easy John Wayne."

Luka steadied his aim in the direction of Lark's voice.

"Or shoot me then. For once, I'm not messing with you. Promise."

He placed his hand on his chest like he was pledging allegiance. Luka held his aim, but his arm quivered as his shoulder strained to keep the weight of pistol extended. He fought. He kept his aim true. The burning in shoulder spread through his back and his vision started to go black.

No, it wasn't going black. It was returning to normal.

Cautiously, Luka pulled the crook of his arm free from his eyes. He opened them completely. The submarine was eerie and dark. The floor was rough, black metal. A muddy glow bathed the walls. Streams of condensation running down the hull shined back at him. He looked up. The lights overhead were fuzzy-red orbs. He dropped his guard and let the pistol hang at his side. Slowly, he turned to face Lark, his shoulders rotating first. He fixed his eyes on him. Lark's empty face gaped back at him.

Lark shrugged. Then he turned back to the cockpit and took his pilot's seat.

"Get your dry bag and your suit. This is as close as we can get and there's only one way into Low City from here," Lark said as he shimmied into his chair.

Luka squeezed the pistol grip until his knuckles turned white. For a moment, he considered raising his aim again.

That path led nowhere.

He exhaled and slid the pistol back into its holster.

He turned his attention to the dry bag at his feet and started shoving his gear into it. It wasn't much: boots, socks, and a lot of ammo for the machine pistol.

He stripped off his desert clothing and grabbed the combat suit from a shelf beside him. He slid his legs into it first and then fed his arms in and shrugged it up over his shoulders. It had the texture of jersey cotton and at first it hung from his body. When he held still, it began to shrink and form to him. It encased him and turned stiff like neoprene. He took the suit's hood and slid it on too. It left a wide oval around his eyes open and had slits for his nose and mouth. When he rolled it down, the neckline of the hood formed a seamless stitch to the rest of the suit.

Lark brought the submarine up to the surface. It hummed as the ballast pumps forced water back into the ocean. When it breached, the craft swayed as waves lolled it from side to side. Luka grabbed his pack and made for the ladder to the exit. A blast of cold ocean air spread through the submarine as the hatch opened. Luka's suit adjusted. Warmth spread through his back and into his limbs. With his dry bag secured to his body, he climbed the ladder and hauled himself through the hatch.

Outside, the wind howled and threw spray into the air. Oil-rich water coated the submarine's exposed hull. Its bulk shined in the night like an old black whale. Across the water, waves tore through the remnants of Old Seattle. They threw up white-tipped spires of ocean where water met rock and metal. Behind them, the lights of Low City cast color into the clouds overhead. They hovered over Low City like bright nebulae in deep space.

He dove into the water, sliding beneath the surface and rising back up in a smooth arc. He began to swim. The suit seemed to brace his whole body. Although his ribs were bruised, he barely felt them. His strokes were smooth and even, despite the rough ocean. He had no more experience swimming now than a few weeks ago, but something bigger had changed in him since the desert. His body felt coordinated and sturdy in a way it never had.

It was a longer swim on this trip. He charged through the first kilometer, but he hit a wall of exertion thereafter. Suddenly, he was breathing hard and struggling to make forward progress against a current. He stroked forward and kicked hard, but waves crashed down on him and pushed him back out into the bay. He was losing a meter for every two he gained. The suit helped to keep his mouth and nose free of water, but there was still a constant threat of drowning. His form broke. He flailed. And then a wave crowned at just the right moment to throw him into the grimy facade of some wrecked tower. The impact knocked the wind out of him. He gasped and aspirated ocean water. The receding wave pulled him back into open water and a wave slammed him into the wall a second time. He coughed and hacked as he tried to get his lungs clear so he could get a clean breath back in.

The receding wave tried to pull out him out and throw him once more, but this time Luka dove under the wave as it rolled overhead. He kicked hard underwater—and though his lungs burned and his body convulsed in protest—he kept swimming forward until he got free of the maelstrom. When he broke the surface, he took in heaving bouts of air.

The current was gentler on the other side of the tower. Waves crashed hard against its outer surface and lost their energy there. They rolled by and lapped up against the broken interior structures of the old city around him. Luka floated for a while, kicking only enough to stay buoyant while he saved up energy. After several minutes of coughing fits and bouts of hyperventilating, his breathing settled. There was a half-kilometer to go before the water receded to a walkable depth. From there, the shallows went on for another kilometer and formed an urban swamp. A few blocks beyond that he would hit the outskirts of LCG territory, near where he entered Low City on his first go.

He took a deep breath and set off swimming again. With his heart rate settled, his form returned. He glided through the black, and increasingly viscous, water.

He stopped to catch his breath again, and when he turned upright to tread water, he realized the bottom was underfoot. He stood. The water was barely thigh-deep.

He scratched at the neckline of his hood, where the seam had been when he first slipped it on, and a small gap formed. He dug his fingers into it like he was searching for the lost edge of packaging tape. The seam widened and he pulled the wet garment free from his head. He ran his fingers through his hair and realized how long it had been since he last bothered with a haircut—or any grooming at all. Sweat soaked strands clung to the sides of his face and hung below his jawline. He threw the hood aside and trudged on through the thick water, skidding and sloshing as he went.

Within a few minutes of walking, the depth waned to a few centimeters. It splashed underfoot and echoed off the concrete surrounding him. The graffiti started to appear. There was not much light, but the orange and pink lines caught is his eyes. They were sloppy cursive symbols and letters: tags—the most base means of marking territory. Ahead, the street rose out of the water and offered the first glimpse of dry—*well, semi-dry*—land.

An apartment building on the left side of the street had slumped into one at the right, and a large street sign hung between them. It outlined the crooked entrance to a tunnel. An elaborate tableau surrounded this gateway. Images of a

Low City style *Dante's Inferno* surrounded him. Its 2D inhabitants were all busy perpetrating some awful act on someone else or having something awful done to them, or were otherwise occupied with doing something nasty to themselves. Unlike paintings of *Dante's Inferno*, however, no demons were tormenting these people. In this scene, the people were the demons.

Luka passed beneath it and moved into the dark corridor beyond the painting. The interior of the tunnel was totally black. It was not only void of light, but painted black too. Luka ducked into a corner and retrieved his socks and boots from his dry-bag, slipped them on, and then fitted the rest of supplies, mostly ammo, into the pockets of combat suit. He kept the pistol in his chest holster, plainly visible, per Lark's advice. He left the dry-bag behind and moved deeper into the dark, taking cautious steps as he went.

Ahead, small inverted crosses lined every centimeter of the walls and the broken scaffolding overhead. They glowed like white chalk lines against dark asphalt. They disturbed his depth perception and made his peripherals go wild with false movement. The disorientating nature of the space and gave it a worryingly powerful funhouse vibe. He waited, vigilant for the punchline.

Then he hit a dead end.

The walls to his left and right gradually funneled him into a single point: a door-sized space, blocked by a sheet of brushed aluminum. He pressed his hand against the walls to his left and right to test them. They were solid, formed of slabs of exterior facades. Luka set a boot against the metal blocking his path ahead and pushed. It gave a little. He pushed harder and it gave a little more. He leaned his full body weight into and it suddenly gave. He tumbled forward through the opening.

He scrambled to back to his feet and clutched the pistol at his chest.

A wide, sloping street of Old Seattle opened in front of him. Glowing yellow orbs of street lights lined the road, and above their thick steel posts, stood moldy-white buildings on both sides. Their empty windows swallowed light like hungry black mouths. The street rose upward and curved left into the distance. Far ahead, someone ran across it. He watched their silhouette pass in front of a light and then disappeared again into the dark void at the side of the street.

He looked down and realized he was standing on a large sheet of aluminum that had once been a street sign. When he stepped off onto and the metal sheeting snapped shut behind him. Powerful hydraulics hissed and it locked.

He started up the hill. As he walked, he became aware of people watching him from the shadows of the buildings that lined the street. They shied away from the glow of the street lamps but the whites of their eyes shined in the blackness. There was only enough light to get a vague impression of their faces but there were a lot of them and there were all sorts too: young, old, woman, man, tall, short. They shared one trait in common, though. They were all skinny, and not the fit-skinny that many aspired to be. They were gaunt in the way that only addicts or starving people could be. From their nervous glances and twitchy movements, they seemed to be as wary of him as he was of them. He kept walking. The grade became steep. He stopped to catch his breath and turned to look behind him. In the distance, he could no longer see the door he had passed through.

When he looked forward again, three men were blocking the path ahead. They looked different from the people hiding in the shadows. They were clean, and portly, compared to the watchers. These men were tall and broad-shouldered. They did not openly display any weapons, but from their imposing stances, Luka doubted they were unarmed. They eyed him and he eyed them back. His hand rose to his chest and hovered over the grip of his machine pistol.

They stood shoulder to shoulder to form a barricade, and as he neared, they crossed their arms over their chests.

A strange, new thought hit his brain when he saw this. It was sharp and crystalline and it spread before he could reason with it.

He pulled his pistol on instinct alone and started emptying a clip in their direction. It was such an abrupt and savage act that no one involved, Luka included, expected it to happen. They were standing lock-kneed with their arms tight across their chest. They had no hope of returning fire, or even diving out of the way, before he hit them. His pistol hummed like a fine engine as he swung his aim across them and they collapsed. He mowed them down like a scythe through brittle grass and he tucked the pistol back into its holster, all without breaking step.

Blood was running into the street from beneath them. It crawled down the hill and collected into little inky pools where the asphalt slumped. They were dead, all three. He did not even bother to look at their bodies as he stepped over them. That icy, crystalline thought urged him forward without concern for his action, and he obeyed. His peripherals, meanwhile, surveilled the dark fields at his left and right. The watchers were there still. He caught glimpses of their faces as they passed beneath street lights while they followed. It might have been the adrenaline in his system, but he thought they looked happier, less anxious or less broken, now that those three men were dead. That sharp part of his mind smiled at this and it spread to his face.

The street eventually leveled out, and the neighborhood it opened to, was where military drone tracked him on his first visit. The impact of explosives had shattered two walls on the building to his right. Below, the wrecked frame of the drone blocked the street. The battery had gone critical and melted its body into the street so it was now a permanent fixture. The carbon armor had been stripped from its skeleton the way carrion birds ripped meat from a carcass. Panels of it clung to frame in the most difficult to reach areas. The electronics had burned away from the inside, leaving only black goop.

Luka tugged at the combat suit between his shoulder blades and a hood pulled loose from what appeared to be seamless fabric. He lifted it over his head, shading his face, and side-stepped around the drone as he went.

He passed the alley where he was mugged. Part of him wondered what became of that man's body, part of him wanted to check, but he already knew it had been stripped and thrown to the ocean. Bodies were a problem here. He knew this now, from the added memories of his biochip. The victims of time, murder, and accidents alike were thrown out into the rough water. Often, they washed back in with the rising tide and became stuck in the swamps and tide-pools of Low City. Locals called them *turtles* for the way their bloated stomachs bobbed above the waterline like the backs of turtles in a pond. Despite the warmth of his suit, Luka shivered.

Viktoria's building was up ahead on the right. He approached the main door, although his biochip already alerted him to the folly of it. The door's surface was a slab of black polymer-glass and there was no response to him. Its biometric readers knew the scents and habits of its tenants. For Viktoria, these doors would simply open as she neared. It knew the biometrics of its tenant's associated persons too. From its algorithms, the doors knew which people had close associations and could be let in without host approval. It knew which were casual associations and required approval. It knew which to turn away with prejudice. Luka had no record with building, so the doors were as quiescent as stone to him.

He back-stepped away from the door and lifted his hood so that he could look upward at the building. He pictured the cat in the window from his memory. He tried to reconstruct which unit was hers.

Then, suddenly, that memory did not matter. It slipped out of focus and he could not pull it forward again. At the same time, he also came to know, with certainty, which unit was hers. He also knew, if he was to enter her building, precisely which front door was hers. In his memory, he had been inside her building twice, but never beyond her door.

Luka looked up and scanned the building. Her windows were dark. He frowned, pulled his hood back up over his head, and began retracing his steps to BLVCKLANE. The shop was the only other connection he had to Viktoria—from either his real memories or his implanted ones. He doubted she would be there, but the staff knew her. They might have a guess where to go next. The thought of asking them hard questions about her whereabouts gave him pause, but there was no other path forward.

As he walked through Low City, Luka's eyes searched the buildings to his left and right. That new, icy part of his brain was hyper-vigilant and he could satiate it only by watching for movement in the pulsing LED's that outlined buildings and glowed along the edges of the streets. As he progressed, the sloppy tag-style graffiti waned and intricate murals sporting unsettlingly violent subject matters replaced them. To his right, a stenciled image of a little girl huddled against a wall bathed in the white glow of a street sign overhead. She held a red balloon in one hand, and a severed head in the other. Her posture said she was afraid, but a fiendish smile curled

271

the corners of her mouth. A gaping howl twisted the disembodied face hanging from her arm. Above her, in neat blood-red block letters, it said *Get Higher.* That phrase appeared in many of the murals around this neighborhood. It was a marking for LCG territory—but it was something more too. It was an ideology he was beginning to understand as his new memories mixed with old ones. It was like Lark escaping the prison where they grew him and killing everyone in his path up to the surface. It was like Luka leaving the military and finding Emma. It was like Michael always trying to lift him out of his depression, to keep him on the mission. It was like the human race trying to find life on Europa. It was the violent hope of leaving the place where you were born.

BLVCKLANE looked the same now as it did in both sets of memory. Its dive-bar storefront glowed in cheap neon red at the end of the street ahead. A group of people on a nearby corner sized him up as he approached. They looked like average inhabitants—which meant they looked alien to him. Even with his new memories, everyone in Low City was strange. They were shadows, dressed all in black—tall, short, stocky, gaunt, pretty, ugly, clean, and heavily armed shadows. Their physical forms varied, but their culture, their look, was homogenous. In their dark clothing, accentuated by pulsing LED's and occult symbols, they looked more like insects than human beings.

As he got closer, he saw that this group at the corner was, perhaps, more threatening than most. Their clothes were more tactical, with carbon armor places in combat-minded places. Symbols ran down the sleeves of their arms in neat lines of chalky white. He recognized one in particular. It was a dagger piercing through a crescent moon that faced upward like an open cup. This marked them as LCG members. The other symbols might have denoted their rank or function within the gang, but he had no knowledge of it. They carried heavy revolvers at their hips. The pistols were an old caliber.

His biochip memory said it was .44 size and that its scarcity meant they reloaded any spent brass themselves. They would not be eager to shoot unless they sensed an easy payday or an imminent threat.

Their heads turned and they watched him as he passed, but the threat implied by his clothing, and especially the machine pistol at his chest, proved to be as effective of a deterrent as Lark promised. It was an exotic and superior weapon, and they knew this. Even between the four of them, this one firearm outgunned them. They eyed him edaciously, but they kept their distance.

Years of cigarette butts stamped out in the entryway of BLVCKLANE had stained the concrete a grimy brown-black. It repelled water and the sheen of mist resting on it made it slick beneath his feet. Luka yanked on the handle on the door and slid backward as it opened. He regained his footing and stomped through the doorway. An unsteady yellow-white light bathed the dingy room on the other side. It was dim and hazy and the fluorescent lighting cast the faces staring back at him in harsh relief. It showed every pock-mark and flaw in their skin. They looked half dead.

Nearest the door was the same man he spoke with on his first visit. He was wearing the same clothing too by the look, and the smell of it. Even over the stench of cigarettes, the sting of body odor curled Luka's nose. The man recognized Luka. Luka watched the reaction evolve in the man's face. It started with shock, his eyes widening, and then moved to amusement as a feeble grin formed beneath his unkempt beard.

"Not often that a gutter mouse like you walks through our doors twice. I gave you a lump of metal instead of a gun and I figured you for dead," said the man. He shrugged and tilted his head to a shoulder.

273

"Who says I'm not dead, come back to haunt you," replied Luka.

Humph, the man snorted. He leaned back in his stool and shook his index finger at the gun holstered at Luka's chest. "In my experience, dead men don't carry pieces like that."

There were four other people in the store: three women and one man. They were watching him, and one of the women stepped closer when she heard him speak. She flattened her brow and narrowed her eyes. She had a gun of some kind holstered on her right hip. He could only make out a sliver of the grip, but it looked like a semi-auto or machine pistol rather than a revolver. She wore tight-fitting black leggings with bright silver buckles at mid-thigh on both sides. She had a blade buckled to her leg opposite the pistol. On top, she wore a cropped black jacket. It was reminiscent of a leather moto jacket, but it sported heavy carbon-armor plates over the arms and chest. A glowing blue tattoo beneath her left eye marked her as LCG. It was a triangle with a crescent moon inside and a thin line passing through both. His biochip memory knew understood this one. It marked her as a descendant of a founding member.

The man looked over his shoulder at them and shook his head. The woman's body eased and she fell back into a conversation with her friends.

The man turned his gaze back to Luka. "What do you want?"

"To pay a debt," answered Luka.

"You don't owe me little mouse. I fucked you. Those drugs were worth ten times what I gave you."

"I didn't mean you."

The man combed his fingers through the wild hair in his beard.

"Her?" he asked with his face twisted.

"Yeah. Lady Luck," answered Luka.

"Not to kill her?" the man pressed.

"No. It's not that kind of debt."

The man nodded and looked down at his feet. He hacked and drew up something viscous from deep within his lungs and spat on the floor beside his boot.

"Alright, little mouse, but I do nothing for free. That's not how I built this fine establishment. No freebies."

Luka narrowed his eyes. "You're not getting my gun."

"Don't be so sure," the man said.

Luka wrapped his hand around the grip of his pistol as he spoke, "I could kill all of you before you draw. We all know that I could. I'll pay you, sure, but you're not getting the gun."

It was a bolder statement than he would like to make, but his new memories of Low City said that a threat would be better received than negotiation. They respected power.

The man smiled again, and this time it was wide enough to distort his shaggy beard and pull it up at the corners of his face. "I guess you are a rat now, not a mouse anymore."

The man scratched at the stringy mane of hair on his chin. "I'll tell you how to get in contact with her if you help me with something."

275

"It has to be something quick."

The man continued stroking his beard. "It will be. If you are hard as you act."

"What is it then?"

"Debt collection. The fun kind," answered the man.

"Shocking," replied Luka as he he pushed his eyes to one side. "Who am I looking for?"

"His name is Richard, but no one knows him as that. He prefers Ricard."

The man brushed two fingers down the inside of his left forearm. A photo of Ricard appeared in the wake of the gesture. It zoomed in on Ricard's face when Luka focused on it. The man in the photo had hair so blonde it looked white against his black clothing. It fell in a frizzy clump to one side of his face. He was androgynous, with delicate cheekbones, but a strong jaw. He was almost pretty, but he also had that gauntness that only addicts did.

"Don't be fooled by his looks. This little grat will do you nasty."

The man paused and spat something murky onto the floor again. "And he'll be hard to pin down too."

"Okay, and what I am I supposed to collect from him?" asked Luka.

"His eyes."

With some effort, Luka kept his expression flat. "So I'm killing him then."

"Not necessarily. He might survive it if you're clean enough about it."

Luka studied the picture more, honing in on Ricard's face again. He saw it then—the hollow space behind Ricard's pupils and the faint mechanical line around his irises. His eyes were synthetic, and they looked to be high-end ones from the quality of the iris.

"And why you can't you manage this yourself?" asked Luka as he memorized Ricard's face.

The man grunted so hard his gut shook. The stool groaned beneath him. "He'd know if I got within a hundred meters of him. The same for any of our crew. You, on the other hand, you are an outsider. He won't see you coming and, well, you just might be his type."

Luka narrowed his eyes.

"Relax. Not like that—well maybe like that too—but I meant you're from up high and you have a perfectly good set of organs in you," added the man.

"You may have guessed that I'm new to this sort of thing, so tell me, how does a one usually go about this?" asked Luka.

"Lucky for you, I have everything you need."

The man stood and disappeared into a back room. Drawers screeched open and clanked shut and he returned soon after.

"This," said the man as he held out a smooth black ring, "is to drug him. The inside surface of the ring secretes an antidote to the sedative. The outside surface will use microderms to inject any skin it comes in contact with. It should put him out in ten or fifteen seconds after contact. Tap the ring three times to activate the sedative."

The man set the ring down on the counter in front of him. Luka grabbed it between his thumb and finger with his left hand and slipped it over his right-hand ring finger. Then he set a small carbon-case on the counter in its place. He snapped the lid back to reveal a hand-held metal tool. It was made of titanium-steel, or some other surgical looking alloy, but its high-tech construction could not hide that it looked rather like an ice-cream scoop.

"And this is to extract," said the man.

He closed the lid of the case and pushed it over to Luka. Luka collected it and tucked it beneath his arm.

"Where do I find him?"

"Dead Man's Hand."

The blood drained from Luka's face. It went beyond luck or coincidence. His path here was somehow pre-determined. He felt it, but he could not connect it. BLVCKLANE existed in the memories Lark gave him. *Did Lark want him to think of this place, to come here?*

"What, you been there before?" The man raised an eyebrow and coughed.

Luka snapped out of his thoughts and shook his head. "No, but I was headed there anyway. Lucky, I guess. "

"Maybe there is some hope for you," said the man.

Luka took the case from beneath his arm and put it into a pocket on his suit. He back-stepped to the door, found the handle, and made his exit. The night air was damp and cold. He took in a deep breath. It soothed his lungs after being in the cigarette-laden air of BLVCKLANE.

The same LCG members were waiting on the corner. Two of them had their backs turned as he moved on to the street, but one nudged the other, and soon they all turned and stood shoulder to shoulder to watch him. It was cold out, and getting colder, but the one standing nearest him wore stupid-looking three-quarter length pants. The strip of pale skin showing between his ankles and calves glared like reflective tape in the light of a nearby streetlamp. His mouth was flat and the muscles in his neck were rigid. He seemed keen to challenge the default authority of Luka's weapon.

The ice spread in Luka's mind again. The cold, sharp feeling welled behind his eyes and hate rose in him with it. His hand twitched and he grabbed the grip of his pistol. He stopped short of drawing it. He hesitated.

It was too late. He already set the conflict in motion. The LCG member with the stupid pants raised his revolver and aimed at Luka. The others behind the man were reaching for their weapons too. Time slowed.

The hammer went back on the man's revolver and then it snapped forward. Luka dove to his left and rolled over his shoulder. A bullet hissed and slapped the ground behind him. Luka drew his pistol, took a side stance, and squeezed the trigger. It hummed delicately in his palm and bullets poured from the barrel. Several rounds struck the man in the chest, but he did not fall. The hammer on his revolver swung back and snapped forward again. Luka watched the fire build and burst out from the barrel, but could not react in time. The revolver found its target. A heavy bullet struck Luka in the shoulder and rocked him back. The bullet ricocheted off him and his combat suit radiated the force through his whole body. The vibrations were uncomfortable, like an electric shock, and it stung in the immediate area of the strike, but he was unharmed. Several more shots rang out and left stinging welts on his abdomen. Luka swept the aim of his pistol across the group. The other men did not have armor. They fell on the first pass.

His adversary recognized that anything less than a headshot would not put Luka down and adopted a two-handed grip for improved aim. Fire rang out and a bullet whooshed by Luka's ear. He mirrored the man's stance, cupping his right hand with his left, and turned his body front on while he aimed. He tapped the trigger twice. He found his target. Two bullets struck the man's forehead and blood and brain matter painted the wall behind him. The man crumpled on to the pavement. He was dead before he fell.

Two of the other men were not yet dead. They clutched their torsos where blood poured out and cursed at Luka as he stepped over them. He thought about killing them, but he saw that their pistols were out of reach, and he did not want to waste ammunition. Something in his mind told him they would not last more than a couple of minutes.

He grabbed the body of their leader by an ankle and started dragging him toward BLVCKLANE. It left a trail of blood and skull fragments in its wake.

Luka opened the door to BVLCKLANE and dragged the dead body inside. The burly man was still sitting on the stool at the front counter. His eyes doubled at the sight.

Luka dropped the man's leg with a thud.

"Is this one yours?" yelled Luka, his chest heaving.

The others in the room snapped their heads around in the direction of the commotion. There was a small delay of shock, then they drew their weapons and aimed at Luka.

"Do you want to die too?" Luka shouted as he waved his pistol in their direction.

They kept their aim, but he saw their conviction whither. Their shoulders rounded and their fingers eased away from their triggers. The man at the counter regained his composure and resumed his stoned demeanor. He folded his arms across his chest and leaned back in his seat.

"He's not ours," he said as he he nodded to the street. "They stand out there and keep a check on us. All I care is their buddies don't bring the war thinking it was me and they'll know it wasn't from the bullets they pull out the bodies."

The man was staring at the body. For a moment, Luka thought it was regret or sadness driving the man's fixation. Then, he understood the deeper motive. *Welcome to Low City*, he thought to himself.

"You want his gear?" asked Luka.

"Hell yes," answered the man.

"It's yours if you drop this errand and just tell me where to find her."

The man scrunched his mouth to one side while considered.

"Fine. We'll call it square. Viktoria is at Dead Man's Hand right now anyway. I sent her on the same errand I sent you. I figured it was kind of poetic. That and it doubled my odds."

He chuckled to himself before continuing, "Keep the ring and the extractor. Help her or leave them with her. Your choice."

Luka turned his back, preparing to leave. He was about to open the door when the man spoke again, "You know, you remind me of someone I used to see around here from time to time. He was the only other person I ever saw carry gear like that."

Luka looked over his shoulder. The man pointed his finger at the pistol in Luka's hand and the suit protecting his body.

He shuddered. He knew exactly who the man was referring to. Now he had confirmation that his new memories of Low City were Lark's own.

Luka turned away and left.

Chapter Twelve

He left the building and immediately the gore of his actions met him. In the heat of it, with adrenaline rushing through him and his pulse throbbing in his ears, he did not stop to consider a parley. He only reacted. They threatened him, so they died. It was an equation that he solved, nothing more. Now, staring at the bodies, the growing lake of blood around them, and the trail of carnage leading through the street, his own instincts dispossessed him. That cold sensation that drove him to such extreme action was painfully truant. He had to process the chaos alone. Bile rose in his esophagus and burned his throat. The pavement pulled beneath his feet. His shoulders slumped. He fell to knees and ejected the watery contents of an empty stomach.

He took his pistol from its holster and pressed the barrel into the hollow beneath his chin. He closed his eyes. He inhaled deep and slow and thought that it was time to let the violence of Low City swallow him back.

But something piqued his ears.

His eyes opened.

Voices echoed down the street, no more than two blocks away. They had that distinctive clipped sound of Low City natives.

"Up here, next corner," the loudest voice announced.

He lowered the pistol and looked around him. The trail of blood leading straight to BLVCKLANE would mean trouble for the owner and others inside, but he guessed they could handle themselves. He didn't owe them anything more than they gave him.

Luka swallowed hard, trying to clear the bile from his mouth. He climbed to his feet. He heard their footsteps. They were about to round the corner. He looked over his shoulder at the empty street in the opposite direction while he holstered the gun. Then he ran.

He needed to cover two kilometers as the crow flies. In the confused street patterns of Low City, that distance stretched to three. He ran flat out, panting to get enough oxygen to his legs. After the first kilometer, he slowed to a jog and tried to recover his breath while he moved. He was settling into a walk, a half kilometer after that when the rapid pop of semi-automatic firearms sounded in the distance behind. The *thwump* of a heavy-caliber weapon punctuated the firefight. He picked up his pace again.

Luka kept running until the buildings changed. Only when the exteriors became clean glass facades and the graffiti disappeared entirely, did he slow. Here, the people walking the streets looked ill-prepared for actual combat. Their clothing had tactical aesthetics, but with diminished functionality. There was no armor, except where it looked good to have it, and they brandished weapons in ways that made them appealing to the eye, but difficult to access. It was an imitation of the harder life in Low City's flooded districts.

He settled into a brisk walk.

Two women ahead of him heard his approaching footfall and glanced nervously over their shoulders. They paused and eyed him with a mixture of apprehension and interest. One was wearing a mixture of carbon-blacks and muted earth-tones. She sported the LCG moon and dagger on the back of her forest-green jacket and had white LED tracing a line from her left ear, along her jawline, and down the center of her throat. Curiously, the other woman was wearing a combat suit that looked similar to his, except that it was a pristine white. She had no gang insignia on her clothing or accent lighting on her body, which also was odd. Her eyes glowed a gentle phosphorescent blue as she watched him, luring him closer like an Angler fish in the Marianas black.

The tension in their bodies suggested that either assumed he would attack them, or they intended to attack him. Luka slowed as he closed the distance between them. He held his right hand up at his side with his palm facing out. His biochip memory held little on the subject of Kinesics in Low City, but he assumed it was enough of a universal gesture to signal that he did not intend to attack.

They were talking to each other. Their lips moved rapidly, but they hushed their voices. He thought he made out the words 'he can't run' in the whispered exchange.

Or did they say 'we can't run?'

They turned to face him.

A voice in the back of his mind warned him they were stalling for backup to arrive. One of the two was LCG for certain. If the people at BLVCKLANE had the opportunity to explain the deaths outside of their shop, then LCG might be on the watch for him. These two could be waiting on a heavy payday.

Without thought, his hand began to float to his pistol.

It caused a chain reaction. The woman in black reached for her pistol too, only he was faster and had a head start. He pulled and trained the sight of his pistol on her before she could even grip hers. He grinned and the icy thoughts bristled behind his eyes. It was an ugly, self-satisfied smile and he imagined himself looking quite a bit like Lark in that moment. He swallowed hard.

He was watching the woman in black so intently that he forgot about her friend. His smile dropped. The woman in white was aiming a large weapon at him. It was gun-like in the way she brandished it but the barrel was wide and rectangular and extended from the bottom of the handle rather than the top. Luka was not sure what it would do if she pulled the trigger—if there was a trigger—but it looked threatening enough that he did not want to find out. Maybe that was the point.

"This is neutral turf!" shouted the woman in black.

"You can't do this here!" she added.

Her voice was firm and she stood strong, with her shoulders squared, but her hands shook.

"Then tell your friend to drop her aim," said Luka.

She did not react. The woman in white was as immovable as a mountain on a far horizon.

The woman in black tilted her head and narrowed her eyes at him. "Wait, you're not Drowned, are you?"

Her accent came through more now that she was not yelling. It was smooth, more High City, more educated. Not typical of LCG.

"No," answered Luka as he shifted his feet and stabilized his aim.

She looked at the ground, deep in thought, and seemed to forget the weapon aimed at her for the time being.

Then she met his eyes. "Okay, what are you?"

Luka opened his mouth to answer, but the woman in white cut in before he could. "I know him," she said. Her cold voice pierced through the tensed air, "He's one of Constellation crew. He's that one that went crazy. The one that attacked that military base down south."

These words hit the woman in black like a heavy perfume. They were a pheromone making her wild. Her nostrils flared as she went mutinous at the scent of opportunity.

In a blink, she drew her pistol and had it aimed at him. Now, her hands were steady. She seemed taller, too, and a sneer curled her lips.

"What, did you come down here to play cowboy with us indians?" she hissed.

He should have pulled his trigger minutes ago, before they started talking. She guessed correctly that he was not prepared to do that and his hesitation cost him. Now there were two weapons trained on him and he had no advantages he could leverage. Down here, the most aggressive, the most biased to action, lived the longest. He made the mistake of using words instead. Now he hoped she would make the same mistake.

"I'm not one of them any more than you are," said Luka.

She scoffed at this, but he continued, "We both know you weren't born down here either. You can cut the nativist act."

She huffed at this and spat on the ground for emphasis— but it resonated with her on some level. She would not meet his eyes now that he called her out. More importantly, she seemed less ready to pull the trigger. Her aim had eased down a few centimeters and her finger was outside the trigger guard.

Luka's aim, however, did not ease. His finger did not drift away from the trigger. He squeezed and three bullets struck her in the torso. He was not sure if they penetrated her armor so he squeezed again and two struck in her in the face.

He dove to his left and rolled.

A blast went off from the woman in white's strange weapon. It was like a shotgun, but with a flat horizontal blast range. Flaming magnesium pellets erupted in a wide arc in his direction. The tail of it caught him. Several struck him as he tumbled and pain flared in his ribs. They burned as they ate through his suit.

He returned a few wild bursts of fire in her direction, but she took cover behind a low concrete wall before any of his bullets could find their target.

Luka went prone and took cover behind a bit of rubbish in the street. It was not solid cover, but it blocked her line of sight.

"LET'S MAKE A DEAL," she yelled. It echoed off the surrounding walls.

"NO WAY. I KILLED YOUR FRIEND," Luka yelled back.

She shouted the words between heavy breaths, "NOT A FRIEND. JUST BUSINESS. LET'S NOT MAKE THIS HARD."

Luka bit his lip. No matter what the proposal, it was a bad idea. He sucked in a deep breath.

"OKAY. WHATS THE OFFER?"

"WE CALL IT EVEN. YOU RUN NORTH. I RUN SOUTH."

"THAT'S IT," she added.

It was worse than a bad idea. She would kill him the second he turned his back, and even if she did not, it meant leaving her alive. She knew who he was and she knew generally where he meant to go. A loose end like that would prove lethal later.

She was too fast, though. And she had a better position. And his suit would not protect him from the magnesium rounds in her gun. He would not survive a head-on shootout with her. His options were bad or worse.

"OKAY." His voice rang into the hollow corridor of buildings behind her.

He waited. His breathing became rapid and shallow.

"ON THREE," she said.

"ONE..."

"TWO..."

Luka scrambled to his feet and took off northward, moving directly into the cover of a colonnade that supported the upper structure of a nearby building. They were ornate Corinthian columns. It had once been an elegant building, but cracks riddled its facade now. Moss grew from the windows sills and draped down in long trails. He weaved through the columns to make himself a harder target as he ran. He expected more magnesium shot to sting his back, but it did not. To his surprise, there was no shot behind him at all. He did not slow to look back and see why.

When he broke free of the columns, he sprinted through the open street to the nearest intersection. He rounded a corner, and another, and with several buildings between him and the woman in white, he eased back to a jog. As the glow of the Light District loomed closer, the streets became more populated. People started to take notice of him. Their bodies turned and their eyes followed him as he darted between groups and sifted his way forward. Faces stared down at him from windows in the apartments above. Drones circled overhead. They kept a high altitude so he could not see them in the night's blackness, but he sensed them following him by the chaotic whine of their engines.

His destination was two blocks ahead when he slowed to a walk. His chest heaved as he gulped in air to satiate his body and his lunged burned from the exertion. While he walked, he patted a hand on his ribs where the magnesium shot ripped through his suit. He winced as his fingers made contact. He withdrew them and studied the result. There wasn't much blood—the burning pellets cauterized most of the wound as they cut—but it was seeping a sticky, clear fluid that now covered his hand. He wiped the discharge onto his thigh and tried to push the stinging from his mind.

Dead Man's Hand was at the far edge of the Light District—too deep in Low City for most of the High City partygoers. It extended six floors down beneath a spired tower that housed Low City's local government. The black glass exterior the building cut high into the night ahead and traced the shape of a dark obelisk against the Light District's purple and red glow. It was a dangerous place for those who weren't themselves, also dangerous. His biochip told him a sizeable crowd coalesced there most nights, regardless. The entrance was not advertised, but the crowd congregating at the end of a street ahead betrayed its secrecy.

Although he had slowed to casual pace, the drones overhead were taking a focused interest in him. They were swarming. Some of them even dropped low enough for him to glimpse their black bodies zipping down to street level and then rocketing back into the camouflage of the night. Attention from them meant their algorithms had marked him, but for what purpose he did not know. In High City, their programming was strictly peacekeeping. There, running erratically through the streets, or wearing combat gear, were both sufficient reasons for them to mark you and trigger a MilPol advisement. Here, he did not know what level of corruption entered their programming. They may be there for public safety, or something more tuned to the interests of LCG and The Drowned. Whatever the case, he wanted their attention elsewhere. As he came within earshot of the crowd, he moved the pistol from the open-carry holster at his chest to a concealed holster at the small of his back. He lifted his hood and brushed his hair back, exposing his face. In the outskirts, his appearance needed to be a warning. Now, he needed to blend in as much as possible.

Those at the edge of the crowd broke into small sub-circles. They chatted eagerly with friends and people they hoped to take home in the early hours. They stole sideways glances at Luka as he approached. Some let their eyes linger long enough to do an up and down of his body—women and men alike. Although Dead Man's Hand was at the fringes of the Light District's safety, the clothing displayed by this crowd showed color and vulnerability not typical of Low City. People wore blues and purples and slick metallic fabrics. Much of it left little to the imagination, which meant few places to conceal a weapon.

Luke moved easily through the sparser clusters of people at the edge of the crowd, but as he got closer to the entrance, the density increased and he had to squeeze through the small pathways left between groups. As much as he tried, he could not avoid contact with people and someone snatched his forearm as he brushed by.

He pushed ahead, ignoring it, but their grip tightened and they yanked him back so hard that he had to turn and face them. He snarled as he prepared to fight, but seeing his captor, his anger faded.

"Oh, you're an odd one," the woman grasping his forearm said. "Come down from on High have you?" she added.

She let go, but Luka stayed. He stared at her, stupefied.

"You know, people down here don't like you Milly's much. I'd watch your back if I were you."

She smiled at him in a way that was both threatening and enticing.

"I'm not MilPol," he said.

She tilted her head at him provocatively. "Well, you have my attention then. Unfortunately, it looks like you have theirs too."

She pointed up to the sky at the drones. "You know that's bad, don't you?"

He shook his head. "Not for certain. Not until now."

"Stumbled into some trouble recently, have you?" she asked.

292

"It would be more accurate to say I provoked it."

He shuddered at the memory but she smiled wider. The whites of her teeth showed and dimples formed in her cheeks. She had dark eyes and hair like night. Staring at her, he forgot his mission.

The people behind her took notice, though, that she broke away from the group to talk with an out-of-place stranger. He felt the weight of their eyes on him and the burn of their skepticism. He remembered himself. He remembered the danger of the moment.

"I need to keep moving. Someone is expecting me," Luka said.

He turned his body and prepared to walk away but she grabbed his shoulder and pulled him back around to face her.

"And where would you go?" she asked with a sly smile. "You're still trying to work out how to get in, the same as all of us. It's obvious you've never been here before and I'd bet the person you're looking for doesn't have a clue who you are."

She released her grip on his shoulder and patted him on his chest. "If I had to guess, I'd say you're here to kill someone."

She dragged her finger across her throat provocatively and pushed her eyes so far to one side that they went all white.

Luka chewed on his lip. Something in his gut told him that he could not just turn and leave the conversation without consequence. He rubbed his thumb along the sedative ring he received at BLVCKLANE while he considered his options.

"That's not far from the truth," he said as he narrowed his eyes, "and given that, is it wise to be standing in my way?"

His words erased the smile from her face and the look between them rose from an ember to a flame.

"Don't play bad. I know bad," she said.

He squared his shoulders to her and leaned in. "You won't let me leave, so tell me, what is it that you're after?"

"I think we could help each other. That's all," she said.

"How?"

"Well, to start have you noticed that the drones buggered off?"

He looked up and listened. The collective roar of voices made it difficult to hear much else, but he did not see any movement. It seemed they had dispersed.

She waited for him to verify before she spoke again, "You and me talking like this, flirting like this, it normalized you. You're welcome for that."

She might have been bluffing, but he knew too little on the subject to call her on it and she was much too socially adept for him to guess if she was lying.

"Thanks, but I could have dealt with that on my own."

She scoffed. "No you couldn't. I saw you watching them on your way over and I saw how nervous they made you,

294

which means you did not know what to do about them. Did you think you would just walk into this place?"

"Yeah. That's usually how it works."

"What you mean is that's how it usually works up there." She nodded in the direction of High City. "Look at yourself. You're wearing a skinsuit, your ribs are bleeding, and you don't have the right accent. In short, you're not the kind of people they let into Dead Man's."

Her friends behind her sensed the rising tension. They broke their old circle and folded Luka and the woman into a new one.

"Okay, then. How do you propose to help with that? From what you said, you and your friends don't have an in either."

"True, but what I do have is quick hands, and a knack for convincing people—and that ring of yours is quite a handy gadget. Quite an expensive one too."

"This already sounds bad," he said as he shook his head.

"Oh, don't worry. It's simple enough."

"Okay. Explain."

"You hang close to our group, don't talk, and you'll blend in. Give me the ring and I'll do the rest." She put her hands on her hips and shrugged. "See? Easy."

"And why should I trust you at all?" asked Luka.

A warm smile spread across the woman's face and those alluring creases formed at the corners of her mouth again. "Hum. You're not as naïve as you seem."

"And I'm not as harmless either."

She tilted her head again. "Maybe I misjudged you. Time will tell."

"What will you do with the ring?" he asked, cutting in.

"If I explain it to you, it won't work as well. Surprise is everything with these monitoring programs. Hand it over."

She held out an open palm and cocked her weight to one hip.

That urge rose in him again, that alarm, that cold-sharp feeling. It tugged at him from those new regions of memory that spread from Lark's upload. Those new voices whispered that she was lying, that she would kill him the moment he gave her the ring. They urged him to reach behind his back and pull out the pistol and start laying waste to her and her friends. It was plausible, but there were plenty of reasons not to draw too. There was a crowd of at least fifty around. Some of them were armed, and even without weapons, the sheer number would overwhelm him.

"Hello?"

"*Hello?*" she said as she snapped her finger in front of his face to get his attention.

His eyes keyed to the motion and shot back into focus.

"I lost you there," she said, wearing a false smile.

296

"Yeah," Luka answered. He blinked excessively, trying to clear the thoughts and put his mind on the present.

"Everything okay?"

"Yes, I'm fine," he insisted.

Even the trace of a smile from before faded.

"Okay, look, if you give me the ring now, then we can go ahead with the plan and I'll pretend you didn't just go deadeyes on me."

Luka nodded in agreement, but she was looking over her shoulder toward the entrance.

"Wait," he said as he squeezed her wrist to get her attention, "Why do you need to get in so bad?"

Her eyes snapped back to him. "You sure you're not from around here?"

"Very sure. You didn't answer my question."

She swallowed hard and clenched her jaw. He watched the lump in her throat bob up and down, and when he saw the muscles in her neck tightening, he realized she would not say it. And when he realized she would say it, he realized why.

"Fuck," he said as he ran a hand through his hair. "You assumed I'm here to kill someone because that's what you're here to do."

He did not mean to say it so loudly.

She recoiled at the truth and her eyes went wide as shock swept over her. When she recovered her demeanor settled to something he had not seen yet. She wet her lips and traced a finger along her collarbone.

"Do you have someone in your life?" she asked.

He froze.

"No. Not anymore," he managed.

"My name is Maeve," she said as she offered her hand.

He took her palm and shook her hand. "Luka."

She withdrew her hand, letting her fingers linger on his as she looked over her shoulder toward the entrance again.

"I'm not going to explain it—just trust me that I'll be discreet and that it will work."

"Okay." Luka wriggled the ring loose from his finger and held it out for her take, "I believe you."

She plucked the ring from his hand and slid it onto the index finger of her right hand. Then she grabbed his hand with her left and squeezed it gently before she walked away and disappeared into the crowd.

Her friends, if that's what they were, never spoke to him or even attempted it. Instead, they stood beside him and stared at him the entire time like he was an alien and this was first-contact. It made his skin crawl, but he forced it from his mind and looked on in Maeve's direction, waiting for something to happen.

He waited a long time—ten minutes or more—but the crowds began to stir. Their voices picked up and tone changed from excited to panicked. People nearer to the entrance began to collapse. It was just one or two at first, but it grew to thirty or more within a few minutes. Drones swarmed in response to the anomaly. Even over the roar of the crowd, Luka heard the whir of dozens of units overhead. Men began to rush out of the club. They dressed in black and they carried submachine guns, but they did not fire at the drones. Instead, they hauled a large device into the crowd, set it on the ground, and then busied themselves with arming it.

The drones had dropped into a low flight pattern. They were less than a meter overhead of the crowd and everyone was ducking as they whizzed by. When the device the men brought out came online, their flight paths became confused. Some even collided with one another and tumbled to the ground. Chaos erupted in the dead-end street leading to Dead Man's Hand as the drones fell from the sky. Some people fled toward the Light District and others rushed the entrance of the club.

Maeve took cover behind one of the security guards as the crowd broke into full panic. Then she too collapsed, but as she fell, she made direct eye contact with Luka.

He broke into a run in her direction, shoving people aside as he forced his way forward against the fleeing tide.

One of the security guards had scooped her from the ground and now held her in his arms like a rag doll. Luka ran to him.

"What are you doing! Leave her alone," he shouted as he approached.

The man holding Maeve was bewildered. His eyes were wide and darted from side to side as he took in the scene. He was only trying to help, but Luka would make him feel like a rapist for it.

"What the fuck did you do to her!" Luka continued.

"Whoa man. Back off!" the man shouted in return. "I didn't touch her. She was falling and I caught her. That's it."

"Sure, a likely story," Luka said.

"Fuck you man. That's the truth," the bouncer said as his hand migrated to the gun hanging at his hip from a shoulder strap.

Luka put his hands up. "Okay. Easy. I believe you. Can you just help me get her inside, somewhere safe?"

Luka forced his right shoulder beneath Maeve's armpit and lifted her legs with his left arm. He carried her like a groom carrying a bride toward a honeymoon suite.

The man nodded.

"Come on, this way," he said as he broke into a jog toward the entrance.

Luka followed at the man's heels, working hard to keep pace in the chaos of people with the added effort carrying Maeve. She was slight but heavier than he expected. Up close, he saw that well-defined muscles rippled through her arms and legs. He shored up his grip and pulled her in closer to him with a shrug. If she was playing unconscious, it was a convincing act. He began to wonder if she dosed herself.

The club doors opened as the man approached and Luka slipped through after him. On the other side was a narrow hallway with an elevator at the far end. Blood-red leather benches lined both walls and the floor was a smooth black marble surface. Hundreds of faux-incandescent bulbs hung from the ceiling at varying heights and bathed the room in a soft glow. The bouncer rushed toward the elevator doors and Luka followed, panting from exertion. These doors did not form a neat vertical seam like most Luka had used in his life. They disconnected in an ornate geometric pattern like a section of wood flooring yanked apart at the random joints of individual boards. It was like being swallowed by the jaws of a huge machine.

They snapped shut as soon as they passed through and then his stomach lurched as the elevator fell and braked to a stop. The doors snapped open again.

The interior ahead was an inverted copy of the one upstairs. Little pools of light riddled the black floor and deep red lines marked the ceiling. In the distance ahead it opened into a wide, black space obscured by a dark mist. Music throbbed softly in the background.

Luka walked through the elevator doors and set Maeve down on a black bench at the right side of the room. One of her arms dangled over the side of the cushions. He pressed two fingers into her neck at a space just below her jaw. Sweat ran down his face and dripped onto her lips, but she did not even twitch. He waited, motionless. Her pulse was strong and even, but he had to sell it. He pulled his hand away from her and mopped his forehead with his sleeve. Then swept his hair back out of his face.

"Do you have ephedrine?" he asked, forcing a quiver of alarm into his voice.

"What? What is that?" the man asked. His accent was thick with Low City and the leading syllables of words were so clipped that Luka strained to understand him at all.

"Adrenaline. A shot to revive people when their hearts stop. Do you have those?"

"Nah. No. None of those kind here."

"What drugs do you have?"

The bouncer bit his lip and looked around.

Luka cut in, "Synth C. Do you have Synth?"

"Yeah, but it's going to cost you."

"No problem, I can pay," Luka said, shaking his head.

"Money first," the bouncer said as he puffed his chest out.
He was pudgy and it made him look like a bird fluffing itself
against the cold.

Luka pointed down at Maeve's apparently lifeless body.
"Do you want her to die?"

He stood and grabbed the bouncer by the collar of his
jacket and yanked him down to his height so that they were
nose to nose. "Do you want her to die?"

It was a risky move, but the payoff was in the sell.

The bouncer licked his lips and shook his head. "Nah,
nah. Not that. Not to her."

Luka let go of his jacket. "Then go get some and come
straight back. If I can't pay, you can have this."

Luka drew the machine pistol he had concealed at his
back and held it out in front of the bouncer's face so that he
could read the make and model. The man's pupils dilated at
the sight and he disappeared down the hallway, moving at a
near run.

Maeve sat up the moment the bouncer was out of view and gripped Luka's pistol by the barrel, yanking it back down to his side.

She locked eyes with Luka. "Don't."

She pressed the pistol in toward Luka so that the shadow of his body hid it. She held her stare. "Don't ever draw that in here. Their drones, the ones in here, don't call for help. They are the help. They'll kill you before your finger can even graze the trigger. Everyone brings weapons into here but not a single person has ever gotten away with using one—and even if you don't mean to use it, waving it around like this is only begging them to find a reason. If just one of them decides you mean business, all will agree and you're dead. You understand?"

"Yes," said Luka as he quickly returned the pistol to the concealed holster at his back.

"Now what? Should we wait for him?" he asked.

Maeve laughed. "You mean the bouncer? Oh no, definitely not. He'll be upset that we're gone and he'll know that we played him, but he won't tell anyone that we made a fool of him."

"What makes you so sure?"

"I handpicked him. I'm a professional, remember? I knew he'd panic and that he was lonely and that he wanted to rescue a damsel in distress in the distant hope that she'd fall madly in love with him."

She spat on the floor. "Men are the same everywhere. There are only a few kinds."

"And what kind am I?" Luka asked.

She smiled. "Oh, you're my favorite sort."

"And what sort is that?"

"Overeager. Over ambitious."

Luka scratched at the beard forming along his jaw and under his neck. "Why's that your favorite?"

"You want to help and you'll take things further than most. People like you are useful in my line of work."

His hand dropped to his side as a shiver ran through his body. They were looking directly into each other's eyes and for the first time, Luka thought to do more than just admire.

Her eyes looked biological, with that randomness in the irises that machines struggled to reproduce, but he thought he saw a rough edge on her pupil. He watched it shift in the fluctuating light and maybe there was a mechanical character to the movement—nothing he could confirm, only a lingering sense of irregularity. If they were synthetic, they were the best quality he had yet seen. If they were, then she was more than a skilled manipulator, she was socially augmented. Every part of her personality right now could have been chosen to push him into this exact scenario.

He broke the stare between them and turning eyes down to the ground. "Can I ask you a question?"

She reciprocated the break, also looking down at the floor as she spoke, "You can ask but I can't promise any answer you'll like."

"Who is he, the one you have business with here?"

"It's not a *he* that I'm after. It's a *her*. Tell me, Luka, why do men assume anything important must involve other men?"

Luka shook his head. "I don't know. I can't answer that."

"No, I don't think you could. You may be my favorite kind, but you have the same blindness as the rest."

"I don't suppose you'd tell me who you are after?" Luka pressed. He looked up in time to see Maeve narrow her eyes at him.

"Don't suppose I would," she answered.

He frowned. "So, what now then?"

"Now we go our separate ways and pretend not to know one another."

Luka let out a long exhale. "Okay."

"Good."

"Ladies first."

He motioned to the dark mist with an open hand. She stood, did an up and down with her eyes, and planted her hands on her hips.

"And they say gentleman don't exist."

"Good manners don't make a gentleman."

Maeve's mouth curled to one side. "You really are my favorite sort."

She turned and she walked away and her hips swished in a way that seemed impossibly perfect as she disappeared into the blackness of Dead Man's Hand.

Luka stood and made his way toward the club. The pulse of the bass swelled with each step and the hallway grew darker as he progressed down it. The effect was not that of dimming lights, but more like he was stepping into a thick fog—except that this fog was not a mix of grays and whites, it was a heavy soot-black. He had to watch his feet as he took each step and it reached a point where the blackness swallowed him so completely that he could not see the toes of his boots. With one more step, it vanished. He stepped through an invisible curtain into the full force of the club. Flashes of orange, yellow, and golden-amber washed over him. The colors danced in geometric patterns overhead like aurora and the pulse of the bass was so powerful he thought it would stop his heart. He raised a forearm to shield his eyes against the lights while they adjusted to the blinding assault of colors.

The music was oddly down-tempo for a club and the vocals were unsettling pitch-shifted hooks from old songs. The mix of old melodies with harsh new synths was like stepping into a haunted space between the past and future. A powerful bass oscillated through it all and held the unnerving music together.

His eyes began to compensate and now he could see a huge bar circling the far corner of the dance floor. Glowing lights marked its outer borders, but the heart of it was swimming in a black fog like the one he passed through to enter the club. He searched the crowd on the dance floor. Between his own memories and the supplemental memories from Lark's download, he remembered Viktoria's appearance well, but in this environment, he had no chance of spotting her from a vantage. There was no avoiding getting in the thick of it.

A new DJ was taking the stage, preparing for his set, and the music lulled in the interim. The sea of bodies settled. Some sifted out of the crowd and into the black fog surrounding the bar. Others faced the DJ's booth and waited for the music to resume. It looked like the best opportunity he would have to search for her.

It wasn't.

The transition between sets took less than time than he expected, and just as he stepped down into the crowd, the lighting in the club shifted from a gentle glow to a disorienting strobe flash. The faces around him moved in a slideshow of momentary captures. A low bass rumbled through the floor as the new DJ built up to his opening song. The ceiling overhead projected a hologram of a building storm. It swirled in the center like a powerful hurricane and added to the drama of the bass. He ducked and looked up as cracks of electricity streaked overhead. While the circling clouds were an illusion, the lightning was not. An intricate pattern of Tesla coils that hung from the ceiling produced real arcs of high voltage electricity. The song broke into the main beat and people erupted into movement. Some danced solo and just bobbed their heads, but most found a partner—or multiple partners—and grinded on each other in ways that bordered between dance and foreplay. Luka pushed his way through. A few looked annoyed at his intrusion, but most were too focused on the music or too strung out to mind the interruption. He made figure-eights through the floor, scanning faces as we went. He was on his third pass when he caught a glimpse of Ricard, the man whose synth eyes Viktoria was here to collect.

Luka turned on his heels and shoved his way through the crowd, ignoring the angry looks he received, as he followed at the man's heels. Somehow, Ricard slipped through the dance floor with ease while Luka lost ground. He could not anticipate the flow of bodies and people kept stepping his way. Ricard got several steps ahead and vanished into a black fog at the edge of the room. Luka tracked the point where he disappeared and slipped through the fog at the same spot.

Several groups of people sitting in luxurious looking booths stopped their conversations and directed hostile glares at him. Luka froze, realizing he had crossed a threshold he should not have. The people at the booths all displayed gang insignias—LCG, The Drowned, and smaller sets he did not recognize. Ricard, though, was nowhere in sight—and neither was Viktoria. He was backing away slowly, like a person retreating from a bear, when a hand grabbed him by the forearm and yanked him back through the dark cloud.

He turned with his body tensed for a fight, but when he saw his assailant, he dropped his guard. Elise smiled at him. Her teeth and her near-white blonde hair shined in the flashing lights of the club. She pulled him in tight against her body and hugged him ferociously. He stood in shock with his arms slack at his sides.

She stepped back but let a hand linger on his shoulder.

"How did you get in?" Luka asked

Elise rolled her eyes. "Really, that's what you have to say? Well, I walked up to the entrance and then the doors opened and then I rode the elevator down and then I stepped through the fog. How did you think I got in?"

"Sorry. Uh. I meant good to see you. I was just surprised," said Luka.

"I'm a hot woman in a nice dress. I'm exactly the sort of person they want in here. What did you expect?"

"It took a bit more trying for me is all. I guess in the process, I forgot that I should expect to find you here," he answered.

Elise wore an asymmetric gray metallic dress with a high rectangular cutout on the side of her left thigh. A band with a small silver buckle stretched across the bottom of the cutout, holding the dress's shape. It was a perfect blending of High City and Low City aesthetics. She wore her hair down with a clean part along the right and her bangs pinned over the left side of her face by an ornate black clip. It flowed down the sides of her face like flowing streams of mercurial liquid. He remembered that ache he felt the night Elise forced her way into his room and left the copy of Dracula that tipped him off.

But realization punched Luka in the gut and the longing vanished. He swallowed hard.

Her tone softened, "It is good though, to see you I mean. Things have been difficult at DA since you left."

Her words drifted through his ears unacknowledged.

Maeve fit the same part as Elise—attractive, well dressed, and well-spoken. *So why did she have to work so hard to get in when Elise did not?*

Elise reached out and squeezed his hand. He snapped his attention back to her and met her eyes. There was a genuine concern in them—a vulnerability that Luka had never seen in her before.

"So how did you manage to get in here?" she asked.

Luka forced back his alarm, "A hot woman in a nice dress helped me."

Elise shook her head and her mouth went thin. "You are intelligent but too gullible to call smart. This woman doesn't happen to be the one over there in the red dress does she—the one casting daggers at me right now?"

Luka glanced in the direction Elise indicated. Maeve was up by the bar, watching them both like an owl on a perch.

"Yeah, actually, it does," he said.

Elise stepped in close to Luka. They spoke into each other's ears, "Well, I think she's here to kill me."

She kept her eyes on Maeve. "I guess there's no accounting for taste with you."

"She can't attack you in here. The drones will kill her before she can do anything."

"Who told you that?"

Luka sucked his lips in under his teeth.

"Oh okay," Elise said as she pushed her eyes to one side, "She did then."

"Point taken," said Luka.

Elise continued, "But in this case, it's not a total lie. I've been here before and if you mean to kill someone outright, the drones will know it. There are workarounds though. You should know as well as anyone that any system can be beaten."

"That's not good," said Luka.

"What now?" Elise asked.

310

"I came here to pay back a debt I owed to someone."

"You what? You were supposed to be meeting me," she interjected.

"Yes, I know. That too, but I was going to take care of this along the way. I was supposed to help steal someone's eyes— synthetic ones. Valuable."

Elise stepped back and raised an eyebrow at him. "Taking to the local culture, huh?"

"Unfortunately, yes."

"Get to the part with the bad news."

"Well, I was given this ring that secretes a sedative so that we could knock the guy out and take his eyes—and that ring, it turns out, works very well. I gave it Maeve when I was outside of the club so that she could make a scene and get us both in. I think that's her—"

"Her name isn't Maeve," said Elise, cutting in.

"What?"

"That woman," Elise pointed in Maeve's direction, "Her name's not Maeve."

"You know her?"

"No, but I've seen her here before and she was going by Alice then. Anything she told you was bullshit."

Elise took Luka by the hand and pulled him into the fog wall at the edge of the dance the floor. They slipped through, back into the VIP section. Two men approached them as soon as they entered, and they looked ready to kill him and Elise, but she showed them a fluorescent tattoo near her ankle and they backed off.

"We need to find my friend," said Luka as soon as Elise turned her attention back to him.

Elise huffed. "Like hell we do. Look things are bad back at DA. Janus has gone mental. I mean, I know he was screwed up before, but it's different now. The mission may be off. I'm out for good and I'm not sure what that's going to mean for my future. I tried to convince Michael to come with me, but he's not right anymore. They did something to him. He thinks you're a terrorist. Most people do. It's all over the news."

"Michael's still alive?"

His eyes went distant.

"I just told you that nearly everyone believes you are a terrorist, and your first concern is what Michael's been up to?"

Gravity shifted and the floor seemed to tilt. His legs shook and knees nearly buckled as the muscles in back clenched and sent fire through his spine. A void was opening in his mind, and from the other side, a cold wind howled. The veins in his neck bulged as it filled him.

Hunched over, Luka spoke so hard that he spat when the words came out, "I don't care what people believe I am. I did all of this, all of it, because they killed him. Or because I thought they did. Now you're telling that he's back in with the group, same as ever."

Elise avoided eye contact. She bit her lip and shifted her weight from one hip to the other while struggled with what to say. She opened her mouth to speak, but hesitated, and closed it again.

Luka clenched his teeth while he waited until she found the courage to speak.

"He is there, yes, but only in body. It's not him in there anymore. They hollowed him out. They did something to him. I'm so sorry, Luka. Please try to understand how complicated this situation is."

He studied his feet while Elise kept talking, "We can help him after we regroup. Right now, we need to get out of here. That woman is trouble. We can't afford to linger."

She put her hands on his shoulders and helped him stand upright. Pain swept through him as nerves fired and spasms wracked his spine, but the tension was easing.

"I know it's a lot to process, but right now we need to focus on getting out or we are both dead. If we die, there is no one left to help him."

He closed his eyes. His head churned with conflicting emotions. He wanted to rage, but she was sincere and her logic was sound. He breathed in deep and pushed his mind back to the present. The pain faded.

"We find my friend first. If she has things under control, then we can go."

Elise exhaled. "Jesus you are stubborn. Why's it so important that you pay back this debt?"

"Elise, I'm going to be living off-grid for a long time and I need to make some friends if I want to survive. She saved my life the first time I was down here. If I can help her out of a pinch, then I'll have an ally. You need to start thinking like that too."

It was a lie. His nagging urge to close the schism between his real memories and the implanted ones was hardly rational.

She frowned. "I get it, I do, but there will be time for that later, and I can help you when that time comes. I know a few people already. For now, let's link up with your safe house contact and get out of here."

Luka's eyes narrowed. "My what?"

"The guy. The one that's supposed to do the extraction."

Elise tapped the back of her neck where a biochip would sit beneath the skin.

The crease between Luka's eyebrows deepened. "I'm not following. I don't know any *guy*. Like I said, I was just here to meet you and..."

Elise cut him off, "You're supposed to have a contact who will get this biochip out of me and then get us both out of Low City."

"Who you told you that?"

"Our mutual friend," she said.

The blood drained from his face. His skin went cold and beads of sweat formed his forehead.

"Luka, what is it?" asked Elise. Her face was ashen now too. It was the first time he ever saw her show panic.

"Lark told me you had some encryption keys he needed to attack DA. He told me this was just a handoff. There's no escape plan."

Elise was looking down at the ground while chewed on her thumbnail.

"He played us," she said.

Luka's eyes darted from side to side rapidly while he replayed memories and reshuffled his conclusions.

"How did you know that Janus was going to have me killed—that night you warned me?" he asked.

Elise looked up. "Lark told me."

His throat tightened. "Fuck,"

Luka started to pace.

"What? What else are we missing?" asked Elise with her eyes wide.

"How could I be so goddamned stupid," continued Luka as he paced.

"Luka, talk to me," urged Elise.

Luka stopped dead and faced her. "The attack on Michael and I's car after the interview."

Elise's eyebrow arched high, "Yeah?"

"That was Lark. It was him."

She narrowed her eyes, acknowledging that buried in those details, was something important. The full the implication did not sink in, though.

Luka continued, "And Michael disappearing, and you warning me to escape. I just figured it out. There was no plan at Daedalus Astrodynamics to kill me ever. Lark set all of that up so that I would go running to him and help him build his weapon. I don't think he wants only to kill them, I think he wants to take control of the entire company."

Elise shook her head. "Luka's there's no way. I've been working with him for years. I—I would have known."

"Think about it. When our car flipped and Michael and I were about to burn up, some private mercs showed up just in time to rescue us. When I was in Low City the first time, a military drone came after me. Just as it was getting close enough to find me, the repulsor went off and killed it. Who else could do that? He guided me right to him and he's been pushing me at every step. He's either got Janus in his pocket, or he fed him bad info that Michael was dead so that I would stop thinking rationally. Then he got you to tell me that they were going to kill me so that I would run and feel like he was my only option. Then he told me Daedalus Astrodynamics was going to kill the whole NASA crew so that I would help him. It's all been scripted, all by him."

Elise groaned and looked down at the ground. "He's been playing us both for a long time."

Luka nodded. "Us, and I suspect, many more."

Then a new troubling thought entered the mix. His face went slack.

"Elise, how long have you had the biochip?"

"Few weeks. Why?"

"Does Michael have one too?"

"Yeah, I think so. Everyone at the facility does by now I bet."

"Oh my god. How did I not see it," said Luka.

"What?"

"Lark didn't explain the specifics to you, did he?"

"No, but I'm guessing it's bad that I have this chip attached to my brain."

"Yeah. It is. He's going to implant a virus that will overload every chip connected to the network."

Elise's eyes went wide and she shook her head incredulously. "There's no way. I don't know much about that kind of security, but I know their networks are too shielded for something like that to work."

"He's built a new kind of repulser and he's got antimatter to power it. They can't shield against that kind of power. He'll overload the network and inject a virus."

"No way he could pull that off. Antimatter is too dangerous."

"Why do you think he wanted me?" replied Luka.

Her shoulders slumped. "Oh."

"I thought he was only going after the executives. He said the virus was coded to only target certain chips—I think he's going to kill everyone that has DA hardware in them. Not just the higher-ups," Luka continued.

"How long do I have?" asked Elise.

"I don't know exactly. He was missing some equipment he needed for the antimatter reactor. We were in New Mexico yesterday trying to get it. I thought we failed, but I think that was his plan from the start. He said they would try to transfer it and he was going to steal it then."

"Where is he now?"

"I don't know. Probably back down South doing exactly that."

"Say he gets everything he needs, how long until he's ready?"

Luka looked up at the ceiling, mentally tallying. "Without me it'll take him a few days to assemble and tune it. He's smart, but this is specialized work and not the sort of thing you get a second chance at if you mess it up."

He locked eyes with Elise. "You win. I can try to help Viktoria some other time. We need to get out of here now and figure out how we're going stop him."

Elise shook her head. "We can't stop him. We don't even know when he plans to do it. First, we need to get this chip out of me."

"Elise, I'm sorry, but I don't think anyone down here could manage it—and I don't know anyone I would trust enough to try. Aside from that, what about everyone else? I was fine with him killing the people that run the show—they've been up to some awful things—but not everyone there deserves this. And Michael too. I don't care if he's not himself."

A strange pattering sound began to bleed through the sound shielding of the fog. At first, he thought it was something in a transition between songs. Now that it was getting louder, it was clear it was not part of the music. There were pulses of a high-pitched whining like a motor being overdriven. They were answered by slower, heavier cracks.

Then the fog wall dropped. It dispersed like a vapor carried on a strong wind and the scene on the other side was absolute carnage.

Chapter Thirteen

An assault team of a dozen MilPol soldiers was fighting its way through the crowd in a V formation. They forced their way through the flood of bodies like a boulder in a rushing river. People peeled around them or were caught in the forward sweep and trampled underfoot.

The club's security drones hailed down volleys of bullets at MP's. The MP's answered with bursts of heavy armor-piercing rounds. Their rifles chucked loudly and the recoil of the over-loaded shells rocked their bodies with each shot. The drones seemed invulnerable, though, and they made themselves difficult targets by moving in erratic patterns and firing from odd angles.

The bouncers got into the mix too. One was unloading .44 mag rounds at the MP's and ducking behind the bar when they returned fire. One racked a shotgun as he ran by Luka down into the fray. In the chaos, he managed to get close to an MP team and ear-holed one of them with a short-range blast. The MP's helmet withstood shot, but the force of it blew him off of his feet. The bouncer racked another shell and aimed for a killing blown when crossfire from a drone struck him in the back. Blood sprayed and he went down, falling on top of the soldier.

Everywhere in sight, people died. No one checked their line of fire. Bystanders got mowed down by the threes and fours. As he looked on, his adrenaline rose until his heart raced and he was panting with anticipation. A cold clarity welled behind his eyes.

Bullets began to find their way up to the VIP. They cracked around Luka's feet and sparked off the floor. His body snapped into action. He rolled backward and crouched behind the metal frame of one of the VIP booths. His legs tensed as he reached behind his back to draw his pistol.

Elise grabbed his arm. "Don't."

Luka whipped his body around to face her and break her grip, but she clamped down tighter and locked eyes with him.

"You're not a target until that comes out," she said as she nodded to the pistol at his back.

He heard her. He understood her, but searing bile rose from his stomach and his face contorted into a grimace.

The point was to be a target and the desire to fight howled in him. The longer he waited, the more painful it became to hold the pressure behind his eyes back.

But Elise wrenched his arm harder. She locked down until his arm throbbed like her hand was a blood pressure cuff. Her eyes burned with determination—and concern. She held her grip and the cold began to recede from him.

He let out a breath and swallowed the thick acid down.

His voice shook as he spoke, "You lead—but we need to fight our way to the exit somehow."

She let go, but a white imprint of her hand lingered on his forearm where she had gripped.

They both looked out onto the main floor studying the movements of the different factions. The drones were choosing a more cohesive pattern now. They clustered

together and concentrated their fire. The MP's had to break
their formation and find cover where they could, but with the
drones grouped, they could land successive shots on
particular drones and penetrate their armor. A few of the
drones fell under the fire like bees swatted out of a swarm.

"No, we don't," said Elise.

He raised an eyebrow and she continued, "I didn't tell the
truth about how I got in here. There's another way."

Elise crouched low and hurried along the edge of the VIP
section, keeping her eyes on the firefight as she went. Luka
followed at her heels, mimicking her form. He tried to catch
up so he could use his combat suit to shield them both but
she was more agile than him and too focused on her goal to
notice his intent.

Both sides were taking causalities and were in a
momentary stalemate—but more MP's flooded through the
main hallway into the club. They replenished their ranks
faster than they fell. The drones did not.

Elise and Luka circled the edge of the room until they
were behind the main bar. With the black fog gone, he saw its
full form. It was a huge L shaped island with a large cutout at
the corner of the L so that bartenders and hosts could move
in and out. Elise passed through the gap into the inner bar
area and sat, taking cover behind the thick bar counters.

The bouncer that took shots at the MP's earlier from the
bar earlier was slumped over a rack of liquor bottles. He bled
from a wound in his neck and his arms hung at his sides—but
he still clutched his revolver in his right hand. Elise scooted
over toward the man, reached up, and pried the weapon
loose. Rigor mortis had already set in. She broke his fingers
in the process. Elise released the cylinder on the pistol and

checked the loads with a spin. Four casings had dents on the primers. She ripped those loose and let them clatter on the floor while she dug through the man's pockets for extra ammo. She found two more rounds, loaded them in, and swung the cylinder closed. Weapon in hand, she moved to an empty space in the center of the bar area. Then she made an odd gesture with her hand, holding her palm out flat and curling her fingers in one at a time like she was closing a fist in slow motion. Two seams formed in the floor and a set of panels a meter wide and two meters long lifted and slid apart. Beneath them was a stairway leading into a dimly lit subspace. Exposed pipes ran along the walls. Water dripped from them and pooled on the steps.

As soon as the panels opened, Elise slipped between them and went down the stairs. She took the shallow steps two at a time. Luka followed. A loud hiss rang through the stairwell as the doors closed behind them and he whipped his head around just in time to see them form a neat seam. They lowered back into place with a fit so perfect fit it looked like they did not exist at all. The noise of the firefight above faded to nothing.

In his peripherals, he saw Elise beckoning him to keep moving. He pulled his eyes from the door and trotted down to catch up. They kept pace until they reached the landing at the bottom of stairs and a cool, still corridor stretched in the distance ahead.

A high tone rang in his ears as a result of the gunfire and made it difficult to hear, but as his blood settled, and his mind adjusted to the quiet, new sounds came into focus. He heard the hum of steam moving through pipes and the patter of water dripping onto the concrete floor of the halls. Elise pressed her back flat against a steel door to her right, let out a long breath, and then slid down into a seated position with her legs splayed out in front of her.

Her voice was breathy and broken when she spoke, "We won't have long, I just—" she said.

Luka looked over from her feet up. There was no visible damage, no blood.

"You're not hit are you?" he asked.

Elise examined her hands and arms, turning them over. She brushed her hands down her torso and legs too. "No, no I don't think so."

He took a sit on the bottom step, lowering himself gingerly with arms. His quads and hamstrings ached from the exertions of the past few hours.

She looked at him. "Are you?"

"No, I'm good."

"You sure about that? You're bleeding, you know," she said as she nodded to his ribs.

He flinched as he pressed his hand in against the right side of his torso again and pulled it back to study it. Sticky, semi-coagulated blood clung to his palm. He was in no danger of bleeding out, but it was seeping enough blood and lymphatic fluid to slick the right side of his rib cage.

"I made a rough go of getting here. It'll be fine."

He scraped the discharge on his hand onto the edge of the stair he sat on.

"What is this place?" he asked.

"Maintenance entrance. They store the liquor in the room behind me."

Elise slapped the door behind her and a hollow clang echoed down the hallway.

"How do you know about it?" asked Luka.

"I told you earlier, I have a few friends here."

Even with this short moment of rest, her voice was already regaining its natural resolve.

"You said we don't have long. We should get moving," he said.

Elise offered a begrudging *yes* and started to lift herself from the floor. Luka pushed himself up from the stairs and offered a hand to her. She took it and pulled herself up the rest of the way. Then she dusted her off her hands and shimmied her dress back down. He turned his head away while she finished situating clothing.

"You ready?" she asked.

He turned to face her and she gave him a peculiar smile in response. His face flushed and he looked away again.

"Let's go."

They walked shoulder to shoulder as they moved into the black distance. His biochip nagged at him all the while, reminding him that they should move in a tactical formation and that they should keep low and hug the walls. He was too tired to care.

Elise was more vigilant, it seemed. They had been walking for less than a minute when she froze and extended an arm to block his path. She tapped her ear. He froze too. He listened. His ears still rang from the gunfire earlier but when he concentrated, he caught whispers of a new sound. There was a person ahead, panting and groaning like they were straining. There was an odd shuffling sound too, like something heavy was being dragged across the concrete.

Elise quietly stepped out of her shoes to approach barefoot. She held her revolver out in front of her and braced the grip with two hands. Luka drew his pistol from his back holster and copied her position.

The source of the sound was ahead on the left. They moved silently forward, pressing their toes down to the floor first and then slowly dropping their heels with each step. Luka inched ahead of Elise. She looked over at him with a scowl, but he gestured to his pistol and she let him take the lead.

The tunnel branched off to the left ahead and the source of the sound seemed to be a short distance down the left-hand path. Luka crept forward toward the corner of the intersection, keeping his body tight against the wall as he approached. He leaned forward only enough to glimpse down the new path. A woman was dragging a body down the side tunnel. She had one of his arms in each hand and was towing him backward in short heaves like a heavy sack. She wore a black dress with a heavy hood that obscured her face. It was an aggressive look for this part of Low City, but a plunging cut out at the back and long leg line softened it enough to make to clear she had been in the club earlier. The man wore a pale violet suit—flamboyant and unmistakable. It was Ricard.

Luka leaned back behind the cover of the corner and looked to Elise. He signaled for her to hold with his palm. She inclined her head, agreeing.

Luka took in a deep breath and pressed his body flat against the wall.

"Viktoria!" he yelled.

His voice echoed down the concrete chambers, cutting through the silence. Elise flinched and shrank into the wall. She glared at him with wide eyes. He didn't mean to yell it. He was deafer from the recent gunfight than he realized.

There was a heavy thump and then Viktoria bolted around the corner like a spooked cat. She had a weapon drawn and she trained it on Luka. He put his arms up with his pistol held out at his side and shuffled over to shield Elise behind his combat suit. The wounds at his ribs cracked and a fresh trickle of blood ran down his side.

Viktoria's eyes narrowed to slits and her face was a mixture of fear and determination. She carried something like a submachine gun, but it had a homemade, stripped-down quality to it. It looked like it could be folded and broken apart into small components. Recognition swept over her as she studied Luka. She tilted her head and her finger slid away from the trigger, but she kept her aim.

She almost spoke twice before she finally did, open her mouth and closing it as she tried to find the right question.

"What're you doing here?" she finally asked.

He kept his arms up at his sides despite the stinging in his side where the wounds had reopened. He spoke even and low, "Would you believe it if I said I was here to help you?"

A deep scowl took the place of Viktoria's curiosity. "That fat asshole at blacklane thought I couldn't handle this on my own? After everything I've pulled off?"

Elise stepped forward and spoke into Luka's ear, "Luka, we don't have time for this."

Though she attempted to be discreet, Luka was sure all persons present heard it.

He shook his head, ignoring Elise and continuing with Viktoria, "No, it wasn't like that. I was looking for you. I volunteered."

"That was a stupid thing to do," said Viktoria.

She lowered her gun and pushed her hood back. It was the first time he saw her face in full. A ragged scar ran down the left side of her head, starting near the top of her scalp and extending down to her neck. She was missing a bit of her left ear. Luka guessed the same downward strike that created the scar caused this too.

Elise put a hand on Luka's shoulder. He glanced in her direction and she widened her eyes at him again, reminding him of the imminent threat above. She was right, he knew. The MP's would breach the drones defense any minute and he had a feeling they would move down this tunnel not long after. He did not know why they were at the club, but he guessed it had a lot to do with him—and possibly that woman in white that he met in the streets earlier.

"Listen, the calvary's coming right behind us. We don't have much time. If you want to do this, we have to do it now," Luka said to Viktoria.

She sucked in her lip and spat on the floor. "It would have been done already if it wasn't for you two. I lured this asshole down into this tunnel and knocked him out. I was just getting started when I heard the doors activating. I had to drag him all the way over here to try to hide him."

Viktoria turned and laid a savage kick into the unconscious man's ribs. Her shoes were a mix, something between a boot and a high heel, and looked like they offered little protection. His body did not budge when her foot landed. It probably hurt her more than it would ever hurt him, but she did not show it.

"He looks skinny, but he's heavy as shit," she added before she spat again, this time on the ground beside him.

Elise stepped between them. "Enough talk. Get it done then," she said as she glared at both of them.

Viktoria did not seem pleased by it but jumped into action all the same. She kneeled beside Ricard and began sterilizing the area around his eyes with murky amber liquid. Luka fished the extraction device given to him at BLVCKLANE out of a concealed pocket and held it out to Viktoria.

"This will be faster," she said as she took the extractor from his hand.

The process was a lot like scraping the pulp from the rind of a small fruit, except grosser, and she made quick work of it. With two quick movements of the device, she removed the first eye. Then, she held it out at her side as she undid the clasps on a small black case hidden high on the inner part of her thigh. Frayed wires dangled from the eyes and the back section shined with an intricate copper pattern. She placed it into a viscous blue liquid within the container and began working on the second eye. It came free with a twist of her wrist and a pop. Viktoria placed it into the same container, flipped the lid closed, and began repositioning the strap that held the container against her leg.

He made the mistake of looking at the aftermath. Fleshy sockets remained where Ricard's eyes should have been. Amber stains from the disinfectant surrounded them like death paint. For a moment, it reminded of Helena's grim makeup.

Elise took his hand and pulled him away.

The trio set down the hallway, moving at an easy jog. Viktoria's shoes echoed down the tunnel ahead with each step. Elise went barefoot, hers a gentle patter, and Luka's suit absorbed almost all sound he made. In the back of his mind, he knew the MP's would enter the tunnels soon, but with the noise of the firefight long gone, he drifted into the rhythm of their footfall. The gentle percussion of it lulled his mind away from the urgency as of their escape and, once again, he ignored the warnings of his biochip.

Until a woman stepped into their path from the shadow of an unseen alcove. She wore a lustrous red dress and a daring smile. They all stopped dead at the sight. The hairs on Luka's arms and neck prickled.

It was Maeve—or the woman he knew as Maeve.

"You really are my favorite sort. Predictable. Easily motivated," she said.

Her hollow voice reverberated off the walls. All traces of intrigue and flirtation were absent from her now. His breath rose as his body prepared to strike. His mind, though, diffused it before he could act. His shoulders slumped and Maeve cocked her head at him curiously. Something was incongruent. The alcove to her right was hidden. Even though they were standing just a few paces away, he could hardly see it was there. Tired, and slipping out of focus, they would have run right past her—and yet she stepped out of its safety to announce her presence well in advance. She stood in front of them now, casually defiant with her hands on her hips in a power stance. If she wanted to avoid them, she had the opportunity, and if she wanted to kill them, they would already be dead.

"She's stalling," announced Luka just as he realized he should not have said it aloud.

A cold expression replaced Maeve's triumphant smile. Her body tensed as she prepared to attack.

Luka pulled his pistol and squeezed the trigger in her direction. Bullets sprayed and ricocheted off of the pipes. Sparks flew and illuminated the tunnel in bright flashes—but she was gone. Maeve had darted back into her alcove before his finger even found the trigger. She was quick—almost as quick as Janus.

He released the trigger and the cacophony died. His vision fizzed with splotches of bright colors where the muzzle flashes had been and the ringing in his ears returned. Elise moved in front of him. He held an arm out to stop her as she passed, but she brushed by without hesitating. Viktoria followed with her bespoke machine gun drawn. She and Elise slipped into a natural tactical pattern. They both had formal training based their movements, and from a similar school of combat, but he had no guess as to the where or how of that. He fell in line behind Viktoria.

Before they could pin her in the alcove, Maeve stepped back out into the center of the tunnel and hunkered down behind a carbon fiber shield. Viktoria and Luka laid simultaneous rounds of fire into her shield without effect. It took the blows and distributed them outward, sending a spray of bullets to both sides. Elise did not join in the firing squad, and instead, sprinted forward when as Luka and Viktoria paused to reload.

She launched a heavy front kick into Maeve's shield. It sent Maeve tumbling backward and Elise fell forward over her. In the exchange, Maeve found a grip on Elise's neck and when they both hit the ground, Maeve rolled on top of her and pinned her down by straddling her torso. Maeve pressed two fingers in deep against Elise's neck like she was checking her pulse.

Luka saw the black ring on Maeve's finger and realized she was trying to force a lethal dose of the tranquilizer into Elise's bloodstream. He raised his pistol to fire, but he did not have a clean angle and the chance of a ricochet hitting Elise was high. Viktoria, dropped her gun, sprinted forward and threw a powerful upward kick at Maeve's face like she was punting a ball. It landed just under Maeve's chin and sent Maeve toppling backward.

Elise scrambled to her feet but stumbled sideways and fell against the wall. She tried to catch hold of the pipes to prop herself up herself, but her legs failed, and they slipped free of her grip. Her head knocked against the concrete as she hit the floor.

Viktoria was on top of Maeve now, landing vicious hammer fists into Maeve's head. Maeve made feeble attempts at blocking the blows, but the kick had dazed her and she had no chance of putting up a real defense. Viktoria switched from fists to using elbows and landed two solid strikes to Maeve's jaw. Maeve's arms fell slack at her sides. She gave up.

Luka hooked his foot under Viktoria's gun and slid it within her reach before he darted over to Elise. He placed a handle under Elise's neck and cradled her head in the crook of his arm. Elise was semiconscious. Her eyes rolled lazily in her head, but her breathing was normal and her pulse was strong—for the moment.

He turned and watched as Viktoria pressed the barrel of her gun to Maeve's forehead.

"Please, no. Please. It's not personal. I just needed the money. The bounty on Luka and Elise. Alive. Please, you know how it is here. We all do things we don't like…" Maeve said to Viktoria.

Maeve looked over at him and pleaded with her eyes in one last, desperate bid. He saw the panic in them as her social enhancements alerted her that Viktoria would kill her. Her absolute fear was the tell. She knew with certainty what would happen next. She was not fast like Janus, she was just good at predicting people's actions. It made her charming and it made her appear inhumanly fast. Her real self was neither.

Viktoria pulled the trigger and a round left the barrel and entered Maeve's brain. Her body went limp, but her bionic eyes shuddered while their remaining electric charge dissipated and died with the rest of her.

Viktoria immediately set to Maeve's eyes with the extractor. This time, there was no need to disinfectant and bother with the pretense of not killing the extractee, so the whole operation took less than a minute. She placed them into the same concealed container with some careful repositioning and then joined Luka at Elise's side.

"Let me," said Viktoria as she kneeled and pushed him aside.

She produced a pill from a hidden pocket in her hood and pushed it deep into Elise's mouth. Her Adam's apple bobbed and the pill disappeared as her swallow reflex took control.

"What did you give her?" asked Luka.

"A stimulant. It will help her fight the sedative."

Luka's brow furrowed. "Is that a good idea?"

"No, absolutely not, but it won't kill her right this moment and we need to get out of here. Immediately."

The pill worked instantly. Elise's eyes came back into focus. Her pupils were dilated to the extent that she had no iris left, but there was an alertness in them now.

"Help me," said Viktoria as she took one of Elise's arms and prepared to lift her.

Luka took Elise's other arm and together they hoisted her up. He wrapped her arm over his shoulders and braced her weight over his body.

"I can do it," Elise insisted as Viktoria and Luka took her weight between them. She slurred her words and her head lolled around her shoulders. She endeavored to walk on her own but it amounted to little more than her feet scraping at the concrete as they carried her.

They hobbled deeper into the tunnel together, suspending Elise between them with the tips of her toes dragging along on the ground as they went. It was slow progress at first. The height difference between him and Viktoria made it awkward to carry Elise. Luka hunched to help distribute the weight onto him, but even with this adjustment, Elise's body leaned to Viktoria's side and forced her to carry more.

With each passing minute, though, Elise's faculties returned. Within a half kilometer, she could support her own weight and their speed improved dramatically. Her mental acuity was returning too, and just in time.

From stairs leading to the club, to the spot where Maeve appeared, the tunnel had been a single straight path—excluding some minor jaunts and alcoves. The deeper they moved now, however, the tunnel branched into distinct paths of seeming equal importance. It was no longer clear which was the main tunnel. At each intersection, a set of sigils marked directions and offered some encoded instruction on which path to take. Luka, however, only recognized a few of the symbols and could not even guess their summed meaning. Viktoria was equally lost. She hissed some nasty words about *little gremlins* that lived in the tunnels but neither he nor his enhanced memory had any clue what that meant. He hoped not to find out.

At the first major branch in the tunnel, they had both stopped and studied the markings for a while and eventually looked to one another with a shrug. They were about to pick a path at random when Elise chimed in and directed them to the left-hand path with an outstretched finger. When they came to the next intersection, Luka and Viktoria again stopped and studied the markings, but they were no more sensical than the last batch. Elise, however, read them with ease. She directed them to go left once more, without hesitation. They encountered five more intersections, and at each one, Elise directed them.

She walked more or less on her own now. She kept one hand on Luka's arm to steady her balance, but rarely needed it. Shades of her characteristic confidence reappeared in her gait. He guessed they had covered several kilometers of tunnels but did not know their intended destination and the combination of darkness and silence was becoming oppressive. A growing unease welled in his stomach.

They came to another intersection. Rather than a simple branch, it was the joining of two major tunnel systems. Elise nodded to the right and started to take a step in that direction, but Luka planted his feet and yanked her back. She stumbled as she recovered her balance.

"Enough. How are you doing this?" he yelled.

Elise and Viktoria both winced at the noise.

"Shhh," Viktoria hissed. "Keep your voice down."

Her eyes scanned the tunnel nervously. She froze until the echo of Luka's voice faded into the distance. She beckoned Luka and Viktoria in close with a curl of two fingers.

She whispered to them, "This tunnel will take us to surface near the Seventh Circle. We'll be a long way from the Light District and we'll be safe from the MP's there. With any luck, it'll be clear, but we may find another kind of trouble."

Viktoria's folded her arms across her body.

"We shouldn't go there," she said.

Elise turned her eyes on Viktoria. She raised her voice, seeming to forget that chided Luka only seconds earlier for the same reason.

"I'm sorry, darling, but we don't have another option. It's the only way out I know," said Elise.

Viktoria's mouth pulled thin and she blinked slowly.

"What then?" Luka cut in.

Elise turned away from Viktoria. "What do you mean?"

"I'm saying what do we do after we surface? We need somewhere to shelter for a few days."

Elise looked down and her eyes darted from side to side as she reasoned through options. When she looked up again, deep worry lines creased her forehead.

"I don't know. This is all is new to me," she said.

"How do you know the symbols then?" Viktoria asked.

"*He* gave me a map of the tunnels," Elise said as she looked at Luka rather than Viktoria and tapped the spot on her neck above her biochip.

"You can stay at my place," said Viktoria, cutting in. "They don't know that we've linked up so you'll be safe there."

Elise whipped around to face Viktoria. "I don't even know you."

Viktoria scoffed. "Do you have another option?"

"We can trust her. Let's move," said Luka as he inclined his head to the next tunnel.

Elise and Viktoria both twisted their mouths in dissatisfaction but started walking, nonetheless. Elise took the lead. She forewent Luka's assistance now. She wobbled every few steps but kept herself upright.

The tunnels became darker and wetter the further they moved into this section. Previous areas had small LED markers every ten meters or so, but these sections seemed older and abandoned. The glow from the trim on Viktoria's hood was their only source of light now and it washed their world in an eerie pale blue. A damp cold took hold in this tunnel too. Water dripped from the ceiling and splashed into pools along the floor. For a while they could avoid puddles, but eventually water covered the whole floor. Elise, who ditched her shoes a long time back, was stuck walking barefoot and fell behind. Her feet were blistered from the rough concrete and probably aching from the wet cold, but she had not once asked to stop or complained about it.

The water level rose as they progressed, and it within than a half kilometer, they were sloshing through thigh-deep brackish water—a mixture of storm runoff and ocean. His suit regulated his core temperature, despite the damaged area, so it was no matter of concern for him. He doubted, however, that Elise's and Viktoria's clothing did much more than weigh them down. They would not last long in such cold water if they stopped moving and he saw fatigue setting in on Elise. She recovered quickly from the sedative thanks to whatever stimulant Viktoria gave her, but the boost it gave her waned now. She stumbled often and soon would need help carrying her own weight again. He knew she was trying to suppress it, but he heard her teeth chattering. She clutched her arms around her body, hugging herself for the little warmth that it provided. She was minutes from full collapse, he thought.

He picked up his pace and took a diagonal to catch up to Viktoria. He walked beside her and their combined wake carved a wide arc in the water.

Viktoria raised an eyebrow at him and he jerked his head back over his shoulder in Elise's direction.

Viktoria glanced back at Elise and nodded in agreement to Luka. Her face was stony, but a concern showed in her intense stare.

They stopped walking.

"Can she take more?" asked Luka, speaking so low over the sloshing water.

"It might kill her—but so might the cold," said Viktoria.

Luka rubbed his forehead. "It'll buy time though, right? The problem is the crash, not the rise?"

Viktoria looked away but nodded yes.

Elise was catching up, only a few meters back now. Her head hung at her shoulders and she took shallow steps. It was more of a forward shuffle than a walk.

"Wh ... what ... what," she muttered as she got close.

Luka made eyes at Viktoria and she produced another pill from the compartment in her hood. He held his hand out and she placed it into this palm.

Luka turned his attention back on Elise.

"You need to take this," he said.

Elise did not react. She was staring at her own feet, lost from the present. He slapped her cheek several times and lifted her chin.

"Elise, you need to take this."

He held the small pill in front of her face, pinched between his thumb and forefinger. The words did not seem to register with her, so he slipped it between her lips. Her teeth parted and he set it on her tongue. She swallowed.

Although his suit would prevent any transfer of body heat, he hugged her body tight against him while they waited for the drug to take effect. In less than a minute, she stopped shivering. She lifted her head and her eyes were open and cogent.

Her voice shook, "How long have we been walking?"

"We're almost there," said Luka.

Elise suddenly realized that she was still hugging Luka and stepped back. "Sorry. Thanks."

He smiled weakly. "We lost you for a while."

"Yeah, I think you did. What did you give me?"

"I don't know, but I do know we need to get somewhere safe before it wears off. You ready to walk again?"

"Yeah, I feel great surprisingly."

"You won't for long."

Viktoria set off as soon as Elise broke away from Luka. For a long time now, she had been their only light source and as she pulled ahead, the blackness swallowed Elise and him. The tunnel did not look like it would branch again, so there was no danger of getting lost as long as they trudged on in the same direction, but standing in the dark in waist-deep water triggered a primal dread that neither wanted to linger in. They both jumped into motion and sloshed forward hard to close the gap.

In a short distance, the water level climbed until it was almost chest high for him and approaching shoulder depth for Elise and Viktoria. They transitioned to swimming, but he kept pushing forward with feet on the ground, knowing that if he did swim, the panic welling in his stomach would overtake him. Elise and Viktoria pulled ahead quickly.

In the dark, the depth climbed to his shoulders. He was breathing hard, not only from the exertion of moving but from the growing alarm in his brain. He thrashed his arms and pumped his legs forward. His movements frenzied, and the harder he worked, the less progress he made. His head swam. Consciousness waned. He slapped and grasped blindly in front of him as he fought to keep his head above water. It sloshed back into his mouth and nose. He gagged and broke into a fit of coughing.

That's when he noticed it—the distinct odor of hydrocarbons. While his body revolved at the smell, his mind elated. It was the smell of stagnant water in Low City which meant they had to be near an exit. He continued coughing to push the contaminated water out. It burned his lungs but cleared his mind.

When his breathing settled again, he let his legs float up, and began swimming toward the light of Viktoria's body in the distance.

It was not far. Within a few dozen strokes, the tunnel ended. A high wall with a wide slot drain at the top rose in front of them. A rusted ladder in a small channel to their left led to the surface. Viktoria and Elise waited at the base of it. They motioned for Luka to go up first.

He drew his pistol and started up the ladder using only his left hand to hold on to the rungs as he climbed. It ended at an antiquated manhole cover. He pushed his shoulder upward against it and it gave a little. Through the small crack between the pavement and steel, he surveyed their landing. The streets were empty, and though his biochip told him Seventh Circle was a flooded district, this particular block was dry. He waited and watched for several minutes through the little crack, but nothing happened. A handful of people passed by but none of them presented an obvious threat.

He slid the cover to the side and lifted himself through.

The air was drier, but colder on the surface. A wind blew through the street and he shivered while his suit adapted. He swiveled his head from side to side, eyeing the streets while Viktoria and Elise made their way up the ladder. Passersby eyed the group nervously as they emerged from the sewer, but when they saw Luka's pistol and the wounds on his side, they turned their attention elsewhere and hurried off.

Elise was the last through. Once she hit the street, he pushed the manhole cover closed and looked to Viktoria to take the lead. Her home was North-East of here, but his chip held little more information on the area. He had no idea how to route it. She directed them to a wet side street a block down, and once they all slipped into the cover of the alleyway, she stopped and faced Luka.

"We should get her warmer clothes. Me too, actually."

Both she and Elise shivered in the wind that rushed between the buildings—Elise especially. Her teeth chattered and her lips were blue. She was looking a bit distant again and did not appear interested in the conversation.

Luka shook his head. "We have to push through."

Viktoria frowned but took the lead on an eastward path.

They stuck to the flooded side streets. Seventh Circle had a large community, but these flooded streets were for the addicts, the outcasts, and those who did not want to be seen. The MP's would not venture this far into Low City but there was a risk that some of The Drowned would be enticed by the bounty on Elise and him. If The Drowned spotted them, they would have to fight their way through. They all had weapons, but their general exhaustion guaranteed they would not fight to their full potential. The risk of losing a firefight was high. Fortunately, Viktoria knew these deserted paths well and they made quick progress. Luka heard the sounds of large groups of people in the distance, but they never came closer than a block.

The water levels gradually receded as they progressed back toward Viktoria's home. Their speed increased as the streets dried out. In less than a half-hour, they were back on streets that Luka recognized.

Her place was just ahead, across the block, and the doors of her building opened as they approached. A welcoming blast of dry warmth hit his face as they passed through the threshold. Although his suit maintained his core temperature, it offered little protection for his face without the mask that he ditched in the tunnels on his way in from the sub. During their long trek, he forgot that his face transitioned from painfully cold to fully numb. It stung in the warm air of the climate-controlled environment.

The entire foyer of the building was black. The floor was a grid of semi-glossy tiles and the walls were a rough-textured substance that looked like stacks of burned paper. Striking green plants accented the room. They had long, wide foliage like the blades of an Agave, but they twisted in graceful spirals as they extended out. In some places, blades intertwined in helix-like strands of DNA.

Luka was reaching his hand out to one of the blades when Viktoria waved them forward into an elevator that appeared from a seamless set of doors built into a wall. His stomach lurched as the lift started.

They moved up several floors and it opened to a foyer identical to the one they just left. Luka froze, wondering for a moment if they had moved at all, but Viktoria exited the elevator, and without hesitating, made for the right-hand wall. She pressed her palm against it and three seams formed in the matte black material. They framed the outline of a door. There was a mechanical clicking and then outlined section of the wall slid a few centimeters back. The door folded down into the floor and disappeared so that a clean rectangular chunk of the wall was missing. Luka and Elise hurried through after Viktoria and the door folded up behind them with a series of clicks.

The walls in Viktoria's apartment were a cream-white with dark trims around an ornate baseboard. It was small and simple, but it was warm and the thick walls offered a sense of security Luka had not felt since the bunker in the desert.

Chapter Fourteen

Viktoria's cat hopped down from its perch at the windowsill and mewed as it dashed over to her. It was a ragged, gray creature, with sharp green eyes. It looked malnourished, was missing patches of fur, and had a crook in its tail midway up. It circled her ankles and she kneeled to stroke its head. He and Elise waited by the blank space of wall that had been the door while the ritual played out. Viktoria seemed to forget that she had company as she and the cat pressed their heads together and nuzzled each other. Luka cleared his throat and Viktoria's head whipped around in their direction. She stood abruptly, remembering her guests, and the cat skittered off back to its window. It curled up in its seat but glowered at them with flattened ears.

She did an up-and-down of Elise. "We need to get her out of those clothes. Things are going to get bad soon."

Even in the warm air, her lips remained blue. Her fingertips were blue too. Though he looked her in the eye, she did not register it. Her gaze was catatonic and her irises looked like gray arctic water. He snapped his fingers in front of her face and got only a twitch in response.

"The metabolites are septic. That re-up might have killed her already," Viktoria explained as she watched him run his diagnostics.

"What do we do?" asked Luka.

She shrugged. "Nothing. Her body will filter the drugs or it will give out trying."

"Given what you do for a living, I'm guessing you've seen her condition before. You've got to have some ideas."

"What I do?" Viktoria said as she squared her shoulders to him.

"What I do? You mean like put myself at risk for you? That's something I do. Twice now. Yeah, I have seen this before, and yeah I do know what to do. We take her to a clinic—but since you can't seem to lie low and keep out of trouble, that's not an option is it?"

She crossed her arms over her chest and sucked in her lower lip so that her upper teeth showed.

Luka shook his head. "Don't pretend you run to a doctor every time something goes sideways. You're a trafficker. You're resourceful. You're self-sufficient."

Viktoria turned her back to him and hung her head.

"Okay. Strip off her clothes, lay her over there."

She pointed blindly to a gray, weathered couch near the window.

"Put the blankets on her. I need to make some saline. We can keep her warm and keep flushing her system with fluids. That's the best we can do here."

Luka mouthed the word *okay* although he knew she could not see it. He wrapped an arm around Elise's waist and guided her toward the couch by putting pressure on the small of her back. It was more like she was sleepwalking than on the verge of death, he thought. Viktoria, meanwhile, disappeared into her small kitchen space and began pulling jars and bottles from cabinets.

346

At the edge of the couch, Luka found the seam of Elise's dress and released it by running a knuckle finger down its line. The garment fell free of her shoulders, but the wet fabric clung to her hips. He pulled it free with a quick jerk. It fell to her ankles and then he eased her down onto the cushions of the couch. Her breathing was labored and shallow and her skin, even near her heart, was alarmingly cold to the touch. Her eyes remained open but were vacant now. He pulled the two blankets from the armrest and laid them over her, tucking in the edges so that the fabric cocooned her body. He stepped back and raked his fingers through the scruff on his neck while he considered the weak rise and fall of her chest.

He turned to Viktoria in the kitchen. "I have to go."

Viktoria laughed, loudly, and poked her around a corner of a cabinet to look at him. "No fucking way. You have to be joking."

"I have to go find a few things."

She scoffed. "What, like your own goddamned sanity? Oh no, you're going to have to do better than that if you want to leave."

Luka took in a deep breath. "Sometime in the next forty-eight hours there's going to be a spike in radiation near the city. I need to know when it happens. To do that, I need to make an ionization chamber."

Viktoria pointed her finger at him like a gun as she neared. "That's going to need a whole lot more explanation before I agree to anything."

"Even if she survives this, she'll die in the next few days if I don't detect this signal. The person I've been working with—well, she and I both work for him it turns out—he is going attack Daedalus Astrodynamics. When I linked up with him I thought it was the right thing to do, but I didn't understand what he was hoping to achieve. I didn't understand *why* he was doing it. Hundreds of people, maybe a thousand, are going to die if he succeeds. Elise among them. My closest friends among them. None of them deserving of it. I thought Daedalus Astrodynamics did something deserving of this, but it was more lie than truth. He's just out for power, like any of the other thugs down here."

Viktoria twisted a stranded of hair between her fingers as she responded, "Trouble doesn't even begin to describe you."

"Fair enough," said Luka.

"What makes you so sure that you can trust me?" she asked.

"Well, as you reminded us earlier, we don't have a better option—so I guess I'm rolling the dice."

A one-sided smile crept onto her face and wrinkles formed in the corners of her eyes. "When I first met you, you were a helpless priss like the rest of your kind. You tried to control. You tried to understand. Now, goddamn if you don't almost fit in."

Viktoria went back into the kitchen and resumed her preparations. She was boiling water and measuring several white powders into a plastic bottle.

"So what are these things that you need to find?" she asked as she worked.

"Not much. some analogs and a reasonable steel drum."

"Right. Simple," she said. Although he could not see her face, he heard the eye-roll in her voice.

"It should be."

She laughed coldly again. "Those things aren't very common down here."

"They aren't in High City either,"

"What I meant is metal doesn't last long in the salt spray down here. If you hadn't noticed, we're fond of c-fiber. It's for good reason," said Viktoria.

"I had. We're fond of it in High City too but carbon fiber can't store every kind of chemical, and no matter where you go, there's always someone collecting old junk."

"Oh great, so all you need to do so if find the one weirdo in Low City hoarding old computers and then rob a chemical plant after that."

"Yes, that. Basically," replied Luka.

"Meanwhile, you leave me to save her life.?"

"Yeah, that about sums it. I am a terrible friend, really."

"Not so terrible. Those eyes I took off the women in the tunnel should fetch me a nice payday. That kind of tech is rare in Low."

"It is up there too," Luka cut in.

"Even better. I'm revising my asking price upward as we speak and I'm guessing it was your presence that lured her in. You played your part as bait—a perfect job for a High City priss like you—and Elise, she did her part too I must admit," said Viktoria without missing a beat.

"Not that terrible in the end," said Luka.

"Not that terrible," replied Viktoria as she poured boiling water into the plastic bottle with the powders. They dissolved and formed a slurry. She capped it and shook the bottle until the mixture turned clear.

"Are you leaving, or what?" pressed Viktoria as the rounded the kitchen counter and approached Elise.

He studied Elise's motionless form.

"Go. You can't do anything for her. I'll give her the best odds I can, but they weren't good to begin with. No promises."

"I understand. Thank you."

He made for the section of wall where remembered the door forming, but as he approached it, nothing happened. He pressed his palm flat against the wall where he assumed the door was. Still, nothing changed.

"Hold your hand up, make a fist," called Viktoria from the other side of the room.

Luka clenched his jaw and combed his hair back. Then, he held his hand out and slowly curled his fingers into a fist like he had seen Elise do at Dead Man's Hand. A chunk of the wall slid back and the seam of the door formed. It folded down into the floor. He passed through and stepped into the elevator.

350

In this situation, the memories Lark implanted proved especially useful. In those new corners of his mind, he knew of a one-stop-shop for all of it. There was a man who extracted gallium and neodymium out of old electronics and sold the metals for profit. His shop would have the electronics scraps Luka needed, and since this man used an array of solvents on his processes, he likely had some industrial-sized metal drums around too.

Luka exited Viktoria's building and set a brisk pace to his destination: an old brewery, less than a kilometer away. Sunrise was two hours ago, but it was dreary out. Deep gray clouds covered the sky as far as he could see in any direction. They blocked out every trace of the sun. There were no shadows. The whole city was flat and gray like the sky above it. No one else was out. Early morning, he guessed, was the least trafficked time for the habitually nocturnal residents of Low City. He stuck to side streets regardless and hugged close to buildings where he had to walk on major thoroughfares. He estimated ten minutes to get there. It took him only eight. A shambled brick behemoth stood in front of him. A black gate with thick vertical bars blocked the entrance and at one side there was a door with a brushed steel handle and an old keypad. He did not have to guess. He punched in the first code in that came time mind—1, 2, 8, 4—and a green light blinked. The gate opened and it rattled shut behind. He flinched and tucked in against the building until the noise died down. He waited and listened, but no one appeared. Nothing stirred.

Luka surveyed the alley ahead. Despite the wrecked look of the exterior, any entry point to the inner part of the building was fortified. The windows were barred and thick steel formed the doors. He saw what he thought were biometric sensors. At the far end of this corridor, however, there were large junk piles. Some of it was separated into plastic bins but most of it was strewn about randomly like it been tossed out of a window. The distinct green hue of 20th century printed circuit boards caught his eye first. Luka jogged over and lifted several large sheets of plastic scrap. As he stretched to pull them aside, a scab over the wound on his side tore back open. He gritted his teeth and clamped a hand over the wound until the stinging subsided.

Beneath the plastic sheets was a huge bin of old circuit boards. He sifted through the pile and discovered that most had been stripped down to a bare board, devoid of chips, capacitors, and even resistors. Fortunately, the parts he needed for his voltage step-up circuit were not exotic and for every few dozen empty boards, he found one or two with a few remnant parts. From his stack of about two partially filled boards, he had enough for his build—with spares. He fished out a small plastic bin from the junk pile and placed his selected boards into it.

He moved to an adjacent junk heap, one filled with broken containers and large plastic drums used to store acids. He dug through this pile, but soon it was clear he would not find metal there. He stood back and planted his hands on his hips while he surveyed the area. A cold breeze blew and soothed the hot skin beneath the broken scab on his side.

Next to a wrecked shed at the side of the building, there was a pile rusty corrugated iron—much too far gone to shape into a drum—but at least it was metal. He hustled over to it and began dragging metal sheets aside. Under these, and another meter of old electronic housings and chassis, he came upon a stock of industrial equipment left from the original brewery. Among it was a metal cylinder about a meter long and half a meter in diameter. The surface of the metal was dull—coated in a transparent film. He did not know if the coating would interfere with his measurement, but he knew he would find anything better in Low City today.

He took a pipe, wedged it under the metal heap and he leaned his body weight over it. The entire pile moved. He repeated the process twice more, repositioning the pipe each time, and by the third attempt, he created enough of a gap to reach down and lift the cylinder free.

He gathered the plastic bin with his electronics under one arm and carried the metal cylinder over his shoulder with the other arm. Although the sky was no brighter for it, early morning had waned into mid-morning. People were moving. He heard boots clacking on concrete and hushed voices. Stealth was not an option with everything he had to carry, so he shored up his grip, and he jogged the whole way back to Viktoria's.

Her building knew him now, and to his great relief, the doors opened as soon as he got near. The entrance to the elevator appeared in the wall when he entered the foyer and it automatically took him to her floor. He stood in front of the section of wall where her door should appear, but unlike with the rest of the building, nothing happened. He huffed and set down his equipment. He held his hand out and slowly made a fist. He waited, but no door appeared. Then he pressed his palm against the wall. Still, no response. He pounded on the wall. The surface of it looked soft from a distance, but it was stone beneath his fist.

A moment later there was a clicking and the door seam appeared in the wall. It ratcheted away and disappeared into the floor.

Viktoria stood in the entryway. "The building knows to let you in this far, but only I can open this door from the outside."

She waved him in. "Come on."

353

He took the plastic bin under his arm and dragged the cylinder with his other hand.

"You did that fast," she said as she moved to the main living space.

Luka set the stuff down in the middle of the room and walked over to Elise.

He tapped his temple with his forefinger. "Lucky me, I knew just where to go."

"I won't ask," said Viktoria

Elise was in the same position he left her except that a plastic tube now ran from a needle in her arm up to an inverted bottle of fluid hanging from a nail in the wall. The lights were low, but her color looked to have improved. Her lips were lighter, more their natural pale shade of pink.

"Don't get your hopes up," said Viktoria as she stood beside him and joined in looking down at Elise.

Luka chewed on his lip while he examined Elise. "This person who buys the synth eyes, do they deal in biochips too?"

Viktoria raised an eyebrow. "Maybe. That's not common fare."

"Would they know how to remove them, without killing the patient?"

Viktoria frowned. "I'm not sure, but I have a feeling I'm not going to like while you're asking."

"Plan B."

Viktoria's shoulders slumped as she let out a sigh. "Luka, you're getting ahead of yourself. I know she looks better, but it's only the fluids. Her organs..."

She stopped mid-sentence. He was staring down at Elise again while he scratched at the hair on his jawline. Deep wrinkles clouded his forehead.

"No one down here could handle a job like that. The tech is completely different," Elise added into the silence.

Luka nodded passively, not breaking his gaze.

"You know that on the news they're calling you a terrorist right? That same lady that interviewed you is plugging a story that you're the head of an anti-government militia now."

He pulled his eyes from Elise and faced Viktoria. "I did. Someone else in Low City recognized me and said something similar. They were very interested in me then. That's why the MP's risked that assault at Dead Man's Hand, I think.. Elise said it too."

A new thought washed over Viktoria. He watched a micro-flash of panic move through her as her eyes flickered wide and her throat tensed for only a millisecond. She buried it and defaulted to her natural stoicism.

"So what they're saying is true?" she asked.

"Yes. I broke into a military base. I tried to steal an antimatter reactor. I killed about nine people on my way here. More than that. I've lost count."

His stomach lurched as he admitted it. He swallowed to keep the bile down and his salivary glands went to overdrive to clear the acid from his esophagus. Viktoria, meanwhile, glanced over her shoulder. She meant it to be discreet, casual, but he saw it before she did. Her machine-gun sat on a shelf about three steps behind her and it was out of arm's reach. She was shifting her weight to her heels, preparing to back-step and reach for her gun.

He drew his pistol but kept his aim on the floor. His hand shook. The cold memories pushed forward and their voices begged him to open fire before she did. He gripped tighter and closed his eyes.

"Don't. You'll be dead before you're halfway there," he said.

Viktoria froze. She held her arms stiff at her sides.

"Who are you?" she asked as her eyes narrowed. She took a step toward him as she continued, "One moment you're some privilege-born scientist and the next a psychopath, bloodthirsty enough for the LCG. So which are you? Because I'm starting to think I made a mistake bringing you here."

His grip on the pistol relaxed as he spoke, "I don't know. Not anymore. Something's changed."

Viktoria took another step, closing the distance. "How much of this am I involved in now?"

"I don't think anyone knows we linked up again. Maybe not at all. Like I said, I didn't understand the scope of it until I met with Elise yesterday. I'm not the bad guy in this—at least I don't think I am—and I am certainly not the leader of any militia."

"You and her both," she motioned to Elise, "have been referring to some mysterious guy for the past few hours. Who is it?"

"He goes by Lark. I don't know his real name."

Viktoria rolled her hands into fists and squeezed until her knuckles turned white.

"We're acquainted," she said.

"I thought so."

"How?"

"Something he gave me," Luka said as he tapped the barrel of his pistol to the back on his neck.

Viktoria nodded, understanding his meaning, but her expression turned colder and a drop of blood fell from her hand where her nails dug into her palms. It hit the floor and left a radial spray of deep red.

"You should not have gotten involved with him," she said.

"I didn't have another option. Growing up down here, I'm sure you can appreciate that," Luka fired back.

The veins in Viktoria's neck throbbed and her eyes bulged. In a blink, she swung a first and landed a hook on the right side of his jaw. It snapped his face around to the side and pain rang through his jaw and teeth. He tasted blood where his molars sliced the inside of his cheek. Although it was a hard strike, he knew she did not want to injure him. He saw what she did to Maeve, when she wanted to hurt someone. This was to get his attention.

"What would you know about growing up down here?" she shouted before she spat on the floor.

He rotated his head around to face her while he rubbed his jaw with his free hand. He recognized how it was a put-down, even when he did not mean it to be. In the past few hours, he began to feel like he belonged in Low City—thanks to the influx of memories from Lark's upload—but he did not. He was an outsider. She was only reminding him of that. Viktoria was tensed like a loaded spring, ready to launch backward and reach for her gun.

He met her gaze. "I wouldn't. You're right."

Viktoria cocked her head and curled and uncurled his fists several times. She cast daggers with her eyes, but little by little, her body easy. She shifted her weight back to the center feet. Her eyes softened.

"That's what he does to everyone he wants. He isolates them until he is their only option," she said.

Luka nodded as he moved his pistol the concealed holster at the back of his combat suit. He could still draw before she reached her gun, but it was a gesture of trust.

"I'm going to put my gun away with the understanding that you will not reach for yours," he said.

"We're beyond that now. How long do you have until this happens?" she asked.

Luka frowned. "I'm not sure."

"And how are you going to stop it if you don't know when it's going to happen?"

"If he's got all of the equipment he needs, and I think he does, he'll run a microscale reaction to test the system first. That'll give off some unusual radiation and I can detect it, I think. If the system test works, he'll strike the next day at peak working hours—for maximum visibility, knowing him. I figure that's nine or ten in the morning our time."

She pointed to the pile of circuit boards and the odd metal cylinder in the middle of her living room. "Hence your pile of junk there."

"Yeah, the test will give off gamma radiation. I'm making an ionization chamber to capture it."

Viktoria looked down at her feet, deep in thought. He waited, motionless, knowing that she was deciding how deep she would go.

"You'd better get busy building," she said.

He smiled, weakly, holding back. He needed her as an ally just as bad as he needed Lark when he first ran from the DA facility—but she taught him not to show it.

He did exactly as she suggested. Luka kneeled beside his pile of junk and started laying out his circuit. Viktoria, meanwhile, walked over to Elise and pressed two fingers into her neck to check her pulse.

First, he stripped the components from the boards that did not look damaged and then sorted them into piles of similar types. He laid out his ideal circuit design on the floor and then from his pile of boards, found a section that best suited it. With the cutting tools in Viktoria's kitchen, he hodge-podged a few boards together, and with a laser device that she used for body-modding, he reheated the old solder on the boards and fixed the new pieces in place. He pulled power from an LED source in her kitchen by tapping into the leads with two old segments of copper wire that had been attached to one of the boards. It took hours, but he had a completed device in the end. He rigged it to send power to an older speaker if there was a spike in the circuit. It would emit a loud alarm if the cylinder detected activity. He could not verify its functionality, so he could only wait, and hope, and trust his design. With the work finished, exhaustion set in. He laid on the floor and tucked his arms beneath his head. He drifted off immediately, sleeping like he did his first nights in the desert.

He woke to the sound of his detector going berserk. Viktoria had fallen asleep sitting beside the couch, with her head laying on a cushion beside Elise. She sat bolt upright with her eyes darting from side to side while her foggy brain searched for the source of the interruption.

The sound was far beyond an alarm. It was a deafening screech. He underestimated the amount of current the chamber would produce and the circuit burned from the power surging through it now. The speaker was shrieking with a high tone that rattled his bones and disoriented him. It rolled off in pitch as the electronics died under the strain of the current, and in a matter of seconds, the boards were smoking. They filled the room with the sharp smell of burning plastics.

Luka scrambled over and yanked the power leads free.

"That's it," he announced.

Viktoria rubbed the sleep from her eyes as she spoke, "It's 3:00 A.M."

"Then I don't have long," he answered.

Elise groaned in the background and rolled onto her left side so that she faced out into the room. Her hair matted to face her and slick with sweat. Her color had drifted back to a dangerous pale-gray. The clear bottle that fed saline into her arm was empty.

"Take the elevator to High City. I can get you access," said Viktoria.

"No way. They'll have my biometrics flagged. They'll just lock it down while I'm inside. I have to take the long way round—same way I got here the first time," Luka replied.

Viktoria stood and collected the empty bottle, removing the tube from it while she spoke, "First, you don't have time. That's too long on foot from here all the way around and back up to the DA campus. Second, I'm not sure you would make it even if there was time. We're all on fumes."

Viktoria showed him the underside of her forearm. Where there should have been a flat surface near her elbow, there was instead an angry, grapefruit-sized welt. Purple-green bruising surrounded it.

"This might be broken, your friend's nearly dead, and that wound on your side is starting to look infected. If you plan to live down here, Luka—presuming you manage to stop this thing you got mixed up in and then get away—you have to drop this ego of yours."

Luka crossed his arms over his chest. "Okay, so what's your plan then?"

"You take the elevator. MP's, DA—none of them will have access to the biometrics on it. It's not a ferry for the rich kids upstairs. It's a tunnel. Like the tunnels the drug cartels used to dig across the border, but this one's hidden in plain sight. The operator is a buyer. They buy the synthetic eyes I bring them. They buy the drugs I bring them. And they buy the organs that LCG rips out of people down here. They do this because rich people want all these things but they don't want to get their own hands dirty. This business survives on discretion."

"Got it?" she added as she pursed her lips.

"Yes, I get it, but the Light District won't be safe either."

"Move quickly. Keep your face hidden. You will be fine," Viktoria said as she set the empty bottle down and began drawing a sigil on the wall with her finger. Her body blocked his line of sight, but it seemed to be a series of intersecting arcs, and when she finished the motion, a small compartment opened. She retrieved something from it.

She turned to him and held out a small brass key in her palm.

"A key? This dangerous black market uses grimy old keys to protect its secrets?"

"It's not a key, that's just someone's idea of a joke. It's encoded. Keep it on you and you will not have any problems with the elevator. When you get to High City, make your way to Northgate Park. I have a motorcycle stored there. This key will give you access to it too."

Luka reached out to take it, but paused, leaving two fingers lingering on top of the key.

"Why are you doing this?" he asked.

Viktoria chewed on her lip and looked away to a distant point at her left.

"You seem like a decent person who got stuck in a shitty situation. I guess I can relate," she said after a long pause.

"No. I'm not buying that."

"Okay then. This, right here," she motioned to her apartment with her other hand, "this is the best I can hope for coming from Low City. It's a prison. Moving any higher means getting in deeper with the gangs. If I do that, I can have more for the short time, but it's blood in and blood out with them. That's a prison too. It's time for change."

Luka's mouth pulled into a flat smile. He pinched the key between his fingers and curled it into his palm.

"I'm not sure it's so different anywhere else," he said.

"We'll see," said Viktoria as she brushed her hair back behind her ears. "I need to make more fluids for her. Take one of the protein bars from the kitchen before you go. Drink some water too. You look like hell and expect you're in for more of it."

They met eyes. "If I make it through this, we'll find a way out of here. They froze my accounts I'm sure, but I've got other means."

He took Viktoria's intense stare to be her equivalent of a handshake.

They both went to the kitchen. There was a stack of packaged protein bars sitting on the counter. Nothing had ever looked so appetizing. It had been almost two days since his last meal and his body had forgotten how hungry he was until now. He ripped one open and shoved into his mouth whole and downed several large gulps of water as chewed it. His stomach rumbled at the return of food. He put down three more bars and a liter of water while Viktoria prepped IV fluids.

When he left the apartment, she was fixing the IV tube to the fresh bottle. Elise was asleep, or unconscious, and grayer than ever.

He did as Viktoria said. Once he hit the street, he pulled his hood low over his face and hurried. The blocks leading up to the Light District passed in a blur, and even the Light District itself was colorless to him. For all the buildup, the elevator was only that. The doors opened, he ascended, and when he exited, he was in High City.

Even though these lower areas were the shabby parts of High City, they were so perfect compared to anything had seen in weeks that seemed like pure opulence to him. The buildings had pristine white brick facades and gleaming black glass windows. Sharp angles and sweeping curves accented their forms. Above all, it was the cleanliness and absolute absence of weathering, or dirt, or garbage or any flaw, that struck him most.

People here followed a more traditional schedule, one based on showing up for work in the late morning and returning home in the early evening four or five days a week. It was too early for even the most motivated joggers and the most ambitious early-to-work arrivers, so no one was out on the streets. Drones, though, buzzed overhead everywhere and he reminded him of his unique vulnerability here. In Low City, people were the threat. Here it was surveillance.

He ducked into the alcove of the nearest building and waited. By 6:00 A.M. people were emerging from buildings. Some walked dogs, some walked by themselves, and some set off on jogs up the hill toward the more posh areas of High City. Under scrutiny, his suit was most definitely for combat, but he decided that at a glance it could pass for running gear— it was tight fitting and designed with mobility in mind. It was not so different from the designer athletic gear people wore.

He fell in line behind a group of three moving at a brisk pace up the hill in the general direction he needed to go. It was several kilometers to the park, but by merging with groups of runners, he was able to blend in the whole way.

Morning was breaking when he reached his destination. It bathed the city in a rich golden light. Bright rays bounced from building to building, and although the air was brisk, the light filled him with warmth. He circled the edges of the park, checking each storage block until one flashed a green light as he approached. He stood in front of it and it rolled out a street bike with a forest green matte finish. When he threw one leg over and straddled it, it came to life. A virtual HUD projected into this field of view and he set course for the base of the road leading up to the DA facility—the final intersection with the streets of High City. He squeezed the throttle handle and the bike took off. It was an auto-piloted vehicle, but it gave the user the illusion of control by allowing them some choice in when it stopped and roughly how fast it went. The computers inside made sure it never collided with anything. He could have let go of the handles and fell asleep in the seat and ended up there all the same.

He pulled up the intersection to the DA facility, powered-off the bike, and rolled it back into the cover of some trees. Then he waited. Between 8:00 and 9:00, the employee shuttles began arriving. They all approached at the same speed and followed the same arc in their turn onto the road. At around 9:15 another shuttle approached. It was moving faster than the others and it braked hard into the turn. The arc was sloppy. He powered up his bike and followed from a distance.

Halfway up the hill, there was a security checkpoint. He had no chance of passing it on his bike, but based on the shoddy mimicry of the employee shuttle's movements, he guessed that Lark's decoy shuttle would not either. He was right.

The fake shuttle pulled off the road about a hundred meters from the checkpoint and stopped. Three men exited the security building and started moving toward the vehicle, rifles drawn and aimed at it. A swarm of drones lifted from the roof of the building and zoomed over their heads. Luka willed the bike to move faster, but its algorithms knew of the checkpoint ahead and it was slowing instead.

He drew his pistol and began firing at the security patrol. It lost its accuracy at a distance. Bullets sprayed around them. A few struck their amour, but none posed a threat to them.

They pulled their attention from the shuttle and began firing their rifles at him. Bullets whizzed through the air around him, and though he squeezed the throttle harder, the bike was losing speed. It powered down and rolled to a lazy stop. With the last bit of momentum, Luka skidded the bike sideways and took cover behind it.

Bullets rained into the side of the bike. He poked his head around the front tire and returned fire, but the security patrol team advanced, undeterred. The bike billowed smoke as bullets shredded the batteries. His time was running out.

Then three shots cracked through the air and echoed down from the hill to the left. The three patrol team members fell in quick succession after as a pink spray erupted from each of their heads. Luka collapsed to a prone position and pulled his body in tight against the bike, even knowing it would catch fire at any moment. The heat from the bike stung his face. He waited until he was certain an explosion was imminent.

He scrambled to his feet and made for the shuttle at a dead sprint, taking a zig-zagging path as he went. To his surprise, not a single shot rang out. He grabbed the emergency handle on the door and ripped it open. There was no resistance. The door broke free from the hinges and gave him an easy path inside. He jumped in and took a deep breath.

Anti-matter reactor and repulser gear occupied every centimeter of the interior. He scanned the equipment, looking for a control panel where he could disable the reactor, but a blinding light flooded the shuttle before he could act.

Then a powerful wave of energy passed through him and burned like acid. A concussive wave hit him next and blew him backward out of the shuttle. He hit the ground and several pops rang through his body as bones in shoulder gave way.

Through the searing pain, he forced his eyes open and caught a glimpse was of the shuttle. It was a wreck of black metal. Much of the structure remained, but the blast contorted it like a giant had taken the front and back of the vehicle in its hands and twisted it ninety degrees. He expected to hear screaming or the hurried yells of emergency workers—and to be surrounded by MP's, but the whole world was quiet. Through the ringing in his ears, all he heard was the soft crackling of the fires consuming Viktoria's bike. He rolled onto the left side of his body and pushed himself up onto his knees with this good arm.

He looked up the hill at the Daedalus Astrodynamics campus. There was no movement at all—no drones, no shuttles, no power. The whole place was dead.

Someone approached from behind. They rested a hand on his shoulder. He fought to his feet, but they squeezed his shattered shoulder and the pain forced him back to his knees.

They spoke, and when he recognized the voice, the fight drained from him.

"I'm sorry, Luka, but you were never going to stop this. You were the trigger," said Viktoria.

END

For updates on upcoming events and new works from Elias, join the mailing list:

www.eliasjhurst.com/mailing-list

Follow Elias on Instagram and Twitter

@ejhauthor

Afterword

If you made it this far, thank you. Growing up, books meant everything to me. They were escapes from the boredom of a small town, insight into other worlds, and time away from my own thoughts. Now, as an author, I hope to that pay forward.

Please leave a review if you can. You would be surprised at the difference a single review makes.

Europa began as a story about a manned mission to one of Jupiter's moons. I wrote a good way into it before I realized I was bored writing it. Then I knew that, surely if I was bored writing it, anyone reading it would be clawing at their face in agony. So, instead of writing a book about a guy going on a space mission, I thought, *why don't I write a book about a guy NOT going on a space mission.*

That is what I did. The first spark for the new concept of *Europa* was that—a failed mission, one that never left. The rest fell into place from there.

Stay tuned for more to come.

Cheers,

-EJH

CPSIA information can be obtained
at www.ICGtesting.com
Printed in the USA
FSHW010503091219
64888FS